ARCOPLEX

Artorian's Archives Book Fourteen

DENNIS VANDERKERKEN
DAKOTA KROUT

MOUNTAINDALE
PRESS

ACKNOWLEDGMENTS

From Dennis:

There are many people who have made this book possible. First is Dakota himself, for without whom this entire series would never have come about. In addition to letting me write in his universe, he has taken it upon himself to be the most glorious senior editor and keep straight all the madness for which I am responsible, with resulting hilarity therein.

An eternal thank you to my late grandfather, after whom a significant chunk of Artorian's personality is indebted. He was a man of mighty strides, and is missed dearly.

A special thank you to my parents, for being ever supportive in my odd endeavors, Mountaindale Press for being a fantastic publisher, and all the fans of Artorian's Archives, Divine Dungeon, and Completionist Chronicles who are responsible for the popularity allowing this to come to pass. May your affinity channels be strong and plentiful!

Last of all, thank you. Thank you for picking this up and giving it a read. Arcoplex is the continuation of a multi-book series, and I dearly hope you will enjoy them as the story keeps progressing. Artorian's Archives may start before Divine Dungeon, but don't worry! It's going all the way past the end of Completionist Chronicles! So if you liked this, keep an eye out for more things from Mountaindale Press!

Please consider giving us five stars on Amazon, Audible, and anywhere else you'd like to spread the word!

CHAPTER ONE

"Get in the bag!"

Ember's hurried outcry and accompanying crazy laughter comprised the first sounds that Artorian heard upon waking. He opened a cautious eye in the care room of the Faith Foundry's central pavilion.

Some scuffling, screaming, and argumentative complaints followed his significant other's flaming wake. He felt the ground tremble from Basher footfalls, Lucia's gait telltale after becoming accustomed to the specific thump of her run. She had a peculiar 'I needed to be there yesterday' kind of footfall pattern, combined with a drive for the zoomies. Given he was an enthusiast of the zoomies himself, this received understanding nods.

Several noises happened in rapid succession. The walls shook from a goblin pile-up barring a hallway. A cry of success. A dissonant *vwump*. The distinct feeling of a Silverwood Bracelet activating. The sensation of loss as Ember swapped from Cal over to Eternia. Likely with a gleeful Lucia in tow, successfully contained in the bag, if the cursing from Basher Sisters was anything to go by.

This told him an entire story from those initial four waking words alone. Artorian silently fist-pumped in solidarity. He smiled to himself, folded his hands, and closed his eyes. It was not time to get up yet. Time to get up was after he indulged in the rounds of gossip provided by both Sisters of the Paw, and the visiting Heavenlies who… Could. Not. Shut. Up.

He hadn't been sure what to expect from an influx of Heavenlies to the common space, but ceaseless chattering had not been it. Artorian admitted to himself that he'd expected a modicum of decorum from the majority of Heavenlies. Some stature. A pinch of self-control. These individuals of great power, the closest connection to the **Laws** that Mages bound themselves to, surely ought to be respectable.

Surely.

Artorian kneaded his eyebrows. Oh, how the turns have tabled! These Tower people had a sense of community and a social rhythm, but appeared to have been outside of a cultural setting not their own for too long. They all became wide-eyed and wonder-filled children outside of their home turf. With accompanying chaos, discord, and the slow, slow grind of them figuring those boundaries out again. He was thankful for the notable exceptions, but Artorian had never expected them to *be* exceptions. "Thank Lunella for Avalon."

He properly began his waking hours today by practicing with his ears. Echolocation outside of Eternia was a different animal than it was inside the game. The same was true for Electrosense, and he was stuck with both. He was also stuck with eyes that were unwilling to settle on either a pink or cyan coloration, but that was a problem for another day. A day where he didn't need a blindfold moments after getting up and escaping his dimly lit room. Aesthetics played second fiddle to being up and running.

The room outlined itself with shapes and borders, boundaries and corners. His range was currently confined to the room and a small piece of hallway, Artorian unable to visualize more. He hadn't yet sussed out why sometimes he had a very broad range of Echolocation, while at other times his range remained confined like it currently was.

The stick figure shapes of energy moving through the hallway were equally vague today. He knew the hallway was there, but he couldn't make a blueprint out of the bonus hints that the seventh sense provided when tacked onto the sixth.

"Time and practice." He had a lifetime to make these senses blend into the background and give him passive information like the other five. "Time and practice."

Opening his eyes to take in the dim lighting as the candles in his room lit themselves, he let himself melt pleasantly into the pillows while taking in the shapes playing on the ceiling. He did like the candles. Creamy vanilla candles were nice. Specifically the ones from Mr. Wick.

Mr. Wick made the best candles.

He would prefer sunlight, but as sunlight was currently constantly winning the eye-stabbing war with such minimal effort that the game wasn't sporting, Artorian settled for the candles.

He smiled when he heard a Sister of the Paw tear a local Heavenly a new one. Something major had changed when he'd left Eternia. An aspect of existence that hadn't been true when he'd entered. Now? Now everyone could see Heavenlies. All could hear them. All could talk to them. It was a glorious mess.

A satisfying *clap* followed a paw's traversal across the cheek of a Heavenly's rear. A bratty one that must have gotten itself into a moping slump, because the Sister's rebuttal was harsh and unforgiving. "Eclipse! Pick yourself up. You want to die? Then throw yourself into the sea! You'll see yourself fighting to survive. You do not want to kill yourself. You want to kill something inside of you. Now get up, give me that jar, and Cal help me that I do not catch you throwing another tantrum for not getting a strawberry tart as a treat before supper. Git!"

Turning to the other cheek, a follow up *whap* across the bottom of that same unruly being preceded sounds of fleeing and calls of unfairness. Unfortunately for Eclipse, they also included commentary that the Heavenly was going to wish the flop-eared Basher hadn't heard.

The Sister rounded on him. "*What did you say?* You think these ears are for show? Get back here, big man! If you think adopting a cutesy or attractive shape will save you from my wrath, then I will educate you otherwise, you ancient piece of sod! You think you're the only Ageless we know acting like this? *C'mere!*"

Artorian pressed his hands over his mouth, cheeks pink as he stifled the giggling. Eclipse the Heavenly fled like a panicked child from the Glitterflit who was most certainly going to catch him. The sight of an energetic, rabbit-shaped stick figure half the size of Eclipse bounding across walls, dive-tackling an energy signature twice her height to the ground was just too funny. Especially when the Sister hoisted him by the scruff as Eclipse failed to keep a grip on the ground while he was dragged away, his commentary and pleas falling on deaf ears.

Eclipse's voice peeped in distress at the results of his own doing. "Not the dreaded kitchen duty!"

Artorian laughed heartily, unable to stop his giggling. Since the day of their return from Eternia by ending the Antelucan Age, life had been like this. Every day, more and more Heavenlies arrived fully fleshed out in physical form, discovering that they could exert personalities they hadn't gotten to indulge in for… they don't even remember how long sometimes. This led to a whole host of ancient beings becoming the most prude, childish, whiny, needy little brats.

Beings with lots of power and zero responsibility.

Lady Duchess would be tempering the back of her iron hand if she knew!

Most of them threw at least one tantrum before learning better, and that the populace of Avalon wasn't taking their pish. Possibly due to the Mages who met the people closest to their chosen concepts suffering a disastrous case of disillusionment.

The disillusionment speedrunning record so far was four minutes and fifteen seconds, when a Tier sixteen Mage bound to the **Law** of **Luck** met Lady Luck. Or rather, he discovered her fondness for all consumables that were both fermented from fruit, and exceptionally strong. The potato drink in particular went down like water, and after four minutes in her presence, he was completely done with her continued claims that some potion seller refused to sell her his strongest potion. For she supposedly could not handle them.

That Mage was later found in a Dwarven tavern being very loud on how they were still dedicated to their concept, because they didn't hold the **Law** responsible... but the person currently in the seat on that node, or however it worked? Could drown on their Abyss-plastered potions. Primarily because they astutely refused to continue accepting the mental image that their **Law**, and the Heavenly of that **Law**, were the same thing.

Everyone's saving grace on the topic of Heavenlies, and their otherwise absurd cosmic power, was that there was a Cal-clad rule in place mediating the allotment for their existence. According to the big rule: Heavenlies had to be as susceptible to events, physics, and actions as any common mortal. Their output and power couldn't be properly contained or restrained, but they could reel it in and play nice. Cal had wanted an Oath, but had to make due upon discovering that this feature didn't work on Heavenlies.

By choice, the Heavenlies agreed to retain an effective power level and rank one level of cultivation below that of the Soul Space which they currently attended. If they moved between spaces, they would drop as necessary before transfer. To Cal's partial surprise, this particular choice had already been agreed upon by the entire Tower before the first one had ever showed up.

Exerting their true power would kill Cal and everyone along for the ride, and all the Heavenlies knew that there were some angry stares from higher **Laws** that would take serious excep-tion to that reality coming to pass. Tipping a toe over the line would end all their enjoyment, and everyone else's. Toes would thus be very carefully kept away from those lines, with consensus swiftly reached.

Feeling more awake, Artorian allowed his morning to continue away from the topic of Heavenlies. Caltopia would sort them.

CHAPTER TWO

Artorian tuned his ears until he found the voice of the Mother Superior.

Her shrill tone was easy to locate, the Mother Superior in the middle of a lecture. "Canoness? Too many people have opinions on things they know nothing about, and the more ignorant they are, the more opinions they have. Prioress? Don't confuse experience with expertise. Having faced a problem doesn't mean you've mastered the solution. Don't mistake expertise for wisdom, either. Having deep knowledge doesn't mean that you know when it applies. So you keep that baby powder tied to your waist and your paw ready to clap!"

He shook his head to forcibly end the attention span, the sound dimming. He needed to try that again, but without a specific voice involved.

Eyes closing, he focused. Just barely, he could visualize the room she was in. The sound coming back like etchings on paper, vague chalk-sketched outlines of pathing, structure, and the size of things. Electrosense gave him a strong visualized indicator of the energy running through a body, strengthened when the heart pulsed, or when an ability was used. The sense allowed him to easily place people, even if he saw them as shapeless clumps of stick figure energy in the rooms sketched out by his ears.

As a bonus, the strength and type of energy running through a person differed with each individual. Like... a Mana signature? Which was extremely appealing to learn since he didn't have access to Mana yet. People would hide their... power level? Was he going to call it a power level? He might as well. There was an obvious difference between Mages and non-Mages. Beasts had their own measurement stick that tracked completely differently from the cultivators he was aware of, discovering that Core quality really pulled the majority of a Beast's weight. Incarnates felt noticeably different from Mages, and Heavenlies were... so obscenely disparate from Incarnates that he currently didn't know the words to describe what an incredible leap it was to separate the two.

There was energy, sure, but Heavenlies were ineffable in comparison to the wonky but still comprehensible mind-cluck that came with paying active Electrosense attention to an Incarnate. He had to stop quickly when trying to keep it active around anything higher than a Mage, for while every energy signature began as a simple stick figure, the more he focused... The feeling of nausea built in a hurry, and the after-effects of upholding active sensors for more than brief moments was identical to being a low-rank cultivator trying to see inside of a Mage with Essence sight.

Instantly hurling generally followed.

A behavior that was responsible for the Goblins and Bashers keeping him in bed. Granted, it was his own fault for having severe bodily reactions when they came to check on him, and he forgot to turn the senses down! Sweeping the pavilion as he did, and tagging several Heavenlies all at once prompted an immediate physical rebuke.

All over some previously pristine robe.

Lisette and the Goblins had laughed, the Sister of the Paw had been appalled but understanding, and all the Heavenlies in the building had simultaneously erupted in applause. Those wretches. They knew, didn't they?

A C'towl with a frosted pastry in its mouth zoomed past the balcony, leaving a rainbow trail in its wake. Music followed, but the creature was gone before Artorian could hear more than a couple of nyans.

Such randomness was commonplace. He would bet a handful of copper that C'towl was a Heavenly. They all had their own, almost insane, incredibly niche sense of humor. Many of their amusements felt like the humor had been misplaced in time. Some jokes were ancient history to him, a few were from his time, but most made absolutely zero sense. A few also went around saying some of those strange words he'd heard before, but had never managed to place. Their antics caused great stories, and his days were all the fuller for it. Once, he'd caught a roaming Heavenly while his mind was on the topic, but the Heavenly—in the shape of some rune-covered squirrel—had glared at him.

Declaring a very apt verdict of: "No spoilers!"

He chuckled at the thought, having caught the tale of the first one to figure out an animal form. They'd apparently lost that Heavenly to the Beast section of Avalon, and hadn't seen the poor thing since. Artorian pressed the doubt prompt that this was a poor circumstance for the Heavenly. That particular troublemaker was likely exactly where they wanted to be.

Artorian placed an additional two silver in the betting pool that it would be one of those future problems he'd have to contend with. Coin he would gladly lose in order to be wrong.

The thought did make his mind wander to a choice he was going to need to make in the near future. "Beast Core, or cultivation technique?"

The dormant Core in him was still that, dormant. His time in Eternia, on the other hand, had pushed him up and out from his non-cultivator origins. The body was still *his* body, but even without a circulation method for Essence, he felt more capable of holding it. That meant some cellular replacement with

Essence had occurred. A process that he felt uncomfortable with, as only when he'd done the entire process himself, having retained control over the what and where, had he been alright with the idea. Now it made him squirm mildly.

That he wasn't able to check on the progress didn't help.

He sighed, talking himself through it. "Possibly Beast Core, but no idea how that works. Possibly sun cultivation technique? Possibly being a guinea pig for whatever Core cultivator technique that Cal or Eternium have up their sleeves. I can't decide."

When he could join Team Sleep in Eternia, he might ask them. Ammy had warned him to not cultivate in Cal. Not difficult. In a rush, he was not.

A smile formed at the team name. Urtu and Hella were to blame. When the war-ladle made a trip through multiple hands, being handed back to Lucia on that first night in the pavilion, they had done zero communicating with one another, and appeared to have instinctively decided that they were all on the same team. Team Sleep!

Urtu and Hella had run with it, as their mostly harmless form of retaliation against Urtu getting ladeled and cubed.

The door to the care room opening ended his train of thought, as a Dwarf in a white coat sauntered in under the strong glare of Lisette, who kept personal watch at Artorian's door. She was short and sharp with him in tone, as she about matched the Dwarf in size. "You have five minutes, McShane. Five. Not a second more."

"Yeh, yeh…" The Dwarf dressed as a doctor closed the door with his foot, cutting off the conversation as he strode into the care room, oversized clinking bag in tow. "Hellur, lad!"

Artorian pushed himself up, but first made sure to reach over to grab the blindfold from the table. He'd been expecting the Mother Superior, or perhaps a Canoness. Stocky Dwarf with schemes written into every hair of his mustache was a surprise addition to the menu. He couldn't wait to see where this was going. "Good morning. If it's morning? Hard to tell with the shutters always closed until someone takes me on my blind walk. I don't think I've met you before."

McShane beamed a fun-loving smile. "Oh, y'have! Sort of. Maybeh. Now am unsure? Meh name be McShane. I'm part o' one of Halcyon's crews. I ran with the Tun's Tavern Team to install and protect Troop Reinforcement Totems. Or whatever they be called, back when ye were doin' yer assault on Mt. Olympus, when Zeus had run o' the place. You came to an Accords with the tarry boys, as I reckon an' recall. Bookin' Demons was a great tale."

The stocky Dwarf performed charades only as long as necessary, as they could both hear the Goblin on the other side of the door stomp away while grumbling. One glance over the shoulder, and McShane had shuffled next to Artorian's bedside, his voice dropped to conspiracy-laden whispers. "Some folks be gettin' a mite impatient about yer visitation, and a wee bit ruddy 'bout the rabbits keepin' ya hostage. So ya know, am no doctor. More of a protein-smith. If ya ever heard of a Dwarf that made snacks for the military called Crayons? Tha' was me! I run Eternium Gym in Nidavellir, with about seventeen branches open at the Coast of Rica. Mighty more popular there than it is back home, I tell ya. Excuse the name appropriation, it brought clients!"

Artorian adjusted his Silverwood bracelet for comfort. He shifted it on his wrist to satisfy a very odd validation need requiring him to make sure that he both felt the bracelet, and that the object was actually there. Satisfied as the odd feeling faded, he then folded his hands in his lap to hopefully discover where McShane was going with this.

Nidavellir getting impatient had been obvious already, with Don's brazen visit. Though... there was no way his friend would ever risk doing that twice. So as coincidental as that link may seem, this visit by the protein-smith had to be about some-thing entirely different, with Don probably not involved. That added spice to the mystery!

He prodded for details about McShane's gym. "Anything fun to do there?"

McShane became the visual representation of a teapot about to burst from excitement when he got to elaborate about his most favorite topic. "My gym? Pains and gains galore! Can't have one without the other. Luckily, Ol' McShane is there with the goods to assist in making the gains. For pre-workout? I've got tons of caffeine in a powdered scoop. They always have a warning about 'do not exceed one scoop,' but no one achieves greatness by following directions. We have lots of fun with crazed, over-caffeinated Dwarves. The stuff's magic, I tell ya."

McShane's face expanded into a wicked grin. "After a good time, not necessarily a long time, I give out BCAAs. Short for branch chain amino acids. This is like pill cultivation, recovery style. Supposed to help you mend the damage you did to yourself faster. See this as a low quality, slow-release type healing potion, if that didn't make no sense. I can see the confusion buildin' on yer face."

Artorian honestly only wanted McShane to get off his railway track and tell him why a Dwarf was here pretending to play doctor, but he hadn't found the moment yet.

McShane's enthusiasm hurled on like a runaway Gnomish machine, oblivious to Artorian's growing need to get back on track. "Protein powder is the golden medium of the Dwarven muscle gods. We mix it with the milk of some unknown beast for extra potency."

He leaned in and cupped his hand to Artorian's ear. "The milk type is not actually unknown, but the ploy is good for marketin'. Only *savages* mix with water!"

McShane then raised back up and wrapped up his spiel when the boy he was starting to irk crossed his arms. "PEDs are last, and optional. Not everyone can handle a Performance Enhancing Dwarf, after all!"

Artorian kneaded the bridge of his nose, out of patience for any kind of subtle approach. He was going to say it as a Dwarf and hit the mountain with a pickaxe. Like a spotter Mage jumping off a cliff to wail on a door made from cursed earth. "Why are you here again?"

McShane perked up, as if having completely forgotten that part of his task. "Right!"

The Dwarf then revealed his massive doctor's bag, sporting an equally massive grin as he upturned it. Wrenches and empty metal jars galore hit the floor. "I'm here to save ya and smuggle ya out! I hear ya know how to do this part, but just for fun, and cuz I've loved the tale since I heard it… Get in the bag, boy! We're leavin'!"

CHAPTER THREE

Artorian's morning ended as a hulk of a hand tugged him free when the doctor's bag unzipped. A Dwarf that he could not see introduced himself all while helping him from his self-inflicted confines. The escape had been a fun ride! "'Ello, Administrator! Corporal Kellen Shadowbeard, dragoon an' dark paladin, bloodmancer extraordinaire, at yer service! Emilia Nerys sends 'er love an' regards, with warm words from the Portal Mages tacked on. Amber was too busy screaming an' runnin' away from swarms o' children whose cookies she keeps nickin', and towards Grace, who keeps teasin' her with new portal tricks she still ain't seen."

Artorian chuckled warmly, feeling excess heat on his skin, while glad for the blindfold as Shadowbeard rambled on. "McShane told me ya may not have met us like we thought ya did, but there's some rumors floatin' about that ya may not be remembering people ya knew from long ago at all. So do be expecting them to try to give you a reintroduction. I ran with McShane at…"

The Dwarf paused his introduction when Artorian was up

and out of the bag. "Oi, what's with the napkin glasses? This be a rescue, not an abduction."

McShane was busy filling a mug, Artorian catching the sound of liquid pouring into a small container. "Not mah gym, not my weights! I didn't do it."

Artorian squeezed the hand still supporting him, steadying himself with Kellen's assistance. "Mr. Shadowbeard? My eyes are the reason I was in medical care. I'm not better yet, so if you were planning to show me something by daylight, I would recommend against that. Soft light, dim light, or night light are what I can currently handle."

"*Awwww*, pyrite!" Kellen clapped a massive stubby hand on Artorian's back, causing a serious stumble. "Tha's a shame, that is! We was planning on takin' ya round the scenic route, and here ya sayin' ya can't see Nidavellir in all its proper gloreh? Well, tha's a coal lump if I ever saw one."

Artorian bobbed his shoulders, face twisted in an apologetic smile. "I'm sure it's still lovely at night? I'm trying to puzzle out if there's a better set of words for that litany of titles you gave me. Bloody Jumper? Maybe Crimson Dragoon. Dusk Knight?"

"Don't worry yer shiny li'l eyes 'bout it none!" Kellen laughed, keeping his arm around both of Artorian's shoulders. Easy to do as they were the same height. "Jus' means some of our information wasn't filling the ale mug all the way. We can still show ya the statues! Had to make 'em by word o' mouth from the bigshots, but it's what we got ta work with when they're the only ones who can see ya mopping up the other world."

"Mopping up?" Artorian wasn't sure what Kellen was talking about, his Electrosense pulsing momentarily.

McShane leaned his particularly active bundle of stocky stick figure energy back into clear view. "Y'know, cuz you're a Janitor class? In Eternia?"

Artorian released a sound of understanding, then coiled his own arm around the Dwarven support's back as much as he could. He felt wobbly from what had been a very noisy and eventful trip off the balcony. Based on the shapes and sounds, he guessed he'd absconded on the back of an oversized Sugar Glider. Clever!

The child-sized Administrator enjoyed the story that would make. "You know they're never going to let you back into the Faith Foundry after this stunt, right? They're gonna come get me, one way or another."

Both Kellen and McShane burst out with heaving laughter, Kellen recovering first to speak. "Aye! An' what a fun game o' cat an' mouse that'll be. We'll just have to keep smugglin' ya about! It's gonna make for an ale-tastic tale with the boys. Now waddle with me, lad. Let's get ya inside so the sun don't kill ya. I know a thing or two 'bout it. Ain't no blood Mage yet, but I've stabbed a vampire or two in mah life. I know all the good gothic nooks and crannies. An' speakin' of, if y'ever find yerself facin' any? Weak point's the heart. Nuthin' else. Just the heart. If it has the vampire tag, ya throw the usual conditions and weaknesses out the window."

Artorian smiled wide in response, waddling along. "I know some of those words!"

More laughter cracked from the Dwarven duo, who helped him all the way to the inside of a structure while making jokes back and forth. Artorian only cringed at some of them. Particularly when McShane got corny. "What's more amazing than a talking wolf?"

Without missing a minepick strike, Kellen caught the beat. "A spelling bee."

Artorian was so glad to hear Halcyon's voice after the puns began to stack that he didn't even properly pick up that it was Cy speaking at first. The soft and sweet cutesy tone was definitely there, but for some reason he'd been expecting Don or Dimi, after all. How a ten foot tall Orca lady managed to have two Dwarves worth of lung capacity, yet sound so small and sweet, was a mystery for the ages. Maybe she chose her voice? He'd known her plenty capable of loud calls and speeches, so perhaps she did it purely out of enjoyment. Or because it sounded cute? Wait, did Cy have a preference for being cute?

Halcyon repeated herself when she got no reply the first time, her hand resting on his head as she did so. "My Dreamer?"

"Cy?" Artorian had to ask just to be sure as he looked up to suss out her stick figure energy shape. She had a golden core where a ridiculous amount of energy coursed, notably different in pattern from the cultivator methods. Did Beasts have meridians and meridian pathways? If that was what he was seeing, then those routes were starkly different from what he was used to. Would this perhaps mean that his own internal energy flow should not be a copy of what he did last time? He was technically human, and being technically correct can be the best kind of correct, but he knew in his gut that it was wrong. Nascent Being boy was going to have to do some deep rock galactic deep-diving into his own meridians.

Her humanized fingers rustled soft and gentle through his hair when Artorian appeared out of it, or at minimum disoriented. "Present and accounted for? Did we steal you away from the bunnies too soon?"

"*You* did this?" He couldn't believe the turn of events, arms going up to be picked up and held. Dwarves coming to nick him? Oh yeah! Totally bought it. No problem. Cy being sneaky? The world was ending. "Cy! The audacity!"

The massive Orca woman laughed with the boy in her arms, already carrying him off deeper into the Art Deco overloaded structure. "Kellen, McShane? Thank you for your assistance."

Both the Dwarves loudly snapped into a salute. "At your order, oh Deep One!"

Cy squeezed Artorian, shuddered in her step, and physically restrained herself from telling them to please not do that. "Yes. Thank you. When he finds out, please tell Don that he can stop worrying about that blue book of grudges? I never had any grumbles to start, but if it makes him feel better to do things this way, then I will accept it. He's considered repaid. All I did was give him a hammer."

Artorian heard the Dwarves refill their ale and shuffle their way out, but when the jokes started up again, he tuned both out at the speed that a Basher could turn their ears. He was glad for the shift in company and conversation. Cy was always a good, safe, welcoming presence. "What's a book of grudges? Haven't heard of those."

Halcyon grinned wide, her teeth on display. Her Dreamer remained unbothered, unable to see the reaction with the blindfold protecting his optics. "The Dwarven bestseller books? A record of past events as much as a story lauding Dwarven grumpiness. You've got the original hit. The Book of Grudges. Then there's the sequel, the Book of Minor Grudges. The prequel, the Book of Major Grudges. Lastly, one surprise addition that took Nidavellir by storm: The Book of It Ain't Really a Grudge but I'ma Treat it Like a Grudge. Very popular. Then there's color variations that each have some meaning I don't know too well. Blue is debts they think they owe."

Artorian thought it would be pleasant enough to let himself see as they traveled underground. Echolocation was giving the design away, and the lack of sunlight was obvious enough. He listened to Halcyon sweetly explain Dwarven heritage as he fumbled with the blindfold.

"They are the accounts of people, places, times, events, and things that have annoyed them. With great details and specifics on how much, and why. Turns out? That's an ancient tradition they're reviving to keep all Dwarves on the same track. Don said, 'To keep us all Dwarven.' I'm still not sure what he meant by it."

Halcyon transferred her Dreamer to her other arm, her body blocking a stronger wind that she knew cut through this particular section of utility halls. "They're having trouble making people agree to keep it all under wraps and act like unwelcome drunken stragglers on visitation. Unfortunately, since the Dwarves living on the Coast of Rica are completely against this wave of old-timey teaching, they have eschewed the old ways, and have instead given themselves to the calls of protein and whey. Did you talk to McShane?"

"I heard his jokes, and his passion for said protein." Artorian mumbled while finally getting the blindfold off. "I was having a good time listening to his enthusiasm for all things gym, but the puns and related content aren't for me."

His response paused when he took in the Art Deco scenery.

Illumination was provided by strips of cloth that ran across the corners and edge the current tunnel network, with the smallest Nixie Tubes he'd ever seen interspersed evenly along the thin band. The gentle orange light added a welcoming glow to the black tourmaline walls, bouncing off the smooth passage as some light in the sequence pulsed, giving the illusions of the lights moving in the same direction that they were traveling.

He touched the wall, running a finger down the glib surface when Halcyon was close enough. She paused in her power stride to put him down, letting him explore. "Warmth? Was not expecting heat from the walls."

Halcyon beamed while hopping on her toes as she watched her Dreamer discover like an Orca calf exploring a new coral reef. She kept silent as Artorian mumbled. "The floor has a grip to it. Same material? Same material."

He bounced a few times, his feet finding a lot of grip on the floor when he came back down. Unlike the wall, the floor wasn't reflecting the Nixie Tube light very well. Was it still called reflection? It might be refraction. He kneeled down to touch the floor, not understanding what the Dwarves were trying to accomplish here. More floor grip was good for running, the halls were decently lit and spacious, but far too wide for generic Dwarven strolling. There was no furniture, no embellishments, nothing but space for movement.

Was this a racing track?

"My Dreamer?" Artorian broke from his trance to look up at Halcyon, who wore an amused curl on her lips as she kept her arms crossed over her chest. Her outfit was the same sporty variant of what she'd come to visit with in Eternia, but the Nixie Tube lights were making a secondary pattern on her outfit glow. "You've been staring at the floor for a while. Ready to see the statues?"

Artorian pressed himself up to be at her knee. "I zone out a lot easier as a mortal. Good call on tugging me back."

He reached an arm up, but unless Cy bent down, he wasn't going to reach her hand. She picked him up for ease of travel, and carried him past the rounded corner. Sure, he could have walked it himself, but the Orca was clearly indulging. Halcyon had wanted the experience to be more of a surprise, but was pleased as a wild ocean current when she got the reaction she'd hoped for after all.

Artorian jaw-dropped when the sight of marvelously illuminated, colorful, mastercrafted soap statues first came into view.

"Crackers and toast, those look delicious." He could smell them all the way from the fancy, geode-studded, arched opening to the round room that broke off from the comparatively stark racetrack tunnels. Here there was plenty of furniture, seats, and plants growing directly out from the walls. All blooming with glowing celestine flowers while delicately adorning a massive brass sign that celebrated Art Deco as an architectural style, with a bold brass art piece of Nidavellir skyscrapers superimposed in front of a rising sun. "Dwarven architecture shining through in all its detail-oriented glory. I like it. Especially that other in-progress piece on the other side that says: 'Welcome to Rapture, beware of bioshock.' Must be one of their new aquatic outposts?"

Were people trying to one-up each other's construction skills? Tim had been very adamant about the little details in Demeter's Dream, and the Dwarves seemed responsible for spurring on a half-rivalry. A set of design sheets or blueprints about a structure called a radiator building stole his attention for a while, but eventually his eyes fell and rested on the centerpiece of the room.

The collection of large soap statues on display demanded

much from his eyes, while a collection of smaller, more thematically conjoined ones along the walls followed suit. Each individual soap carving was locked to a recess in the ground. For
support, perhaps? Or had that been part of the block of soap
that had been pared down to become the works he currently
ogled?

His senses weren't letting him delve any deep details, but
Artorian guessed that the skeletal metal supports hidden inside
kept these soap people upright and properly shaped. Since he
was grasping at straws, he wriggled until Halcyon let him down
so he could zip over and inspect them.

The Nixie lighting in the noticeably dry area was sharper.
Between the celestine floral hue and the change in tubes, the
domed display room didn't have the warmth that the hallway
did. No pulsing flickers either. Was this perhaps an observation
chamber? This room had many openings that connected to
many of the racing halls. An Air Essence wall to block out the
sound and gust of racers zipping by would make this a great
vantage point. The spiral staircase next to the brass sign led to a
more illuminated area, but he couldn't see what it was. "I'm
going to look at some statues first."

The first statue he recognized and stopped at was Lucia's.
Part of a set along the wall, it was separated from the others by
oversized plants. The likeness was remarkable, the soapy scent a
mixture of geranium and cedarwood. "The quality is incredible. This carving looks just like her! Dwarven crafters did this
with nothing more than a description?"

Halcyon shook her head, taking a seat on a metal bench
made from bent pipes. "The Heavenlies are boasters, with the
Dwarves easily in the runner-up position. Our visitors show
their screens. Most everyone who wanted to watch had a front
row seat to your trials and tribulations. Your speech about
utopias was particularly memorable."

Artorian turned beet red, standing just as still as any of the
statues present. The understanding that he'd been correct, and
that their group had been watched with more intensity than

he realized, turned his insides upside down. "You… saw… that?"

"In detail! Followed by the solar ignition." She grinned, watching her Dreamer sink into himself. "Loved the light show, oh child of light. There was much rejoicing, followed by a huge debate on why the extension systems weren't allowing anyone to reselect you as a deity option. There's still a brawl going on upstairs between a vast number of Beast rescues from Eternia and the Dwarven locals, per why it's unfair that players can't benefit from your health regeneration buff, but non-player characters can. We're calling that faction NPCs for short. The Dwarves started the argument by being greedy, and the rescues came to your defense in numbers counted by the horde."

She looked up at the glowstone-coated ceiling, able to hear what Artorian could not. "They're having a great time up there. I think they're going for the longest and biggest bar brawl in history? Some Dwarf named Guinness is recording it all. I'm very interested to see who the last Dwarf or Beast standing will be. Though, in this ultimate showdown of ultimate destiny that Nidavellir is trying to weather, I believe that the victor will be Mr. Rogers in a bloodstained sweater."

Artorian became a very small ball, releasing a meek keening sound. Halcyon's idea that this could have been a fun prod was turned on its head, shooting from the bench to immediately curl arms around her Dreamer before she picked him right back up. "No, no, it's okay. It's alright."

The voice of Zelia interrupted Halcyon's spike of worry, her rambling attempts to pull the discomfort back out of her Dreamer wildly unsuccessful. The teleportation Arachnid took one additional step after entering the display room, slipstreaming right over to them. Her order was short and to the point, Zelia having the solution that Halcyon didn't. "Give."

CHAPTER FOUR

Halcyon stuck her lower lip out at the five foot five, Kimono-wearing secretary. "I can—"

"*Give.*" Zelia's sharp, unyielding rebuttal and open, outstretched hand made Halcyon lean down and hand the sad bundle over. Young-torian wasn't much smaller than Zelia, but she carried him like he weighed exactly two grapes.

Instead of trying to talk him out of his unpleasant feeling of incredible embarrassment, Zelia had more effective solutions. Artorian's current difficulties as a mortal boy were going to require a lot of time to cope with. Facing these problems directly was not always the best course of action. She walked him to a set of statues showcasing a humorous event.

"My Dreamer?" Artorian turned his head while pressed to Zelia, his expression a copy of Halcyon's. Complete with a stuck out lower lip. "Look at these four statues for me."

Artorian did as asked, observing the first statue in a sequence. The pose and story reminded him of Cal's embarrassing statue collection. He flicked his sight to the next few in the sequence, then found it difficult not to smile. When Zelia pointed out that plaques accompanied each piece with description, his discomfort began to fade as he puzzled the story together.

The collection portrayed the actions of a lovable fool. On his third go-through, Artorian narrated the scene. "I strike my wizard staff on the ground and immediately duck behind a rock. There's a flash of light, and my ritual chamber is covered in extra saucy spaghetti. I open my grimoire to make another tally under the column labeled 'spaghetti.' The other column is labeled 'harvest god,' and is completely blank."

He wiped his eyes with his sleeve, then slumped in Zelia's arms. "What happened here?"

Gliding across the ground like she was skating across the single line of a web, Zelia moved towards a different wall. "College student antics. You laughed, and your thoughts became preoccupied. Do not be concerned about the observation of your adventures. Anyone with uncouth commentary will be mine."

Artorian tensed, shooting her a look.

Zelia did her best to reply with a most innocuous expression, and innocent tone. "Mine for humble conversation, my Dreamer."

Her Dreamer didn't buy the ruse. "Is that before or after your mandibles are glossy from drooling?"

Zelia covered her mouth with flushed cheeks, the hanging cloth of her sleeve covering her expression. "A mere nibble, my Dreamer. Harmless."

Artorian chuckled hard. "Who are you trying to convince? For that matter, how did you know Halcyon was going to be here? This abandoned racetrack with its hidden-away oasis of soap is pleasant, but I don't believe for two seconds that there isn't something else going on. I have the powerful notion in my head that the Dwarves are being made to take the fall for something they aren't actually responsible for."

"Astute, my Dreamer." Zelia pulled her sleeve away, a broad, proud smile in place. "That is correct. You are in the Nidavellir Underground, where many have a need for speed.

However, neither Hadurin Fellhammer nor Don Modsognir are currently aware that you are here. They will likely know soon enough."

"The plot thickens!" Artorian motioned at the ground, and Zelia played the game of putting him down just to see when he was going to need to be picked up again. He brushed himself off, observing the soap statues while his head felt like it was clearing. "So what is the plot? What are we doing today, Brain?"

Zelia picked at his care-house attire with her claws, her attention drifting to making necessary replacements. "The same thing we do every day, Pinky. Make your life easier since it's too convenient to take over the world, and that's just no fun. We're going to sneak you into Incursus for some game-related item and skill improvements, and be all set for your second leg into Eternia. Better prepared than the first time, and I want some events to occur without Tim's orderly eye on it. A bit of **Chaos** never hurt anyone. Terribly."

Artorian let himself be posed as a mannequin as he studied a series of statues organized by size. Zelia was present! Zelia was in fact located next to the initial depiction of Lucia, and this time he knew to look for a plaque as he went down the line of sculptures. They each had some mysterious measurement on them. With hatch marks? "Lucia - 5'. Zelia - 5'5". Tatum - 5'8". Artorian - 5'9". Brianna - 5'10". Yuki - 5'11". Adam - 6'. Dawn - 6'. Dasein - 6'5". Eri - 6'5". Halcyon - 10'."

"Must be a height system? One Halcyon is exactly two Lucias." Artorian then looked at the line of figures again. Zelia's statue was an umbrella-holding beauty, Tatum a plague doctor holding a very mean burning cleaver, followed by himself in mid-flight! Portrayed as an aged, long-bearded grandpa in the most party-rific beach attire he'd ever seen.

He read the plaque, the creators listed as originating from the Coast of Rica. "Blow me to Bermuda? What an outfit name! Love the vibrancy."

Brianna was depicted in a long, flowing dress that reflected the surroundings to hide her own form. Yuki was positioned with her back facing the viewer, her glare just barely making it over her shoulder. Adam had both his arms and his wings out wide like he was glad to see everyone. He sighed wistfully when turning his head to see Dawn. She had been posed to stand as military commander. Artorian focused on the intensity radiating from her expression. "At the minimum, I can say the Dwarves did my dearest justice."

Dasein…

Artorian stepped right in front of the motherly figure of the Heavenly that he wasn't sure he'd properly seen before. She looked real. The careful detailing of soap carvings was nowhere to be found. The skin was flawless. The lighting on her black and white attire was too smooth. He could swear the statue moved to look at him and wink, but when he rubbed his eyes and moved to touch the piece, this depiction of Dasein was a soap statue after all. "Fascinating."

Eri was an individual he had not met yet, but she was clearly Oni in nature, and matched Zelia in clothing style. Some touches were distinct, but the rope belt around the Oni was a big centerpiece to her look, to the point where he almost didn't spot the horns. Lastly, Halcyon towered over everyone, a wide Orca-toothed grin on her face as if she was completely aware of that fact, and proud of being the big strong one.

Artorian noted the detail of pink blush on her statue's cheeks. Someone else had picked up on Halcyon enjoying cute things. He then rubbed his forehead, turning to his Chosen when he could see the forest for the trees. Zelia's words were filtering in, the detail about skill improvements turning in their ticket after standing in line. "This art is a pleasant distraction. Something was said about Incursus? I know that's a dungeon where explosive ordinance tests happen, and forts get built."

Halcyon crossed her arms, nodding furiously before happily elaborating. "We needed an easy-to-place meeting room, prefer-ably under lots of cover, so we could sneak you out and do some administrative work. In Eternium's space, Dawn and Lucia are setting up to get your feet back onto some solid ground. Your bracelet exit point in Eternia is currently empty space, next to an active sun. Dawn had a way around that, but I don't know the full plan. I do know that, with the Dwarves taking the heat and everyone's eyes off the prize, Zelia can enact what she had in mind. There's some political complications happening behind the scenes, and this was to get around that."

Zelia pulled an honest to the celestials pocket watch from the inner part of her kimono, and clicked it open. "Currently, all is proceeding according to Keikaku."

Artorian kneaded the bridge of his nose. "Let me… Give me a minute. I was nicked from the Faith Foundry by some Dwarves. On account of a Blue Book of Grudges. The owner of which does not know that blue book was called in. In order to sneak li'l ol' me out to the catacombs of the Dwarven capital. So that Zelia could enact a secret plan that somehow required all this subterfuge?"

He felt like he was missing several pages of events, and his guess was off. Yet both his Chosen were nodding along as if his deduction was insight into the greater mysteries. He dropped his hand towards Zelia. "Why?"

The Arachnid lady cocked her head, had gears turn behind her eyes, and covered her mouth with her sleeve again. "My Dreamer, you are certainly aware that I am a dungeon. You are aware what my **Law** is, yes?"

Artorian searched both his feelings and memories, but came up blank. "I… remember that you were the dungeon located in the Fringe, as the **Portation** Core. Then there was the Blessing of **Argent** after I found you in a vulnerable state. Was there more?"

She bowed lightly, then politely motioned at herself as she was as she provided Artorian a quick breakdown to more conveniently explain the steps. "I am Zelia, the Chosen. My strongest connection is to the **Law** of **Argent**. That being silver. This came with your grant, during a circumstance where little of myself could exist. I grew from this connection, reestablishing myself to more correct concepts."

Zelia then grew in size as she adopted the shape of a Drider, allowing her main body and many legs to seamlessly develop from the bottom of her kimono, while her torso, head, and six arms remained dressed and human. She motioned at the alteration. "This is Spider Lady Zelia, Drider form. Controlled and mastered. My strongest connection is to the **Law** of **Portation**, of which **Teleportation** is the most common form. That being the translocation or movement between place A and B. This second step brought me closer to my greater whole."

The Drider shifted a second time, Zelia adopting a full and proper void-swirling Arachnid form that had Artorian take several steps back as she filled the room. He'd never seen such a ferocious version of a spider. Color was no longer the right descriptive form to detail what he was looking at. Translucence was a better marker to describe the shifting, ethereal nature of cosmic milkiness that filled Zelia's current form.

She stretched out before speaking, her mandibles clicking when she spoke. "Full-fledged dungeon boss, inhabited by my dungeon mind directly. I am the web of **Chaos**. No other name shall fit these confines. I have become whole, and found myself."

Satisfied with her own performance, she compressed herself to the size of a copper coin, voice no different than it had been moments ago. "Hand, please."

When Artorian upturned his palm, she teleported above his hand, falling the remaining few inches to land in the center. "Are you following, my Dreamer?"

"I... could use more explanation. I'm sorry. I'm not able to place why you're showing me the forms. Though I'm feeling pleasant that you have become happier over time. That means a lot to me." The tiny Arachnid slipstreamed through the ether, vanishing from his palm. Zelia reformed into her human shape mid-transit, arriving behind him with bore-smooth teleportation as the well-dressed secretary that Artorian had come to recognize the best.

She twirled her umbrella with a twinkle in her silver eyes as she walked around to be in front of him. "My preference, as a subset of **Chaos**, revolves around **Portation**. **Argent** is a small pebble in a big pond, honored to have been included in the sympathy connections that returned me to my proper place."

Artorian stood there with his mouth open, half-pointing as the copper dropped when she said it a second time. The emphasis hitting him. "Did you say **Chaos**? Like the Hawthorn child? I thought **Discord, Chaos,** and **Entropy** were with the Hawthorn saplings."

His secretary hummed her approval. "That is correct, my Dreamer. When the Hawthorne trio connected to the Tower, they did so from the opposite end as normal, because that's where Cal was connected as he worked his way down. I will mention that, with **Chaos** specifically, nothing is ever as it seems. Much like **Nature**, multiple locations of the Tower are there for **Chaos** to hold. The different spots merely differ in Essence affinity combinations."

She smiled sweetly. "Do not fret. The Hawthorne boy did not lose his connection. When he was shown what the position he held would entail, he requested to be swapped to a lower node on the Tower. Less responsibility. Less headache. He is still of **Chaos**, but found more comfort in the simpler combination of Infernal and Celestial. In relation to power, to us who live through this concept, our location in the Tower is particularly irrelevant. In relation to responsibility, we occasionally pass the baton, but know where we belong."

Artorian ground both his palms over his temples. His mind was running into all sorts of unhappy error messages. "Zelia, you are one of the most well-ordered, organized, planned out, efficient people I know. **Chaos** is a *difficult* sell. Your entire line excels in keeping populaces neat and tidy on a global scale. Anansi is enamored with Alexandria, for crying out loud, and it doesn't get much more **Order**-aligned until you get to Tim."

The Arachnid made a long and elegant kiseru pipe appear in her hand, smoking holic vapors in delight. The exhaled cloud hung heavy and lingered as mystic fog. "What is **Order** to the spider is **Chaos** to the fly, my Dreamer."

She swirled the tool in her hand, circling the statue room. "If **Order** is the sensical and understandable, derived from a universe of ineffable truths, then what is **Chaos**, except an **Order** that is yet too vast to grasp? **Order** is, to a degree, imperfectly captured by our limited conceptions. What **Chaos** accepts that **Order** does not is that there is always something beyond the patterns we conceptualize. The way of things as we perceive them, or accept them."

Zelia exhaled an entire cloud of inky mist, her clawed hand turning the pipe to poke pinpricks of light into the vast black and purple churning mass. "A finite mind cannot fully capture the pattern of **Life**, or **Nature**. Too much is forever vague, nebulous, and unknown. **Chaos** transcends our best attempts to make these ideas concrete. Unless dedication to such a concept itself is at play. Even then, those concepts choose to be blind to the workings of all other things outside of their domain."

A twist of her hand caused foggy, shadow-gray grass tinted with purple bioluminescence to grow across the entire floor. "If one looks at **Nature**, for example, one finds it Abyss-near inde-structible. **Order** seeks to make what is known presentable. Easily consumed, and confined to its preset, accepted phases. Yet, no amount of **Order**'s attempts to control, corral, or curtail **Nature** can stop it. **Nature** always finds its way around the limitations of an imposed order."

A rising motion of her hand added trees formed of magenta fog to the scene. "Tim would tell you that **Order** is the better way, because it is the sensical way. It is what has been under-stood. What has been grasped from the cloud of the nebulous mysteries. Carefully unpacked, studied, and agreed upon so others could have their foundations to exist in a realm of the sensical, and concrete. A realm not steeped in **Madness**."

When she had poked enough pinpricks of light, she connected them with lines of brightness. A sudden pattern emerged out of otherwise irrelevant points in space that held no correlation. Unifying and forming the image of Artorian as a grandfatherly figure, holding his beard, studying some esoteric truth. "Just as no man was ever wise by chance, there is no genius without a touch of **Madness**."

The glowing constellation overtook the full breadth of the central chamber, billowing out to claim all available space while adding in additional details. Such as the book he was scribing into the fabric of the very stars, the tome held open in his other hand. Illuminated within cosmic pages, great truths of the universe were written. Zelia read an entry before turning the page with the back of her pipe. "As long as you live, keep learning how to live."

When the cloudy page turned, she pressed her kiseru pipe down upon its inky surface, reading one more entry before she returned her attention to her topic, and her bewildered Dreamer. "Time heals what reason cannot."

Artorian gawked, and could hear in her voice that she was proud of this scenic accomplishment. "Does that mean **Order** is unreal or imagined? No. All that which is not orderly still exists. Forming its own patterns. Its own devices. If you ask Eternium, he will tell you the words 'Ordo ab Chao.' They mean **Order** from **Chaos**. That being, the amount of sense he has been able to grasp out of the cosmic web that we call the greater whole. The simple truth is that it does not matter if the **Order** is unreal or imagined. If one believes it is there, then one will grasp at endless straws in order to form it."

Zelia dismissed her pipe, but left her foggy galactic creation in place. "I understand that it is difficult to see me as one of **Chaos**, my Dreamer. I do not stand for the lesser versions of bubble-bubble toil and trouble one expects from that concept."

Her circular pacing paused when she stood right in front of him, Zelia ever so sweetly bowing and extending her clawed hand. "That does not mean, my Dreamer, that it is not where I stand, and where I feel whole. Did this injure your view of me?"

Artorian frowned, but took her hand. "I trust you, Zelia.

DENNIS VANDERKERKEN & DAKOTA KROUT

You've been nothing but good to me. Yet, if that is what you stood for all this time, why be so kind to me? Why the dereference and the Dreamer title? You eclipse me."

Zelia took a knee, lifted his hand, and pressed the back to her forehead. "I decided this long ago, my Starlight Spirit. On the day where you opened your heart to me, and offered me all that was **Love**. That **Chaos** is but empty star stuff. Undirected, and sown as a field of complete disorder and confusion, without the right star to pay attention to. The right guidepost to follow. **Order** and I will always butt heads, but we will both turn our gazes to catch and carry the concept that allows us this passion to drive forward."

She looked up at him with a worried frown, a mixture of affection and deep concern filling her silver eyes. "Because nothing in this existence, my Dreamer, nothing at all, neither **Chaos** nor **Order**, is worth the least of an expended candle, without the light of **Love** to brighten the way."

CHAPTER FIVE

Artorian slam-hugged the Abyss out of Zelia, refusing to let go as his hands clawed biscuits into her back. She was taken aback by the sudden motion, remaining on one knee so her Dreamer could more easily embrace and attempt to squeeze the life out of her. She felt him hiccup in her arms, a moment passing before it registered that she had overwhelmed him with emotion.

Her lips parted to speak, no mandible in sight as she kept her shape fully under control. Yet she did not speak, choosing instead to allow this great Dreamer—in the form of a small child—to grow where he felt safe. That he felt safe in her embrace, when she was feared across all Caltopia, meant the world to her.

When the words came, she let them flow. "I am unspeakably ancient, my Dreamer. I have seen the world turn and fill with majesty. I have seen it all fall, to rise again, and fall. To rise again, and fall. Both with me and without me, the world has burned and risen from the ashes. When you were but a speck of dust living at the outcrop of one of my many extensions, I had long given up. Of **Chaos** I may have been, but my purpose was burned out. My goal lost to time. My endless schemes were either so easy to bring to fruition that they were not worth doing, or had succeeded so long ago that there was no further thrill in their pursuit. I am capable of galactic influence. Cosmic stratagem. Yet even before the third moon fell, I was lethargic. Uninterested."

She swallowed, her human voice cracking. "I was never provided the door to take over for **Chaos**. That door will never open. Yet I yearn for one still. A path of upward momentum and purpose. The current individuals of **Chaos** are exactly where they need to be. Exactly the right minds for the purpose and placement of their nodes in the Tower. My capacities were fruitless. I did not fit. I had Incarnates willing to brave my dungeons, but no peers, and certainly no friends. My automation kept going all that it needed to. By the end, I had taken from myself all reason for life and growth to matter."

She pressed her cheek to his forehead since he was curled against her. "There is a story called The Ocean On His Shoulders. A man plods down a sunken hall, under the weight of all the seas. He's tired. Every day, he goes through a routine for which the 'greater purpose' of doing so is long since gone. Nothing left to do but survive now. He walks through wreckage, burned, buried, washed over. He is wracked with guilt, and the memories of what once almost was. A utopia, nearly there, before it all came crashing down."

A squeezing hand on her back gave her strength to continue. "He rides up a rickety little elevator through all that's left. Even if what's left is a crumbling, leaking wreck. There are no threats that can assail him, but there is a void of which he is the epicenter. Inescapable, internal, irreparable. For all his unassailable strength, there was one thing this man feared above all. That one day he would stop. Stand in place. Look behind him. Then fail to perish from all the regret, all the loss, and all the guilt. As he walks on, yet no others walk with him still."

She swallowed again, frowning. "This is what I was thinking of when a hand so seamlessly slid through any and all passive protections I had in place. Under a small hill, in a most irrelevant, innocuous hideaway. I could not tell you what truly possessed me to go and be there. Only that this is how the universe moves, and I was there."

Artorian held her tight, protecting her head with both his arms.

"I was mad, then. I lashed. I sent my children. I lost. What a feeling that was. Loss. All the power in all the worlds, and a fresh incarnate of **Fire**. Tier *one*, **Fire**. Bests me. Has **Chaos** pranked me? Then, I find that, no, **Chaos** did not prank me. Of all the intentions that could have pushed me from my main dungeon, on another layer no less. Into a little hole in the ground, to be grabbed by my face and have eons of work ripped to pieces? I never would have guessed that the intention was **Love**. Someone up there did not want me to quietly die when the world did. I certainly would have. I'd have run out of Essence, Mana, and Spirit. Even cannibalizing all my children, and my entire dungeon, I would have run out of it all long before Cal reached his exit point, because I know for certain that I would have run out before this current point."

She hadn't noticed her Dreamer rubbing her head before now, but she said nothing of it. "I knew hope at first, when I was lesser. I found a tiny throw pillow filled with a feeling that mended an emptiness in me, that I had either never known was there, or had never grasped the means or knowledge to know how to fill. Then there you were. The Wandering Sun. Cleanser. Destroyer. My clever ruses and obstacles but layers of cloth for you to push away. Then you looked at me, and you changed. I watched you change. I watched you choose, that to this creature of which you were most afraid, you would not be lesser. For you, mercy was victory. You sacrificed, you endured, and when given the chance, you forgave."

Zelia improved her speech even if she still had to speak slow, the comfort of being held strong. "**Argent** gave me a floor. It let me stand. Even if I no longer knew who I was, it let me stand. Then when I felt the emptiness within me return, your arms were open. Your heart welcomed me. I felt emotions that I never encountered as a dungeon. Never conceived of by a normal spider."

She motioned at Halcyon, who had taken a knee next to her. Her own large hand added to Zelia's lower back. "Then there was Halcyon, and Yuki, and an unconditional acceptance. Even when I looked at your back, and your mind was far away. Your Aura is so endlessly gentle. I saw the **Love** pulsing in your chest, blooming out from your being. I cannot describe to you, my Dreamer, what it was like for you to turn in that moment and look at me. For me to read the expression on your face, and know without doubt that you see me as someone you loved. When you had no idea that you were doing it. When you had no intent of doing otherwise. When you saw me as just a person who deserved the affection and care you so freely gave me. Not as what I was, but who I could be. You saw in me a potential for growth I had abandoned. You had no idea that your Aura turned, reached to me, and surrounded me in the warmest of hugs. For it had already learned, even then, who you are, and what you are."

She softly bonked her forehead to his, her words weak. "I do not eclipse you, my Dreamer. You are the living example of who the man, who carried the ocean on his shoulders, should have met. For him to be able to walk out of that ocean, and be able to look back. Because that is what you did for me, and not once did you want anything from me, except for me to be happy. You are a dream made manifest. You are a hope that breathes life into the fallen. You are a hand that may reach for me at any time, and I shall be there. For you are, to me, the embodiment of care, and stand for all that is worth living for in this life."

She reached for him, and squeezed her arms around his shoulders. "You are my Dreamer, and I choose to call you so. For in the dream that you let me live in exists a reality from which I do not ever desire to wake. I do not care about your form. I do not care about your power. I do not care about your age. I do not care about your species. I learned long ago who you are, and what you strive to be. Your pattern claws into the void, screaming to reach for the one way in which majesty that rises, shall not fall."

Artorian nodded while keeping the mutual embrace, at a hearty loss for words.

Zelia slowly let him go, but wiped her sleeve over her face before she allowed him to see it. "I am never bothered that you cannot spend all your time with me. I am never bothered that I miss out when I hear stories of your ventures. Your tales make me fiercely proud, each time I hear of them. You prove, again and again, that you refuse to be lesser. You ceaselessly continue to place yourself into the line of fire. You cannot stop. You will not stop. You staunchly believe that if someone must stand in the front that it will be you. So it is someone else who does not fall. Because to you, Artorian, you are the least important person in the entire universe."

She stood slow, composing herself. "So while you claw at the universe, my Dreamer, helping where you can, and with what you can, as the whims of the dungeon and the circumstances of life whip you around in the whirlwind, your Zelia will turn her eyes in the direction your back faces, and you will find no daggers pressed against your spine. Unseen, there will be a network of support that my webs tangle together. For you have the **Love** of a spider on your side. Whatever your task. Whatever your struggle, or your need."

Artorian swallowed to wet his own mouth, his eyes wet and cheeks stained. "Can I do anything for you, Zelia?"

Her expression twisted, wrecked by emotion as she reached out a hand for him to take. She squeezed when he did, closing all her eyes to breathe as she lost control over her face. "I tell you of my pain, and even as a mortal child, you cannot help yourself. Yes, my Dreamer, there is something you could do for me, if it pleases you."

He nodded, laying his other hand over the one she was gripping. "What can I do?"

"Let me help." Her expression was that of a forced smile, but neither Halcyon nor Artorian was going to mention the detail. "If you're going to throw yourself into the game, into the role of Administrator, into the circumstances of life where you think you can help the people you want to be there for. Let me help. That's all I want. As a dungeon, I do not experience the world, or feel things as a human does. We are different. Which is why it is all the more important to me that you understand the weight of my next words."

She squeezed his hands. "I love you, my Dreamer. Yet there is no shred of romantic love in that statement. I do not experience it, not as Tim does for Yuki. Not as Dawn does for you. You are fond of speaking on the topic of **Love**. May I give you how a dungeon sees it?"

He let her go when she was ready, very gently making a hand motion to request she continue, throwing in a light bow for a pinch of flair and to make her smile.

She cocked her head, recalling the terms. "Where you are Agape — Selfless Love. Wanting nothing in return? I am Pragma — Enduring Love. Matured over many years. Halcyon, Decorum, Alexandria, and all your adopted from the Fringe and the Old World give Storge — Familiar Love. You are family to them all, endlessly accepting, deeply trusting. Yuki, cold as she may appear, gives Philia — Affectionate Love. A love without romantic attraction, between friends or family members. Built when both people share the same values, and respect the other. Dawn, bless her fire, is both your Eros — Romantic Love, and Ludus — Playful Love. She adores you for all the world to see. Voltekka is Mania — Obsessive Love. The boy cares only for your company, and when he can find it, he will remain there. Dumb he is not, but a box of rocks might give him a run for his copper. He is so happy to play Pylons with your two Squirrely friends in Eternia that he'll likely be there for as long as you intend to return. He loves being your lightning."

That got both Halcyon and Artorian to break from their

demure facial expressions, a small laugh freeing itself from them both. "What I know you lack, my Dreamer, is Philautia — Self Love. I have spoken to Scilla about this at length. She fears it will be your true hurdle that prevents you from becoming an Incarnate. Neither of us have any doubt that you will make it to the zenith of Magehood. Both of us expect you to be very stuck at it, as well."

Artorian quickly lost his smile, going quiet. He looked at his feet, frowning as he thought. He then looked back up at Zelia, holding his own wrists. "Is this what you want to tackle when you say you want to help me? To be there when I stand before that hurdle. Out in the real world. Having reconnected to the Tower directly. At the platform where my soul becomes manifest."

"I would like that. Yes, my Dreamer." Zelia folded her sleeves together, lightly bowing to him. "If you wish to become an Incarnate, that is a desire of mine. Though I currently have no answers for you. I require permission to begin such a venture. To engage in this against your knowledge and without your consent... would not do. It is not your way, and while you have never heard of it, it is also against the way of Heaven's River."

Artorian frowned, but Zelia was waiting on him to let her explain, if he wished. He felt her reaction more than noticed it, nodding gently. "Please tell me, Zelia."

She did so gladly. "The way of Heaven's River references rules you will undoubtedly have heard of in another format, for they are wise, and ought to be shared. Bob was the only other person I knew to have known them, but he was close to the Beavers of Bobiverse. The Iron Rule: Treat others less powerful than you however you like. The Silver Rule: Treat others as you'd like to be treated. The Golden Rule: Treat others as they'd like to be treated."

"That's a pleasant phrasing of those rules." Artorian agreed, somewhat biased from how it involved Bob. He rubbed the back of his head, his feelings abating as a sense of calm and peace held him. He'd been expecting discord, to feel unsteady, and to have emotion run rampant. Yet, no. He was not conflicted. He did not feel an imbalance. Zelia was giving him the kind of information that his way of thinking, his pattern, thrived on. He didn't even feel poorly about her statement concerning Philautia.

She was simply right.

Artorian collected his words, and shared them. "I don't understand how a heavy talk like that somehow improved and increased how pleasant, confident, and stable I feel. I'm no longer bothered by the knowledge that anyone who is anyone saw my speech to Lady Duchess. Your experiences weigh heavy on my heart, and I can't help but feel that now that you have said what has burdened you, it feels lighter than a feather. I feel that tears should be running down my face from hearing how you feel about me, but all I feel right now is a sense of peace. The calmness of a still lake. The warmth and heat in my chest of how grateful I feel that you'd share that with me, and that I want to hug you."

He frowned ever so slightly, opening up with honesty. "I don't think that I really deserve you, Zelia. Nor how adoring those I once called Chosen are, as you all continue to treat me with such affection. None of you have to act like I'm special. You've all powerfully outgrown the tiny naming gift I was able to give you, and have shot past it in style. What I did feels so minor. What you all did by yourselves is what I'm proud of."

Halcyon brushed her hand over his head, repositioning herself to be kneeling next to him. "That's part of the point, my Dreamer. We do not adore you because once upon a time you gave us names and positions. We adore you because, in addition to that kindness, you have proven to be the kind of person we would willingly put this effort in for. Not because you gave us a jumpstart, but because we genuinely believe you are deserving of our adoration. Our time. Our effort."

Cy bumped noses with him. "I love you as well, my Dreamer. Zelia explained it better, but you are family to me, and you always will be. Regardless of that being in the shape of a large noodle, a tiny child, a fussy old man, or a ball and bundle of energy. We want to be here for you, Artorian. You are important to us. What is important to you, by extension, becomes important to us."

Zelia leaned into Halcyon, adding a comedic shift as she placed her own hand on top of Halcyon's while she kept her palm on Artorian's head. Her tone returned to her confident, usual self. "I am on this team until you rebuke me, or find someone better. Good luck with either option, my Dreamer. If you wish to tackle the problems in Eternia, then that is your choice and we will support you. Let us sneak you off into Incursus, fix your half-baked skill and ability entries, update your gear for it to actually be fun and useful, and then have you fondly think of us when you go play with it. You are not the only person in Eternium trying to solve all the problems you have set out to solve. You are not alone."

She patted Halcon's hand, then walked away as she began to dismiss her nebulous creation and sculpture of light lines of Grandpa-torian holding his beard. "It matters little to us that there are issues in the Soul Space of Cal. There will always be issues in the Soul Space of Cal, or Tim, or the real world outside. That is the nature of issues. They will self-generate. What is important to those who love you is just that. You. You matter to us. Remember us. Include us, my Dreamer. Share with us your goals. Your dreams. Your aspirations. A Heroic Age cannot be built on your back alone. Carrying the ocean on your shoulders will only leave you lonely and wet. The majesty of an age not built from your spirit will spend far too much time on the floor."

She smirked wide, the joke coming to her as she peeked over her shoulder. "So perhaps it is time we call upon Ellis? I am looking behind me, and I find myself in need of a door."

CHAPTER SIX

Artorian clapped his hands together, matching Zelia's speed and wholesome mood, all on board with this call for upward momentum. "Then we summon Ellis, the door of worlds!"

Kra-kow!

Ellis appeared on command and on cue, accompanied by the crack of a whip as Artorian dove behind Halcyon. The wooden, battened and ledged barn door smoked with heat on arrival. As Artorian peeked his head out from behind Halcyon's knee, he remembered how unpleasant Ellis had been before he'd turned the man into a portcullis.

To many, the sudden appearance of a door being yanked through space via a rather unfriendly teleportation-tug would be unsettling. Young-torian merely chuckled as the shape of the barn door altered into a thick wooden frame adorned with simple saloon doors, forming the facade of a building complete with windows, accompanied by cantina music leaking through from the dark areas that he could not see through.

Zelia smirked, patting the frame in praise as she slid over to Ellis's cantina doors. "I hung him out to dry in Incursus, but he has developed a sense of humor over the years. Less ego. I do not know if you recall Nong the Elf, and Tex the Dwarf, but they are doing work in Incursus for me. They have changed since the days of throwing mountain tokens onto the Jotunheim ground, giving Cal leeway to drop in multiple icebergs and tilt the landmass like a spiteful gesture to a good painting. We may encounter them. We may not."

Artorian rubbed his temples. His memories of those days were vague at best. The Chosen were his strongest, most prominent recollections. Dawn throwing him across a few sandy deserts for combat training? Hard to forget. What else...? He was sure there was more, but Kellen Shadowbeard's comment on people reintroducing themselves suddenly carried greater merit. His non-cultivator mind had the shovel in hand and was going to town on burying things. Forgetting might be healthy, but a synchronized cleaning crew was currently having a dance-off in his head.

The janitor slide combined with Astrea's sick beats, dancing to the Fooly Cooly and making his memories poof by ironing out the wrinkles of the brain. "Shall we go ahead and head in? I've had my fill of inner turmoil. Child-torian would like some toys to play with."

Halcyon pushed herself back to her full height. "I enjoyed having this talk with you both. This was liberating. I must part with you both for now, but I leave my Dreamer in Zelia's most capable claws."

She pointed at his bracelet. "I am aware that you are currently holding on to my Tonfas, but please keep them, my Dreamer. They require a slight adjustment in their description block for them to be properly useful to you, but Zelia has someone on the inside who is an expert on bugs and is ready to report. I do not know if you have met Kowsky before."

Artorian nodded, remembering the three-inch masked bug that Ember had called out a projection of. He'd had some very good things to say the last time. Artorian expected this next time to be no different. He extended his arms up to request a hug, received it with gusto, and squeezed Cy back as hard as he could before following Zelia into Ellis's held open door. "See you when I see you, Halcyon. You are an adored member of the family."

She clicked her tongue at him with a wink, beaming toothily with a pink flush on her face as she watched him step through into Incursus.

The transition for Artorian was easy.

Gone was the soap statue room. On the other side of the door existed a blasted landscape covered in endless ruins of all shapes, sizes, materials, and remnants thereof. Wherever anyone had built a fortress, someone else had made sure to blast it to itty li'l bits. The space had that same not-light effect going on as The Pale. Nautical twilight present all around.

When Ellis vanished with a *vwop*, Artorian performed a small hop on his toes, feeling no different from being in Incursus's dungeon. He kept expecting to feel sick or something. Entering with a mortal body must be some kind of key for ease of transition. "Status."

His character screen successfully came up without issue, showing his current attributes and statistics from Eternium. A star was present next to several entries, but a quick tap brought up the explanation that all functions and features originating from a greater or upper-typed Soul Space game setting may not translate or function properly in a limited-typed setting. Incursus simply did not have the means that Tim did. "Does the dungeon know we are here?"

Zelia wordlessly pulled her own screens up, most of them a deep black in color, adorned with white text and silvered filigree. "He does, but is likely to stay put unless called. Incursus was forewarned. I required his setting, and he graciously thanked me for considering him for this project. I am aware you are not informed of all the Cores that live on the Silverwood Tree, my Dreamer, nor the social activity between them. The short version is that they are forming their own culture and mini-society. They are all very aware that when exodus time comes, they will all part ways and fill the roles they need to.

Until then, the local hierarchy is set. There is a standing agreement that they will be taken care of, and are encouraged to use either some allotted space in Cal, or their own Soul Spaces if they have them, to experiment freely and engage in dungeon-craft. They are, however, limited to assaulting only other dungeons unless someone explicitly comes to bother them."

Artorian nodded and tugged his weapon entries to the forefront, curious about what was off with the Tonfas. He hadn't seen a problem before. He did glance back and forth between his own powder blue screens, and Zelia's more imposing ones, but didn't want to ask about the colors yet. "I am aware that I'm missing out on several development tracks inside of Cal, but that is bothering me less and less as time goes on. Eventually, I am sure that I will run into someone who will give me an update on how life has been. I lump my Wood Elves in that boat as well. There are multiple groups of people who would love to steal me for years and years. So when life takes me to their shores, I will gladly lay on the beach with them. Until then? Between problems to solve, there are things to do and people to help."

He motioned at the Tonfa weapon entry. "I'm really not seeing this supposed problem here, though."

"That is a task for later down the line, my Dreamer." Zelia held up a yellow-covered screen with a fancy blue border. "Please take this title first. It is necessary for us to make any changes and improve your quality of life."

He pushed the accept prompt when it showed up after taking hold of the screen.

———

Notice!
  Title Acquired.
  Title: Architect.
  When designing, editing, or updating system functions—including attacks, or other mechanical entries—you will be allotted system time up to

the maximum rate of frames that the system is able to provide. This time will be experienced normally, but the world around you will appear to slow to a crawl. Taking any actions that alter your intent away from this process will end this effect, including attacking, casting, and ability use.

———

"Helpful!" Artorian was instantly glad to have this title until he noted a hidden drawback. "This says nothing about it costing me no energy, or not making me tired by doing so. This title merely compresses the time in which I get something done, but it appears that the time spent will be treated as real time to me. So even if I wake up and eat, then spend eight hours compressed down to a few seconds, if that's even possible? This task is still going to make me terribly tired, sleepy, and hungry all over again when those seconds have played out for everyone else."

A polite nod from Zelia confirmed his worry. "That is correct, my Dreamer. This is why you are venturing out with a party, instead of soloing the world as you did during the alpha version. I would also like to direct your attention to the special character traits that we currently cannot get rid of."

He glanced, groaned, and sat on his butt as he reread his Glass Cannon trait. "I forgot my HP was set to onnnnne. A measly one! That's going to be... I'm actually going to need to think about circumstances before I blindly run into problems! Lucia is going to save my life with those shields of hers. I really don't want to take the game too seriously, but that effect is harsh."

"Indeed."

Zelia's short reply had Artorian look at her, a cold feeling building in his chest. "I don't like that you agreed so fast."

Zelia sat on a charred husk of wood that used to be a teak tower strut. "The impetus remains with you, my Dreamer. Only you can be responsible for avoiding the fate that taking a single point of health damage would cause, and you lack many necessary tools to protect yourself. It is not the end of the world if you were to perish in the game, but it would certainly be very annoying for the rest of us."

He nodded, crossing his legs and arms to pay attention to all the new screens Zelia was placing in front of him with flicks on her wrist. "Then I will try not to die. I hear that's important."

Artorian motioned at one of the red-colored screens Zelia had placed near him. "Are these some of your notes?"

He read off a few lines when she didn't reply.

———

Description Issue: Core text - Trans Am deactivates only when the player's Stamina or Energy bar bottoms out. Is incorrect. Provide the descriptor in the written entry that it is possible to manually disable this feature from the Player's end, to match the mechanical end.

Circumstance: There is no air to breathe in Eternia space - Player is vacuum immune, still requires air for core functionality. No solution found.

Optimization: Supreme Weapon Mastery makes high variable, top-heavy maximum damage weapons very enticing due to automatic maximize. Critical Fault: If a player scores a critical strike, Supreme Weapon Mastery dictates that the opponent dies. This makes the actual damage on any piece of gear unimportant for the purposes of removing threats, on successful critical tally. Auxiliary systems keep crashing violently during formula tests. Pylons may be damaged, the effect may not be functional.

Optimization: Halcyon Days Tonfa set effect calculations are occurring in the incorrect order. Damage from natural strength that any other melee weapon receives is not tallied. Damage from strength in the effect entry is tallied instead, but should not have replaced the original mechanic. Bonus damage from tallied effect is counted as base damage, not bonus damage, making critical tallies impossible. Provide an update or reforge equipment.

———

Artorian held his chin, pensive as he read the rest of the entries in silence. The list was thick. Zelia did not interrupt until he asked her a question, busy with preparations so he could accept a host of prompts in the correct order. "Zelia? What's this at the bottom about mundane weapon importance? It's underlined and precedes an entry about LFB's? Light Fusion Beamers? Beamers for short. The detail about them being miniature Essence cannons caught my eye, but now I'm stuck on this prior entry."

Zelia glanced at the text, recalled flawlessly what it was about, and recounted her initial thoughts while her six arms each remained occupied and undisturbed from their current roles. "As a Mage, did you notice that weaponry and armor of all kinds became either moot, unimportant, or irrelevant?"

Artorian moved the screen blocking his clean line of sight away, folding his hands as he watched Zelia work without one hiccup to her movements, her face trained directly in his direction as he spoke. "I am aware that their relevance fell off a cliff, yes. I've become aware that the C-ranking Dwarves who kept the Mage-level friars at bay in the Old World used some exceptional runed equipment to do so, and that without that equipment it would have been a one-sided slaughter. In any other circumstance, save for Adam and his conceptual weapons that I hewed through Demons with, or Dawn assuming a weapon form, I consider you to be entirely correct. In a world of Mages, mundane weapons are sort of... *nyeh*?"

"*Nyeh* is the best qualification." Zelia turned one of the screens she was in the middle of modifying with a swirl of a claw. "Answer me this, my Dreamer. If this became true in Eternia, would the game still be fun?"

Artorian had to parse out some bits of her unspoken question. "You mean, the equipment becoming irrelevant because people exist that ignore their value purely by existing?"

A silent nod made him ponder and continue. "I'd say that would be pretty terrible, and not fun. I'm now thinking how Tim doesn't allow Mages in his setting. When I tried to use cultivator tricks during the first foray, the system shunted me into forced alternatives. Like Empowerment. For the better, I think. This way weapons will always matter?"

Zelia highlighted segments on her prompt. "Weapon-making in Eternia has more to do with, 'we have this resource now, can we do anything with it?' For as people increase in realm difficulty, the old material may not do anything of substance against the current monsters in that setting. Think of... a Resistance bonus against materials from lower Realms. Half damage from steel, purely because it's steel, or such."

She highlighted a different screen, showing cultivator values if they hadn't been subverted. "When your basic Mage can pick up a mountain and play ping pong with it, weapons become difficult to keep important. My solutions in that instance diverted to: the people are what's special. The people are taking on the role of weapons, literally, in some cases. Players will need more than the basic triangle of hammers smash, swords stab, and axes cut. The sprinkling of 'ranged pointy sticks are better in place X than Y' does help, but that only gets us so far. None of these tools are useful when you are up against an individual who has the density of Celestial diamond. Kindling is in posses-sion of the ability with the closest similarity, and while it changes her appearance, all it does is add her hardness to her damage reduction."

Artorian nodded, once more pensive until he got stuck on the name Zelia used. "Who?"

She held up an image of Ember embossed on a prompt. "Dawn. I call her Kindling in this current format. She's a firestarter."

Artorian sputtered from Zelia making a joke. "I did see her turn diamond while dancing in New Haven, I think."

Pleased, Zelia turned her screens back towards her, repur-posing them. "I see you are satisfied. Would you like informa-tion on Beamers, or shall we get to work?"

Artorian cocked his head, expression unchanged. "Are there any other reasons we need to rush into work? Can I not do this in Tim?"

His chosen one bobbed her head apologetically. "No, my Dreamer. You cannot."

That got his attention. "Can I know why?"

"Of course, my Dreamer." Zelia smiled like a pleased spider unfurling a scheme. "The moment you enter Eternia, you will commence combat. There will instantly be fighting. You cannot escape this. We either handle the administrative work now, or you do it mid-fight while fleeing on Lucia's back. An option you are guaranteed to need."

"*Ah.*" Artorian pruned his lips together. "Let us commence the great work."

Zelia's expression turned sweet, speaking as a seasoned secretary. "Of course, my Dreamer. Let us begin by going over every single entry in your character sheet, altering the phrasing, and lessening the burden on your personal Pylon hold. Your synthetic crystals are bursting at the seams after what the Task Manager did to them. We cannot alter the core effects of your character traits, but we can clean them up. I will now call in our little hollow knight. I demand his presence, and expertise."

She upturned one of her claws. Her six black arachnid eyes filled with focus and fury as she summoned the bug with a call. A swirl of small, glittering orbs formed on her open palm; bright pink hues mixed with the comfortable colors of a deep, resplendent dream. Ever-shifting shapes representing the fleeting view of a kaleidoscope rose in a tight column, shattering into snowflakes of radiant light. From another Soul Space entirely, Zelia teleported her intended target directly into her open grip. "*Come. Kowsky.*"

CHAPTER SEVEN

Pop.

"...And one more thing!" Kowsky stumbled as the ground changed under his tiny feet. The three inch bug stopped swinging a needle around, focused on stability. He froze in place with both his arms reaching out, knees bent. "I'm good? I'm good."

Artorian didn't notice anything different about the bug finder. Kowsky was tiny, wrapped in a cloak fashioned from a moth's wing, and carried several nail-sized weapons on his back. The one in his hand was stowed to join the prior two as Artorian greeted him. "Hello again."

The mask tilted up, Kowsky needing a lot of time to let the surroundings filter in, but he did recognize the friendly face. "Administrator?"

Kowsky's voice was breaking less than before, but still sounded distinctly genderless. Spoken by a teenager, filled with that seasoned civil service worker cadence that gave away this was life number two for this individual. "Bug finder eight-five-nine-eight, reporting in. How can Kowsky be of service?"

Artorian glanced at Zelia, who had the most wicked smirk

stuck on her face. When he glanced back down, Kowsky had puzzled out something was amiss. A spider sense of sorts was tingling in the tiny bug, as if a large amount of predatory eyes were on him. The mandibles of the most dangerous insect in all of history within striking distance.

With Kowsky frozen, Artorian nudged a leading question. "Are you, by chance, afraid of spiders?"

"Of course I'm afraid of spiders! They are the perfect apex predator of the bug world! No matter what size, they——" Noticing the shape of what he was standing on, large droplets of sweat formed on his mask and began to pour down his face as panic swirls became visible behind the eye sockets of his mask. He hand-twitched towards the nail with the grappling hook enchantment, because his senses were screaming at him to fleeeee. While the more intelligent portion of his mind was tackling the panic portion to the ground and trying to muffle that screamy voice, saying that if they fled, they would perish.

Ever so slowly, Kowsky looked over his shoulder to find the imposing gaze of Zelia bearing down upon him with the weight of worlds. He fell upon his hands and knees, prostrating himself with a yelp. "Good health to the Autarch!"

Zelia chuckled, having forgotten that Autarch was how many of the non-Arachnid Beasts and others saw her. "I have questions, bug finder eight-five-nine-eight. Will you answer?"

"At your pleasure, Higher Being!" Kowsky slammed his forehead into Zelia's palm. "How may this humble hollow knight be of service?"

Artorian frowned. "First he's afraid of Ember. Now he's afraid of you. I'm not liking this pattern here. Just how much fear is going around?"

Zelia hid her expression with her kimono sleeve. "My Dreamer, there are troublemakers, and then there are those who would make trouble for the sheer enjoyment of it, if a Damocles did not hang above their heads."

While that didn't answer his question, Artorian was eager to get on with it, distracted by the weapons Kowsky had. "Well, let the poor boy up and please stop crushing him with your gaze."

Zelia became the picture of politeness, doing exactly so and letting Kowsky breathe without being blanketed by increased gravity. "Of course, my Dreamer."

Kowsky trembled while getting back on his feet, but found his courage, providing the Administrator a crisp salute as he waited for instructions.

Artorian motioned at his weapons. "Would it be alright if I see those before we begin? I'm very curious."

"Of course, Administrator!" Kowsky swiftly removed all three bug-sized weapons from his back, holding them up.

"Thank you, Kowsky." Artorian waved a hand at the weapons, directing his intent along with the command word that he was pretty sure was the right one. "Inspect."

———

Name: The Debugger.

Rarity: Unique.

Damage: 1 – 6 Kinetic.

Weapon Type: Nail.

Weapon Size: Insectoid.

Material: Everglow.

Internal Note: Everglow = Osmium + Celestial Corruption.

Material Effect: This metal is identical to Osmium's properties with the exception that it self-repairs, and can hold 'Charges.'

Special Qualities: Self-repair is faster if the weapon is holding a Charge, and consumes that Charge while sheathed, repairing 10% condition per Charge. A Charge takes 1 hour to consume regardless of quality.

Special Effects: Everglow releases a constant, pale blue light. The intensity of the light increases by 50%, stackable, for each Charge the weapon holds. This denotes how close the weapon is to self-destruction, with the blue color darkening the closer it comes to 0% condition.

Special Ability: For each Charge this weapon holds above 1, its condition is damaged by 20%. If the weapon's condition reaches either zero, or a negative number, it explodes and permanently destroys the item. Try not to be in the vicinity, you may join it.

Description: Everglow is next to indestructible with its constant self-repair.

Enchantment: Dynamic Exchange.

Internal Note: Infernal Essence Enchantment Variant.

Special: Effect-Eater.

Description: Effect-Eater allows the absorption of any effect it is intended to strike at. The user needs to be aware of the effect to absorb it. Absorbing a spell will consider the weapon to be 'Charged,' allowing the use of either its Special Quality, or an ability from the user with matching keywords. Non-spells do not generate a Charge.

Internal Note: If weapon condition, the same statistic as durability for this weapon, reaches either zero, or a negative number, then unlock the Achievement: Splitting the Atom.

Flavor Text: Up close and personal. While you're holding it. Boom.

Internal Note: 'Boom' scales with physical weapon size. Test version limited to bug-sized Nail weaponry. We don't want to make another lake, Jerry.

Internal Note: Weapon functions are intended to 'shut off' errant, unwanted effects. Like a pebble rotating at thirty-thousand rotations per minute. Without taking the effect upon yourself, Jerry. We're still cleaning your vomit off the clouds. How did you even get it that high?

————

Artorian chuckled. "Jerry doesn't seem to be very suited to his job."

Kowsky's mask gained glum lines. "You don't know the half of it. How do you find the first nail? Satisfactory?"

"Convoluted?" Artorian rubbed his chin checking the entry over again. "I grasp that it's meant to stop errant effects in a roundabout way. Effects that shouldn't be going off being hard-stopped, and such. The method is strange, but I'm of the assumption that this odd workaround was needed in order to make the end result work."

He moved on to the second nail.

———

Name: King's Antler.
    Rarity: Unique.
    Damage: 1 – 6 Kinetic.
    Weapon Type: Nail.
    Weapon Size: Insectoid.
    Material: Jotunheim Hercules Beetle Antler.
    Special Quality: Herculean Strength.
    Internal Note: Her-cu-les, Her-cu-les!
    Special Effect: Herculean Strength, calculates your strength attribute as if you were a creature of Huge size.
    Lore: The horn of an area boss.
    Enchantment: Wings.
    Internal Note: Wind and Earth Essence Enchantment Variant. Grant Basic Flight Transmutation.
    Special: Scarab's Vengeance.
    Description: While held in the main hand, this weapon provides Scarab Wings to the user, or improves existing wings by one step. Shell included if the user is wingless. Existing wings will instead gain the 'Sturdy' Quality.

———

"Curious." More interested in the next weapon than exploring the wording in the second one, Artorian skipped to the third and last nail entry.

———

Name: Ignition.
    Rarity: Rare.
    Weapon Type: Nail.
    Weapon Size: Insectoid.

Material: Sparkflint (blade), Furnace Mite Carapace (hilt + scabbard).

Internal Note: Sparkflint = Flint + Earth Corruption.

Material Effect: The stone is identical to regular flint, but requires much more force to chip or break. Furnace Mite Carapace is a strong insulator against heat.

Special Qualities: Friction causes the Sparkflint to heat up and release sparks. Furnace Mite Carapace protects the wielder from the heat.

Enchantment: Spider Silk Shot.

Internal Note: Earth Essence Enchantment Variant.

Special: Sling Sword.

Description: The user may expend mana to create a thin, durable strand of spider silk at the hilt, connecting to their hand. This allows for swinging and spinning motions over long-range.

Internal Note: This enchantment is otherwise most commonly used as a kind of grappling hook to traverse cliffs and chasms.

————

The naming convention made the Administrator shoot Kowsky some side-eye. Particularly after his own foray into the Eternia beta. "I think some of these Pylons are perhaps being… What is a nice word for overused?"

Kowsky turned a touch red, looking away to maintain innocence. "The Ignition Pylon is queued for repairs, Administrator. After a certain minor, highly visible hiccup where an effect caused an entire inert sun to catch fire, the bug finders find themselves down a surprise tool. The problem should be mended before you return to Eternia, sir."

Artorian grumbled an *mmm* from the throat, but dropped the issue and ended his Inspect. He was also a little sad that he would not have access to that surprise tool anymore either. Luckily they were here to update his equipment? If they could patch out those scarab-nibbles and slot in something more useful, that would make him happier in the end. There were only so many instances of bending system rules and vulnerabilities before he couldn't look the other way anymore. "We called you here because you, I am told, are the expert on the problems in my toolkit. Can we get directly into them?"

"Of course, sir! How may Kowsky be of service?" The bug finder sat down on Zelia's palm and pulled out a map that appeared to have the same functionality as Artorian's screens.

Zelia moved her hand to a wooden post, gently depositing the bug. "Before that, bug finder, do you have an update for me about the token debacle with the giant mosquitos?"

Kowsky swiftly flipped through map entries when Zelia made her request. "I do!"

Artorian quietly asked for some clarity with a lift of the hand.

Zelia answered while Kowsky browsed for her update. "Giant versions of creatures are not entirely new entities where the system is concerned. Large, giant, huge, and gargantuan creatures are created by adding a new set of tokens to pre-existing templates. This didn't cause too many issues for normal creatures, but for a certain class of creatures bearing the pest token, it notably did not remove their corresponding swarm token."

She pulled up a screen with those tokens on it, giving Artorian a visual representation of their respective icons. "The result? Whenever the game wanted to generate a creature of a certain threat level, it could land on the Giant Mosquito as an option. Which the game saw as the same threat level as any number of other giant creatures. The problem with this was that whenever the game spawned a creature with the swarm token, it spawned not one entity, but a literal swarm of them. I don't recall how many, but if in an appropriate biome, it was possible to suddenly be overwhelmed by hundreds of mosquitos the size of large wolves, or houses, or small hills. The name change should have given it away."

Zelia shifted on her seat, not particularly comfortable. The scenery and seating was sub-par. She was starting to be bothered about it as Artorian asked a follow up question. "Name change?"

She nodded, creating a visual representation of a mosquito. "The suffix '-ito' means 'small.' Which hints at the existence of something bigger and greater than 'Mosquito.'"

Kowsky sprang right up, mimicking a pose of a truly horrifying being. "El Mosco!"

He stumbled and fell on his butt, but barely noticed. "Somehow made even scarier by the Invictus version where they have claymores and zweihanders instead of forearms? I think flamberge was the correct word. That vampire template is nasty as well, but the numbers have been rolling in since the sun turned on and the death count is staggering. They either blot out the sun, or fight in the shade. They're dangerously Spartan."

His map went *ding* as he found the news that was requested, and handed that screen to Zelia with a bow of the head. "Your update, Autarch."

Zelia took it, read it, and filed it. "That is unfortunate. My Dreamer? It appears you will be needing armor after all."

Artorian pulled his eyes away from the screens, then checked to make sure he still only had that single hit point. "*Uh*, I cannot take the spank. I will not be the tank."

CHAPTER EIGHT

Kowsky hissed out a sound of pain when he went through Artorian's current character sheet. "*Ouch.* That's gonna hurt. Tank or not, Administrator, you are in dire need of protections in front of that proud single health point. What's with these titles and character traits? They are horrifying."

The bug finder tapped his map, encountering an error sound. He tapped it again with no difference in outcome, then slapped his tiny hand furiously on the repeating prompt as the error sound played over and over. He then pulled free a piece of coal and drew angry eyebrows on his mask. "What do you *mean* no access?"

Zelia hid her laugh with her sleeve, turning her own screen towards the bug finder for him to gasp and gawk. "*You* have no access? *What?* Who dares stand in front of the Autarch?"

She chuckled fondly. "The corpse of a crispy Task Manager. That chalk outline may not have been the most threatening triangle in the box, but he was certainly skilled in the ways of system management. We have encountered endless rough seas of troubling difficulties because of that crossed out poster. We will manage, of course, but as we do not have the luxury to grow an entirely new synthetic bank to place Less Than Three's character information on, we must contend with the gordian knot of the existing system, and its troublesome entanglement. What an ugly web this creature wove."

Kowsky felt enraptured by the information he was diving through. "I understand now what you needed me for, Autarch. Navigating these waters is my specialty. I shall do my utmost to be of assistance."

Artorian stood in place, stunned, too busy grappling with the knowledge that the Task Manager was dead. "Wait. I got him? I actually got him? Last I recall, Ember told me that party member number four was mighty displeased. I recall thinking that Taskie was out of commission for a while, but the orange traffic cone is dead-dead?"

Zelia's mirth bled through, an enjoyed cruelty briefly visible when her expression slipped from behind her sleeve. "Dasein turned him into one of his own crossed out posters, my Dreamer. She twisted him from existence after he spoke of trapping you in a cycle that she most definitely did not approve of. Otherwise, that Heavenly has been content to operate in the background. The recordings are plentiful, should you ever wish to see them."

"No, thank you." Artorian blinked away the thoughts, pacing in the destroyed surroundings to find somewhere to sit that wouldn't be rubble. "I... Alright, to begin, is it possible not to sit in rubble?"

"Incursus." Zelia summoned the dungeon's attention with the use of his name. The pressure in the environment grew, becoming noticeably heavy as a baroque-style castle of wood and stone broke from the ground, cracking away both rubble and the damaged remains of other structures as a colossal, hunched golem stood. Incursus towered above them all as a literal castle emplaced on a turtle's back.

The tolling of bells preceded the massive being's speech. The words slow, deep, and deliberate, but not particularly bright. "You. Rang?"

"Your sense of humor always amuses me, Incursus." Zelia's sudden change of voice to one of sweet playfulness drew the ears of both Kowsky and Artorian. She was overly polite with Artorian, and somewhat cold to Kowsky. Yet to Incursus, Artorian could have sworn she was flirting. "We are in need of a less discordant environment to do our work. Can you build us anything?"

A bell tolled a single time, Incursus answering with a rumble. "Make. Camp."

The star-lit night sky of Incursus dulled as lit campfires rose from the debris fields around them. Rubble sank into the earth like rocks through quicksand, replaced by the accelerated sprouting of walnut trees that formed a full and complete canopy above them. Tents, chairs, and expedition equipment all followed. The supplies rose from the ground until Artorian's surroundings could no longer be distinguished from an adventuring camp where half the party was too wealthy for their own good.

He sat back down in a plushly padded wooden chair, testing the seat with a wiggle before extending his feet towards the fire. "I like this a lot more already. All that's missing is some food."

A metal cooking grate fell onto the fire with a *clang*, kicking up embers and coals that singed the fresh grass. Pre-chopped slabs of meat followed, whole racks of ribs piling onto the metal grate and feeding the flames as the fats began to seep. The meat glistened as chunks hovered back up all by themselves and turned in place.

Artorian wiped his mouth with the back of his hand, the aroma causing some well-deserved salivating as different mixtures of spices launched themselves at the scintillating slabs. The fire pit smelled all sorts of wonderful. "Now I'm just being spoiled. Thank you, Incursus."

A bell tolled, the dungeon pleased as the moving castle it was using as a host body set itself down, plunking the baroque-styled castle in the middle of a brand new forest. "Company. Pleasant."

"His alternatives have been Geese, Wisps on a mission, and Gnome teams hungry for more ordinance tests." Zelia patted the chair to praise the dungeon for his quality work before sliding into the seat. "He does well. He has interesting patterns when it comes to being a dungeon. Rare is the case when a heart such as his comes by. Incursus, for all his uncanny comforts with explosions, things blowing up, and being on fire, has proven to be thoughtful and kind. The initial designs of Demeter's Dream were made here. He volunteered for Ammy's Silverwood Bracelet project. Small things for people to do, but for a dungeon? That is a heavy extension of care."

She ran a single claw up the chair's arm support. "I find myself weak to such accommodating touches. To find affection in those one does not expect it from. Incursus, therefore, is a bit special to me. Many dungeons would eschew care in favor of the pure pursuit of their goals. That is part of the way of being an intelligent dungeon."

Zelia reminisced. "Before sapience? Us other dungeons tend to hand-wave their actions and not pay much attention. A Core still developing as a fledgling dungeon and thrashing against the limits of the world should be left alone to do such. They were all Beasts before, after all. The survival of such a dungeon to a full-fledged sapient Core is, culturally, one of a dungeon's barriers to entry into our overarching social structure."

Artorian crossed his arms, wondering about a random thought. "Does that work the same for all the Cores grown on the Silverwood? I think they grew there, at least. The limit of my knowledge on Cores is… that if you have one in you when you die, there's a good chance that you will come back as a Beast… No. No, I got that wrong. That was if you had a culti-vation technique in you that happened to be the Pattern of a Beast, because the completed patterns of beings are highly potent. The Cores…"

He rubbed his forehead, troubled by how difficult it was to remember. "The Cores happened because… No. All Beasts have Cores. A Beast without a Core is just an animal; that's how we get the Beast designation in the first place. The Core of a Beast that dies has a chance to become a dungeon… and then I lose my mental thread."

Zelia counted on her claws, providing a short list rather than an explanation. She had prompts that she would like to get to. "Natural. Manufactured. Synthetic. Silverwood Genesis. And a category I like to call: 'that shouldn't have happened.' When Occultatum was still The Master, that whole endeavor with plunking human minds and souls into Cores was a rough, ugly business. Would you like this conversation now, my Dreamer? Or did you wish to begin going over your character sheet? Ribs will be done shortly. Vegetables may have to be grown."

Artorian stared into the fire, nodding absently. "Sheet? Yes. Best if we did. Focus is difficult. I was never a mind that didn't dart between what could hold my fancy. Cultivation helped me keep the clarity on a task for longer, but that all feels like such a nebulous dream now. One day, that will be back. For now? Yes, please. Being kept on task is the better way. I'm still surprised Yvessa isn't here to be glued to my shoulder. She must be fighting a small army for her to be detained from appearing and commenting."

Zelia gladly organized every entry of his character sheet into an individual prompt, restructured into a floating circle around them as the screens slowly gained some spin. Rotating around them with the fire as focal point, their trajectory smooth and slow, to be freely plucked and attended to. "She does not know you are here, my Dreamer. Like many of your fold, I can assure you she is dedicated to your health and wellbeing. What you do not know is that she is working on that project through other means. I am certain you will have the time to see all your loved ones again. For now, shall we begin with your attributes? You do have a bonus waiting."

He squinted at the fire. "Did I earn it? I'm not feeling keen on accepting system freebies. It already feels off that so many tools I could be getting through gameplay are being wrenched in beforehand. I know that's a sudden thought, but it was on my mind."

"An understandable thought, my Dreamer." His chosen one pulled his attributes screen from the circle. "I will inform Tim that, when able, natural growth is a factor you prefer. Are you against building the tools to complete your current objectives in Eternia?"

He shook his head and held up a hand. "No, I didn't mean that. There's a… a disconnect? On one hand, if I'm going to play Cal's game, I would have more fun if it were the case that my effort and energy being spent produced results of new and additional toys being provided to me. I would feel like I earned them. I would have a sense of progression. Enjoyment in the fulfillment of goals and growth. That has been a difficult thing to do in Cal, and I am aware that I have been more privileged than most in my advancements and momentum. So if I still feel like this regardless, I imagine it must have been much worse for everyone else. I'm losing my thread again."

Artorian got himself back on track. "On the other hand, I have this need in my chest that I want to clear the roadblocks in Eternia. That I have an obligation to all the starsouls trapped in that realm. Now that the sun is on, I suppose there are many more who can shoulder their way in and solve issues, but I still want to do my part. Tisha, especially, is a voice I hear ringing in my ears. My shark boys are in there somewhere, as well. Yiba and Yorn have both held on. What kind of **Love** would I be if I didn't grab my shovel and rush to dig them out?"

He straightened up in his seat, reaching for a rib that seemed done. "To that end? I will accept any and all toolkits, up to what I can get away with. So while, yes, I would have more fun with natural progression, I want my shovel. I want my Administrator tools. I want my Deity options. I want my broom. I, however, reserve the right to fuss and toss away toys that I do not want to play with, if I am endlessly handed them. I want some control over my comfort. Afterwards? We see about an iteration of my game character that stands more rooted in natural progression. Until that time? I shall rip and tear, until it is done."

He thought of the broken broom Shaka had dropped, and pulled it free from his Silverwood Bracelet while letting the cooked meal float. "Speaking of. Can we do anything with this broom handle? It was partially on fire when Shaka dropped it, and it's been used in a brawl or two. Still, a Janitor should have a mop!"

Zelia claw-motioned for him to drop it on the ground. "Give it to Incursus. Let him play with it."

Artorian did so, watching the handle vanish in the soil like he'd dropped a rock in water. "Fascinating how easy it is for Incursus to do that. I remember making earth act as water being decently difficult. Especially when other aspects are interacting with earth Essence and still need it to act as if it had the same conditions as before, like being properly solid. I'm not sure I can do that."

He thought of the other items he'd obtained from the Task Manager and procured them. "Kowsky, would you happen to have the time to tell me if anything suspicious happened to this bow, and if there's any terrible things going on with this Owl cloak? The source I got them from is dubious at best."

"Yes." Kowsky gladly received the bow and cloak as the latter was hung from the pole he still sat on, the weapon leaned against it. "I'm checking them out."

He moved the attribute prompt that Zelia wanted him to focus on in front of him, leaving Artorian's hands the freedom to handle the roast ribs!

Like a hungry Beasty, the boy tore into it. A happy noise caused by an excess of savory, juicy flavor was all he needed to make for people to grasp that he was pleased with the rapidly vanishing meal. He swallowed, motioning at the prompt with the bone. "*Mmm*! Don't hold up on my account just because I'm enjoying the cooking of Chef Incursus. He knows what he's doin' with fire! I'm not sure what exactly I need to do here, so please do tell."

Zelia bowed courteously. "First, would you like an account of the old entry, and then an account of the new entry? Or merely the updated entry with some hints as to what changed?"

Artorian waved his bone at the second option. "The latter, please. Let's not repeat information too often. I'll get confused on which is which if I have to read big chunks of the same text twice. Show me the tasty numbers!"

CHAPTER NINE

Zelia was adamant they tackle these screens in order. "First, your new character sheet. It was deemed that you should earn something from turning the sun on, regardless of means. Ten attribute points have been assigned to you as a system reward in all entries. Not at all because we wanted cleaner, more even numbers. We will move on afterwards with your rephrased titles. Followed by your updated race entry. Each entry will recount your personal Pylons that are spent, as they represent your actual limit of available tools for the moment."

———

Name: Less Than Three
  Character Level: 1
  Race: Nascent Being
  Class: Janitor
  Specialization: Crit-Fisher
  Profession: Scribe
  Characteristics:
  Strength: 750

Dexterity: 750
Constitution: 750
Intelligence: 750
Wisdom: 750
Charisma: 750
Perception: 750
Luck: 750
Karmic Luck: 0

———

Artorian leaned in, his hands full of food. "Looks like those ten points bumped all the growth and flat values by another category again. Can I see the end results of what that currently looks like? Non-Trans-Am, please."

———

Characteristics: Improvement Choice.
  Strength: Pattern A: Flat
  Dexterity: Pattern A: Flat
  Constitution: Pattern B: Growth
  Intelligence: Pattern B: Growth
  Wisdom: Pattern B: Growth
  Charisma: Pattern A: Flat
  Perception: Pattern A: Flat
  Luck: Pattern B: Growth

———

Characteristics: Threshold 750, Total Bonus:
  Strength: 6,000 Base Stamina Pool.
  Dexterity: 600 Stamina Regeneration.
  Constitution: Multiplier of 10, replaced by Multiplier of 25.
  Intelligence: Multiplier of 10, replaced by Multiplier of 47.5.
  Wisdom: Value of 25%, replaced by Value of 40%.

Charisma: Bonus Language slots: Plus 15.
Perception: View distance clarity: Plus 15 Kilometers, or 9 Miles.
Luck: FIF chance, Plus 15%.

———

Calculated Values:
Hit Points: 18,550.
Mana Pool: 35,625.
Mana Regen: 300 / second.
Stamina Pool: 13,400.
Stamina Regen: 787 / second.

———

Adjusted Values:
Hit Points: 1.
Other:
Language slots: 16.
Note: Language slots are poorly utilized and fail to account for existing languages known. An update is in the works.
Vision Range: 18 Kilometers.
Note: Vision Range is considered poorly worded, as it has less to do with the actual range of one's vision. Instead, this value dictates the range at which both clarity of vision can be brought to focus, and indicates the maximum range of certain Abilities.
An update is in the works.

———

Alteration:
Your Mana Pool has been renamed to: **Nuts**.
Your Stamina Pool has been renamed to: **Bolts**.
Main Calculation node: Incursus.

———

Artorian made a pained noise when he saw the calculations roll in. That one in health was going to eat at him. It took the prompts much longer to populate with information since it seemed to be Incursus doing the math, rather than the Nuttelator. He pressed two fingers together out of curiosity, finding no electricity connected between them when he pulled them apart. That must only work in Eternia, due to Voltekka playing with the Squirrels. "Alright. One health. Fat mana pool. Ridiculous stamina regeneration. How does this compare to an average baseline?"

Kowsky and Zelia looked at each other, hoping the other had the answer. Artorian picked up on the awkward sudden silence, deciding it was time to pull in more people. "Who can we ask to join us for help?"

The bug finder grumbled when pulling out a second map. "Blue is around, but spotters and bug finders have an… iffy work relationship. We hunt for scarabs, signs of Pylon damage, and patch connections while taking down errant effects. They… they lick rocks."

Artorian kneaded his forehead. "Blue… is he an Axolotl by chance? Dwarven spotter otherwise?"

"That's him! You know him?" Kowsky put his map down in surprise. "The spotters are very reclusive. I know you're the Administrator, but they're the type of people to stay away from anything that isn't their field of study. His puns kill me."

Artorian nodded sagely, understanding on a fundamental level the agony that was caused by rampant punnery. "As they do to us all, Kowsky, as they do to us all. Yes, I was there during his… decanting? I'm foggy on the details, but I pulled him out of an Axe-shape that he was stuck in. Never did ask how he got stuck as a weapon in the first place…"

Kowsky chuckled. "A pun-related incident during rune tests."

He held the bottom of his mask, wanting to give a clearer answer. "Administrator, do you recall what Lady Dawn's lectures were on the dangers of turning into weaponry, and how you can get stuck? No amount of her warning people not to do this stops everyone. Spotters being the prime example of people who do not care how bad of an idea something is. They're going to try it. Personally. While the rest of their group watches with *ooohs* and *aaahs*. Spotters then frantically all take notes while the prime mover among them lies in a smoldering crater, trembling a hand to the air with a thumbs up. They're as mad as Gnomes, I tell you."

The slow fizzle of aquamarine-colored electricity refracted from Kowsky's mask before a Dwarven voice peeped clear and smooth from a small set of lungs. Blue, the spotter in six-inch tall Axolotl format, stood on Zelia's open claw, having been there just long enough to catch the tail end of Kowsky's blind rant. "Hah! Ah do drive Kowsky up the tavern wall! Ah seem to bug him with me puns. He den threatens to blue us to smithereens with his wee Debugger. An' yeah, some folk do show us the most interesting things. Like with Lady Dawn, where 'pon we do ignore small details like warnin's. To us spotters, warning labels tend to be interpreted as instructions."

Blue saluted Artorian. "'Ello, Administrator! Good ta see yah! Lovin' the younger format you're trying out. Can say Ah've grown fond of bein' the wee li'l blue one mehself. Now, s'cuse me for a moment."

The Axolotl turned around to figure out his surroundings, bowing deep towards Zelia the moment she came into view. His tone instantly became far more respectful. "Good health to the Autarch. How may this humble spotter be of service?"

Zelia placed him on a nearby tent pole with a wide top, then took one of her black screens and gently slid the information into Blue's hands. She said nothing, and gave no instructions.

Blue reverently took and studied the exceptionally rare high-sec access screen, muttering under his breath like a normal Dwarf. "*Hmm.* These here be Muspelheim values. You'll breeze through the realms up 'til then, but you'll get your teeth kicked in if ya cross to Asgard. When they're all fixed, I mean. Muspelheim and Niflheim are where ya belong, Administrator, challenge ratin' and attributes-wise. Ya be painfully behind on the specializations front. Late Vanaheim might give ya trouble, if the secret purpose of what that realm is for doesn't stop ya cold in yer tracks first. They each have a special li'l something they try ta teach the player ta overcome. Again, I mean when they're all sorted. I'm working from design documents, not the current state of the world."

Artorian folded his hands. "Is there a chart of sorts you'd be able to show me? I need some kind of reference point."

Blue glanced at Zelia, her response sharp as she didn't share Blue's reverence for the value of the black screen he was holding. "You give the Administrator everything he requests."

The spotter instantly ducked his head in deference, combining a 'yes ma'am' and 'at your order.' "I happen to have such a chart. Please don't fuss 'bout the details on rough cultivation equivalent none, that's there specifically to rile up A-rankers an' get them up and at 'em to Asgard. Where they get smacked in the face with a heavy dose of game reality, an' have to tuck and run back to a lower realm with their tail 'tween their legs! Attributes ain't everythin', an' that's a hard lesson to learn. We knew what we were doin' by giving A-rankers a bonus of only seven-twenty in all attributes, leavin' 'em just shy from the next door over. For the folks coming up from the bottom, it's the opposite story. That measurement becomes something to strive for."

Blue formed globs of water into flat sheets to get the prompts solidified, before he cautioned Artorian. "I warn ya ta be careful, Administrator. Most people go in at your level with the mindset that the place is a game, and only a game. They don't take it serious none, and can't until something bites them real hard in the arse. If ya ever feel the switch inside of ya that allows ya to take the place more seriously? I advise that ya capitalize. It'll only help ya. Please pardon me for taken yer attention. Your list is ready, sir. Here ya go, Administrator."

———

Maximum attributes, organized by location, with rough cultivation equivalent.

150 - Midgard - F to D rank.

300 - Alfheim and Svartalfheim - C rank.

450 - Jotunheim - Low B rank.

600 - Vanaheim - Mid B rank.

750 - Muspelheim and Niflheim - High B rank.

900 - Asgard - A rank.

Uncapped - Hel - S rank.

———

Blue sat on the edge of his pole, legs swinging as Artorian glanced his eyes over to the Axolotl, silently requesting some more chatter while he read the list over again.

Blue relished the opportunity. "There be talk of redoin' specialization requirements. Some folk are adamant that the second and third specializations ought to be limited by first obtainin' the Midgard maximum of two of the player's CRAs. That bein' Class-Recommended Attributes. Then the fourth specialization be locked until the player obtains the Jotunheim maximum of two of the player's CRAs. What's actually been happenin' is that multiple systems are bein' made to apply to different kinds of players an' people. Not all people are fit to be players, an' not all players are going to be people."

Blue tossed Artorian another screen. "Here be the current results of the arguments in progress. Expect some changes? The first two entries be set in stone, though. Cal went and deemed it so after the Nidavellir Dwarves got into a feud with some Elves from the Old Guild. They're gonna need to work that out somehow, and Cal got wind of it. The big man himself gained a big, wide, evil grin on his face per how he could get each to… What'd he say? 'Experience life from the other's viewpoint'? Don't know what he meant by it, but we ain't gettin' in his way on it. There might be a *wee* war in Eternia soon, and Cal already said that if it don't sort the problem the first time, then history gon' repeat until it do."

Artorian hummed in understanding, then read the prompt.

———

Realm Unlocking, plus Requirements.
  Midgard - Enter the Game.
  Alfheim and Svartalfheim - Specialization 2, plus completion of the tutorial.
  Jotunheim - Alfheim and Svartalfheim are made whole.
  Vanaheim - Specialization 3.
  Muspelheim and Niflheim - Access the hidden Bifrosts in Jotunheim.
  Asgard - Specialization 4, plus defeat one hidden world boss from each prior realm.
  Hel - Defeat Odin in Asgard.

———

"Defeat Odin?" Artorian blew air from tightly pursed lips. "Good luck? I could barely do that! Even then, I don't think what I did counted in terms of game checkmarks. Do I have to go through all of these steps? Feels like I already mucked some of them up. I do recall the gravity-squishing two-minute timer. Is that gone?"

Zelia shook her head. "No, my Dreamer. Those functions will be restored over time. What you read is merely the intended, current plan. Circumstances will require us to change that list and its stated thresholds. We simply don't know *how*, until there is an overabundance of players to give us that data. When it comes to requirements, New Game Plus individuals worry about none of them regardless. You are considered to have finished Hel's last challenge as far as any checklist is concerned. You equally do not need to be concerned about the two-minute timer. That feature is currently inoperable."

She smiled so wide that her human expression broke, her

face swiftly hidden with her sleeve before Kowsky or Blue could turn pale. "Tim is adamant about not annoying Dasein. By giving her leeway and the permissions of a moderator, he does not have to grant the same liberties for the other Heavenlies clamoring to play. They will have to begin as new player characters, with all the limitations thereof. If they complain, they may direct their whining to Dasein, who has already agreed with quite the smile that she would be delighted to intervene."

Her expression under control, she dropped her sleeve. "What she did to the Task Manager alone put the fear of nonexistence into any Heavenly who sees the recording. Particularly during the part where she looks straight at Tim's perspective. The visiting Heavenlies all suffer this tense, fearful little shudder that they do their utmost to hide. It's a delicious detail."

Artorian held his own hands as she savored recounting the moment. "Zelia, I'm starting to recall why everyone is frightened to bits of you. I'm so glad you like me."

The Arachnid in human form beamed, pulled an adorable paper umbrella from storage into her hands, and twirled it with satisfaction. "Of course, my Dreamer. Shall we continue on to your titles?"

CHAPTER TEN

Artorian moved some prompts around to make space, accepting the blank one that popped up as the updated titles and character traits started rolling in from the top of that screen.

Character Trait: World Boss.

You have been designated as a Roaming World Boss. You may claim an area as your dungeon or base of operations. On defeat by another Player, you will drop all items in your possession as lootable objects. You are permanently limited to a maximum of 10 items on your person, and in your possession.

Until you claim an area, the 'Roaming' suffix will remain attached to this Title. If defeated while under the effect of the 'Roaming' suffix, then your Player Pylons will be wiped clean.

Artorian held his chin, growling. "That item limitation is even less generous now!"

"Apologies, my Dreamer." Zelia highlighted that section for him within the entry he was looking at. "Part of the trickery of the now-deceased triangle. The mechanical effect was always set this way, the wording simply did not reflect it. We have removed the less than truthful phrasing, and updated the entry to reflect its actual effects. Other titles have also received a quick pass of the whetstone as well, including Architect."

He sighed, scratched his head, and nodded. "Thank you, Zelia. What does this mean for my storage bracelet?"

Zelia glanced at the Silverwood piece. "Currently? You can take items out, but not place them back in. I would recommend emptying its stores to have full control. I heard you had some difficulty accessing its current contents? I can sort it for you."

Artorian waffled, but agreed in the end. He slid the object from his wrist, casually tossing the bracelet to Zelia when she offered to empty it. "Let's continue."

————

Character Trait: Glass Cannon.
Your maximum Health Pool is set to 1.

————

Title: Administrator.
Cal assigned. Cannot combine. Can be toggled on and off. Grants deep system access. Bugfix access. Player character modification. World modification. Inspect quality: All.

————

Title: Overdeity.
Eternium assigned. Cannot combine. Can be toggled on and off. Grants: Deity System Access. Deity features. Divine energy point access. Divine energy shop access.

———

Title: Cultivator.
  Cal assigned. Cannot combine. Gain ATB based on personal cultivation rank. F-rank: 1. E-rank: 2. D-rank: 6. C-rank: 24. B-rank: 120. A-rank: 720. S-rank: 5,040.

———

Title: Architect.
  When designing; editing, or updating any functions, you will be allotted system time. This time will be experienced normally, but the world around you will appear to slow down to a crawl. Taking any actions that alter your intent away from this process will end this effect.

———

Cursed Title: Focused Caster.
  Curse: Cannot be removed.
  You cannot cast in any way, shape, or form, without the proper and correct focus item. Your focus item, once designated, will demand the use of another title slot.

———

Title: Focus Item.
  Curse: Cannot be removed.
  Casting Focus: The left leg of Exodia, The Forbidden One.

———

Artorian sighed, dropping his open hand at the last two entries. "That's just silly. Can we do anything about those? They don't say I can't combine them. Free up a slot?"

Blue and Kowsky looked at each other, communicating with

expressions and hand motions before the bug finder raised a nail for attention. "On that topic, Administrator, there is no entity called 'Exodia' anywhere in the game. Pieces or otherwise. Your required casting focus doesn't exist, and was only allowed to be slotted into that entry because a Log Pylon exists that happens to have that name present in a note. We may actually be able to do something here."

"Please go on." Artorian leaned heavily in Kowsky's direction. He momentarily looked at his hands to wonder why they weren't dirty, wet, or sticky after he'd finished a whole racks of ribs, then noticed that his cleaning effect was active and rolling out at full blast. Good enough!

Kowsky leafed through several maps before pulling out the correct one. "Here we go. This is a rules issue. Limitations can't be instilled through values of which the threshold condition cannot be satisfied. Therefore, you are currently holding an illegal title. As we currently cannot remove the title, our options are twofold. One, to change what the key is supposed to be. As in, no longer a leg, but an object that is attainable. Two, do nothing. I would recommend not merging them, and instead using the provisionary system allotment to alter the Focus Item title."

Artorian crossed his arms, mumbling begrudgingly. "I listen to my experts. How do we change the entry?"

The small ones looked to the Autarch, who was already working on it. She then held up a bar of soap in confusion, the object having been present in his inventory. "I'll have it done shortly, my Dreamer. I simply need to have the item. Preferably in hand. I have no idea where this soap came from."

Zelia inspected the object, getting no results. Not even a prompt. She shot a questioning face at her Dreamer while motioning at the bar of soap, utterly baffled.

Incursus helpfully chose that moment to push the repaired broom up from the ground. The mahogany instrument of mighty cleaning hovered in mid-air, ambling next to Zelia's seat.

She looked to her Dreamer for approval of this substitution, but he was too busy breaking down with sudden laughter.

To Artorian, a Janitor using a broom as a focus item was too funny. "Ha! You know what? Yes. Let the broom be the casting focus. Bedknobs and Broomsticks as foci. Next thing you know I'll be making up spells like Treguna Mekoides Trecorum Satis Dee. Every magician needs a good substitutiary locomotion spell."

Ding!

Title: Focus Item.

Curse: Cannot be removed.

Casting Focus: The broom of Shaka. The Boom Shaka Laka.

The Administrator howled, slapped his chair, and wiped tears from his eyes. "*Ahhhh*, and suddenly it's a good day. Yes, that will do wonderfully. Even if I collapse into a giggle fit when once more casting 'To Whom It May Concern.' I need to increase the blast range of that one. That spell is more of an 'Abyss that person in particular,' right now."

Zelia attempted to make additional adjustments, encountering the same error noise that Kowsky had been fighting earlier. She frowned deep, her irritation rising when repeated attempts reproduced the error. "This displeases me. Do I need a Gnome for this? A Wisp? One of my children? I have already summoned a bug finder and spotter. Shall I simply call a full table to order?"

Artorian made grabby hands at another glistening rack of spiced ribs that gleefully floated its way into his hands. "Go for it! The more the merrier, and if they all have slightly different skill sets, all the better for problem solving."

Power crackled around Zelia, a chaotic medley of colors

suffusing a billowing cloud around her claw. "Summon-Porta-tion on one person at a time is child's play. Three at once takes some focus. Two would ease the strain. Come, my son."

Mr. Webb stepped seamlessly from the ether via a rudimentary Slipstream, and faced his mother upon being called. The young male Arachnid arrived in a mostly human guise. He pressed a hand to his gray-suited chest, fingers touching the lapel as he bowed low at the hips. Adjusting his mulberry-colored vest as he rose, Webb spoke smooth and gentle, a mixture of deference and calm patience in his voice. "Good health to you, Mother."

A crack of power later, and an orange Wisp popped into being, followed by an ink-skinned, well-dressed, red-bearded Gnome. The duo had been in the middle of an argument, frozen in their combative poses. They both hushed as a disorganized pile of papers and other data recording material floated to the ground around them. They weren't in the Archives anymore, but still crossed rolled up paper templates as makeshift weaponry.

Feeling the pressure from Zelia's gaze, both of them began to sweat as the chaotic cloud around them dissipated. Their heads slowly turned before they panicked and dropped their improvised armaments. They both said the same words, but the voices were distinct.

Aleksandr spoke first. The orange Wisp, whose color and affinity type excelled in being soothing, spoke soft and gentle. His voice never raised in volume. An excellent hallmark for those who helped dungeons focus on quantity instead of quality. "Good health to the Autarch!"

Turk, the feisty Dark Gnome who smelled of habaneros, tucked his bright red beard into his dapper attire where a tie would ordinarily go. His speech was gruff for a high-pitched Gnome. The deference to Zelia kicking his professional grumbles with Aleksandr from the first place pedestal. "Good health to the Autarch!"

Between bites, Artorian mumbled commentary, amused by

the sight at this point. "They're all so polite. Hello, you three. I don't believe I've met you all before."

Webb, Aleksandr, and Turk turned, the recognition slow as Artorian didn't match his grandfatherly description. Kowsky cheated by hurriedly holding up a sign with his title on it, at which point all three newcomers politely greeted him with a light bow, before being directed to take a seat in one of the many chairs pushing out from the ground.

After they sat, Zelia handed out copies of screens, getting the Wisp, Gnome, and Arachnid child up to speed. Much like Kowsky had been starry-eyed at the sight, great reverence was shown for the black screens that ended up in their hands. There was silence as eyes ate information and fingers scrolled through data.

A pleased noise from Zelia made Artorian look in her direction as she pushed a confirmation prompt. She then smiled at him, and motioned at his own screen.

Artorian focused his attention, and watched changes roll over his character sheet like a red tidal wave, a large amount of edits occurring all at once. A sense of loss filled him, followed by a dumb idea. He then stood as if attending a wake, adopting a preacher's pose. "Dearly beloved. We are gathered here today to mourn the death of this character sheet. For, 'Oh Lawd, there's a fire.'"

Zelia shot him a dry look for being silly. "Very good, my Dreamer. Anything else to get out of your system before we resume work? I know you too well for it to not be the case."

Artorian sheepishly stood there as the grease on his fingers cleaned itself away, his immaculately pristine hands scratching the back of his head. The tingling sensation between his teeth did feel weird, but he wasn't about to complain about his ability being thorough. "Yes. Sorry. I can't really stop thinking about what the Wisp and Gnome were arguing about, before being teleported to us while in the midst of a dueling state."

He turned to them and gave a light bow. "Apologies, Aleksandr, Turk. Could you indulge me?"

Aleksandr pulsed a deep orange, tripling in overall size to become a large beach ball of a Wisp. "Of course!"

Turk raised his small hand, needing to insert a preamble. "Administrator, a warning? Our entire conversation is the definition of the quote 'Never argue with an idiot. They will drag you down to their level and beat you with experience.' I will not have you enter this debacle without proper forewarning."

Artorian sat, holding his own knees to watch the replay of interactions.

Blue the Axolotl had a Nixie Tube moment. "What 'bout that one growlin' match you two had 'bout 'no amount of skill is going to protect you from the sheer luck of a chronic dumbass'?"

The Gnome and Wisp silently communicated through looks, not wanting to do that one. Turk held his flaming beard. "How about from the point of conversation where I said, 'I want to poke things and see what happens'? Or the later topic of organization?"

Aleksandr pulsed a soft yellow, swaying in place. "The later one."

The Gnome agreed and cleared his throat, recreating the scene from the Archive. He knew exactly where he wanted to begin to light the fire all over again. "Shine ball, it's not my fault Wisps don't know how to organize records. The burnt or damaged entries from the incident are obviously the most important, as they were blatantly taken at the most interesting point of the experiment."

Remembering to breathe, he cracked on. "You glow balls keep going on about alphabetical order or some sort of nonsensical moisture decimal system. Just because you're all glowing dots of light doesn't mean there gets to be the dots in the middle of every entry. Clearly, and as any decent Gnome knows, you want to access the fun parts first, so those should be the most easily accessible!"

Getting right into the swing, Aleksander matched Turk's fire with Wisp-fueled ire. "Don't know how to organize records?!

Abyss, please! How are you going to find anything if you don't categorize and sub-categorize via alphabetical order!? For your elucidation, oil dweller, the Dewey Decimal System is fantastic. You can't grow a tree without developing the root foundations first!"

Turk returned fire. "That only works if you know the title of what you're looking for!"

Aleksandr didn't accept that cheap shot. "That's what categories are for! You make a category. You shove all the related items under the category, and then you make any needed subcategories and organizational systems. Easy, step by step, and reliable!"

Turk pressed his fingers together, dropping both hands forwards with the full weight of his frame. "And where does that end? We can categorize and sub-categorize and further refine until important documents are nowhere near each other! Then you have to sort through miles of aisles and mountains of fluff until you find the important bits. Have you seen how big the Archives are? We need to make the most interesting stuff available, so we can share the experience and spectacle."

The orange Wisp grumped at that rebuttal. "With a properly organized system, one is able to find all the information they need efficiently and accurately. That includes your category of 'spectacle.'"

They both looked at Webb, who needed a moment to realize he'd been part of that conversation during a walk-by. It took Webb a second, but he remembered what he said and added it to the replayed script. "I personally don't like the Dewey Decimal System."

The Gnome and Wisp both nodded in approval, pointing at each other to figure out who had the next line. When Webb answered that by pointing at Turk, the Gnome stuck his tongue out at Aleksandr and took the spotlight. "If we left it to the spiders, you'd all want to stick the information in endless webs, safe and hidden away high up in the clouds. Just think. Information stored in a web network, and written on clouds? Ridiculous!"

The orange Wisp made muscular arms of light appear, purely to cross them in front of his ball. "At least the spiders have some sense of organization…"

Turk slapped his chair. "That's why we have memory stones!. The Archives aren't just for notes, they're for prestige! Notoriety! They're a trophy hall and a declaration of who had the most interesting ideas!"

Webb grinned wide. "Seems like a perfectly logical system to me!"

Aleksander let Webb's comment slide, but couldn't abide by the Gnome's words. "Memories are useless if you need to access a document you've never seen before, you rusty sprocket! Therefore, when we need to find and read a file new to us; a lovely, structured, consistent, and well thought-out system is needed to organize data for future reference."

Turk was not on board. "Memory stones, glowball, memory stones!"

Aleksandr once again believed the Gnome to have missed his point entirely in favor of letting the fire roil. "Memory stones are unreliable! While we may now have quite the stock-pile, there likely will come a time where we run out, or cannot spare them for every little piece of data. Additionally, how are you going to find the correct memory stone?"

The Wisp played *ba-dum-tss* drums on the air. "Through an organized system!"

Turk needed a few seconds for the reply to that one, but grinned wide when it came to him. "Then you're gonna hate what I did on aisle 13.4.3.1556."

The Wisp had forgotten this part of the conversation, his reply too crisp and quick for it to be a continuation of the script. "Oh, Cal. What did you do this time? As a side note, we only know it's aisle 13.4.3.1556 *because* the aisles are marked via an organized system."

Turk cackled, his arms crossing as he could smell victory. "Ya find it by finding the right shelf, and the right shelf is always the one that catches your attention first! It's not worth doing unless you find it interesting!"

Flustered, Aleksandr moved his manufactured arms so his fingers pressed to where his forehead would be on the glow ball. "No! You can't just jump to the fun, juicy parts of a topic and expect to navigate the discussion and work like an expert! You have to learn the fundamentals first. Scattering information around based on how flashy something is will just confuse people!"

Since the conversation had derailed, Blue added his two coppers. "Jus' dun look for a system in the spotters guild. There ain't one. We just love Runes."

Turk rounded on the Axolotl spotter, his fire redirected. "That was you lot? Your nonsense and Runic notes got so bad, one of the filing rooms rebelled and evolved into an infernal info dungeon. You were fabled in the old legends to have the best notes!"

Blue carefully pressed his fingertips together, mumbling. "Easy ta have the best notes when you're the only faction with any public notes at all. Before Spotterton was taken over by fungus, it was the primary testing site for all our best ideas. Ya could say the passion really grew on us. That new dungeon mushroomed right out of the ground."

Turk chuckled, his flame tempered. "I attribute this to an inability to organize."

Webb didn't agree, the young Arachnid defending the spotter. "Just because you can't comprehend the system doesn't mean it's not organized."

In a stroke of madness, the Wisp came to the aid of the Gnome. "Comprehension is not the issue, my multi-legged friend, it is the utter lack of any uniformity."

Zelia, who was very much done with this banter, had summoned an effigy of a different dungeon to be present on her palm, the Celestial Harris Hawk holding a wing over its face after having listened in to most of the script.

"Curator Caladrius." Zelia addressed the Celestial dungeon's image in her claw, the Hawk turning its head to regard the Autarch. "End this."

CHAPTER ELEVEN

Curator Caladrius, in Celestial Hawk Harris bird format, still spoke as they otherwise did. With slow enunciation. Pausing unnecessarily between words. A soft, breathy tone delivered through the nose, as if they were yelling with their inside voice. Not displeased, but certainly disappointed. As an art curator to a guest being purposefully rude to a hanging work.

Caladrius turned his beak toward the orange Wisp. "Uniformity is elegant and efficient but boring overall. There is no use to it if you lose yourself in trying to find what you need, because the way the information is organized has so many subcategories you need a lesson on just how to use it."

Caladrius then looked down upon the Gnome. "That said, having all the interesting bits front and center may draw attention, but would lack the basics of what's needed to get started on any given project. It is possible to have the interesting things as a footnote of the main category one desires, with a linkage to the base information on what's required to get started."

The Hawk swung a wing outwards like there was a painting being presented. "You can add a flourish to any title. That's merely a few more words to help guide those prepared. Those who already have an idea of what they want, but may not know the proper jargon. Subcategories become much more streamlined from that point onward."

Curator Caladrius then glared at them both, driving home the important point that both of them were missing. "We aren't building this system to be used by us… *right?*"

Turk took off his tiny dapper hat in apology, and consigned himself to defeat. "The dungeon, and I say this grudgingly, does have a point."

The members of the conversation then turned to Zelia as one, and joined Turk, bowing in apology as Curator Caladrius was dismissed with a glorious huff. The Autarch hummed with approval at this gesture, then tapped her prompt. "Excellent. Provide me some answers to this as able? I am moving on to equipment so I can return my Dreamer's storage item, then we are tackling the racial entry."

Artorian clapped his hands after receiving both the broom and his emptied Silverwood Bracelet back from Zelia, opening his arms for the new prompt. She had opted to keep the soap. It might fit well in someone preoccupied with running their mouth. "Ten item limit! Here we go! What have I got?"

Ding!

———

World Boss Limitation: Item list.
Silverwood Bracelet - Storage Item.
Boom Shaka Laka - Casting Focus Broom.
Item Set: Autarchy's Warmth.
Items in set: 7.
Pieces: Boots, Pants, Shirt, Mittens, Parka, Scarf, Beanie.

———

Artorian released a subdued unhappy noise. A grumble from the throat that wasn't given enough effort to turn loud. "So… *one?* I can have one more thing on my person, and then I'm considered full? That's… not ideal. Between the mystery cloak, the bow I need to return to Lucia, and Cy's Tonfas, which I'm not even sure counts as one item or two… *ouch.*"

Zelia frowned at that list, then flicked the prompt from where she sat.

Ding!

———

Item added: Spider Autarch's Brooch.

———

"That's what I thought. I was expecting that one to be trouble. It's too complicated for most non-Cal or Eternium systems." She slid her fingers back and forth across the chair she remained seated in. "Don't fret, Incursus. You're doing well. Quantum entanglement is magic wuju to you still, and that's alright. Take your time for me? It would make me happy if you didn't rush into this."

The tolling of a bell rang in the distance, but no words accompanied the sound. Zelia's face softened, pride oozing from her face. "Look at him being so good."

Artorian held his face. "Zelia, I want to be happy for Incursus and how well he's doing, but I'm very stuck on being at ten out of ten items, while I don't have a weapon in my pocket. Is there a way to increase the number, or do I have to give you this item set back to mitigate this setback?"

A silent group of people around him scrolled through screens and wordlessly dug for solutions. When the first ten minutes rolled by without anything being said, Artorian tried to relax with another rack of ribs. Eating solved discomfort, right? He bit into the meal and kept on munching until someone had a fix. He was currently very glad not to have jumped headlong into Eternia, because this would have been a very annoying hamstring to discover mid-dive.

The toll of a bell got Artorian's attention, but everyone else was too absorbed in finding a solution through their particular field and method of expertise. Incursus, instead, was trying to give him a new title to solve the problem outright. Artorian read over the prompt, blinked at it, then began to slowly clap. "I need everyone to stop what they're doing and look at what Incursus just did."

Ding!

―――――

Title: World Boss +

Requirement: World Boss Character Trait.

You may no longer claim an area as your dungeon or base of operations, and will always be considered a Roaming World Boss. Maximum item limit is set to 20.

―――――

Applause joined Artorian as people read over the entry, as while that downside hurt somewhat, it solved the immediate problem thoroughly. Artorian patted his chair, and pressed the acceptance prompt. "Good job, Incursus!"

A bell tolled as a thank you, with that bell blushing. Incursus then cleared Artorian's item list, refilling the entries with the expected equipment.

Ding!

―――――

World Boss Limitation: Item list - 13/20.

Silverwood Bracelet - Storage Item.

Boom Shaka Laka - Casting Focus Broom.

Item Set: Autarchy's Warmth.
Items in set: 7.
Pieces: Boots, Pants, Shirt, Mittens, Parka, Scarf, Beanie.
Spider Autarch's Brooch - Communication sigil.
Heartstring Bow - Weapon (1)
Halcyon Days Tonfas - Weapons (2)

———

Artorian sighed in relief. "*Ahhhh*, that's much better already. Could I see the Autarchy set again before we address the robe?"

Zelia nodded, but paused. "While I have the opportunity, my Dreamer, I am adding the socks to the set, and combining the brooch into the mixture while I'm at it. The effect is minor, but it does allow me to increase the set rarity to unique, and improve the set effect by two comfort levels, rather than one. Plus, I can remove the cold conditions limitation of the original set. This will increase your inventory number to fourteen, leaving you six slots."

He beamed brightly at her. "Yes and please!"

Ding!

———

Item Set: Autarchy's Wonder.
Pieces: Boots, Pants, Shirt, Mittens, Parka, Scarf, Beanie, Socks, Brooch.
Rarity: Unique.
Set Effect: Extra Fluff - You are loved by the Floof, your comfort level is always two categories higher in adverse environmental conditions.

———

Item: Boots
Name: Snowsteps.
Material: Spider Wool.

Rarity: Special.
Effect: The user does not sink through snow.

––––––

Item: Pants
Name: Everwhite.
Material: Spider Wool.
Rarity: Special.
Effect: Cold Resistance - Ignore the first 100 points of Cold typed damage, then a flat 20% of remaining Cold typed damage.

––––––

Item: Shirt
Name: Less Than Three.
Material: Spider Wool.
Rarity: Special.
Effect: Exist comfortably in any temperature. Resistance to temperature based conditions. Such as: Frostbite, Heatstroke, Hyperthermia, and Hypothermia.

––––––

Item: Mittens
Name: Object Permanence.
Material: Spider Wool.
Rarity: Special.
Effect: Once equipped, these mittens exist only when paying attention to them. Otherwise the user has full use of their hands, as if not wearing mittens. User's hands will remain warm as per wearing normal mittens.

––––––

Item: Parka
Name: Jurassic Cage.

Material: Spider Wool.
Rarity: Special.
Effect: Frost Resistance - Ignore the first 100 points of Frost typed damage, then a flat 20% of remaining Frost typed damage.

———

Item: Scarf
Name: Shinobi Run.
Material: Spider Wool.
Rarity: Special.
Effect: Endurance Bolstering - All Stamina costs are cut by 10%. Might make the user run funny. May also cause others to cringe.

———

Item: Beanie
Name: Happy Ears.
Material: Spider Wool.
Rarity: Special.
Effect: Ice Resistance - Ignore the first 100 points of Ice typed damage, then a flat 20% of remaining Icet typed damage.

———

Item: Socks
Name: Sock-em.
Material: Spider Wool.
Rarity: Special.
Effect: You may punch with your feet and kick with your hands.

———

Item: Spider Autarch's Brooch
Name: Entangled Web.
Material: Iridium.

Rarity: Special.

Effect: Seat of the Senate - Speak with any Senate members in your vicinity who also wear this insignia. The correct position of the brooch is on or in the left segment of the collar.

"Autarchy's Wonder? I like it. Warmth was a nice word, but I do like wonder. Makes me feel special. Thank you, Zelia. That was a pleasant treat." His attention was then claimed by Kowsky and Blue both holding up the Owl-themed robe.

He motioned for the bug finder to explain, worried that if he designated Blue, there would be more puns. "You were right! A real trout of a trap. We untangled the robe from the problematic pylons that would have turned you into a C'towl on wearing it. So technically it's a C'towl robe? A lightning-based trap was attached that would constantly zap you while in the cat form. Nasty piece of Pylon work."

Blue the Axolotl brought it over to Artorian for him to take, his inner Dwarf bleeding through rather heavily. "Archimedes here be a right piece o' good fortune, he is. The worst thing the cloak'll do to ya is give ya kitten ears when ya pull the hoot—I mean hood—up. Warnin' ya ahead o' time, Administrator, Archimedes be a living item. That there cloak be a person we haven't gotten unfurled yet. It'll take some doin', but the lot of us can sort it. Just won't be today or tomorruh. Yer current item count is fifteen."

Artorian stood when accepting the robe. Cloak? Robe. Cape? No, it was more of a cloak. He was just going to go with what the description said. Swinging it over his shoulders, he got the cloak snug, and then pulled the hood up. "How do I look?"

Zelia hid her expression with her sleeve. "Like you need head-scratches between those adorable ears, my Dreamer. Notably, because I can see the question written on your face, the main difference between cape and cloak is their length. Capes are shorter, and typically reach the wearer's hips and thighs.

Cloaks are often longer, and reach below the knees. In terms of design, both capes and cloaks are sleeveless outer garments made of a single piece of fabric that hangs loose. However, a cloak tends to have no sleeves, being secured only by a string or a clasp of some sort. I suggest using my brooch for this. Anyone who gives you lip for the brooch not being in the designated location can come see me."

She removed her sleeve when her smile was gentle, curious about the living item. "What does Archimedes do?"

He'd not thought to pull up the item description, and did just so. "Let me find out."

Ding!

Item: Tribal C'towl Cloak
Name: Archimedes.
Material: Darkwind Storm C'towl.
Rarity: Unique.
Ability: Shunpo - At will, lightning-themed, short-range teleport. Maximum 50 meters. Costs 5% of a mana bar per use.
Cooldown: None.
Toggle: The effects listed below can be toggled on or off at the user's preference.
Effect: 1 meter radius area damage-effect on arrival, equal to mana cost.
Effect: Afflict any damaged valid targets with: Stun - minor - 1 second.
Note: While Stun trigger is guaranteed, the effect is easy to resist.

Artorian rubbed his chin in lieu of a beard, performing a dance jig for fun, and placing his hands next to his head to make caramel cat ear motions. "That's frankly incredible. Are we sure that ought to be merely unique rarity? That's some incredible potential tucked away in a cloak. Were any large changes made to the bow? I know the tonfas are a full rework."

A prompt popped up to answer his question.

———

Name: Heartstring.
  Type: Bow.
  Material: Dinosaur Bone.
  Rarity: Unique.
  Damage: Investment.
  Special Qualities: Inevitable Betrayal, Glitterflit String, Heartlock Keychain, Chalk Scribble.
  Description: This bow deals kinetic damage to enemies, equal to an amount of mana invested in each shot. This bow functions as a normal recurve short bow, and its conjured ammunition is subject to physics. Heartstring is covered in many mementoes, and the chalky paw marks of children. Inevitable Betrayal allows the wielder to heal allies equal to the normal amount of damage dealt.
  Glitterflit String doubles the amount of healing that Heartstring applies.
  Heartlock Keychain applies bonus true damage to enemies spotted by Lifesense, equal to one percent of final damage.
  Chalk Scribble allows the wielder to see both weaknesses and weak points on their targets. Either to guide their shots toward them, or the veer their shots away from them.

———

The entire group, save for Zelia, shot him the equivalent of a thumbs up. The bow was clean, mostly identical to the original entry, save for some grammar and punctuation patches.

Artorian nodded, moving the bow's prompt away to take hold of the tonfa prompt. All the red text made him blow air from tightly pursed lips. "Alright, let's get into this. I'm not going to ask what happened. I only want to see what they do now."

———

Name: Halcyon Nights.
Material: Gravity Iridium.
Rarity: Unique.
Damage: 1 – 1.
Special Qualities: Graviton, Maneuver, Calculation Priority.
These tonfas have a strength requirement of 500 each. Not meeting this strength threshold makes a person entirely unable to lift a single tonfa. A strength of 1000 is required to wield both tonfas. If wielded as a set, their special qualities activate.
A single Tonfa weighs two tons.
Special Quality: Graviton. This material is a variant of the Iridium base metal. Gravity Iridium quintuples in weight when striking an opponent. To the user, these Tonfas feel five times as light, regardless of being at rest or in motion. A Graviton weapon does not cost stamina to swing. Repeated attacks will still incur the normal stamina strain penalties, calculated based on the weight of the weapon versus a user's strength attribute.
Note: If meeting the prerequisites to wield a single tonfa, then under Graviton's effects, that single tonfa will always qualify as a light and finesse weapon. As its comparative weight uses less than, or equal to, one-fifth the user's strength value. The light weapon quality allows the user to apply their dexterity attribute to calculate damage instead of strength as base damage. Whereas the finesse quality allows that same mechanic, but with wisdom. This interaction is a required prerequisite for the Special Quality: Calculation Priority.
Special Quality: Maneuver. All martial arts maneuvers can be used in conjunction with this weapon.
Special Quality: Calculation Priority. This weapon set follows a customized damage calculation priority. The user's attribute value for base damage is not added to this weapon's calculation order. Instead, the average of all the user's attributes will be used to calculate bonus damage that is

added at the end of the formula. This bonus damage is not considered in the critical chance formula.

————

Artorian read the weapon listing again with his arms crossed, doing some napkin math in his head. He wasn't sure if the numbers held, but if five-hundred strength translated cleanly to being able to pick up two tons worth of weight... That meant a two-fifty in strength could pick up one ton, or about a thousand of the kilograms? Chop off a zero, and twenty-five strength meant being able to pick up about one-hundred kilograms. That was a lot, but it was easy numbers. He liked easy numbers. He weighed what in kilograms, forty? Fifty? Twenty-five strength to pick up two Young-torians? Seemed good if the numerical average was a ten, which could lift about one of him with some struggle. Even if his napkin math ended up not being accurate, a baseline to hold onto was good.

Artorian commented on the entry. "Enjoy your sunset, Halcyon Days. Good evening, Halcyon Nights! You look ready to *party*. Shame that I do not meet the qualifications unless I'm in Trans Am. I suppose that's what they will be for, given they cost me no stamina to swing, and Trans Am locks out my regeneration values. Not great for a new daily driver, but wonderful to have in the pocket. The bow I will be returning. This unfortunately means that I don't actually have weaponry to use that aren't my abilities and spells."

He considered a desire, and looked to Zelia. "Can I earn one instead of being given one?"

His Chosen bowed her head gently towards him. "Of course, my Dreamer. I have already informed Tim and Kindling. I recall she previously had a host of weapon tickets from Eri's Emporium at her disposal, but I do not wish to diminish your desire for earned achievements. That is a desired game aspect, particularly when we are still heavily in the swing of balancing weapons and ability mathematics to appropriate realm limitations. The more you test, the happier we will be. As a note, she may have needed to do as you did, however, and dump her entire inventory. Kindling is also limited to her ten slots. I'll contact her about the title solution, and see if that's a route she'd like to take."

Artorian liked that a lot, his mood chipper and voice cheerful. "Excellent! Onto the next thing! I'm craving being back in game-land already and turning some health bars into melt bars."

CHAPTER TWELVE

Melt bars got him some odd looks, until the Wisp poked people to look at the Shining Ray entry, at which point the Administrator's mention made sense. Though, Shining Ray was in the cue for reprocessing. That ability would have to wait.

It was racial entry time!

Ding!

———

Race: Nascent Being.

As a Nascent Being, you gain Electrosense and Echolocation as new empirical senses on a base level; along with sight, hearing, taste, smell and touch.

As a Nascent Being, you are always considered Well Fed and Well Hydrated. You can breathe in any environment, and are immune to the effects of depth crushing, thin atmosphere, vacuum, harmful gasses, inhaled venoms or poisons, and cloud or vapor based attacks. Note: The environment does require breathable material.

A Nascent Being is never lost, and always has a vague idea of where to go, regardless of what it is currently looking for.

———

Artorian saw nothing different. Glances at the rest of the group did not give him anything new to work with either. This entry was either unchanged, or what had been changed was so minor that it wasn't worth the mention. Moving on.

———

Advancement: Truesight.
A sensory advancement to see all as it actually is. Ignoring all forms of obfuscation, invisibility, guise, and illusion. This extends to creatures, objects, and effects. The true form of a creature will be betrayed by the shape of their shadow.

———

Advancement: Profound Sight - Complete.
A sensory advancement that denies a greater power. Complete Profound Sight allows the use of Truesight on Heavenlies. While there exists a greatest power that Complete Profound Sight cannot pierce, no other mighty shall escape your awareness.

———

"That one's new." Artorian put a hand over one eye. He squinted as his vision wobbled, stabilizing when he intended his focus on the surrounding individuals. Kowsky's shadow was an exact duplicate, while Blue the Axolotl had a larger, Dwarven-shaped shadow. Webb and Zelia both didn't appear to have shadows at all, until he noted the tiny spider shapes. Interesting.

Aleksander the Wisp had no shadow at all, probably because light sources did not cast shadows, while the shadow of Turk the Gnome matched him exactly. "Feels just like Essence Sight. Intent driven goodies are the best goodies. I was worried about an instant headache, but feeding some intent to the eyes may have been a step I've been missing all along. My eyes do not hurt at all."

He paused and cocked his head, observing the stars nested in twilight. "Incursus? Could you turn up the brightness ever so slightly?"

The toll of a bell answered, the sky filling with the edge of a sunrise, without an actual sun ever rising. The sky became a very pretty piece of work to look at, and most importantly, Artorian didn't feel like he needed to squint. "Thank you, Incursus."

Out of curiosity, he then checked himself for a shadow. Maybe he would sneak some insight into what a Nascent Being was. To his incredible annoyance, and much like the Wisp, he had no shadow whatsoever. Zelia snickered at his commentary, knowing exactly what he was trying to do. "*In-con-ven-ient.*"

When he stopped using the special sight to discern his shadow, it bled back into reality like that shadow had been there all along. Artorian rubbed his forehead, and gave up that avenue. "Let's move on."

———

Advancement: Bone Scripting.

Bone Scripting Effect: Advanced Freedom of Movement.

Advanced Freedom of Movement provides full three-dimensional acuity of movement in any environment. Included but not limited to: land, water, underwater, air, high atmosphere, and vacuum, separated by two methods.

Method one: mundane locomotion, amended by platform footing.

Your feet will always find purchase, surface or no.

By applying a platform to every step, tumble, or hand movement, you will no longer destroy landscape or buildings when launching from, or traversing over, these floor types. Elevation is a matter of choice, but can only be sustained so long as movement is constant.

You remain subject to gravity.

Method two: Wisp flight.

While you are able to freely combine methods one and two, this method of flight allows you to no longer be affected by gravity, as per the movement form of a Wisp. This provides true and full three-dimensional movement, not hampered by water or vacuum. However, this method of locomotion is not calculated by the same standard as method one, as you are no longer using your body and related attributes as a measurement base.

Your top speed is limited by what you can withstand, measured by force. Attempting to move more mass, with increased velocity, will vastly increase the cost of the attempted flight.

Math at the Novice rank: A cost of 6 mana per second equals 1 kg of weight moving at 1 meter per second for 1 second.

If you double the mass, then the cost doubles.

If you double the velocity, then the cost quadruples.

———

A church bell tolled, Incursus providing Artorian a bonus prompt. The Administrator took the screen in his hands, and quietly read the entry.

———

Notes from Incursus:

Bonescripting addendum: As this change is applied to your actual body, this feature will remain with you on leaving Eternia. Please keep in mind that game mana does not scale or compare to either real Mana, or Essence. Game mana is a carefully crafted, unique energy type specifically suited to the functions and purposes of the game. Matching in similarities to the existing energy types both for the ease of transition of cultivators entering a game world, and the transition of turning non-cultivators into cultivators without harm. Game mana is intended to ease an individual's exposure to the true energies. Improving their comfort during the development and growth of a center, and resistance to the eventual side-effects of typed Essences. The exposure to, and use of game mana, will also indirectly improve one's comfort and control over Essence, Mana, and Spirit.

Commentary: Administrator, you are currently at 4'11" in height. With your equipment included, you weigh almost exactly 50 kilograms.

Moving 1 meter with Wisp Flight, for 1 second, would cost you 300 mana per second. Moving that same weight over a distance of 2 meters, for 1 second, would cost you 1,200 mana per second.

Moving a weight of 200 kilograms, over a distance of 1 meter, for 1 second, would also cost you 1,200 mana per second.

Note: This math has been updated since your last major recorded use. When you hovered into New Haven from the Murim Woods, doubling the mass did not double the cost. Do not be concerned about this current math's cost formula not matching the time and available resources it took for you to ascend that prior distance.

At the Novice rank in our shared game setting, this ability is five times as expensive as the Journeyman rank, which is considered the average base-line of cost and effectiveness. At the Journeyman rank, expect the text of the cost to alter to a cost of 1 mana per second equals 1 kg of weight moving at 1 meter per second for 1 second.

We are currently not concerned with individual levels between ranks. Ordinarily, the ranking system only affects the output of a particular tool. Wisp Flight is an example of an ability that follows the spirit of the intended system, but not the established rule.

Not all dungeons currently have access to all the same tools. Expect to see a mismatch between the similarities of tools and entries, and how some are calculated or designed.

For many offensive tools, the damage is modified and scaled to match the user's rank. A common-quality Midgard-origin Frost Bolt, as example, normally deals 10 damage. A novice Frost Bolt will only deal 2 damage, whereas a Journeyman Frost Bolt would deal the ten damage as normal, and that same Frost Bolt at the Sage level would instead deal 50 damage.

———

The chart modifiers for ranks function as follows:
Novice - 0.2
Beginner - 0.4
Apprentice - 0.6
Student - 0.8
Journeyman - 1

Expert - 2
Master - 3
Grandmaster - 4
Sage - 5

———

Note: There are several skills that can be gained to benefit the Wisp Flight ability, either further reducing the cost, or increasing the output received. Do not be discouraged by seemingly unattainable numbers. We, as dungeons, have yet to move the game project into the balancing stages. When that occurs, expect costs and outputs of skills and abilities to become far more reasonable.

We intend to segment them based on—at the minimum—rarity, power, and realm.

For now, we thank you for your time and effort to test entries that are developed from the Pylons available, and to provide us the results of that data for future balancing. This is a difficult portion of the task for us, and we could not do it without you. Simulations only do so much, and do not reflect real world applications of some of the created entries.

I can't talk well, but I'm glad you came to visit, and you are welcome back anytime.

Regards - Incursus.

———

Artorian took his time to look up from the prompt at Zelia, who was grinning at him while resting her chin on her claw. "I understand now. Incursus is a *sweetheart.*"

"*Uh-huh!*" Zelia beamed, in full agreement. "He overexplains by a good margin, but I find that endearing. Additionally, we are finished with the racial entry of Less Than Three, and related physical modifiers. Nascent Beings do not have attribute modifiers like Dragons do."

A thought occurred, and she indulged in a light dabbling of **Chaos**. "I'm going to give you the hint, my Dreamer, that the important function of Wisp Flight has less to do with you having the option to exchange energy for velocity. Rather, it allows you to ignore gravity. You can run significantly faster than you can fly, and a well-timed jump that is then no longer subject to a constant downwards force, by itself, can accomplish much."

She tapped the side of her nose mischievously. "Platform running also has no associated cost, unlike Wisp Flight. That may change in the future, so let's make good use of it while it doesn't. They must construct additional Pylons."

Artorian loved this, his hand swirling in a circle. "Alright, this mutual scheming that we are doing? I adore this. This is great. What's next?"

"Why don't we ask the wiki team?" Zelia sat back and looked at the group, each member of which was currently very prepared to hold up their own prompt with a differing topic.

Artorian, of course, gave her the 'please explain' look.

"Wiki is an acronym for 'What I Know Is.' They are the team that knows." She motioned to each member of the newly assembled wiki team in turn. "Son?"

Mr. Webb, the young spider, had the shortest to-do list, barely a note's worth of content present on his screen as he held it up between two fingers. "Professions."

Aleksandr the orange Wisp shot their screen up when Webb's went down. "I have class, so I handle classes!"

Turk followed the flow of organization, with a notable Dark Gnome grumble when he realized what pattern they'd suckered him into. "Skills."

Kowsky and Blue needed to work together to hold up their screen, as it was easily the largest of the bunch. Blue nose-shoved his face at Kowsky, wanting the bug finder to speak. The hollow knight had no problems with that. "Abilities."

Zelia folded her hands, assigning her son to go first. "Webb. If you'd please."

CHAPTER THIRTEEN

The young spider in the nice suit rose fully from his seat, politely walking over to Artorian to directly hand him the prompt. "The single profession you have as your character, Administrator. I was hoping to tackle your deity options, but Mother has taken that task upon herself, and she is infinitely more skilled than I."

He then turned to his mother with clear reverence and respect, politely bowing. "May I be excused, Mother?"

With a nod of approval, Webb Slipstreamed away, a visible distortion left behind in the air. Zelia scrutinized the after-effect, silently making a mental note of Webb's progress. "Satisfactory, for now."

Artorian was of the mind that he wanted to learn how to do that. Properly, this time. He'd half-used portation perhaps once or twice with Zelia's direct guidance. Particularly to escape a storage hold with a dragon body? Or was that to break into one? He couldn't remember. His intent turned to Zelia to ask for lessons, but a booming explosion in the distance that sounded like a soundwave collapsing in on itself rocked the trees and trembled across the ground.

There was work to be done, but the entire group turned to watch hosts of birds take off from their newly grown perches. Artorian did not have to ask what that was, as Zelia was long out of patience, and the object of her current ire was already in the same layer and bubble of existence as her.

Axon the Chronomancer, in the form of his game character Tchaikovsky the Gnome, was standing in front of her with a solemn *pop* to his name a mere moment after she reached out. While a human Mage outside of the game, Axon had opted for rolling a Gnome Bard named Tchaikovsky, with his instrument being a temporal crystal cannon. The crystalline end of which still smoked with heat as the Gnome moved exceptionally slowly, his words warped and unintelligible from how laboriously they were being spoken.

Artorian quickly checked the Gnome's status and character screen, discovering all of these details, and that Tchaikovsky was currently afflicted by a debuff named Temporal Slow. Which… Tchaikovsky seemed to have been the cause of? "Did you aim that cannon down, by chance?"

The Gnome heard him at accelerated speed, but was still responding in slow motion, leaving Artorian without a reply, and watching Temporal Slow be the kind of condition he immediately wanted to be immune to. He was used to seeing opponents in slow motion, but when only one person was afflicted by the condition, the sight felt strange.

Blue inspected the temporal cannon that Tchaikovsky had dropped, adding commentary. "A temporal crystal cannon probably is better for music, as you can delay the sound until you want it? The log on this says he tried to fire it twelve times, instantaneously. There's a note attached from a background team that says: 'Tchaikovsky, no!' His reply being: 'Tchaikovsky, yes!' Fittin'."

Artorian nodded, but instead looked at the screen Webb handed over. Tchaikovsky was being helped by Turk. Gnomes of a feather sticking together. It did not appear to matter to the Dark Gnome that Axon was only a Gnome due to playing as the Tchaikovsky character? Interesting. Gnome unity was something else. The camaraderie built in the before times of the Wisp Wars.

———

Profession: Scribe
You are a record keeper, jurist, and vessel of bound knowledge. Through your carved and painted words, eternity is cataloged, and remembered.

———

With Turk no longer available for banter, Aleksandr hovered over to hand the Administrator his screen. "Classes are all sorted. Please have them, Administrator. Wouldn't want a Gnome to Wisp them away! Am I approved to head back to the Archives?"

"Please do. Would you be able to check on Yvess—I mean, Titania—while you're at it? I haven't heard from her and I'm getting concerned." Artorian nodded in the process, but looked to Zelia since he had no method to take the glowball home. She snapped her fingers when Aleksandr snapped to a salute. The orange Wisp was gone with a **pop**.

Turk slapped the slowed Tchaikovsky on his back. "No Gnome goes a-Gnome! We travel in packs. Maybe if we shot it a second time, it would cancel out the first?"

Blue loved the pun as if he'd made it himself, but couldn't agree. The spotter needed to adopt the role of the Wisp since Kowsky was frantically at work, and their pool of candidates was dipping. "That would only increase the duration. We dun tried that already."

Artorian hummed in response to their chicanery, inspecting the class entry.

———

Class: Janitor

"Bless the cleaner and his broom. Bless the coming and going of him. May his passing cleanse the world. May he keep the world for his people."

- Shai-Hulud, First of the Allsand.

All cleaning-related abilities have their cost negated.

"In his way, there was only the cloy. In his wake, there was only cleanliness."

- Shai-Hulud, First of the Allsand.

———

Scrolling down the prompt, Artorian noted that the Wisp had also tackled his specialization entry. Best to read that now and understand what he was working with,

———

Specialization: Crit-Fisher.

A Crit-Fisher attempts to create instances of critical chance, in favor of other ancillary effects. Your critical hit chance is quintupled. Critical chance is determined by taking the numerical value of a tool's rarity, dividing by the averaged base damage, and rounding down.

System: A one-hundred sided die is then rolled. If the roll is lower than your threshold, you achieve a critical hit. Your critical hit chance is always set to a minimum of one percent, before modifiers.

You may mentally auto-toggle your critical hit effects.

Slotted critical effects:

Explode on Hit.

Double Damage.

———

"That improved my day." Artorian poked the addition of the minimum percentage. "This means that there is always some chance a critical effect can occur, and other people using this system aren't locked out of critical hits purely because the formula puts them deep in the black. Is there more to classes and specializations? The text in my prompt stopped."

He looked up to see Tchaikovsky had recovered and had been pulled to the side by Turk. The Gnomes whispered to one another aggressively, with their hand motions betraying what they were talking about. Didn't… didn't he do that too? *Uh oh.* Well… maybe not really a problem, in hindsight.

His eyes caught a small black and red prompt working in the background near his other screens. He frowned at what it was called, pulling the pocket-sized entry in front of him. "What is a Daemon process? I think the only time I've ever heard of that word with this spelling is in reference to Yasura. That S-ranked Daemon with the six arms, where the additional A in the word Demon changed the meaning. Thinking of it, the Orkharn we met in New Haven also had six arms, and I did wonder how Oni ended up there. Coincidence?"

"I think not." She soothed his concerns when he frisbee'd Zelia the screen as she made a motion for it. "That *is* Yasura, my Dreamer. In Pylon computing, a Daemon is a function that runs continuously as a background process. Yasura used to operate independently in The Pale, but after being caught smuggling… Daemonettes? No. Succubi. That's what it was. After he was caught sneaking no-thank-you-byes into taverns for company, he was reminded of the Accords situation."

She couldn't contain her smirk. "Yasura was punished accordingly. As such, he is the only entity performing this function. I considered it fitting. The Orkharn and Oni were excusable, but non-booked Demons? That was a dangerous faux pas. My children have already visited to make the ladies aware that their behavior is to be considered in their actions, regardless of what their nature may provide them as cravings and inclinations. I was promptly informed that Kindling had beaten them to the punch, and had put the fear in them."

The Autarch enjoyed her momentary amusement as understanding of the pun dawned on Artorian's face, his expression souring by the moment as it ebbed in. "I have been informed you have already encountered The Generator? That Mechanicus Steamlord boss encounter will be one of the first fights you will have to contend with upon your return, my Dreamer."

That brought joy back to Artorian's face. "*Ooooh*, a fight! I'm itching to get to it! Hopefully it won't take as long as some of the fights in recent memory? Barry, Odin, Henry, and Marie all took very dedicated portions of concentration. Taskie and Moonmoon don't count."

The brooch currently keeping his C'towl cloak together crackled, Ember's voice cutting through. "Sugar? You there?"

Artorian took hold of the Spider insignia, squeezing it to reply even if that didn't do anything. Like all great items, it was intent-based. Holding the brooch made him feel better, and that counted. "Honey! I'm with Zelia, sorting my character sheet out. Good to hear from you. How is your end?"

"Great!" Ember's voice was chipper, pleased, and excited as it came through clean and smooth over the Senate connection. "We're all set, but when I came to get you from the Faith Foundry, there was uproar instead of my boy in his bed. Are you good?"

Artorian felt his cheeks go flush and pink. Something about hearing Dawn's voice just made him happy. "I'm healthy, and talking to you is making me happy. Zelia and company have sorted through a lot of trouble I would have otherwise needed to contend with. We have skills and abilities to go, but after that, I believe I would have been set to return to that bed. If you're telling me you're ready, I'm having cravings for that straight hop and skip into the age of the rule of cool era in Eternium. I will gladly throw myself through the void for you two to catch me! Lucia is there, I believe?"

The Glitterflit's equally happy voice laughed in the background. "Momma's here, sweet boy! You give the medic a heads up before you hurl yourself, y'hear?!"

Artorian bent forward, laughing. "Ha! Yes, Momma Bun! Be with you both in a bit! I hear we have a boss fight to get to."

Ember cackled from the other end of the connection. "A

boss fight? Sugar, we haven't *stopped* fighting since we got here. The whole place is a free-for-all. Enemies are unthawing and self-spawning from preset triggers all over the place. I have never had this much *fun*. Finish your sheet! Get over here! Lucia has shields for you and I've got **Pride**, **Sorrow**, and **Compassion** all asking for some game time. I'm making them form a party and be independent until you can cross paths with them. Shaka and Tom have also formed a party! They passed us while setting up a personal competition about who could get to the edge of the world first. We—*Bun*! *Left*!"

Artorian overheard sounds of combat, laughter, things exploding, and Lucia bouncing around as her shield ate impacts and the swing of a swordspear cleaved foes in twain. As their connection ended with a crackle, the look he shot Zelia was one of pleading and hunger.

"I wanna gooooo."

CHAPTER FOURTEEN

Zelia wasted no time. With a flourish of her claws, prompts in the vicinity cleaned themselves up, returning to the slow-spinning cycle around the fire. "Abilities."

Kowsky released a high-pitched scream as the screen in his hands fought him for control, wrenching itself free from the bug finder's grip. "I wasn't done!"

He hurriedly unfurled one of his many maps instead when he lost the fight, working on that same prompt remotely while his little hands slapped onto the entry fields like he was playing the tiniest set of bongos. Blue rushed back to help Kowsky while Zelia prepared the entries to be consumable by her Dreamer.

During that process, Artorian received mail.

Ding!

———

Message from: Titania.

Sunny? I just had an orange Wisp zip up to me at ludicrous speed to fill me in on events in Incursus, and relay your message. To the dismay of my personal guards, which did amuse me. I'm well, my dear friend.

I'm working on getting game screens functional for real cultivation, rather than improving the game screens currently active for Eternia use. By the time of exodus back into the real, it is the Wisp's grand master plan to present you with a better tracking method for your status and achievements.

I would have come to check on you, but you're in good hands, Grandpa. Now don't disturb me, if you can? The work we're doing is sensitive and demanding. I want to get this right for the time when it's important.

Call for Genevieve or Aleksandr if you need a line of communication. If you are going into Eternia soon, do consider a detour to a particular dungeon? Lair of the Far Squid. An eldritch squiddy beast from the void lives there. Specifically, you're looking for Louis, the Voidsquid. You'll know why when you get there. Have fun!

Ever your caretaker,

Yvessa.

———

Artorian sighed in relief. The message destroyed itself when he'd finished reading, rather than him needing to dismiss the prompt. An interesting development, but not one he was going to fuss over. Zelia was already placing screens in front of him.

No reason to dally!

———

Ability: Ink to Bolts, Bolts to Ink!

Where you write, your words remain forever.

Effect: You may use your Bolts meter to write using any tool, and on any medium, including system prompts. Your digits count as tools for the purposes of this mechanic. Your Ink has the properties of copper, cobalt, and lightning.

This ability can be used as a linking mechanic for other abilities.

———

A nod from her Dreamer made Zelia scroll down to the next entry, as she currently held proprietary control over that particular screen. Shining Ray was next! He'd been looking forward to this one. She paused him before getting started. "Shining Ray has improved from the Student rank to the Journeyman rank. Would you prefer a power boost, or one of your special qualities? With the removal of the Ignition bug, this entry qualifies for bolstering."

Artorian closed his eyes and crossed his arms. From his allotment list, two came to mind. "Pierce and penetrate matter to me more than the damage does. The damage will matter little if I can't cut through a swarm. I remember my dearest saying: pierce physical armor. Penetrate esoteric magic. Although you can pierce magic barriers, and penetrate physical protections, those keywords won't work as well for those purposes, compared to using them in the correct word order."

He was going to mull over choosing one, but Zelia surprised him with the sound of a confirmation prompt being pushed. "Done."

He quickly leaned in to read what had happened with the entry. He hadn't chosen one!

———

Ability: Shining Ray.

Rank: Journeyman.

Special Qualities: HitScan, C-Laser, Ranging, Critical, Pierce, Penetrate.

Output: Deal thermal damage per second proportional to the energy invested.

Rate of Fire: One ray per second.

HitScan: This attack is instant, occurring when the ray comes in contact with any object in the line of fire.

C-Laser: A continuous-wave operation laser is a ray that continues to operate so long as it is fed energy. C-lasers have no cooldown triggers between uses.

Ranging: The maximum range of this ray is determined by the player's vision clarity metric. See prior entry: view distance bonus.

Critical: Critical chance can apply to each instance of a ray.

Pierce: Ignore 50% of physical effects that would reduce the damage of this ray. If the opponent has no such effects, and has no armor value, then this ray will travel through that target as if it did not block line of sight.

Penetrate: Ignore 50% of magical effects that would reduce the damage of this ray. If the opponent has no such effects, and has no mitigation value, then this ray will travel through that target as if it did not block line of sight.

Note: Due to having both Pierce and Penetrate on this ability, if either of the conditions of these special qualities are met, then the ray will travel through the target, regardless of the target having a value that would prevent the ray from doing so, or not.

———

"Well, having both is nice, but…" Artorian barely believed what he was seeing. "That's it? Where'd the giant blocks of text about HitScan mechanics go? Wasn't this a massive thing?"

Zelia shook her head. "New and improved, My Dreamer. New and improved. Some Pylons had to be sacrificed for integrity, and the cleaned up entry of Shining Ray had unused allotments. Please note that Shining Ray does not list what *kind* of energy it takes to create a thermal damage-typed ray."

She winked at him when he ooooh'd at the realization, rolling the prompt into the next ability entry. "I do have to apologize for Luminous Gatling. We were forced to replace several connections that weren't viable, and no longer have the option for another special effect allotment. You have the choice to improve the output, or modify the cost."

Artorian scanned over the entry, much of the text blinking an angry red. "Let's drop the cost this time, even if that's not the best choice. Then, if I end up needing to swap out sets, your scarf won't end up being the math-breaker. I remember it blinking at me that it was helping with costs. I'd rather mitigate that instead of bolster damage, when damage—so far—has not been a problem yet."

His secretary gladly abided, altering the entry and watching with her Dreamer as all the red text resolved into a happy neutral text, no longer blinking in distress.

———

Ability: Luminous Gatling.

   Rank: Apprentice.

   Special Qualities: Gatling, Homing, Critical.

   Shape: Laser.

   Description: This ability fires rapid bolt-type lasers that home in on a designated target.

   Output: Luminous Gatling requires 3 Energy per special quality to fire a single bolt.

   Current Cost per Bolt: 9 Energy.

   Ammunition: Ink to Bolts, Bolts to Ink!

   *Luminous Gatling considers both the **Nuts** and **Bolts** bars to be valid Energy meters to draw from. Ink to Bolts, Bolts to Ink has a cosmetic effect on the ammunition created, mimicking the visual properties of copper, cobalt, and lightning.*

   Luminous Gatling may be spun up to fire a maximum of 60 bolts per second, at the user's control, minimum 1. Each bolt deals 1d10 worth of kinetic lightning damage. Cost will be calculated per second, and detracted from the player's Energy regeneration, until that value hits zero, at which point Luminous Gatling will draw from the Energy meter.

   Special Quality: More Dakka.

   More Dakka: If Luminous Gatling is firing bolts at its maximum output, then its projectile count is doubled.

———

Artorian whistled. "Now that's good dakka."

His attention was then stolen by some of the Trans Am

description already poking in from below, his inner Goblin speaking out loud. "*Oooh*, shiny! Can I see the shiny?"

Zelia chuckled and flicked her wrist up.

———

Ability: Trans Am.

Rank: Novice.

Exia Pylons operational. Color codes: pink, red.

Trans Am doubles a player's core attributes, at the cost of removing all Energy regeneration metrics. Trans Am deactivates either when any of the player's Energy bars bottom out, or when it is manually deactivated.

Trans Am has a cosmetic effect, shrouding the player in a pink glow, with red particles.

———

"Glad to have it." Artorian nodded sagely as he read that entry over twice. "Shame the color is red. That's more in line with Ember's theme. I'm more of a Blue's Brother? Original eye-color, and whatnot."

Zelia pursed her lips in thought, her claw tapping on the chair as she considered the change. "Yes. Choose two. As a note, your iris color is currently a bright blue, my Dreamer. Your use of intent appears to have sorted the swirling."

Artorian did just so as the prompt scrolled on, glad for the tidbit. "Well, the entire party so far is a main color, and then white as secondary. So set me as blue? Or celestine. That's softer. Teal or cyan is good too, it's whatever the Pylons can handle."

Zelia worked her magic juju. "Done. Exia Pylons reconfigured, color codes now set to white and blue. Blue glow, with white particles. Your next ability is up, my Dreamer."

"Thank you, Zelia." Artorian turned his gaze, reading up.

———

Ability: Cleaning Presence.
   Rank: Novice.
   Special Qualities: Aura, Clean.
   Shape: Orb.
   Description: A field emitting a constant cleaning effect, centered on the caster.
   Output: One meter in diameter of cleaning effect per percentage of maximum Energy bar invested. This field cleans, but does not cleanse.
   Note: You may only have one Aura-type effect active at any given time.

———

Cleaning Presence appeared entirely unchanged. He toggled it on and off, but regardless of the output going full blast, he didn't feel a difference. He dirtied his fingers while it was off, observing them. Sure enough, dirty hands remained dirty. As if that was normal. Because it was. That took a moment to sink in, then he flicked Cleaning Presence back on and watched the magic happen, his hand getting cleaned particle by particle. Paying such close attention, it kind of tickled!

"That is all for the abilities, My Dreamer." Zelia began folding up the prompt, returning it to the flock around the fire.

Artorian heard his own brain play an error sound. "What? No? Nono. What about 'To Whom It May Concern'?"

"About that." Zelia called a different prompt to her circling web. "These next two spells were Pylon-coded… poorly. Listing them as abilities was incorrect. Please review them."

———

Spell: Abyss That Person In Particular.
   Rank: Novice.
   Special Qualities: Explode on Hit, Cast on Target.
   Description: This ability causes a designated target to explode, possibly destroying it.

Output: A designated target will explode, taking explosion damage in a five foot diameter equal to one-fourth the energy invested.

———

Ability: To Whom It May Concern.
Rank: Novice.
Special Qualities: Explode on Hit, Cast on Target.
Description: This ability causes a designated area to explode, possibly destroying it.
Output: A designated area will explode, taking explosion damage in a fifty foot radius equal to one-tenth the energy invested.

———

Artorian carefully read both entries over. "On one hand, yay spells. On the other hand? I'm going to need to be careful. One is measured in diameter, and the other one in radius. I'm fairly certain a circle's radius is half of its diameter, but it's been a long time since Dwarven Math class."

Zelia smirked. "Do remember that you need your broom for them, my Dreamer?"

Artorian made sure to have the Boom Shaka Laka Broom in hand, then held it up, grinning right back. "I'll sweep them all! Cowabunga calls for my foes to fall."

Zelia laughed openly and with heart. "*Ha-ha!* Let us make that your third spell, my Dreamer. I have such fond memories of your unyielding use of that statement in your bout against both Zeus and Marie. Let us add it to the to-do list, and move on to your skills. I wish to see you play in the snowy Midgard fields. Let us culminate. We can skip the deity options. That will not be a swift discussion."

Artorian stowed his broom. "Skills time!"

CHAPTER FIFTEEN

Zelia's fingers prepared a snapping motion. She glanced in the direction of Kowsky and Blue, both of whom snapped to instant salutes. Kowsky beamed under his mask. "A pleasure to serve, O' Higher Being. May the Radiance fill your days."

At the snap, Kowsky vanished with the same dream particles he'd arrived in.

The spotter, in large part, copied the bug finder. Though sans smile, as his expression wouldn't be conveniently hidden. "Call 'pon us anytime, Autarch. May the radiance fill yer days."

Another snap, and Blue vanished in a whiff of wet smoke, leaving only Turk, Tchaikovsky, Incursus, Zelia, and Artorian present in the encampment. Holding Tchaikovsky by the scruff, Turk walked the other Gnome over to help him bow and apologize, as Tchaikovsky hadn't really figured out what toes he'd stepped on yet. Tchaikovsky was a good boy, enjoying the labors of relative time and chronology. If he wanted to keep enjoying then, being polite to the right people would pay off. Not because those people would take offense directly, but due to it oft being the case that many others took the offense for them.

The Autarch might say nothing about the Chronomancer

being an interloper in Incursus as he did some testing, while they happened to have this meeting, using the Gnome character or not being rather unimportant. Yet all of Zelia's children, and likely a fat host of Dark Elves, wouldn't see it that way. Turk bowed his head while forcing Tchaikovsky to do the same. "A thousand pardons, Autarch. Please excuse me to teach this young'un the error of his ways."

Zelia quietly smiled at the antics caused by background politics. One snap, and both Gnomes were gone, leaving only the skill screens that Turk had finished. She summoned them close with a wave of the hand, checked their entries, and then moved them to be in front of Artorian so her Dreamer could read them. "Skills."

Artorian was stuck watching the empty space the Gnomes had been. "I'm really not sure how to feel about this politicking. No matter how exempt I appear to be, I feel a deep concern for everyone living within the system. This really is too much fear for my liking, but at the same time, Avalon is the best I've been able to help with. Which, compared to this global, cross-faction, multi-race balance you're playing with? Feels so small…"

"You have done wonderfully, my Dreamer." Zelia laid her hands across one another. "Avalon is a shining beacon of what the world as a whole could become. A beacon that I, with all my strings to pull and webs to weave, would not have been able to accomplish."

Warmth and care filled her words. "Do not diminish yourself, Artorian. I am not actually in charge. I am merely the reminder that we are all stuck in the mess together, and that there are lines in the sand. Their choice of respect is just that, a choice. That my children are zealous is acceptable. I have given them strict instructions not to take their intentions too far. A little discomfort goes a long way. Actual harm has… reservations, and requirements. When possible, I look forward to you being in a seat where the Love of Avalon spreads."

She winked when that made him feel better, purely to be coy

and supportive. "Until there is no patch of grass left that does not know how much you adore it, and no person on it who is unaware that their wellbeing is your great happiness. The fall of many nations occurs during the exchanges of power. It is thus my great pleasure to know that you will live exceptionally long."

Artorian rubbed the back of his head, still worried, but placated. He didn't know what to say, but Zelia gently pushed one of the screens closer, not needing a reply if he did not have one.

———

Skill: Critical Luck.
Rank: Novice.
When rolling the event of a critical chance, roll the die multiple times. If any of the resulting rolls result in a successful critical event, then the critical hit occurs.
At each new rank of this skill, one die is added to the pool.
At Novice Critical Luck, your pool consists of two dice.

———

Skill: Freedom of Mind.
Rank: Static.
Freedom of Mind provides full immunity to possession, mind altering states you do not allow, and grants a powerful boost to any speech-related activity. This does not provide a numerical change, and will instead put you on equal footing with any who use oration of a superior skill level, regardless of your respective skill level.

———

Skill: Flash Runes.
Rank: Primer.
This skill will improve to Novice when Flash Runes, the ability, can be

introduced to the player. This skill is a primer and placeholder for when the system is ready to engage.

———

Skill: Luminous Gatling Mastery.

Rank: Beginner.

When engaging the use of Luminous Gatling, the hidden burdens will be lessened. When all the burdens are mastered, this skill will provide hidden benefits instead.

———

Once at the bottom of the list, Artorian attempted to keep scrolling, but there was no text remaining. "*Uhhh...* Zelia? I think there's a small problem."

When she didn't reply, he looked up to find her holding her chin. One of her legs shifted over the other as a claw tip tapped against her lips. The missing entry for Supreme Weapon Mastery was in front of her, but the entire entry was flashing red. Every last bit of it. "I see you have already found the small problem."

"It refused to populate." Zelia had no issues saying the words, but Artorian had plenty trying to understand them. He reached weakly for her prompt, hoping he wasn't about to lose that skill.

Zelia laced her fingers. "I have good news, and bad news."

He winced. "Tell me I'm not losing the critical hit autokill."

Zelia refused to do so. "You're losing the critical hit autokill."

Artorian shot both arms to the sky, shaking his fists and lamenting loudly. That was the one thing in that entry he did not want to lose. His entire build was going to be based around that mechanic! His game plans were ruined! "*Nooooo!*"

Ding!

He closed his eyes, inhaling deeply. He didn't want to read

the new entry. He did, but he didn't. It was a conflicting desire to both want and not want something at the same time. Peeking open an eye, he cautiously treaded these murky waters.

———

Skill: Supreme Weapon Mastery.
  Rank: Static.
  Supreme Weapon Mastery provides proficiency in all weaponry, of all types. Instead of variable damage, all damage rolls are considered maximized. Attacks no longer cost stamina. Skills applied to attacks have their costs halved.

———

Had he not already been sitting in a chair, Artorian would have dramatically fallen down into one. Grasping his heart, he placed the back of his other hand across his forehead. "Oh, the inhumanity! It's gone! It's all gone!"

"Just like the rum." Zelia nodded at the statement. A bell tolled, some crates of rum pushing up from the ground and adding themselves to the encampment. She chuckled, and petted the chair. "You're sweet, Incursus. I was making a silly jest to lighten the mood. The Administrator did just lose a favorite component of one of his skills. An imported one, no less. When he was forced to avoid choosing his more potent options to begin with. This is a blow to him, as this writ of Supreme Weapon Mastery doesn't feel so supreme anymore."

"That's certainly a way to say it." Artorian moped. This hurt. This hurt a lot. "I mean, it's still good. Easy math for damage is nice, and not fumbling about with what I pick up is going to be a solid boon. Still doesn't feel... I feel like a piece of my chest is missing all of a sudden. I know I didn't lose anything physical, but it feels like I did."

A bell tolled in the distance, a few new screens appearing.

Artorian was going to dismiss the dungeon, saying he appreciated the efforts but now was maybe not a good time. Then before his mouth could doom him, his eyes saw the words on one of the entries, voice dying in his throat as he lurched forward to grab hold.

Five entries later, and his whole mood turned upside down. "Incursus! You *gem!*"

———

Skill: Critical Mastery.

    Rank: Novice.

    Your minimum critical chance value is 5%, instead of 1%.

    Each rank of Critical Mastery will increase your minimum critical chance value by 1.

    The calculation from weapon rarity adds to this floor, before the class multiplier is applied.

———

Skill: Critical Stack.

    Requires: Critical Luck.

    Rank: Novice.

    When rolling a successful critical event, additional successful results from Critical Luck will cause additional critical effects to apply.

    Each rank of Critical Stack will increase the number of your possible additional effects stacking onto a single critical event by 1.

———

Skill: Critical Clarity.

    Rank: Static.

    You have access to the critical calculation screen. You are able to see and modify your critical effects and associated priorities, including the actual effects of what that critical effect accomplishes.

———

Skill: Critical Conversion.
   Rank: Static.
   You may reduce the damage of any weapon you are holding to 1. All damage a strike would have incurred past 1 is instead doubled on a successful critical hit, and applied as bonus damage before critical effects are tallied.

———

Skill: AllCrit.
   Rank: Static.
   You can successfully land critical hits on anything. Targets that would otherwise be immune or resistant to critical hits have that quality negated.

———

Skill: SpellCrit.
   Rank: Static.
   Spells benefit from critical chance, based on the player's minimum critical chance value. Current: 25%.

———

"It's not autokill, but this is very nice! I can work with this! Now it no longer matters what weapon I'm tromping about with, I can maximize my crit with this. SpellCrit also does me good, and I'm guessing there's a requirement with abilities where it currently needs to be listed as a special quality." Artorian beamed, happy with this development. "Was there anything else, or can I be hurled into Eternia? I can work with this!"

Zelia closed down every single screen around the campfire, dropping the illumination of the general area down to half. "Plenty, my Dreamer. Deity options can wait. I don't have a solution for keeping you breathing in vacuum yet, but I will not be detaining you. So, yes. I can *hurl you*, if you wish."

Her wicked expression made him giggle, grasping hold of

the communication brooch to check in with the team as requested. "Momma Bun! I'm coming in hot!"

He then jumped right off his chair, adopting a wide stance like a surprised Goblin, his expression certainly matching the energy of one. "Ready! Forget the bag. *Toss me!*"

Zelia smirked, finding this incredibly amusing. Without a word—but with plenty of flair and show—she appeared behind him, grabbed him by the fluffy scruff of his parka, and full force hurled the screeching Goblin-torian into Eternia with a snappy *vwop*!

CHAPTER SIXTEEN

Within the realm of Eternia, constellations lit up across the night's sky. Ancient history, written in images of light. They flickered, lived bright, and dimmed like a dying Nixie Tube.

The sky above the realm of Midgard rumbled. The cracks of a storm breaking, rumbling to be free as the clouds fractured. Lightning popped, and icy rains poured forth.

Upon the rimward march of New Haven—part tower and part glacier—stood Lady Duchess, named Lady O'Dachi by those who lived in New Haven. The legendary weapon itself was never far from her, the purity-seal adorned sword resting on two silk-covered pillows carried by her personal assistants, two Kitsune dressed in sanctified shrine maiden attire.

This tallest, physical outcrop of New Haven provided Lady Duchess a crisp, clean line of sight to the skyward disturbance. She watched as Fuyu No Arashi, the Eternal Thundercloud, beat its bright drums once more on the horizon. The lights alive and fighting within her, however, shone a color other than the icy aquamarine that the cloud loved to spew forth.

On that far horizon, a peal of purple lightning cracked, Fuyu No Arashi broken from within as four distinct lines of light descended from the sky. Aquamarine electricity chased them down to punish their impertinence, but found no purchase. As each mixture of colors lost their trail and tail on the way down, comfort filled her old bones. There had been many strange visitors to New Haven of late, but these were the ones she'd been looking forward to.

The Eminence, Astarte, Lady Death, and Less Than Three had returned.

Good news for her. Their arrival signaled an addition to a stream of existing good news that had been flooding in since the ignition of the sun, and the stellar return of their Child of Light. While others appeared to be having some difficulty with the thought, Lady Duchess had no difficulty separating the Child of Light, an overdeity, from Less Than Three, a transmigrator to this realm of theirs. She needed a better word for that.

To many others of New Haven, the people clung to the highest available designation, failing to see the boy for what he was, or for who he was, and instead clung to what they hoped he was. She had great doubts that the ancient grandfather filling the memoirs of her mother would fail that task. Younger form of not, she had no doubts of this. The Child of Light would shine.

No, it was Less Than Three that occupied her mind. Wise ancient or not, Three was but a boy. And a mere boy ought not to be expected to carry the weight of all the realms on his shoulders. She steeled her gaze, gripping her forearms behind her back as she maintained a rigid, iron posture.

The lights of differing colors were no longer descending straight down, playfully racing from the sky as they escaped the great cloud. The red and white dot had bumped into the blue and white dot. Their playful scuffle was broken by the yellow and white dot that, swift as light, zipped between them, with the black and white dot the only to remain steady and unbroken.

She could infer the conversation from here. Astarte, the girl of war and fire, was teasing her cute boy. Three, realizing that this was an invitation to play, prepared to match her energy in turn. This attempt was then broken up by Eminence Lucia, while Dasein, colored in black and white, was likely amused and happy to observe.

The colors intertwined and attempted to circumvent the yellow and white line a few more times, but that effort was thwarted. The yellow and white dot took the blue dot by what was probably the scruff, and hurled it realmward. The blue dot traveled significantly faster, hitting the horizon hard before the other dots could catch up. This impact kicked up a massive snow cloud as Lady Duchess became aware of just how different Midgard looked now.

Ice had replaced many segments of snow. Slush was everywhere, gooping its way into crevices and holes of the world, freshly opened up from the new heat that blanketed their snowy realm. Major sections of Midgard were still coated in white sheets, but the land had obvious shape to it now. No longer evenly sloped and smoothed to perfection as far as the eyes could see, with only the trails of their hunts carving paths.

She calculated how long it might take this party to reach New Haven, but felt her vision drop, eyes lingering on a massive canyon that no jump would ever cross. That same canyon had inadvertently protected them from all of the... nonsense crawling out from the muck. A combination of natural defenses, and visitors, had certainly helped matters.

Not that it compared against particular visitors. Transmigrators looking for 'fun.' Or, as she had deduced, 'fights.' There was some chatter about 'experience points,' and that had told her enough. Access to the Voice of the World had been gone for a long time, but now? Trickle by trickle, it was all coming back, and so much was waiting for her. So much control. Options. Information. Screens filled with maps and values and numbers and truths. Whole panels *specifically* for quest and kingdom management.

How she wished she could have had such luxuries in The Pale.

Instead, she had an influx of visitors. So many that the

amount of taverns in New Haven had suddenly tripled. That their glorious food stock was diminishing too rapidly for her liking due to this was an arrowhead that she was mid-process of biting. The visitors were most helpful when directed to a task or need, little rivalries existing between them, as she was still swallowing the bitter medicine that they were all here for 'fun.'

The word was bitter. *Fun.*

After the Abyss of a life she'd lived through to claw and tear out a future for every person here in this frozen fortress. Reduced to entertainment. She tensed, her old bones aching as she squeezed her wrists too hard, the irritation slowly bleeding away as the accidental damage caused the warmth of blessed health regeneration to kick in.

A calm bliss followed, her sharp nose drawing on the cool air. She relished this tiny gift from the Child of Light that he likely hadn't been aware of. Particularly the limitation to only extend his gifts to those who refused to be players in their realm of theirs. An affection for those who lived here, and were one with the land. To lay his hands on the shoulders of those who had clawed to survive, and not those who had come clawing to take more.

The thought, cruel and selfish as it might have been, brought a smile to her face.

There would be other Divines that would come.

Others who would, in one way or another, make their way up to such a platform.

Yet, Sunny would be theirs. *Only theirs.*

The Sovereign of the Sun, Overdeity of Eternia. The one who did not wish to get involved, but came back for them anyway. He would only ever be theirs, and that brought a comfort to her iron heart. The name would probably change or, more likely, be buried in obscurity. Or both? Both would be good. Other Divines could have their glory. She knew Sunny would be content to walk with her and her kin, uninterested in the scuffle of shrines and temples. Those were but means, never his ends.

She believed so with certainty, squeezing a patch of cloth tight in her grip. Her own personal, hand-sewn sun sigil. Her symbol. One just for her. Made with the person who would look upon her, and love her without reservation in mind. Without condition. He would let her go with warmth, and would accept her back just the same.

There was such beauty in those words.

That freedom of agency was liberating.

"No strings. Only an eternal welcome." How rare it was for her to have something to hold on to that wasn't her own strength, and iron will. She basked in the sun, barely noticing the icy rain falling on her face between the warmth fervently permeating through.

A crash, bang, and commotion behind her made Lady Duchess close her eyes and inhale the strength to deal with the newbloods. She was relishing happy thoughts, yet the world demanded her attention once more. As always, she spoke with both exceptional clarity and the bleating volume of a sheep that wasn't about to be ignored. "Form up!"

The kerfuffle below her quickly found a way to make ranks, even if Lady Duchess was convinced that many of these individuals had her well and truly beaten in both age and power. Were they humoring her? Or was this part of the game they were playing at her expense?

No... *no*. She shouldn't allow herself that avenue of thought. While to these new people, her world was a game, to Lady O'Dachi, this was all still deadly serious work. Her people needed food and shelter. A change in conditions didn't alter those needs. So, she was as stern and sharp-tongued as any scorned grandmother who didn't have time for uninvited guests.

She had even lumped them into groups they were making by themselves, complete with a unique, silly team name. The act had either amused them, or greatly improved their day for some reason. Just for fun, she had also provided each team with an otherwise pointless hunk of metal, hammered into the shape of an iron sheep. Allotments was how she'd spun the story. There were a limited number of tokens, for a limited amount of... to use their own words, 'adventurer' teams.

Have a token? She would allow them these 'quests' they were supposedly here for. If they were going to act as if she were in charge, then she was going to continue to act as if she was. That half of these madlads and ruffians had already shown the kind of powers and prowess that put Less Than Three's artillery bombardment to shame?

That would remain quiet.

"Hear me." Lady Duchess raised a bony hand to the air. "Hear me."

The clamoring and conversations on the rung under her tower simmered down, allowing her to speak without having to yell over anyone. "The quests are open, and assigned as follows. The groups Nightshade and Predator's Territory have access to quests in the north. Beef and Book, alongside Team IcyHot, have access to quests in the east. Magnitude and The Old Wood have access to quests in the south. Four White Mages *Not* in a Trench Coat—that name is too long—are allowed access to quests in the west, alongside Beasts and Beauties. This, I decree."

A large gong was hit behind her, Lady Duchess standing firm as the groups gathered below broke out in applause and excited whooping. She leaned her head to the side when a Kitsune shrine maiden moved in to whisper about the... missing group that she had tactfully not mentioned.

The Lady had to compose herself before replying to the innocent maiden. "The group known as You've Yar'd Your Last Har, as far as I am concerned, has yee'd their last haw. If they're going to be more chaotic than what Magnitude seems capable of, then I don't care where they go. So long as where they go isn't *here*."

CHAPTER SEVENTEEN

Digging himself out of a mound of wet snow that clung unpleasantly to his clothes, Artorian shook his hands before coming face to face with a massive creature. He slipped instantly from being too close, tumbling right down the incline of the snowy hill. The large horned beast covered in granite and permafrost looked down upon him with beady eyes of coal that slowly turned white. This large, lumbering creature that looked incredibly slow must have come to inspect what had fallen from the sky.

Perhaps it had hoped he was food?

The great horned beast stood its ground on the top of the hill and stared at Artorian tumbling until the boy hit a hard patch of frozen ground. A glowing shell around the small creature in fuzzy blue and white fur blipped out of being, expended at the damage taken.

"Ow." Laying on his back, Artorian watched the Beast fold its ears against its head as the icy hair on its hump raised up. The Beast smacked its mouth at him, licked its lips, and clicked its teeth. Artorian could not decipher why it whipped its head back like a horse as he slowly got up, but did feel some concern when it lowered its head at him and began to advance.

Cleansing Presence made the ick and the stick go away, but it was doing nothing to halt or slow this advancing Beastie that picked up speed far faster than seemed reasonable. Needing some information on what was going on before the rest of the party could get here to help his single digit health point behind, he waved his hand and threw out a simple inspection.

He didn't need a lot of information, but a name would certainly help.

Ding!

———

You have encountered: Jotun Bull Moose.
Detected Trait: Revenge of the Herd.
Detected Ability: Cold Fusion Charge.
Detected Ability: Power Antler.
Detected Skill: 360 Hooves.
Detected Skill: Turn and Burn.
Detected Skill: Snow Mastery.

———

"That's strange formatting. I've never seen a prompt give me information that way before. Is someone else in charge of my prompts again?" His comment should have waited, because the Moose did not, and his response was panic. "Shining Ray!"

The granite and permafrost charging Jotun Bull Moose shone a cold, vibrant blue as it attacked with Cold Fusion Charge without any hesitation. Power Antler shrouded its glowing antlers in a cloudy pale turquoise light as it barreled towards him, the Jotun Moose increasing in speed before cannoning towards him at a very sudden Mach one. The sound-breaking bang that this caused was silenced by the persistent beam of burning light erupting from Artorian's open palm, vaporizing the icy Moose from existence, along with the entire chunk of landscape that had been behind the creature.

Ding!

———

You have triggered Revenge of the Herd.

———

Artorian barely noticed the prompt, both his hearts busy pounding in his ears. "*Fwhoooo…* that was close! I done went and booped his snoot, and then he was *gone*! That was way too close. I only just made it back!"

Three impacts slammed into the ground nearby as he caught his breath.

Thump!

Thump!

Thump!

As the bursts of snow cleared, and each party member entered his view, Artorian saw a pleasant sight. Dasein smirked with her arms crossed, content to watch. Lucia fussed and stomped her way to him, a charged Shield spell already in hand. Ember had landed closest, and was helping him to his feet. She was smiling, but it was one of those 'you're in trouble' smiles. "Sugar? Do you at all remember why you weren't supposed to use Shining Ray?"

He stumbled once he was on his feet properly, the snow under his boots slightly giving way, but not remotely as much as he expected that it should. His boots pulsed with a soft light, barely noticeable at all as their effect remained active. Artorian quickly checked what his boots were supposed to do before his mind could turn onto Ember's question.

———

Item: Boots
  Name: Snowsteps.
  Material: Spider Wool.
  Rarity: Special.
  Effect: The user does not sink through snow.

――――

Satisfied, his mind immediately snapped to an answer. When his more conscious mind then reviewed that answer, Artorian slapped himself on the forehead. "Because we didn't wanna get the attention of the moon?"

Ember squeezed his shoulders. "Because we didn't wanna get the attention of the moon. Y'know, the moon that eats people? The moon that is currently dressed in chunks of Vanaheim? The hungry Ecumenopolis in the sky? That one."

He winced slightly. "Did we get the attention of the cheese moon? Or did I get away with it, free from its fondue tentacles?"

They both looked to the sky, finding it very difficult not to notice the whole of Vanaheim laboriously, but certainly, turning toward them. Ember patted his shoulder, smacking her lips. "*Mmmmyup!* Brother Moon noticed it, alright. Looks like Vanaheim was facing the wrong way entirely, so you may have just *barely* gotten away with it, buuuuut if you do that again while it's looking this way?"

She clicked her tongue while looking down and shaking her head, saying nothing with her lips tightly squeezed. Ember then tactically got out of Lucia's way when the Momma Bun got within Momma-reprimanding range. "Boy!"

She placed her paw right on top of his head, borderline exasperated after the stunt it took to get him out of space. He glowed a faint yellow when she added her first buff, Artorian noticing that everyone else in the party shared the sudden addition. "Greater Sanctity."

Her Glitterflit paw reformed into a human hand as she

controlled herself, the second effect blooming out more of a pink hue that coated them all for a moment before fading over time. "Greater Lenity."

Artorian felt the damage absorption shell surround him, layering on top of the Sanctity effect that protected him from a slew of nasty status effects. He didn't directly feel any different, and the sensation faded when the visual effect did. Lucia's third cast took a bit longer, adding more involved whispers and hand motions before she patted him on the head again.

This time he glowed a strong green as Momma Bun verbalized her cast, recognizing the spell as the heal over time effect that triggered if Lenity took damage. "Greater Prosperity."

Satisfied with her work, she looked him up and down, then trained her eyes above his head to read a status screen only she could see. When remembering that tidbit, she flicked him right in the nose. Soft enough not to eat up the expensive spells she'd just layered on him, as her flick did no damage save for making Less Than Three stagger and grab hold of his own nose as Lucia gave them all heads up displays. "Greater Acuity."

He illuminated with a dim, warm light, but couldn't discern a color. He was instead focused on not sneezing, and Lucia inspected her paw. "While I'm happy some of the cosmetic effects are returning, I can't help but feel like some mechanical effects were changed. That felt different to cast? Hard to explain."

"No, I get it, Momma Bun." He raised his own hand, flexing his fingers open and closed. "I didn't get hit with any backlash from Shining Ray at all. Not a spell, sure? I still felt a noticeable smoother experience. Like my hand was coated in water instead of sand while the effect was going off. A minor and strange difference, but it was there. I think they're getting Pylon banks in order?"

A coruscating arrow from Astarte's Damocles bow whizzed past them, turning a chunk of snowy landscape into a burning pit as not-so-sneaky gathered Moose in that location turned into flying giblets. The local area rained burning blood, the liquid actually on fire as it all came back down like a colorful summer shower. Ember snapped them all back on track. "Conversation later. Combat now. We haven't actually stopped in between fetching you from orbit, sugar. "

"Right!" Artorian jumped into formation as the unity settled in, awareness of his surroundings bleeding in as the threats became visible. The Moose herd approached at ludicrous speed. "Those are way too fast for Midgard! That's so unbalanced!"

All three of the women around him stopped mid-combat-prep to look at him. Dasein couldn't contain her soft rise in giggles, hiding her face as she said what they were all thinking. As she grasped that, in their current situation, that was a special kind of silly statement. "The audacity."

Dasein then lifted her own hand up, adding to the group's cohesion, adding a spell as her foresight reached far and wide. A darkness surrounded the four members of their team, blacklight humming and clinging to them all just as Lucia's brighter spells did. Nobody was going to ask where the Heavenly had picked up spells. Popular guesses were that she had a sit down with Tim and a few other participating Heavenlies to build a starter kit, because the alternative would have likely involved some blatant cheatery.

Copying the healer's nomenclature, Dasein chanted her spell, using the same designator to turn a single target spell into a group spell. "Greater Momentum."

Curious as all Abyss as to what that one did, Artorian looked at the top left of his vision to see the effect add itself to the bottom of the list under his energy bars and health... dot? Where was his health bar? Or was that measly sliver supposed to be it? No, that was probably it... He mentally tapped the entry while reaching for it with his left pointer digit, the prompt helpfully jumping to the forefront of his vision as his other hand began to spin up Luminous Gatling.

―――

Spell: Momentum.
   Affix: Greater.
   Rank: Student.
   Description: A party normally travels only as fast as its slowest member. No more! Momentum allows the designated entity to move at the same speed as the fastest member of the current party.
   Output: Momentum tethers your current speed to that of the fastest member of your party, compensating for lack of attributes. Momentum also provides a flat 20% reduction on stamina costs while the spell is in effect.
   Warning: Momentum does not grant you the skills or abilities that the leading party member uses in order to more efficiently traverse. No active abilities of the speed leader will transfer to the tethered targets.
   Gnome note: Affixes. The 'Greater' designation either amplifies a specific component of a spell's effect, or adds to the amount of maximum targets. Least and Lesser designations diminish a spell's effects, while Greater and Greatest improve it. The 'Greater' affix adds an additional three entities to the maximum number of targets affected.

———

He glanced at the Heavenly for a question, but her gaze was drawn to the sky. Dasein's black lips curled into a knowing smirk as she crossed her arms, enjoying the light breeze flowing through her short blonde hair.

Artorian indulged in more curiosity as Luminous Gatling finished spooling up. "Do we have anyone watching?"

Dasein, Heavenly of **Existence**, kept her gaze on the sky a moment longer. She sharply jabbed her nose off in a dismissive direction, as if telling an observer to get the celestial feces out of here. She then aimed those same pale blue eyes over her shoulder at him, and winked.

CHAPTER EIGHTEEN

Lucia hopped on her toes, bouncing in the snow boots that prevented her from sinking through the white fluff. She was answering the same question for herself that Artorian had silently asked, and found the effect satisfactory. "Astarte? You're the team lead. What are we doing, and who is the speed lead?"

Ember threw that directive right back at her, her compound bow pulled taut to release a flurry of arrow-shaped flames at some of the Jotun Moose that were getting too close for comfort, picking them off before they could fully lean into that speed boost effect of theirs was crucial. "That would be you, Momma Bun! We're going in the direction of New Haven. Get your zoom on, take point, and take us out. Three, you're taking up flanking positions with me. Lady Death? I know better than to tell you what to do."

Dasein enjoyed the wildest smile at the use of her newly earned nickname.

She, as all the Heavenlies did in Eternia, went by her own name, having profusely refused game names of any sort. They were in no way trying to be someone else, and were all dead set on recreating their personal power sets in this game space, one way or another. The nickname, though? She did not mind that accolade at all, her words smooth and sugary as ever. Even as a massive, onyx black and Tuscan yellow scythe formed in her hand. "Lady Death will take the rear, and bring death to moody deer."

Adding flavor to her actions, the Lady stepped into the flow of the game world, and spoke the name of her attack into being as she kept up with the group's rising speed. "Rarely Violent. Always Fatal."

She danced subtle, aggressive movements, flourishing her death scythe with blasphemous dexterity. A trail of Vantablack night followed the weapon's mesmerizing crescent patterns. As the flourish flowed, unreal darkness followed in its wake. Like the universe was sewing itself back together behind each strike. Ashen black lines cut the space around her, but vanished before seeming to do anything truly dangerous.

Or so Artorian thought as he fell into a jogging stride with Lucia and began to spot for targets. He found a Moose to blast, then saw it bisected by a Vanta-edged ashen-black scythe slice, as if that attack had occurred exactly where the Moose had been.

The effect's resolution was instant. Off with its head!

Instead of a number, a black skull appeared above the slain Jotun Moose.

"What?" He blinked in confusion as the pace increased, Artorian looking over his shoulder at Dasein with a curious frown as his voice turned momentarily shrill. "What was *that*?"

Lady Death was most amused, indulging the boy with the interesting stele. "The strike of a weapon through space does not need to match the location of where the effect of that strike happens. I performed the motions, but know how to cleave only that which I wish to cleave. I completed the cuts, but I did not cut the air around me. I moved the execution, the real cut that happened, onto the enemies around me. One cut, one kill. The effect guillotining through them with the difficulty of cutting air."

Her expression curled toward the indulgent. "For this flourish, I struck them not with damage. I struck them with Death."

Artorian wanted twelve. "Is there a range on that?"

Lady Death purred. "No. It is a lesson. There is no escaping a woman's wrath."

Flabbergasted, Artorian shot his head to Ember, pleading with a look that he wanted to learn how to do that.

She rolled her eyes at him before turning a hill into a burning crater with a fiery *boom*, a host of red numbers rising up from the enraged wound in the snowy world. "Sugar, *I* can't even pull off Death effects. That save-or-die attack style is not my toolset. How am I gonna teach you? I don't rely on attacks that allow for attribute protections, saving throws, endurance rolls, I-Frames, or invulnerability saves. I just deal damage. Lots and lots of *damage*. You'd have more luck picking up the speed technique these horned ballistae with an anger complex are using than what Lady Death is currently dancing around with. I can teach you the flurry, how to cut space, and how to transfer intended damage. Not the instakill. Not like that."

Artorian felt sad for about zero point two seconds before the idea of stealing a Moose's ability snuck in from around the corner. "Oh. Well, I'm gonna do that then!"

Ember and Lucia both had a moment where imaginary sand moved through a spinning hourglass, before they both tried to tell him not to do that particularly dumb idea. They got as far as breathing in before Artorian, with a huge dumb smile on his face, was feeding his Nuts and Bolts energy meters into the plan, fueling his intent as he went ahead and tried it. Because why not! "Cold Fusion Charge!"

Several error noises and unhappy orange 'Stop' prompts accompanied his successful theft of the Jotun Moose's toolkit. Before that could be addressed, the party that had slowly been accelerating and gaining velocity as a four-point diamond-shaped team now lurched forward. Less Than Three turned the diamond-pattern into a triangle as his sudden burst of Moose-y speed shot him ahead of the pack with a *wheeeeeee*!

The team matched his speed due to Greater Momentum, while a coma and tail of bright blue and white fusion light poured off of him. The landscape sped by, turning into a snowy blur made of valleys and hills. On their warpath, valleys and hills gained burning craters, Vantablack cut marks, and glittering gold paw prints. From Astarte's Damocles bow, Lady Death's scythe, and Her Eminence's Luminous Rail Paws, respectively.

Ding!

———

Notice!

Message from Eternium: Boy! On one hand, thank you for finding out that was possible. I don't know why nobody has tried that before until now. That worked far too easily, and the Pylon hold is glowing a whole host of new colors. I'm going to ask you to give that one away in the future. It would do poorly for you to keep it. I would also ask you not to do that again… but we both know you will. I will assign you a slight bonus for each of these unwanted interactions you happen to find. This really should have been gated with something. Anything. Enjoy your zooms, my friend. I know you like them.

Do be aware of the upcoming pack of Heavy Assault Unicorns.

———

"Heavy assault *what?*" Artorian slowed his roll, the fuel to Cold Fusion Charge tapering off because he was quickly running out of resources. The speed boost ability was meant as a sudden buff to charging speed, not a constantly fed effect to keep accelerating to infinity and beyond.

He fell back to his position in the four point diamond as speed allowed, the back of his head cuffed by Lucia who shot him a look. A look that was short lived as the huge grin of enjoyment on her face betrayed that the sudden case of zoomies had been a good time.

He laughed the bop to his glowing shield off as it ate the damage for him, then asked again when his question went unheard the first time. "Why did Turnip just warn me about Heavy Assault Unicorns?"

That turned Lucia's expression sour. "*More* of those? They're enemies who have Execute-type abilities. If you have less than X percent health? Instakill! It's not as critically dangerous as true damage, or as cheesy as the Lady's death effects that instagib if your wisdom can't defend you. At least Heavy Assault Unicorns aren't as bad as the *clouds*."

Lady Death and Astarte both joined with matching sour expressions at the mention of clouds. Ember spat in distaste. "Ugh. *Clouds*."

The litany of question marks living above Artorian's head must have been invisible, because he had enough of them to bury a Rock Squirrel. That nobody was forthcoming with the information wasn't helpful either, but he did not have the time to ask as a Jotun Moose—whose sudden angry existence was triggered by Revenge of the Herd—burst out from the snow directly next to him.

The Jotun Moose's own Cold Fusion Charge was already engaged, with antlers glowing and ready to gore targets galore. Activating Turn and Burn, the Moose—without losing any speed—sharply turned ninety degrees to intersect Artorian's trajectory and bowl him over.

Artorian didn't think, he only yelled. "Luminous Gatling!"

Cacophonous blasts of kinetic lightning tore into and through his barraged target, but he couldn't see any of the resulting gore that happened. Damage prompts decided to take that moment to block his field of vision, filling it with glorious numbers made of delicious damage. The back of the screens were plenty red and chunky, but that was nothing Cleaning Presence couldn't wipe away.

Riding the adrenaline, but having no targets to unload on, Artorian exhaled a hot breath and read the prompts to clear them. "*Whoo*! That's two close calls now! This isn't good for my health!"

Projectile: Luminous Bolt.
    Modifier: Rapid.
    Type: Kinetic Lightning.
    Special: Homing, Critical.
    Series: 1.
    Number: 1 / 120.
    Raw cost: 9 Energy.
    Discounts applied: Greater Momentum, Shinobi Run scarf.
    Cost discount: 30%
    Actual cost: 6 Energy.
    Take from regeneration value first? Yes.
    Damage roll out of 1d10: 8.
    Critical 1d100 roll one: 93 - Fail.
    Critical 1d100 roll two: 88 - Fail.
    Total damage: 8 KL.

Projectile: Luminous Bolt.
    Modifier: Rapid.
    Type: Kinetic Lightning.
    Special: Homing, Critical.
    Series: 1.
    Number: 2 / 120.
    Raw cost: 9 Energy.
    Discounts applied: Greater Momentum, Shinobi Run scarf.
    Cost discount: 30%
    Actual cost: 6 Energy.
    Take from regeneration value first: Yes.
    Damage roll out of 1d10: 7.
    Critical 1d100 roll one: 5 - Pass.

Critical 1d100 roll two: 6 - Pass.
Critical Stack: Engaged.
Critical effect 1: Explode on Hit.
Critical effect 2: Double Damage.
Total damage: 14 Explosive.
Explosive Modifier: Damage all components on the affected target with the listed numerical value, rather than only the location struck.
Critical recount: Pass. Base value for ability critical effects is 2%. Class quintupling modifier applies. Actual critical threshold for permissible abilities: 10%.
Log and continue.

———

Projectile: Luminous Bolt.
Modifier: Rapid.
Type: Kinetic Lightning.
Special: Homing, Critical.
Series: 1.
Number: 3 / 120.
…

———

Artorian spent four seconds looking at the screens before complaining, his ability to target new threats nullified from a wall of stacked information. "This is terrible! *Who* is doing my prompts? Who thought I would want information this way? Summarize this! Summarize it!"

CHAPTER NINETEEN

The prompts self-terminated when the call of a new herd burst from the snowbanks, each Bull Moose that perished triggering its own death trait, forcibly keeping the spawning ball rolling and fueling the cascade. In no time at all, their surroundings crawled with Moose, like ants fleeing a flooded nest. Artorian was glad not to be the speed leader as he became very busy with priority targeting, Moose being ex-Moosed left and right. "This is madness! Where are they all coming from?"

Ember growled as she added burning craters along both sides of Lucia's route, the giblets flying. "In addition to their ridiculous trait? The spawn Pylons are busted! They all grew together in a big amalgamation. We need to get a whole new bank up and running before we can stop supplying the old one with power, or a bunch of other systems will collapse. It's going to be Abyss-mode everywhere we go unless the location is already flooded with monsters, so long as players are active in that zone. We need to get to a zone that isn't tagged as a spawn-able area. That's why we're hoofing it to New Haven. Other-wise we have to flood the overflow buffer in the relevant Pylon for the enemy generation to end."

Artorian riddled several Jotun Moose with holes when they leapt at him, the braying Beasts spinning in circles with their abilities active as their 360 Hooves skill came by to play. This turned the hostile rage-Moose into rolling pinwheels of Dark Souls misery as streams of damage numbers flooded out of their heads and vanished skywards.

Artorian's hands snapped to new targets, but his head was screaming for better alternatives. "Can't Lucia take us like last time?"

The Momma Bun rail-slapped a unique ice-sculpture Moose out of the way as she led the pack, turning the beast into a crumpled mass of crystals and... vanishing particles? All the others had been made of meat. What happened to the gore? "No can do, bunny boy. I only fit two, and new updates are putting us in a bind. If I go Beast mode, the area boss gets spawned for electric boogaloo. Suddenly it's a territory war between high-attribute Beasts, and Highlander rules get tacked onto our encounters. Very bad time! No likey!"

"When did that change?" Artorian turned a Moose into a holy pincushion while rushing by, the group now teeming with speed at a very comfortable half of Mach one. A solid five-hundred feet per second that their outfits made a rather unbothered experience to zip through. The windchill, without a shield, would be tearing them apart otherwise. That same speed, on the other hand, was keeping rogue snow out of their faces via sheer air displacement, the area around them blasted sideways.

Lucia backhanded another Moose to keep the choo choo going and train on through, answering her kit's question. "Sun's out!"

Ding!

———

Notice!

Message from Cal: Hey buddy! Good to see you're up and running! Guess what! I've got a connection! Also, Dale is tromping around in

Eternium, and no, it's not a problem with recursion, or us all blowing up like what happened when I tried poking around in your Soul Space while you were in mine. Good times.

Dale is his own person, that fragment of my soul is uniquely his, and he's got a fully separate mind. No issues. That aside, sun's out, puns out! I'm taking a break from work to have some fun. This is your forewarning!

Pretend I'm cackling evilly? Thanks bud, have fun storming the castle!

Your princess is in the Vanaheim one, I hear, but Tisha's a trooper and holding her own against… Arachnoids? What are Arachnoids? Are those like Arachnids but with bad spelling or…? Woooow! Those are cool! Somebody give Dale one of those laser beamer things, we're going Arachnoid hunting! Button the hatches and bolt them down! No, these mini-cannons are not using bolts… beaming? Lasering? Beaming. Light Fusion Beamers remind me so much of my old, original Infernal Cannons. I loved proving that Ghost type was weak to Darkness! These are so much more compact, and tame. I like it. Very baby-cultivator friendly. I really shouldn't be comparing C-ranked cultivators to babies…

Love the interaction notes. Beams function identically against Aura shields as if they were Essence Techniques? Neat. I picked the Blue one! We're going Beaming! What's a Klendathu? Oooh, these beamers can handle this much juice? I'ma go blow it up. Baiiiiii!

Dale! Dale it! Take the Mobile Infantry Class. Yeah, that one! Mwahahahahahaha!

―――――

Artorian chuckled with swallowed panic. "Well, I just heard from Cal. He's in a euphoric mood. We're all in the celestial feces now. Who knows what we're in for."

He then aimed his palm at a newly apparated Moose, and let loose. This time, with the intent that he actually wanted to see his numbers. Both in the hopes of a nicer summary, and so he could stop thinking about Cal using Dale to influence the game by hitting it with a whale. Or whatever insane stunt that duo was about to pull. He didn't know what a Klendathu was, but it was certainly about to no longer be anyone's problem.

Klendathu was about to have Cal as a problem. Poor Klendathu.

Ding!

———

You have hit: Jotun Bull Moose, #43,978, with: Luminous Gatling.
Impacts: 43.
Non-Critical: 40.
Single Critical: 2.
Double Critical: 1.
Damage One: 323 kinetic lightning damage.
Damage Two: 21 explosive damage.
Multipliers: None.
Total Damage: 533.

———

He waffled on that damage prompt, but wanted it even cleaner. The math also didn't add up? The math did not add up at all. Since it was clear that someone was listening, he vocalized his need. "Even more summarized, please! Also, could I get an explainer on where that final damage number is coming from? Either something is wrong with explosion damage, or it's not getting counted the way I remember it being counted. If that has something to do with the critical hits instead, assistance would be helpful."

Ding!

———

Notice!
Explainer: The explosive modifier, even when not acting as an area of effect, causes damage to all components on a target using the listed numerical value rather than only striking and dealing damage to the location of projectile impact. The common denominator of components on mass-

spawned enemies is considered to be ten. The terms 'explosion' and 'explosive' are considered identical in effect. Explosion damage caused by critical events will be counted to each component, therefore, damage is multiplied by ten before being compiled in the final formula. Explosion damage caused by explosion abilities will be counted as normal damage of the explosive type, no multiplication by parts.

A note has been made of this odd discrepancy.

Elevating issue for streamlining.

Amending damage prompts.

———

You have hit: Jotun Bull Moose, #41,448, with: Luminous Gatling.

Impacts: 72

Kinetic Lightning Damage: 553.

Explosion Damage: 52.

Components affected by Explosive Damage: 10.

Total Explosion damage: 520.

Total Damage: 1,073.

———

"Excellent, thank you, mysterious prompt controller!" Redoing the math in his head on the prior formula made a happy chime whistle in the back of his mind. "Momma Bun? How much health do these invaders with their questionable and short-lived Moose-y fates have? Are we tearing through them too fast, or on par?"

Lucia laughed heartily at the head of the pack, leading them around bothersome terrain and onto more stable, smooth snowbanks. They'd passed a mountain or two already, one of them being some kind of colossal corpse. Their Autarchy brooches carried the brunt of their conversation at this speed. "We are most definitely above par for this area! These Jotun Moose have been scaled down to Midgard values, and shouldn't be showing up here at all. You already know that the Pylon amalgam is on the fritz. Currently, these Moose have about… five to seven hundred health a pop? We're overkilling most of them by a good margin, but most Midgard natives would be having one Abyss of a time."

She then answered his follow up question before he could ask, knowing it was coming. "For their actual Jotunheim statistics? Multiply by three, after their other bonuses kick in. Multiply by two for Svartalfheim and Alfheim; the curve used to go up smooth and easy like that. Don't ask me what's in Asgard. I never made it that far. Niflheim and Muspelheim were my hard limit, and that was with a good party. There was a Valkyrie boss in front of the Gates of Asgard that had to be defeated before you could enter. The world bosses weren't implemented. I think her name was Valhalla? She hits like a mountain! I couldn't out-heal her damage at all."

"Can do." Artorian's voice crackled through her brooch, joined by muffled dakka. "Any other goodies?"

Ember took over for a moment. "The region multiplier affects their core bonuses too, and their static health points pool gets a nasty boost the higher the realm you find them in. All the enemies have a Midgard version, called a base template. That base creature template gets altered based on realm, region, terrain, a circumstance, and a local event. With a random chance for unique properties, or in the case of meddling? Racial templates. We actually got lucky to find these Moose in Midgard! Now we know their assault kit. These are not starter-friendly mobs, and they're not even smart!"

The Glitterflit quickly shared some knowledge that she felt was prudent when Ember mentioned the surprise difficulty. This was not the walk in the park they should take for granted. "That sharp left turn of theirs has already caught me off guard twice, and I'm only alright because my shield ate the damage. I had the stats to shrug the physics off, but my shields don't prevent the sensations that physics causes. Pain is diminished by my shields, not mitigated. Had I been hit with Power Antler in a higher realm, we would be getting slobbed and mobbed right now. We would be shattered as a team, or stuck in place from lost party cohesion, and they would have piled on us."

Lucia made the party as a whole dodge left by altering her vector, ignoring some newformed crags that were making miles of terrain in front of them sag and sink away. "We're only keeping the advantage by keeping our train on the tracks! If we stop or slow down, it won't matter that they aren't tough right now. They *will* overwhelm us with chip damage, and those charge attacks when all their toys are active do well over a thousand damage."

Artorian ran the numbers. "How much protection is this shield worth, before Lenity and Prosperity?"

"Lenity *is* the shield, kit." Lucia appreciated the easy question as she clapped another Moose out of the way.

"Overheal!" Her glowing golden paw turned the meaty Beast into frizzed particles as the system simply did not have the resources to keep up with all the gore. Her enemy had been filled with such an overabundance of vivacious energy that it exploded brilliantly. The bodies of everything Lucia hit became charged so full of Light energy from her Overheal paws that they outright detonated in brilliant flashes.

After clearing out an entire line of foes, she recovered the mental bandwidth to answer. "Your shield is made up of ten times the value of my wisdom score, which is a flat eight hundred. You can take eight sequential hits, probably less. With Lenity and Prosperity combined? Maybe twelve, so long as you don't take the hits too fast. I can't fix the shield if you break it, and while I have the perk that a shield will break before it eats into your health, that's a one hit wonder away from misery. Keep in formation! Astarte, should we update that now?"

Ember was a professional at crossing terrain and leaving her upper body to independent movement, her bow flurrying burning shots in every direction. The explosions had become so common that everyone had tuned them out, barely noticing the effects anymore between the flashes they caused. "Sugar! Expect to be saddled into the center sooner rather than later. Especially when we're in a group. You're a damage dealer, and as Glass Cannon as they come. We need you dealing damage to priority targets, followed by anything you can see that might be a problem. Unless I tell you not to unleash? If you see it, you blast it! But you blast it from behind the bulwark provided by the rest of us. Got it?"

Artorian saluted mid-run, resolving to maybe take the game a tiny bit more seriously. He'd been high on excitement for getting to play and unleash the toys, but his party made good points, and he listened to experts. "Ma'am, yes, ma'am!"

He angled his aim to the next closest Moose not already in a line of fire, and let loose the Abyss of war. His glowing hand cycled back and forth between the projectiles being released from around his wrist when he didn't have a smooth and proper line of sight to his target, followed by palm-based shots when he did. The thunder shelling from his hand bothered him less and less as he kept using his regeneration statistic to fuel his homing bombardment, already starting to shift between targets before he had confirmed the initial Moose he'd been aiming at was dead.

The effort was costing him seven-hundred and twenty stamina for a full salvo of one-hundred twenty bolts, but his regeneration metric ate that cost easily. Though something felt very off, and he wasn't sure what felt wrong. Quick-checking information, he found something new to grumble about.

While he was most definitely firing off the full one-hundred and twenty bolts per second, his prompts were telling him that not all of those bolts were hitting home before the target in question had been felled. The remaining bolts went wild, losing their homing feature and flying off before either smashing into the ground or winking out of existence.

Artorian checked a damage log.

———

You have hit: Jotun Bull Moose, #39,679, with: Luminous Gatling.

Impacts: 45.
Kinetic Lightning Damage: 340.
Explosion Damage: 27.
Components affected by Explosive Damage: 10.
Total Explosion damage: 270.
Total Damage: 610.

————

He looked at the prompt between targets, seeing that on average, between forty to seventy bolts were being used to bring down a Midgard Moose. Calling them Jotun Moose seemed silly. "This isn't so ba—"

Bang!

Straight in his path of travel, a Jotun Moose appeared from the ground, activated both Power Antler and Cold Fusion Charge at the same time, and crash-slammed Artorian right out of formation like the juicy target that he was. His yellow shield indicator took a whopping three-thousand plus damage! Coating the energy field around his body in nasty yellow cracks as his own momentum got turned against him in a two-thousand points of pain kind of way.

Physics hurt!

Artorian instantly lost all his velocity and directional movement, forcibly slammed back the way he came. A litany of negative status effects momentarily lived on his Acuity heads up display before they were all slapped down by Lucia's protections and Sanctity winked out from his effects list. Sanctity then reappeared, flickered on and off, and didn't seem to know what to do with itself.

That partial moment of active debuffs had been more than enough to knock the wind out of him. He felt the unpleasant effects of bruised ribs and an aching midsection before the soothing measures kicked in and those sensations died. Artorian tumbled down the snow banks as he quickly lost speed and control, knowing the rest of his party had to turn and double back to catch back up to him.

His bolts flew wild as his ability to focus on or designate a target was nonexistent, his body suddenly turned into the ball of a Speedball game, as multiple other Moose erupted from the snowy woodwork to bat him around like an orb they were trying to keep in the air.

The first came from behind as his tumbling stopped and he scurried to his feet, sending him face first back into the ice and snow as another thousand-damage plus angry crack appeared in his health shield.

He winced trying to keep an eye on it, not liking the results one bit. Two hits in, and he was down to half a shield, with Prosperity barely having had time to do its job.

———

Lenity Shield: 4105/8000.

———

Prosperity was hard at work both keeping the shield present and in recovery, but the follow up Power Antler from another Moose knocked him straight into the sky.

———

Lenity Shield: 3115/8000.

———

"*Ow!*" Having a shield was not preventing him from feeling a majority of the pain, like Lucia had warned him. His vision was blurry and body was sore, as he felt like he just got run over by a massive animal. Which had then backed up, and ran him over again. Regardless of his dot of health not being what took the damage, it hurt!

He hit the snow hard, bounced from the impact, and immediately got Power Antlered into the Power Antlers of another Moose that had already been coming the other way, eating a brutal two-thousand plus more health out of his barely recovered shield. A shield made of more cracks than actual protection at this point.

_____

Lenity Shield: 1215/8000.

_____

"*Ow!* Alright, that's it! Playing with physics! Flight!" The next Moose missed him whole, as the target it was going to hit stopped falling and instead hovered in the middle of the air. That Moose crashed into the Power Antlers of another Moose, as this group seemed intent on double-teaming him until his final breath.

Artorian, with an understandable amount of upset from the pain he kept being smashed with, tapped into his knowledge of system mechanics. He forcibly channeled the use of Luminous Gatling to both of his hands. An effort that was rapidly joined by more unhappy error noises, and a few more orange 'Stop' signs. He'd never tried dual casting before, but he'd also never been surrounded by a field of targets playing the bounce game with him as the ball.

He combined that effort with the genius, possibly above his head idea to not designate one target at a time. The effort hurt his head, but it was either implement the crazy idea, or get Moosed.

Ding!

Artorian ignored the host of prompts and notices that came up. Their contents were not important right now. What was important were the upgrades! Targeting reticles appeared in his vision, a circle with a crosshair overlaying each designated target as new skills rolled in.

Artorian howled to the sky, energy spinning around both his arms with a roaring, bright fury. "Double Luminous Gatling!"

CHAPTER TWENTY

Soft blue information screens enveloped Artorian that he only found marginally worth his attention. Targeting information. Enemy statistics. Damage expectations. A data point added itself to one of them, a timer counting down with an altering rough estimate? He figured it out fast as the Double Gatling hummed with heavy burden, considerably slower to charge as the energy spun up to maximum revolutions. That timer was the duration it would take his team to get back to him. Very soon! Yet not soon enough.

The Midgard Moose brayed, lunging up at him with Cold Fusion bursts to knock him out of the sky. He was still too low to the ground to be out of harm's way, and they wasted no opportunities amending that problem. Artorian felt no pity for them, or what he was about to unleash as he remembered that he was wearing Archimedes. Intent was all it took. With an electric frizzle, a shunpo popped him higher into the sky and out of their range without the charge of his twinned gatlings being lost.

A nice detail to learn! Plus the tidbit that even with Cold

Fusion Charge, no amount of hurling themselves at him was providing the Moose the extra distance, denying them the needed melee range to break the rest of his shield.

The additional height eased his targeting methodology, and he shelved that knowledge away as the reticles locked themselves in. Less Than Three brought the thunder, speaking into his brooch to give his team a heads up that the DPS was bringing the dakka. "Position secured. Commencing bombardment."

Buh-du-du-du-du!

Bolts of kinetic lightning burgeoned from both his hands, the pristine snowy landscape of ant-crawling Moose below turned into a walking war crime. The act was a mix between catharsis and vengeance. He was angry. Angry at the warning being proven true. Angry at these Moose for being responsible. Knocking him out of the dream that this foray into the game world could all have been good, simple fun.

He considered this return fire to be just desserts. This near-instant threat and treatment of taking him out of the game so soon after entering it. He was aggravated. More at himself than he wanted to admit, so the grievance released itself with the Moose as those to blame.

It was their own fault for aggravating a roaming world boss just trying to get from one place to another, really. Artorian had the momentary thought that if this was what the beta was going to be, by not letting him be, then he should fill the shoes of his title and trait. The fear used by Dawn and Zelia found footing as something that made more sense.

He'd come here for fun, and to help! Then his first major encounter was getting beat down in a zone that should have been a warmup?

He wanted More Dakka. Double Gatling was more expensive than he could reasonably pay for very long, but he didn't care right now. "More. Dakka."

Moose exploded by the dozens. Homing kinetic bolts tore

through his enemies, riddling the irritating Beasts with holes as their yet unexpended counterparts retargeted onto another reticle-locked entity. Curving, these smarter bolts zipped right over terrain, circumvented fallen foes, and slammed into a still-living, valid target. No longer would bolts go wasted as a now very upset Artorian would remind the world just how frightening he could be, if the world so demanded it of him. "I call this fury management!"

More Moose immolated into particles as explosion damage did them in. The riddled remains of the others barely had the time for their corpses to fall into the snow. The intended mechanic was for the bodies to sink underneath the treacherous snowy surface before vanishing from sight. Instead, enemy bodies never even hit the snow before all their particles were expended.

Artorian, his fire and anger slowly fading as the number of reticles diminished, began to feel better about life. With this current wave of annoyances mopped up, he took a breath and lingered on some of his presented information before inspecting his surroundings. He was starting to feel the strain, and allowed his arms to relax when a sudden wrenching caused the bolts to stop firing. The Luminous Gatlings didn't spin back down so much as their effects shattered right off his arms, as both his Nuts and Bolts meters hit zero.

Wisp Flight didn't stop its gravity defying effect, but he did hang in the air as some sparkly, rainbow-colored vomit came out of his mouth.

What had been a flawless snowy landscape was now an icy rent of broken trenches, where explosions had flash-fried snow to become sharpened ice by sudden heat. The picture formed a rather fetching fractal pattern.

Artorian recovered fast, likely thanks to Lucia. He cocked his head at the pattern as he wiped his mouth with the back of his glove before his cleaning Aura made all the nastiness both inside and out go away. The picture was pretty, but something bothered him as he hung nailed to the sky while his bars refilled. He noticed a strangely large amount of square hatch shapes from where enemies had populated. Being on the ground, he likely wouldn't have noticed the spawning pattern, but up high and hovering? That spawn pattern was clear and easy to see.

He mulled over what to do with this information as his head cleared, and the timer on that side screen hit zero. As his team showed up, he decided that he would rather help the greater good, than deal with his current dilemma. Yes, he was upset at getting kicked around... but at the same time, if he could prevent this from happening to someone else? That was worth the bite in his butt, so he would bite the arrow and elevate the issue.

He called this in. "Prompt person? Can a Wisp be sent over to my current location? I do mean to include the height. I'm able to see the exact spawn points of enemies, and unless that gets updated, I'm going to know exactly where I need to aim to trivialize any encounter from this point on. I think someone thought they were going to be very clever by using the endpoints of a hatch cross shape? But all the distances are in the same range."

A confirmation chime played next to his ear, and given that the spawning occurrences seems to have ended, he stopped paying the flight costs and used platforms to staircase walk himself back down to ground level. "*Pffff...* That was a frustrating adventure all by itself."

He then held his brooch between his fingers so he could talk to the team. "Did we hit that overflow buffer? Also, yes, I'm alright. Had a bit of a scare there, and *yes*, Momma Bun, you have thoroughly proven your point. Though, I would like to make a few suggestions on grand strategy moving forward? The Moose were focused on Lucia for the longest time, and then suddenly when they decided it was me, our formation got instantly busted."

His voice filled with resignation as he continued stairway-walking to ground level. "I'm not particularly fond of being relegated to mounted cavalry, but how about I stay on Momma Bun? I have been given a sufficient-enough scare to want to be under a bubble shield if I can at all have one. My single health point wasn't damaged, and the shield did its job, but pain sure still works as normal! Also, Bun? Check Sanctity? Its effects lasted beyond a single hit, and my Acuity is being weird. Some of the values are flickering, and even now it's acting up."

If the girls were going to fuss at him, there was no sign of it when he got to ground level and collapsed into Ember's open arms, ignoring the hovering screens and breathing hard with his face buried in her neck as all the strain from bottoming out both his Mana and Stamina bars ate into him. She rubbed his hair, running her nails over his scalp while keeping a firm grip on him.

He didn't hear any conversation, but had plenty of intuition to grasp that nonverbal versions were occurring. Mostly, he noticed that his arms hurt, and that he had a headache which a sudden helping of Momma Bun Veracity was fixing.

Ember kissed his temple soft and easy. "All we care about is that you're okay. We had a little scare, you got yourself into a safe spot. You got a little angry, but that's okay. There's a time and place for anger, and that was it. You got bushwhacked, you got out of it, you hung in there until we could get to you. You did well, sugar. You did well. Don't be too fussed about a Midgard critter suddenly getting the better of you. Attributes aren't everything. You're not used to being here yet. You don't have a good grasp on footing or balances, or expectations, or how to comport yourself. That's all okay."

She continued to purr in her comfort voice, petting his head as the pain and throbbing tension in both his arms went away. Someone was taking his arms and moving them around as well, but he recognized the paw hands of Nurse Lucia by now. Some healing effects were being applied, and he was in no mood to be snarky or unhelpful as Ember talked. He felt unsettled, and this was helping. Her words very on the nose on his twisted feelings about what just happened. "Your idea is good.

We can do that. It just means that we'll be fighting area bosses as we pass through segments on the way to New Haven. Is that fine?"

He nodded into her neck and shoulder. "I'd rather deal with area bosses and be under a double shield than get stomach-slammed from below and knocked out of formation. That was very unpleasant, and you're right, dear. I was suddenly very bothered that these supposed easy enemies that we've been waltzing through nearly offed me when we're trying very hard to avoid that. I want to remain flexible with encounters, but, if it is reasonable for me to stay under the big shield? I should."

Ember hummed in agreement, still rubbing his head. "We had several ideas, but adapting based on what we came across wasn't mysteriously not on the table, sugar. I too am not particularly happy that you vanished from the formation, because turning around while going that fast is not a quick process, and we had our own Moose to fight on the way back over here. We've killed a critical mass of them for now, and the Pylons have overheated and overloaded. Like you guessed? Buffer's full. When they cool off enough, this is all going to happen again. We can keep amending our tactics until we have strategies that always work."

He nodded into her shoulder again, then pulled away to find Lucia replenishing his shields and associated protections. He heard her whisper the words Sanctity, Lenity, and Prosperity as soft colors glowed on his being, the effects refreshed. It ended the flickering, but he considered escalating if that happened again.

Child-torian gave her a silent hug after, and got one right back as she put her chin on the top of his head and ground down hard. "You did good, bunny boy. I'm going to assume my big Glitterflit Basher form now, and you climb right into the same spot as last time, you hear? I want you to check those screens and tell me if anything odd is in them. Make sure you're up to date on if anything changed, or if you got new abilities, because it looked like you did even from far away. You were scary for a moment there, precious. Momma Bun is worried about you."

He said nothing to feeling her chin grind into the top of his head again, then bashed his forehead into her chest to affirm her question. "Yes, Momma Bun."

She mushed and squeezed him tight, copying Ember and rubbing her paw over his head. "That's my boy. Now hop on. Your shields are fixed and your status conditions are patching up. Don't look at those yet, just know that the stunt you pulled damaged a lot of things that weren't your health bar. Try not to dual cast again anytime soon? You took mana bar damage."

Artorian had never heard of mana bar damage, but wasn't about to argue with the healer. Obeying the medic, he weakly moved to make a silly salute, then used platforms to walk his way up to the new height and sink into the assigned space once Lucia finished going Beast mode, the massive Glitterflit doing a stretch and wiggle to get a sense of her proportions.

A quick check confirmed Lucia's mention, but he was confused on why his mana bar was the damaged one, when Luminous Gatling primarily took energy from his stamina bar. He tried to puzzle it out in a hurry, but whoever was helping him with prompts took over as more screens than expected zipped to the forefront with some upsetting text.

Calculated Values:
   Hit Points: 18,550.
   Mana Pool: 35,625.
   Mana Regen: 300 / second.
   Stamina Pool: 13,400.
   Stamina Regen: 787 / second.

Adjusted Values:

Hit Points: 1.
Mana Pool: 28,500.
Note: 20% burnout damage.
Shield: 8000.

———

Luminous Gatling expenditure Information:
Raw cost: 9 Energy.
Discounts applied: Greater Momentum, Shinobi Run scarf.
Cost discount: 30%
Actual cost: 6 Energy.
Full Cycle Cost, Gatling 1: 720 Energy per second.
Full Cycle Cost, Gatling 2: Error Detected.

———

Error Log: More Dakka doubles the output of bolt projectile count, not the count of projectiles fired. Values incorrectly fed into the Nuttelator. Recalculating. Prior cost of 6 Energy per bolt was tallied as if firing 120 bolts per second.
Actual bolt count valued for energy consumption: 60.

———

Notice: Error caused system overdraw. Player mana circuits damaged.
Elevating issue for compensation.
Recalculating costs.

———

Luminous Gatling expenditure information:
Raw cost: 9 Energy.
Discounts applied: Greater Momentum, Shinobi Run scarf.
Cost discount: 30%
Actual cost: 6 Energy.

Full Cycle Cost, Gatling 1: 360 Energy per second.
Full Cycle Cost, Gatling 1: 360 Energy per second.

———

Nuttelator Notes on Luminous Gatling:
Single Gatling Draw: 360 Energy per second.
Double Gatling Draw: 720 Energy per second.
Pending: Triple Gatling Draw: 1,080 Energy per second.
Pending: Quad Gatling Draw: 1,440 Energy per second.
Combined energy regeneration metric: 1,087 / second.

———

That didn't answer what he was hoping for, so the mana bar damage was a mystery for later. The note of triple and quad functions caught his eye… but weren't those features in Ember's toy box right now? Or was that a limitation he had unknowingly been imposing on himself and shouldn't have? That… that was not a great thought.

If he was shoehorning himself into a corner because he was looking at his tools and kit the wrong way… he should change his kit. That soured his stomach. His options were already so limited and… and he was already starting to sink into relying on a select few abilities. That was either potentially dangerous, or told him that the alternatives he had to work with weren't alternatives he really wanted to work with.

He glanced at his spell list, and pondered.

They were great to have, but what was the point of having them if he was always going to favor other solutions? He would forget them, and effort would be placed in keeping track of them, causing unnecessary work for people in the background. Being able to do too much wasn't good either. In the alpha run, he'd gotten to use the majority of his kit, but much of it he had only ever used once.

With the majority of his attention shifting to other, more

favored toys, a bigger kit was not a better kit. He'd been given fun tools based on jokes, but he was starting to feel like they weren't the right tools, and that seed twisted his stomach. A conversation for later, perhaps. Maybe sooner rather than later. He felt movement and saw his elevation shift when Lucia stretched out. For now, it was time to return to reality and get a move on.

CHAPTER TWENTY-ONE

With Artorian saddled in, Lucia's egg-shaped hexagonal shield formed over and around them, building and knotting together one hexagon at a time as the light panels interlocked, laced, and merged. The shield thumped with a repulsion effect when Lucia took her first step, the beat matching the cadence to her footfalls as she checked her ovoid protection.

Lucia was pleased. "There we go. Your senses might muddle a bit, but there won't be any issues firing projectile spells out from inside of the shield. If they double back though? The shield will take damage and eat it. I saw your bolts doing all sorts of acrobatics earlier! Fancy show off."

That prod got Artorian to laugh as he ran his hands through the softest of Basher fur. "Alright, yes. I do have a bit of flair for the dramatic, but those were all pragmatic effects at play. I'll check my screens, and if anything pops up that I can see, I'll do as team leads advised and get blasting. Do we need anything else before carrying on?"

Dasein was the only one who remained a silent statue, content to be there. Ember observed this behavior, then shook her head no and made the decisions. "If Lady Death can take your other flank, I can cover this one. If you're able to slap down pursuers, even better. Our new formation is an arrow pattern. You're right. The Moose did seem to be targeting Lucia unfairly. The area bosses will be annoying, but I'm also happier with you walled under double shielding until we can all get the hang of things. I wish I knew why our spawn modifier was insane, but if it's like this for everyone, then… fine. I'll continue laying waste. My guess is that the realm is trying to compensate for our high attributes."

After Dasein winked with a sly smile to affirm her part of the formation, Astarte motioned two fingers at Lucia, dropping them into a forward movement pattern. "Go. Greater Momentum will keep Lady Death and I on your track."

The Glitterflit nodded, dropped her ears back with a snap, and activated the nyooms! In no time at all, they were rolling over brand new landscape and snowy fields at great speeds. With Artorian safely under the shield, she even kicked it up a notch and tore into Mach one with a *k'bang*! Cracking that sound barrier as neither Lady Death nor Astarte appeared to be having any difficulty with the speed, environment, or strain.

It then occurred to Artorian that, out of the bunch, his attributes were probably the lowest. What a strange feeling. There had been talk that the Heavenlies were supposed to start from scratch, but it was now abundantly clear that this had not happened for Dasein. Equipment set or not, she was unphased by the journey.

He shrugged, leaving the politics and reasoning to the dungeons, and checked his screens. He had a lot of them, and some light reading might make that pulsing Astrea theme party-beat in both of his hearts simmer down as they tried to match the thumping cadence of Lucia's run.

That Moose to the face had been a hefty reality check, and regardless of how he thought he'd been clearing through this beta test, he was clearly not as almighty as he'd assumed. A Midgard critter had almost ruined his day. A *Midgard* critter. He shook himself, trying to get the crawling feeling off from his shoulders, and out of his head. To no avail, as he was still bothered when he'd already tried to put this out of mind once, only to have it all come flooding back. "What's the use of these high attributes if I'm going to be a fool with them?"

He'd mumbled the words, receiving no reply. The reality of the situation on the other hand, slowly sunk in. The numbers meant nothing if he used them poorly. The game was useful for something, it seemed, and that something was to sharpen him. To take the eternal rusty spear that he seemed to be, and apply the whetstone to its dulled edge.

He sat up straighter, his spine no longer allowing him to slouch. His fingers kept a tight grip on Lucia's fur, but some of the fog that had gathered in his head was starting to clear. The beating of his hearts, while still heavy, no longer pounded in his ears. His eyes trained on the distance, sharpened, and turned to his prompts.

He flicked them momentarily to his flank, noticing that Dasein was observing him in eerie depth. She made no effort to turn her gaze away, her pale blue eyes trained on him as she watched him settle internal struggles. Watched him decide who to be. Watched some lines on his stele deepen, while others dulled.

He found amusement in it, for some reason. The corner of his mouth lifted up as he cracked a joke. "Is there something on my Soul, Lady Death?"

For some conversations, it was never a good time.

It was simply time.

"Yes." Her curt and to the point answer caught him off guard, but there was a warmth in her words. "I had worries about you, precious boy. Yet I watch, and I watch, and I see why the light loves you so. I see why **Love** so protectively holds you close. I see why she swirls around you, everywhere you go. Your body means nothing to you. Your mind is everything. You are endlessly flexible. Your thoughts are welcoming, and adaptive. You change as water, you flow as wind, and you stand with the earth. You breathe hearthfire, you strike as lightning, you find a prize in higher thought, and you balance your obsessions."

She smiled at him, sharing his amusement as she remained enraptured with the movements on his stele. She was not there to guide him, but seeing the constant, healthy improvements on his record did something for her own wellbeing that she cherished. "Your Soul, the canvas on which your experiences are carved, deepening with repetition and time, speaks freely to me, Merli. It speaks of your experiences, Tsu. It speaks of your choices, Elder. It spins tales shelved in archives, Artorian. You fear loss as much as any man. Yet you face that loss, over and over again. You bite through pain. You fall. You choose to get back up. You get back up. You get back up again."

Her voice lost parts of its warmth, the intensity of her slow speech increasing. "Your Soul wounds, your Soul heals, you make yourself anew from the **Love** of others. You stand before them, a bulwark before **Eternity**, your arms spread wide. Daring it to come at you. Daring it to get past you. Your Soul is weighed with baggage. Your Soul is heavy with regret, and consequence. Your Soul looks over its shoulder at me, smiles, tells me I am always welcomed behind your bulwark, and that all will be well."

She reached for him, but merely pressing her pale hand to Lucia's shield had the same effect as if she'd placed her palm right on his head, making the gesture that all three of them had adopted to soothe him. "All will be well. Continue to make choices. Continue to craft your Soul with experiences. Continue deepening the pattern of who and what you are, allowing it to reflect on the canvas that you paint. So that when you one day Incarnate, the person formed by your Soul, over eons of time, is the example of the pattern you wish to unleash into the world. For once you make that leap, that is the pattern of who you will always be."

When Dasein pulled her hand away, the feeling on his head went with it. "There is much on and in your Soul, Less Than Three. I am glad that you have one, and that your experiences have been carved upon it. Your stele is all the better for it, and I am pleased to see certain strains resolving themselves. A Soul embosses itself upon a stele, and when needed in crisis, the stele provides the carving that is to be reflected back onto the Soul."

She then pointed at him, as if the rest of the world did not exist, her finger pressed against his very center. "I had the concern that your stele would impress back upon your Soul when the conditions of your being were no longer that of a Mana-formed. Harming you. Destroying you. Yet, your stele, knowing of **Love**, gives your Soul only that which it can handle as you grow back into your ideal shape. Your ideal self. Your Soul now grows and is shaped from two directions, and while your stele may hold more information that you may one day decide to forego. Carvings you no longer desire to be imprinted back upon the person you will become upon Incarnating? Your stele, like the most exemplary of their kind, waits for you to choose who you will be. Judging not, as it happily releases the embossing of the patterns that you refuse to repeat. Over time, the choices of your mind will be at one with the pattern inscribed upon your Soul. Then, your Soul will emboss your stele once more, and one day, you will come to stand before our door."

Dasein momentarily sounded exceptionally proud as she pulled her hand back. "When you are Incarnate, and your mind, body, and soul are one? I would hope that you take the time to learn how to see and read your own stele."

She sounded momentarily coy before a hint of the somber slipped in. "**Existence**, for one, would adore your company in the Tower, if you would ever choose that path. I will be sad to see my friend, **Love**, ascend greater heights. Yet I have always adored each and every one of her forebears, and it appears that I will continue that pattern, and continue to adore **Love**'s successors as well. So few are willing to fight **Existence**, and I wish that so many would."

Her smile then turned predatory, her eyes wide and full of hunger. "So, come at me, Grandpa. Find me anytime, challenge me anytime. For while I am not against happiness, **Existence** adores those who defy convention, and claw at the emptiness. Just as life fights to improve, I crave this sight that you have promised, old man. For if it is a crime against existence that everyone would get to win, and everyone would get to be happy? Then I wish you to play the adjudicator, Artorian. Show me just what *that world* looks like. *I want it*, Elder. Show me this utopia you would pull out of your empire of dirt, Administrator. Show me! This dream that I have never seen come true. Show me, *Architect*!"

Artorian felt paralyzed, gripping Lucia's fur as neither Ember nor the Glitterflit seemed to dare intervene. Dasein's pale blue gaze remained trained on him a moment longer, her fury and intensity palpable on the tongue.

Lady Death's voice dropped to its prior, softer register. Her words a request, rather than a hungry demand. "Will you do that for me, precious boy?"

His double hearts beat harder, rather than calming to beat softer. He swallowed, and his thoughts raced. That was not the segue he'd been expecting, but then again, he never really knew what someone was thinking. Or what they might want to say to him. He searched himself, but did not have to search far. Resolute resolve was waiting for him. The answer was easy. The answer was his. The answer was why so many with luminous hearts looked upon him, and saw a back to press their hands against. From the depths of his psyche, at the very bottom, where an old grandfather picked himself back up, and then picked himself back up again. A fist shot to the sky in defiance of what it meant to fall. A fist from a weary old man that looked over his shoulder, and smiled as that fist turned into a thumbs up. "Of course I will."

He swallowed again, his hands tightening on Lucia's fur as he pulled his gaze away, training it back on the approaching horizon. He found a strength in it, Dasein's words and intensity swirling in his chest as the answers clicked into place. "**Love** will get its day in the **Sun**."

"Good." A momentary hand on the head from Dasein helped Artorian turn his eyes to the prompts still hanging around him by the droves. Lady Death appeared content to leave him be once more, having said her piece. She turned her attention back to dividing local threats into multiple pieces instead when the Pylon buffer cleared, and the hordes of foes returned.

Some prompt reading sounded like a fantastic breather right about now.

CHAPTER TWENTY-TWO

Artorian checked his character's updates, pulling his statistics screen next to him so that the impending napkin math would be easier. He rubbed his chin while going over his character sheet, then moved new screens to him one at a time, starting on the ones that had easy updates, or were simple new skill additions.

———

Statistics:
    Hit Points: 1.
    Mana Pool: 28,500.
    Note: 20% burnout damage.
    Shield: 8000.
    Mana Regen: 300 / second.
    Stamina Pool: 13,400.
    Stamina Regen: 787 / second.

———

Skill: Luminous Gatling Mastery.

Rank: Apprentice.

When engaging the use of Luminous Gatling, the hidden burdens will be lessened. When all the burdens are mastered, this skill will provide hidden benefits instead.

―――

He wondered why he got a mastery update, then figured the rank must be higher than last time, so he moved right along.

―――

Skill Gained: Dual Casting.

Whether casting a spell or activating an ability, as long as you only need a single hand for each effect, you are able to evoke two at once!

Effect: Increase casting time by $51-1n\%$ where 'n' is skill level. 33% chance of failing due to faltering spell stability, $+1n\%$ spell stability per skill level.

―――

"*Huh?*" Artorian stopped and frowned. Not moving to the next prompt in the queue, he pulled the entry for Dual Casting close to his chest so he could squint down at the screen. He mouthed the words, still didn't understand most of them, then spoke them out loud. Doing so got him confused ear twists from Lucia, and concerned frowns from Ember who was developing the same confused expression he was wearing.

Ember made a grabby hand for it, and Artorian shoved it into her grip right away. He had no idea what to do with this thing. "What the Abyss. This is... fully furnished? Sugar, this skill is dependent on features that are still being built, but aren't... remotely ready. We don't have levels up and running yet, we only have ranks. Where did you get this?"

Artorian threw both his hands clear into the air, motioning at the waiting prompts. "It was in the pile! Part of all the sudden new toys I got when I was governing and rezoning the landscape above the meaty pile of Moose I ended up shredding like cheese. I got a bunch of them all at once. Wait, are they all like that?"

He pulled the others in that bundle to him, groaning instantly. "*Ohhh nooo.* They're *all* like that."

Ember grumbled to herself, the gears turning behind her eyes. A Nixie Tube flickered to life, her hand finding her forehead with a slap. "*Caaaaal!*"

Laughter broke from the sky as they continued to advance across terrain in an arrow formation, hordes of Heavy Assault Unicorns visible in the distance as lesser Moose died around them in droves. Appearing as a geometric shape while matching Team Sleep's speed, Cal's voice melodically crackled like a cheap villain. "*Mwahahaha!* You rang? It is I, the great me!"

Ember full force chucked the entry for Dual Casting at the smug geometric shape, **thunking** Cal's gimmick straight out of his local orbit. Impacting at Mach speeds, the hexagon-looking thing tumbled down into the snow. Solidly whapped by the improvised slipper. Cal sputtered as he lost control, coughed like he was breathing in dry water, and ack'd loudly every time his rolling path hit a sharp rock. Bouncing him back up as momentum was far from done with him. "*Ow*, I, *Ack*! Dawn, I —*Ack*!"

Dasein extended her hand, the noisy object ceasing its tumble. With the pull of some very powerful telekinesis, Cal's temporary housing effortlessly appeared in her grasp. Holding the momentarily muffled dungeon by his face, she inspected the multi-sided die with casual disinterest while remaining on the move. "This shape is known as a truncated octahedron. Contrary to assumption, this is a fourteen-sided die. Calcifer? Are you speaking through this toy? I know you are not truly here in any capacity."

The dungeon sputtered back at the Heavenly as she turned him like an apple, allowing him his words. "Not Calcifer! Just Cal! Thank you. I mean please. Please and thank you."

"Cal, why did you give Artorian these?" Ember rolled her eyes as she pulled the topic back to the difficult prompt, Damocles peppering incoming enemies until her bow played a chime, signaling readiness.

Unleashing virulent walls of explosive volcanic arrows, she preemptively blotted out the sun to politely provide their foes some cool time in the shade. As she rained down death from above, Ember fueled her Army of Vesuvius ability with a grin. Descending in waves, her shots caught pyroclastic flame, causing each arrow to expand in size and destabilize from their given shape. This conflagration transformed entire arrow walls into carpets of burning orbs composed of rage and heat.

When the comparatively merciful impact struck, Ember knew glee. The Army of Vesuvius meteor shower mulched her foes and sent their remains flying before they had a chance to take any initiative.

Astarte enjoyed acting first, burning the land, and boiling the seas.

Her bombardment flattened the land and compacted anything that may have been on it, paving the way forward for Lucia. The Momma Bun *nyoomed* right through all the dissolving, smoldering particles, her ovoid shield rebuking the shimmery remnants.

Cal waited for the volcanic cacophony to die down, then spoke all chipper and self-satisfied. His plot had succeeded, after all. "The complex prompt entries? To test if they worked! Tim and I made a small test batch over at my place. We ported them a bit ago, and saw you were being accosted. I admit, I was *joking* about inconveniencing one of you and slapping the skill in, but then a Moose went and bodicd my Administrator out of formation all on his lonesome. Tim and I were gawking! T.C. is still laughing, in case you can hear that. He's making a statue of the event for his tulip garden, because your face was priceless! We then scrambled to assign these Pylons to Less Than Three, which, *adorable name* by the way. Then pop! They worked! What's the problem?"

Artorian pressed his fingers together, his body tense and voice terse. "They. Make. No. Sense. Simplify this, Cal. *Please.* I am not this good at math. I can do napkin math, and Dwarven numbers if I have sit down time and formula references. I looked at this, and felt so confused that someone might as well have run into the room and yelled '*Naked Grandma!*' before bolting out in a blind rush, leaving you just enough time to panic and jump for cover."

"*Relaaaaax*, you moody Belgian waffle." The sounds of hands clapping together preceded the text and formulas in all of the prompts updating. "There, all of them are fixed. You fussy baby. You're lucky I like you! Oh, Dale made it to Klendathu? Wonderful! Time to scour a bug planet. Gotta go! We're testing the baby Infernal Cannons, I mean, the Beamers toys with the mobile infantry class! Really odd why we called it that. Isn't infantry always mobile? What are they gonna do otherwise? Stand there in lines and take turns? Ha! *Baiiiii!*"

Artorian buried his face in his hands while the rest of the party tore through Heavy Assault Unicorns like they were holding up targets with 'pick me' signs on them. The heavily armored, gray-plated, double-horned lumbering beasts barely had the time to turn as Team Sleep tore through the herd at a steady Mach one.

The Assault Unicorns faced their great horned weapons towards the intruders in time to be replaced by a bloody mist. "Is it fixed? Someone please tell me it's fixed."

Without an answer, and left to suffer in silence as everyone else was too busy keeping his fussy baby butt alive, he peeked between his fingers to find great relief. Ember had placed the prompt back in front of him, the updated information patiently waiting for his courage. "*Oh, thank Cal.*"

Dasein pocketed the fourteen-sided speaker device to muffle the dungeon before Cal could return with a sudden moment of snappy snark. She glanced over to sneak a peek at what the precious boy was so happy about all of a sudden. Dasein could hear that his heart rate had calmed, her moment of evoked emotion processed by Artorian.

———

Skill: Dual Casting.

Rank: Novice.

Whether casting a spell or activating an ability, as long as you only need a single hand for each effect, you are able to evoke two at once!

Effect: Your casting time is doubled. There is a one in three chance that your intended effect fails to activate. The activation cost will still be collected, regardless of outcome.

———

That update was indeed more fussy-baby-friendly.

Dasein nodded in approval. Flourishing her scythe, Lady Death continued combat, sending Talons of Darkness forward. The crescent, onyx energy blades carved up through the snow from below and grew in size as they hunted, racing ahead of the speeding party. Slaughtering Heavy Assault Unicorns by the score as they trucked on to New Haven, the Talons became independent hunters. Hungrily seeking out targets, the Talons grabbed and dragged their caught armored morsels under the banks of snow. The sounds of crushing and meaty things going squish followed, for the few moments they were audible.

Mach one travel left little time to savor the details.

The support from Lady Death and Astarte provided Artorian plenty of time to read his remaining messages, or would have, if they didn't change again right in front of his eyes and squish themselves together into a single panel.

Artorian grumped as his grip on the existing screen was nullified, the prompt merging with the others. He reached out for the new one so it flew into his open hand. "I'm going to remember this Calcifer comment."

———

Skill: Visual Tactics.

Rank: Static - Temporary.

Some people need training wheels, some wheels need training. Visual Tactics provides a struggling player temporary system assistance, allotting basic, minor information at a glance. Including, but not limited to, damage expectations, a guesstimate on enemy statistics based on the player's hidden Inspect value, and the targeting of multiple opponents.

Note: This skill will remove itself once a player has achieved immersion level 3 with the game world. Current immersion level: 1.

———

Confused, he flicked Visual Tactics on.

Less Than Three gained targeting awareness of a critter behind him. A clever one that was chasing the group while lurking below the snow. He turned that critter into Swiss cheese by keeping his focus on it while thundering out some gatling bolts in front of him that all re-vectored and slammed into the hidden foe with a very satisfactory mid-air curve.

Pleased, he flicked Visual Tactics off and looked behind to notice a lack of snow-bulge chasing them. That was pretty convenient.

Electrosense had picked up the Lurker Assault Unicorn, but there had been too much going on for him to be able to parse out the correct information. Echolocation and Electrosense were currently responsible for a buzzing in the brain more than anything else. Like bad, untuned static. "Useful, and not littered with math terms. I can work with it."

He dismissed the screen, then summoned the rolodex of damage prompts. Flipping through them, he got a sense of how helpful multitargeting had been. Verdict? Significantly.

The targeting solutions had been tracked independently from both lefty and righty, but aside from the obscene chunks he'd torn out of his Nuts and Bolts bars for flying while firing, the data he was looking at was nothing less than spectacular when it came to improved efficiency. Had he even been losing mana for flying? He didn't think so. That got him no closer to what caused the mana bar damage. Crackers and toast.

"Helpful to have the damage prompts. Wish I could... Wait. One moment! I remember how to change the formatting from my item fixing days." He altered the information formatting by pressing all his fingers down on the prompt and twisting his wrist. The prompt in the rolodex clicked at him like a safe being opened, the presented information changing designs and shapes with each click. "There we go!"

————

Calculation: Left Gatling, continuous burst 22.
   Target: 7.
   Impacts: 42.
   Result: Target eliminated.

————

Calculation: Left Gatling, continuous burst 22.
   Target: 8.
   Impacts: 51.
   Result: Target eliminated.

————

Calculation: Left Gatling, continuous burst 22.
   Target: 9.
   Impacts: 27.
   Result: Target damaged.
   Expanding entry.

————

You have hit: Jotun Bull Moose, #39,551, with: Luminous Gatling.
Impacts: 27.
Kinetic Lightning Damage: 147.
Explosion Damage: 23.
Components affected by Explosive Damage: 10.
Total Explosion damage: 230.
Total Damage: 377.
Collating cohesive damage log, transitioning to the next entry.
Priority: Relation to the current target.

———

Calculation: Left Gatling, continuous burst 23.
Target: 9.
Impacts: 5.
Result: Target eliminated.

———

Artorian took a moment before rolling through more result prompts in the rolodex. "Five impacts? Five? That's it? What were these impacts? That seems awfully few, even for a target that had already taken three hundred and seventy seven damage. Here it is. Let's have a look."

———

You have hit: Jotun Bull Moose, #40,001, with: Luminous Gatling.
Impacts: 5.
Kinetic Lightning Damage: 0.
Explosion Damage: 29.
Components affected by Explosive Damage: 10.
Total Explosion damage: 290.
Total Damage: 290.
Result: Target eliminated.

———

"All crits? Must be Crit-mas! That works for me!" He dismissed the entire rolodex. All the remaining damage prompts were going to be more of the same. "Honestly, what I need is probably something I can keep laying into for a while. Really work the Nuts and Bolts bars. A challenge that can take all this heat. Didn't someone mention an area boss?"

The sky laughed. Distinctly Tim-toned. The word 'jinx' was written above them using clouds, before that word mushed into itself, coagulated, and called for momma.

Ember looked up and scowled. "Timmm, not more clouds!"

Lucia and Dasein both joined the groaning complaint that Ember had begun, knowing what they were in for.

Fuyu No Arashi, the Eternal Thundercloud, appeared when summoned, dramatically entering the field like some unsuspecting isekai protagonist with a casino's worth of chips burdening their shoulders.

The living thundercloud unfurled in the darkening sky like elephant paste, consuming all available space. She beat her bright drums in rage and anger as a peal of thunder cracked. Her frozen rains fell as icicles, and cold-typed lightning struck the snowy ground. Furious at the rude summoning, Fuyu No Arashi took stock of the region.

The living cloud discovered the carnage left in this party's wake, recognized the annoyances, and responded by dropping a People's Elbow! Fuyu No Arashi knew exactly what kind of fate was to befall Team Sleep, and vindictively slammed an area boss down on them like she was dunking a ball of pure ice through an open hoop.

Or rather, much like the Lurkers, the area boss ascended from below. Bursting and breaking free through the ground of ice and snow like a frosty volcanic eruption, Gargantua Storm Mole 'The Bends' Barotrauma instantly took the situation from zero to a hundred by appearing on the battlefield, joined by thunderous drums from Fuyu No Arashi as the area's color scheme changed entirely.

A moment of civil twilight preceded a heavy dose of astronomical twilight as the Storm Mole unloaded its boss-quality toolkit, applying its unique Barotrauma character trait to the region!

Activating its field effect on first appearance as astronomical twilight settled in, heavy boss-music erupted to match the pulses of sky-lightning that signaled the start of the match.

Their snowy surroundings were flattened in a purple flash, slammed by fluctuating, extreme changes in pressure that knocked both Astarte and Lady Death clear out of formation from their hands slapping over their ears and their eyes snapping shut. He heard the start of their cries, but the yelps ended instantly as Lucia was moving far too fast to keep up with the sound.

That wouldn't do, and an emergency plan quickly formulated. "Abyss! Momma Bun, double back! Slap a personal shield on me against this storm! I am a dumb-dumb, and we need the full team for this. Get them under your big shield! I'mma make it angry!"

"In progress! Tell me you're not doing what I think you're doing!" Her ears flicked fast, glowing with runes to cast several spells. She leapt mid-stride, landing sideways into a mighty power slide. Her golden paws skidded across snow and kicked up a massive wave, going far too fast at Mach one for an easy turn and burn maneuver like the Abyssed Moose could. She'd be sliding wild until she could come to enough of a stop to blitz her way back. "We can steal tools, right? I want Turn and Burn!"

Lucia recalled that foul play was fair play in this beta version, resolving to steal that tool for herself before the motherly instincts kicked the door in. "Kit, remember that you have spells!"

"We sure can, and—Abyss! I forgot!" Artorian did no such thing as comply with telling the Momma Bun what he was up to, in too much of a rush to create the conditions that would restore party cohesion. The moment that the new Shield spells against Barotrauma and similar effects were on him, it was time for action. "Thank you, Momma Bun!"

He shot straight into the sky as a blue and white blur as he took the moment to check his heads up display. Artorian didn't know what Integrity and Tenacity did, but he trusted Lucia. He assumed that, like the expenditure-trigger for Sanctity, it was best if he just didn't get hit. He'd apologize to Ember later, because he was stealing her role as the dodge tank, and was breaking formation immediately after saying he'd be better off staying in the shield.

The best laid plans rarely survive contact with the enemy.

That reasoning was pointless now. It was adaptation time, and he knew exactly what his new role actually was. "I *am* the distraction! Cold Fusion Charge!"

CHAPTER TWENTY-THREE

Artorian grimaced hard. He ate two-thousand-five hundred damage to his shields from the physics reversal he forced on himself by slapping in Cold Fusion Charge. Willingly, this time, as he shot the other direction without needing to wait for Lucia to skid to a halt.

It hurt, but he needed to get there first! A distraction to annoy the Mole-thing so Lucia could pick the ladies up and get them back into the fight. He did not like that, without the shielding, the two heavy hitters of the group might as well be down and out. An assumption he would gladly overturn if the situation proved otherwise.

Cold Fusion Charge seemed to instantly set his velocity to a specific speed in the vector that he was facing, with a gradual speed up the longer it was sustained, and that pained him as much as it was useful right now. Turn and Burn sounded mighty useful if that let someone get around this injury before flaring the boosters.

Summoned from his Silverwood Bracelet mid-flight, the Boom Shaka Laka Broom appeared in his hand. He was then quickly reminded just how expensive Flight was, as his mana bar already flashed red at him. When he didn't immediately stop combining it with Cold Fusion Charge, the bar started flashing far faster, and it started to *burn*.

Ding!

———

Warning! Mana bar damage at 21%.

———

"*Yeeeeooowch*! Oh, come on!" He cut the feed, then realized that by just suppressing the grip gravity had on him, his Bonescripting kept him moving at the same speed and velocity in his current direction! Useful! If he could get this trick tucked good and well under his belt, he was going to be able to accomplish all sorts of fun acrobatic and speedy treats! Not to mention the cost it would save him on accelerating and gaining more zoomies!

Zelia had been on to something with her tip.

Feeling that his spells would be out of range, he reminisced and pointed two fingers at the oversized Gargantua Storm Mole, his eyes training down the imagined rail. "Abyss, I miss Accelerator. I miss it badly. What I wouldn't give for a Mass Driver right about now…"

He dropped his hand, and considered his spells. Abyss That Person In Particular sounded useful, but still not remotely as useful as Luminous Gatling might be. Some gears turned in his head as he used Cold Fusion Charge in the short bursts they were intended for to alter his angle to the direction of the area boss's current rampage.

Astarte and Lady Death were holding their own based on the visual spectacle of red and black blades cutting up the surrounding landscape, but they were in clear retreat and on the defensive from being hammered by that Barotrauma effect. The area boss also didn't seem to be taking a lot of damage from their attacks?

That boded poorly.

The good news was that both Lady Death and Astarte were up and at 'em!

Assumption smashed!

Artorian didn't fully grasp what the field effect did yet, but if it was making both his heavy hitters back up and play with extreme caution, then he was going to take the effect seriously. Just as he was starting to take this game more seriously in general. He had tools, but too much that required attention. Once again, he felt like he had too many tools to easily remember, and he supposed that might have to do something with his abysmal immersion rating?

He looked at the broom in his hand, a wonderful solution to a sudden problem coming to mind. Cold dread filled his stomach when the question that he realized he wanted to ask hit him. "Tim?"

He spoke the word with such dread that time around him directly slowed, the whole world dropping in speed frame by frame as if he were going faster with Mage dilation.

Eternium's voice popped into being in front of him from a hexagon similar to the one Cal had used to speak. The Dwarven Rhys cadence was heavy in Tim's voice. "That sounded anything but good, Administrator. What's wrong?"

Artorian did not address the change in dilation speeds. He got straight to the point. "What would I get for giving up spell-casting entirely? The whole thing. I can't keep up. I know I have it, and they're great tools, and that I have Conditional AllSpell waiting for me. But I can't keep up. I appreciate that you're letting me play with Cold Fusion Charge, and this is not the best time to ask, but this is the time where it's suddenly eating at me."

Tim seriously considered Artorian's request, not diminishing him in the slightest. "A full lockout would change the Janitor class. It would no longer have access to spells, and be reliant on other tools. You would lose both of your current spells instantly, but… now that I'm looking at it that way, you wouldn't qualify for either of your cursed Titles, and they would be purged from your Pylons. They'd have no ground left to stand on. As a minor mention, I appreciate in turn that you mentioned the cross-hatch spawning pattern. It was part of the reason I helped Cal slap you with the earlier skills; you were due some kind of help or reward. My apologies that you will lose Visual Tactics, but it really is meant to be used as training wheels."

He nodded peacefully. "That's fine, my friend. Spells?"

Tim's hexagon wobbled left and right with difficulty as the dungeon figured it out. "Doable. Busywork for me, but the effect would be instant for you. This is a rather sudden and strange request. I'm keeping time slowed; can you tell me what caused this?"

"Too much on my plate?" Artorian struggled with the response. "I'm aware I barely have any tools, but I'm obviously not using a whole wall of them because I already have abilities that I use far more frequently, that use the same resources? I realized that just now when I was holding this broom. My mana bar is movement fuel. It also hurts. That same bar fuels my spells. Flight is pricey, but I wouldn't trade a moment of flight for so much as a single spell. Which I say without wanting to get into the topic of the mental attention it would take for me to do that. Swapping from focusing on flight, to casting, back to flight? I can't do that right now."

He pulled up his character sheet purely to turn it around and show the dungeon. "Character attributes are nice, but they clearly don't correlate to my actual reality, because I do not feel like I have an intelligence of whatever seven-fifty is supposed to be? As a Mage, I have memories that would definitely feel on par with that kind of a number, but as a mortal? I am *struggling*, Tim."

He then made a swirling motion at his own stomach for another persistent issue. "I am also very aware that I've been having some severe emotional fluctuations lately, and they already feel like they happened yesterday. They happened only a bit ago, and I feel like I've gone through a week of coping after what Dasein said to me. Is there a secret ongoing effect on me? Or players? Once was an occurrence that I didn't notice, but now I'm at several, in a row no less, and I feel *nothing*. I am the definition of okay. I just now had this garbage feeling in my stomach, and I can't help but notice that it's already gone."

Tim snapped his fingers, Artorian feeling like the dungeon was pointing at him. "That is in part due to your attributes affecting your being, and yes, you currently do not have a specific type of mental manipulation resistance in place that Freedom of Mind isn't helping you with."

Tim cleared his throat. "The effect is minor, but its specific purpose is exactly what you just mentioned. That is what immersion levels should be doing. I'm expecting an influx of people who are afraid of any kind of injury, danger, or threat. Diminishing the impact of what they experience, and the duration of that negative experience, will bolster their will to keep moving forward in adverse conditions. If this is something you do not wish applied to you, I can turn it off."

Artorian held up a hand, and shook his head. "No. Do not. All I wanted was an explanation, but right now these Pylons of yours are being immensely helpful in keeping my thoughts clear and my hearts calm. I thought going into Eternia was a partial vacation? I was very wrong. I am no longer here to have fun. I am currently starting efforts to take your playground seriously, and that comes with equally serious consideration to what I can and cannot do."

He spoke with his arms and hands as much as his mouth, his gestures flying. "I have Flash Runes coming, and I already needed Momma Bun to remind me that I had spells. Until she said it? I had once again completely forgotten. Zelia went over them with me moments before I got hurled into Eternia, and *I forgot*. I cannot handle my toolkit."

He asked his question again, purely to be certain, even as

his voice wavered. "Can I give up spells in trade for something else? I would like to, Tim. I would like to, right now."

The hexagon was silent for a moment, then with a small piano note playing in the background, Less Than Three lost his spells, two titles, and one skill. A box appeared before him that was the exact shape and size to fit the broom in his hand. "Relinquish your focus item, Janitor of Shai-Hulud, and it is done."

The broom went into the box before it truly had a time to shine, but its sacrifice dropped a weight from Artorian's hearts. He felt better without them, as odd as that seemed. He then thought of another component that Tim may feel happier to have back in his hands. "Do you want my allotment list? I've sort of had it trying to make my own abilities. The concept was good, but the execution is… not making me happy. I liked Artifacting? I liked having some kind of guideline, and giving titles and tools to other people."

Artorian shook his head in apology. "However, I am not having a good time making them for myself. I'm sorry. I am happier earning them. And I now feel like so much is being handed to me, that the gifts, and the gifting process itself, is feeling sour. If I truly need thing A to solve problem B? Yeah, I understand. But, I am no longer truly needed to solve any particular problem B, am I? Unless I understood wrong, you may be riddled with problems, but the specific instance I was needed for was turning the sun on. I have a really good grip on thematic and sympathetic connections. That task made sense to me. I understand hunting down Barry's evil little gifts, and mop up protocols, but do you need *me* for it?"

"I do not." Tim's reply was curt, professional, and clear. He was thinking this topic over himself as the components list vanished from Artorian's pool. "I have rescinded the allotments. I am ruminating. You are correct, my friend. I may have started to perhaps take your activity for granted. Everyone at the high table knows that it is never the case *if* you are going to help, but rather that it is always the case that you *will* help. You are correct. All the factors that Ammy spoke of can in fact be handled by other groups, and some may even be more suited to the task. Could I ask what it is that you would currently like to focus on?"

Artorian nodded, grateful. "Thank you, my friend. I want to go to Vanaheim's Arcoplex, get Tisha out of her predicament. Possibly pull Decorum in to help me since I am burning up to see that **Love** reunited, and go rescue all the people I used to know. This is what I want to do."

Tim mulled over the response. "I understand. I recommend you keep your party down to four people, but Dasein has already communicated to me that she is intent on leaving your party upon reaching New Haven. There are other Heavenlies she wishes to see, now that more and more of the obscure ones who would otherwise keep to themselves are being forced to arrive. Do recall that their appearance here is not voluntary, and that a lack of the energy needed to keep them alive is what's making them manifest in the first place? Most of them are acting out because for the first time, in a very long, very certain existence, a lot of them are looking at the real possibility of true death. They are all on a timer, and neither Cal nor I have any means of extending their timers."

That fact hit Artorian like a brick to the head. "*Excuse me? Timers?* Are you telling me that the reason a lot of them are being complete babies is because they're trying to do whatever they can to find some happiness before they kick the bucket?"

"For many? Yes." Tim affirmed the fact without sadness in his tone, but Artorian was not deceived. The hint was there. Tim knew all too well what it was like to be a grand being, and then suddenly get threatened by an unopposable force that calmly took its sweet time walking toward you, giggling and undulating with **Madness** at the certainty of your impending demise.

The Administrator inhaled deep. "I see."

Taking a few seconds, Artorian quietly focused on his breathing until the emotional effects once again ebbed away.

"Bud, these Pylons of yours are… something. I'm alright again. I'm sorry for taking up your time with this. I should be all set and fine to go and play whack-a-mole? Unless you had anything you wanted to address?"

"Yes, but I have comforts to provide you first." The hexagon chuckled in gentle amusement. "Do remember I'm here with you, Artorian. I'm not here against you. No more freebies, but don't blame me for pulling an Oberon once or twice. You may flip over a rock and find a strange hatch, or the like. Treasure chests the size of horses may appear from the dead bodies of small rodents. Don't question physics. Merely accept the box I had to use to stuff your reward in."

Artorian saluted without fuss.

CHAPTER TWENTY-FOUR

Eternium took this chance to share some of his own concerns, making a list appear. "First. You're overloaded on Pylons, and it's making your mana bar burn up when you push your abilities beyond their constraints. That thing you like to do where you force the system to adapt to you? That trick is not without a cost. Have a look, and know that this is a major reason why I went against my grain and approved the removal of your spells. I do not normally approve of tools being taken away directly. We've got the Soul Forge for that. In this case... Well... if you wanted to give up something else, now's a good time. This list shows the numbers with your recent removals already accounted for, sans Cold Fusion Charge. That one is a whole box of different problems."

He paused to let the Administrator absorb information, then trekked on with more screens. "Second. The cause of bar damage is a recent find, so please don't blame Zelia. We successfully tracked down the source when your numbers started rolling in. The numerical value of personal Pylons available in your hold ended up being important."

Tim sounded terse, and worried. "Your Pylon hold is

running *hot*, and may make your effects or tools go on the fritz. I have a log showing this happened to Sanctity already, and while that one happened to be in your favor, the next fritz may not. Pylon overload is how we ended up with the spawning amalgamation problem. That whole synthetic bank *melted*. Your hold showed us what the initial stages of going over the limit looked like. The spawning Pylons? We got to those after the catastrophe. Speaking of, if you want to help with something after you're done with the Arcoplex, come see me about that Amalgam."

Tim then turned some of his screens around, showing Artorian what the numbers currently looked like. People always loved something tangible to hold on to.

———

Less Than Three, Pylon allotment:
  Titles and Traits: 268.
  Racial: 445.
  Profession: 24.
  Class and Specialization: 162.
  Skills: 574.
  Abilities: 605.
  Total: 2,078.
  Available: 1,703.
  Warning, overload!
  Overload Value: 375.

———

Artorian winced. "How do I get more Pylons?"

Tim answered calmly. "Not easily. This is your adaptive Pylon bank, and everything was shoved into it by the now-deceased Task Manager in an attempt to kill you slowly, should he fail to kill you quickly. Skills and abilities rooted in the system won't cost you Pylons from your bank. To get more Pylons directly... I'm sorry, my friend. I'm going to have to give you quests."

Artorian's grumble was minor. "Then quests are what I will complete, Tim. What else? Before we get to other things to give up."

The hexagon bobbed in approval of the Administrator taking that news in stride. "Second, you may have noticed that you're gaining no experience points, have been getting no drops or achievements, and there's no random gains to be found? This is unlikely to change, but permit me my indulgences? When you attempt to work on a skill, ability, or a new toolset, that is when we will begin making checks and balances per what to do about letting them roll in."

The hexagon twisted in place, twirling. "I am in your boat. I want gains to take *some* effort, but it does not escape me that many tasks that are borderline impossible for others are going to be as difficult as breathing for you. One does not make it as an A-ranked Mage without a particular set of skills, after all. I'll see where the Wisps are on Artifacting, Flash Runes, and Accelerator. Don't... don't expect good news on that last one. Mass Driver by itself is blowing up several Gnomish labs when they attempt to replicate it with current Pylons. The synthetic ones just... don't..."

The hexagon shook itself as if Tim had crossed his arms, sorely shaking his head from side to side in disappointment. "They just don't have the flexibility that the others did. More ethical, certainly! Far worse in a way? Definitely. The only good thing is that, with Cal's help, I'm able to grow these new batches like bamboo. They're just so celestial feces flammable! They explode, too! Worse than they used to, and I still haven't gotten that *smell* out of any of the healy ones. You enter that Pylon hold and you can taste the monosodium glutamate scent. It's terrible! Well, I mean, it does make meat very tasty, but that's not the point. Healers are going to get mobbed by game monsters, there's just no way around it."

Artorian was plenty happy to let Tim vent. The effort made

him feel useful, and trusted. "You're doing well, bud. Thanks for telling me the pattern report did you good. I'll try to keep reporting problems as I find them. I might play with them for a round or two first, but I'll hand them off. Do I give Cold Fusion Charge to a person? Or can I give it to you and point it at someone later?"

The hexagon bobbed with a sigh, partially relieved. "I can take it. That would be easier."

"Nab it. I'll run my way down on platforms, and… if you ever give those a cost, please tell me. That's going to radically change my movement dynamic if I start getting used to it."

Tim's energetic flailing paused.

"Your Bonescripting has no cost for method one movement?" The dungeon went to check, an act that was followed by the sound of a hand hitting a forehead. "How do I keep missing things like this! First it was Supreme Weapon M— *What happened to Supreme Weapon Mastery?* Where is all the text? I thought the Wisps said it was fixed! It's just gone! What is this piddly little pizza party pretending to be leftovers? I can't feed a Pylon hold rat with this, much less a player!"

Artorian couldn't stop himself, he laughed. He laughed hard. Wiping away the wet from his eyes when he could catch his breath, he hovered in place with a dumb smile on his face. "Ahhh… You're great, Tim. That was great. I needed that."

"*MMMMMmmmm!*" An aggrieved noise erupted from Tim's hexagon, followed by heavy breathing as some blue Hades flames flared out of the top of his hexagon. "I'm good. I'm alright. I'm fine. I'll flag your entire character sheet for review again. An… No. Know what? *Ey!* Oberon! Your favorite tricky li'l human has other people messing with his character sheet again."

From deep in the background, something heavy hit a table. Followed by the sound of an insulted Wisp not being particularly happy about that news as Oberon threw a fit. "What?! No! Unacceptable! Ten years dungeon!"

Artorian once more lost himself to the laughter. "Ha! Ha…

sen—send me on my way, bud. I have a boss to beat. Or can we talk about overload mitigation?"

Tim took hold of Less Than Three's character sheet. "We could… We could actually feed most of your abilities into Flash Runes once we get that up and running. Which we can run system-side if we're lucky. I almost want to ask for what's left of Supreme Weapon Mastery. There's just nothing left to it, and that was an import slot. I am vexed. Those were supposed to be meaningful, now… Look at this mess. I'm glad your Bone-scripting is malleable, because it looks like that's going to need to be updated again. *Ugh…* Let me know if your bones feel like they itch at any point?"

Artorian frowned, but nodded while squeezing his arms. "I'm sure it'll be a scream of a good time."

He then sighed, and rubbed the back of his head since he was able, thinking that he would much rather have less tools in the kit than end up as molten, crystalline slag. "Take… Take all the goodies you just gave me back. Dual Casting. Visual Tactics. Take Supreme Weapon Mastery since I'm not exactly in a position to use weapons anyway, and lift my Flash Runes skill out since that's a primer. The build I wanted to make is now a build I can't make. Because that single health point is always going to bite me."

He opened his inventory, motioning at the contents. "I can't have fun with tonfas when I can't take a hit without Lucia's shield, and while I don't mind this DPS lingo, I really did want to learn martial arts with Ember again. I can't do that right now. I'm locked into a corner to stay at range, and behind a wall. That's not great for me. Trans Am is a cute get out of jail card, I can't use Shining Ray without major consequences, and I have no idea what else to give up. I need Bolts to Ink as a gateway for Gatling, so that needs to stay."

Artorian dropped his arms, taking a breather. "I very much did not want to give up my New Game Plus Weapon Mastery, but here I am. What's my overload value at?"

Ding!

———

Less Than Three, Pylon allotment update:
  Skills: 356.
  Warning, overload!
  Overload Value: 157.

———

Tim mulled it over. "Since we still can't get rid of World Boss and Glass Cannon... we can lose another eighty-one points by dropping Critical Conversion and Critical Clarity. While we are on the topic, please understand that I will be feeding these back to you as Pylons allow. I appreciate you standing by my side on the field when it comes to the precaution of not blowing you up, if your Pylon hold happens to go. I was going to approach you about this when you got to New Haven, but you reached out first. I thought something may have already gone wrong when you did. Glad we could catch this early."

Artorian nodded with difficulty. "That's... That's where my mind was. I made a promise to Dawn that I wouldn't blow myself up again. This is giving me that... itch, as you called it. Remove them, Tim. I need to be within the allotment, regardless of how annoying it makes the situation."

———

Less Than Three, Pylon allotment update:
  Skills: 275.
  Warning, overload!
  Overload Value: 76.

———

Tim bobbed at the sight. "Progress. If you give up... Well, first off, do not give up Shining Ray. I also need to know why using it is a problem. The Architect title is currently doing you no good if you are not intent on making your own things anymore, and Critical Mastery doesn't affect your ability calculation… for some reason… That's odd. It should. Why is your base calculation for abilities set to two percent? That should be a five at base for you with Critical Mastery."

Artorian shrugged, his attention pulled to the boss fight that he was eager to get to. "Bud, remove them, fiddle with my Bonescripting and specialization as needed, and get me those quests when you can. Sounds good? I want to minimize my points of failure, before I maximize my performance."

Tim turned his screen as a happy chime played. "You're in the clear."

———

Less Than Three, Pylon allotment:
   Titles and Traits: 219.
   Racial: 445.
   Profession: 24.
   Class and Specialization: 162.
   Skills: 229.
   Abilities: 605.
   Total: 1,684.
   Available: 1,703.
   Note: Pylon hold within safe values.

———

The dungeon dismissed the screens. "What's this about Shining Ray and consequences? The entry looked great. I'm going to work on Supreme Weapon Mastery and see what I can do with it, but I owe you an Imported New Game Plus tool, when it's safe to give it to you. Many of these tools are tagged… Incursus? *Bhah*! Now I can't even be mad. That dungeon is such a good boy. I like turtles."

"Vanaheim gon' eat me?" Artorian wildly motioned at the planet in the sky above them. "Brother Moon turned our way when I used Shining Ray right after dropping in. I was honestly expecting some Nootingale Assassins by now. Those sharp fondue-sticks seem to be able to be anywhere and everywhere."

Tim's hexagon was suspiciously silent, before he broke with laughter. "Ha! That cheesy blob playing dress-up? Brother Moon dressed in city plating has his tentacles full right now, and isn't going to give you a string cheese lick's worth of attention. He's got a major bug problem trying to eat him alive right now. Use Shining Ray. You have to go to Vanaheim for Vanaheim to be a problem to you, at this point. Let 'er rip!"

That cheered Artorian up just a little bit. "Off I go then!"

Before Tim could release Artorian, Cal popped a brand new hexagon of his own in to say hi. "Hello, friends!"

Eternium's hexagon turned toward him, far too slowly for Cal's appearance to have been kosher. "Aren't... you supposed to be somewhere else right now?"

Cal had no such worries! "What Dani doesn't know won't hurt me."

Unfortunately for Cal, Dani was hot on his heels as she personally popped in. The Wisp was a rolling minefield of colors as she replied dangerously sweet. "What do I not know, Cal?"

Silence hung in the air before a violet tendril extended from Dani's orb. Dani gripped Cal by his metaphorical ear, and tugged him away with a cryptic message. "You. Me. Bot. Bot."

Artorian instantly made confused hand motions at the empty space when Cal and Dani popped out. Tim had to stop laughing before he could reply. "Dani wants to play League. Speaking of, they likely haven't had a chance to tell you yet, but Grace has a little brother! The name is uncertain for now, but I think they're leaning toward Maximus? Macintosh? Mak? Regardless of what the name ends up being, he's a precious Wisp boy."

Tim paused from that train of thought, suffering a pressing

DENNIS VANDERKERKEN & DAKOTA KROUT

idea which he needed a random roll for. His voice turned big-dungeon serious. "One moment, my friend. Curator Caladrius? Dark Gnome Turk? Your time, please."

A Dark Gnome with fiery red hair, and a Celestial Harris Hawk promptly arrived from a black and white, Kings-and-Castles Gate of **Order**. In a much more controlled and genteel fashion than when Zelia had plucked them from the Ether. They both strolled over solidly lit flooring, taking their places before bowing, taking their assigned positions on a platform of hard light, complete with extended perch.

Tim's hexagon bobbed to make a nodding motion. "I require a dice tower and an eight-sided die."

Caladrius instantly formed an artistic tower that expanded downwards like an unfolding puzzle. The Gnome saluted, pressed his hands together, and dove from great height into the tower's top hatch as if it were an Olympic swimming pool. Mid-drop, he turned into a smoky, garnet- and soot-colored octahedron. Several clatters, bangs, and at least one explosion later... It was a four!

"Thank you both, you are dismissed." Tim bobbed again, the Gnome and bird becoming their original forms once more. They bowed, and walked out of existence the way they arrived. In an **Orderly** fashion. "Right, it seems we've calculated how many 'nopes' the Creeping Death Squirrel is worth. Blast that Pylon cabal of yours, Artorian. Barely any time in the holds, and they have a faction, with *champions*. They're helping the Rat problem, but still. A *cabal*."

The hexagon spun in place before settling, expanding on this cabal when Artorian's face turned into a tapestry of questions. "There's Yuki's Rock Squirrel, Hulk. Kronk, the Lever-mancer. Ratatoskr, the Messenger—who may or may not be a Heavenly fooling everyone—Bullwinkle, the Air announcer. Odin's Chosen: Ikkar the Revolutionary, who as you can tell from his title didn't like the man very much. Then finally... *Nibbles*, the Nibelung. First of the Death Squirrels. Grand

Gooserider. With Voltekka, honorary squirrel, as a bonus entry."

Tim grumbled as he undid the time dilation, sending Artorian on his way when the boy touched his fingers together to pull them apart at the mention of Voltekka, the electricity back between his fingers where it belonged. "Stupid Squirrels and their stupid Nuttelator and its stupid, accurate results and good calculations... I want it!"

Stifling laughter from the mighty dungeon being refused a calculation engine, Artorian smiled and sighed a fresh breath of relief. Normally he'd be upset about losing tools, but this time he was happy about it. This happened by his choice; for his health, happiness, and well-being. Vocalizing his personal choice also did him well. Being dragged along with the tide was one thing, but he loved having his own boat and paddle.

Speaking of! There was whack-a-mole-ing to do! "I'm Barotrauma-proof. If I keep my distance and lay on the damage, I should be able to buy enough time for Lucia before I'm a pinball. I suppose I should be lucky that Cal left, or he'd roll out the pun carpet and suddenly it'd be Bearotrauma."

Mad cackling erupted from the sky. The voice of Cal was both obvious and distinct. "Dani! I'm doing it! That's such a good pun!"

A *whap* clapped across the sky, the connection breaking afterwards as some space in the living thundercloud parted. Unfortunately, not before the Gargantua Storm Mole turned into a Gargantua Storm Mole-*Bear*.

Artorian held his face. "Why do I say things?"

CHAPTER TWENTY-FIVE

Ding!

———

Quest Notice!
You have been offered the Quest: Bear-o-Traumatic.
Objective: Eliminate Area Boss: 'The Bends' Barotrauma.

———

Quest Notice!
You have been offered the Quest: Lair of the Far Squid.
Objective: Visit Louis. Make a friend.

———

Quest Notice!
You have been offered the Quest: The Archmage Of Bonkmancy.
Objective: New Haven has a Mechanicus Steamlord problem.
Resolve it.

Quest Notice!
  You have been offered the Quest: Arcoplex.
  Objective: Rescue Tisha.
  Bonus Objective: Help Decorum Rescue Tisha.

Artorian glanced at the prompts as he entered freefall, his prior speed and direction retained from before Tim surrounded him with dilation. He slapped all of the quest accept prompts in a single clean swipe, and would check them later. The first one had to do with what he was already going to do, so why waste any time.

He flicked on Wisp Flight so gravity stopped having a hold on him, then altered his orientation so he could run horizontally. Planting his foot right down on an angled panel, he propelled himself forward and took off.

The Running skill tried adding itself to his character sheet, but an upset error noise rebuked it. That same error noise went off as several other skills felt their requirements had been met, only to be rebuked as well.

Artorian paid the system resolving itself no heed as the ex-Mole came into view. He had a Bear to brawl. His new shields flickered into high activity as they fought back against the area boss's character trait, negating the negative effects of purple flashes that filled the area. Integrity and Tenacity were both doing work! He'd figure out what those actually did when he could.

Deciding on his attack pattern, Artorian checked his distances.

He was still decently high in the sky, but below Fuyu No Arashi's layer. A bright cold snap passed by his head, making him miss a step in his run. That moody cloud that was throwing ice-flavored lightning at him? How rude! Time to check his offensive options. Gatling had been a mainstay, but he trusted Tim when the dungeon said that he wasn't going to draw Brother Moon's attention if he whipped out Shining Ray.

That would certainly poke the bear.

"Whipping time!" He would inspect the boss after this surprise attack, aiming a digit at the soon to be upset mixture of claws and fur. "Shining Ray!"

B-v-uuuuummmmmm!

A beam of thermal heat shot from his finger as a fat laser. The reddish-white beam appeared coarse and rough, wider than usual as Less Than Three kept his eye on the prize, and his aim true. He thought that was odd, so focused on the beam. His intent altered the laser to a finer, thinner, more concentrated beam. One more white than red, to the point where it appeared pink.

Instantly, the HitScan laser slammed into the back of the Bear's head, an easy one-thousand stamina invested in the first second of continuous-wave operation, dealing a thousand damage.

Artorian smiled wide when his attack hit, the boss staggering as his laser refined itself to his intent. He wondered for a moment if he could make it blue, but first he had to celebrate. "Ah-ha! Gotcha!"

The Bear roared in trauma, trying to bat and paw away this line of hot light busy carving into its health bar without pause. As Artorian approached, the area boss tried to snap at the line only to earn a mouthful of tongue-burning pain, which caused the first instance of a red number to float out from above the Bear's head. A measly one-hundred points.

Biting the heat line proved equally fruitless, and any attempts to smack the attack away only changed where the Bear was gaining burning laceration marks. Laceration marks that didn't look very deep at all.

Artorian couldn't spot any damage that so much as went through the Mole-Bear's fur. "That's barely a sear! I want a flambé! Ignite!"

The Bear did not catch fire, another measly one-hundred floating up from its oversized head.

"Right, that was patched."

He did, on the other hand, accomplish his goal of making the area boss very angry, specifically at him! When he realized that the Bear had stopped playing chase with the heavy hitters on his team, he altered the vector of his run, turning a sharp ninety-degree angle to lure the roaring thing and its attached area effect away. "So far so good!"

He gripped his brooch with the hand he wasn't using to keep contact with the enemy. "Bun! I've got its attention! I'm luring it over to those crags, but Growls-a-Lot over here is more zoomy than me. I'm hoofing it as fast as I can, and he is gaining somehow. That's ridiculous! Someone balance that!"

He saw Lucia's bunny-nyoom spear of light tear up the landscape behind the area boss, her vector on direct approach to a winded set of streaks in black and red color themes. She replied to him in an equal hurry. "I'm almost at them! Buy me more time, then circle back! Are you doing any damage to that thing? It looks angry and that's about it. That Bear's health is barely moving!"

Artorian didn't like that. "What? I was seeing that correctly? I've been spot on with my laser for… *Oh, whoops!*"

His stamina bar flashed. "I need to lower my output. That's a dangerously low stamina bar. Dropping my output to seven-hundred! I'll turn at the crags and inspect the thing, see what I can find. I noticed earlier that dark talons and red blades weren't doing much to Bearsy either. Checking back in when able!"

He blew the heat off his fingertip when seven hundred expected damage seemed to do just as little as one-thousand, though he had succeeded in turning his laser blue. Small victories. Ceasing Shining Ray to recoup some energy, he looked over his shoulder mid-sprint while breathing deep. "Still on me? Outstanding!"

The Bear roared at him, in full sprint and chase mode as it

crackled with purple power, gaining on the pipsqueak that had burned its tongue. Artorian wasn't sure how it planned to close the vertical gap, even if Bendsy could close the horizontal gap. He could remain airborne, but Bendsy the Baro-Bear did not seem to have that capacity. An edge!

"Alright Mole-Bear, let's find out what your gimmick is, and why you're not taking damage. Shining Ray should have ignored half of all your protective goodies, and was still only doing one-hundred on a thermal beam of one-thousand oomph. What's the deal? Full inspect!"

Ding!

———

You have encountered: Area Boss: 'The Bends' Barotrauma.
  World: Eternia.
  Realm: Midgard.
  Region: Beyblade Crags.
  Terrain: Snowy.
  Circumstance: Area Boss Encounter.
  Local Event: Fuyu No Arashi Storm.
  Unique Properties: Gargantua.
  Racial Template: Bearification.
  Species: Mole-Bear.
  Detected Trait: Barotrauma.
  Detected Ability: Burrow.
  Detected Ability: Purple Rain.
  Detected Skill: Rubber Banding.
  Detected Skill: Snow Mastery.
  Detected Skill: Molehill into a Mountain.
  Protection: Immunity to Pressure Damage.
  Protection: Immunity to Dark Damage.
  Protection: Greatest Resistance to Heat and Fire-themed Damage.
  Protection: Resistance to Cold and Ice-themed Damage.
  Protection: Lesser Resistance to Sonic and Electric Damage.
  Vulnerability: Lesser Weakness to Thunder and Lightning Damage.

Vulnerability: Weakness to Kinetic and Melee Damage.
Main Attack 1: Maul.
Main Attack 2: Directed Ice Thunderstrike.

———

Properties unlocked, revealing localized information.

Local Event: Fuyu No Arashi Storm. This Local Event causes Cold and Ice Damage Lightning to strike the battlefield. The impact zones become brighter before the lightning strikes.

Unique Properties: Gargantua. This property guarantees that this creature is of the Gargantuan size category, which cannot be altered by Spells, Effects, or Abilities.

Racial Template: Bearification. This template evolves an existing template with the Bear Type. Providing the creature a Maul attack, increased durability, additional Health, one Resistance bundle, and one Vulnerability bundle.

Protection: Resistance to Cold and Ice-themed Damage.

Vulnerability: Lesser Weakness to Thunder and Lightning Damage.

Effect in Progress: Barotrauma. This effect deals sensory damage in a wide area, by chaotically raising and lowering the air and water pressure of anything within the affected zone. High chance of Discombobulation. Extreme chance of Nausea. Extreme chance of Vertigo. Extreme chance of temporary deafness.

———

Properties unlocked, revealing Ability information.

Detected Ability: Burrow. This Ability allows a creature to move as freely underneath the ground as it does on it.

Detected Ability: Purple Rain. This Ability allows a creature to call down a purple colored, Cold themed Thunderstrike onto a designated enemy that it cannot otherwise reach with its claw or bite attack.

—————

Properties unlocked, revealing Skill information.

Detected Skill: Rubber Banding. This Skill allows a creature to match speeds with the target it is currently chasing, then add its own speed on top of the matched velocity to catch up.

Detected Skill: Snow Mastery. This Skill allows a creature to move on or through snow without difficulty, as if the snow was solid ground, or normal water.

Detected Skill: Molehill into a Mountain. Mole-Specific Skill. This Skill allows a Mole to ignore terrain density when burrowing. Including Bedrock, Metals, and Minerals.

—————

Properties unlocked, revealing Protection and Vulnerability clarity.

Note: Affix and Suffix values replace standard modifiers.

Immunity: Complete Negation of related effects.

Resistance: Mitigation of related effects, Resistance reduces damage taken.

Weakness: Amplification of related effects, Weakness increases damage taken.

Least: A two times modifier alteration.

Lesser: A three times modifier alteration.

Weakness: A four times modifier in an unfavorable direction.

Resistance: A four times modifier in a favorable direction.

Greater: A seven times modifier alteration.

Greatest: A ten times modifier alteration.

Example: Greatest Resistance to Fire, will cause all Fire-themed damage to deal one-tenth the expected damage.

Note: A creature with specific resistances; Such as Heat, will tally that Protection rating against that specific Damage type, in addition to any general protections that it may have listed. A creature with both Greatest Heat and Greatest Fire protection will take one-twentieth the expected damage, from an attack that is both Heat and Fire themed.

Example: Thermal Damage.

Note: Matching types cancel out.

Example: Lesser Resistances cancel out Lesser Vulnerabilities if attack types match.

———

Artorian gawked, dismissing those screens. "Celestial feces, full inspect, my boy! You are dangerous! One, that's some good information. Two, that is a *ridiculous* amount of protections and vulnerabilities."

He took the amount in as best of a stride as he could, then focused on what he could do about the situation with this new information he had uncovered. "So, I was ignoring half of its protections, but half of one-twentieth means Bendsy is still ignoring my damage down to one tenth of the expected oomph? That's painful! For me! So much for Shining Ray. Those weaknesses and resistances are definitely going to need fine-tuning... Even *one* of those would make a drastic difference in an encounter. That many of them on one critter? Ludicrous."

He then flexed his arm, cocking it playfully as a humming built back up around his wrist. The Inspect had given him solutions. "So, I need kinetic damage? I *have* kinetic damage."

Taking another sharp turn so he could extend his arm to get a clean line of fire on Bendsy, Artorian grinned wide. He hadn't seen the boss's attributes or health count come up, but he had wanted something beefy to lay into with Luminous Gatling! And wouldn't you know it? She was all charged up. "*Showtime.*"

CHAPTER TWENTY-SIX

Buh-du-du-du-du!

Bolts of kinetic lightning unleashed from Less Than Three's open hand, peppering Bendy with a hailstorm of impacts that clearly did not tickle like Shining Ray had. Artorian laughed as he ran circles around the Gargantuan-sized Mole-Bear from above, the boss roaring, jumping, and swiping in an attempt to maul him. No dice!

The DPS was up far too high, and able to stay up there indefinitely as Artorian tore actual chunks out of the Barotrauma boss's health bar. Seeing that he was finally effective, Artorian was suddenly having a good time! Outright giggling as he kept playing distraction. "I love it when a plan comes together!"

His free hand gripped his brooch. "Momma Bun! I have this thing in a holding pattern unless it gets real clever, real quick. Am I doing more damage to this Bear on your measuring thingy than I was? My Inspect didn't give me its health, and while I think I'm laying down the smack, I don't trust the visual representations."

Lucia's voice crackled back through, her voice hurried. "No time!"

"I'll wait!" Artorian responded quickly, whistling for a damage rolodex as the Bear did in fact get clever, and purple rain started pouring down while the massive area boss pulsed with equally purple flashes. In tune to the beat of the music no less!

Less Than Three dodged mid-air when they came down, the pulse on the boss betraying when a strike was imminent. "About a two second delay between cast and effect?"

He watched for a flash, then counted. "One... two... dodge!"

A well-positioned foothold let him dodge left and freefall slightly, feeling the purple crack of lightning miss him entirely. He formed a new foothold to get him back on track, and back up into his higher layer of elevation. Convenient to do when there was little distinction between where he planted his feet, and the location of the road. "*Wooo-hooo!*"

Artorian cackled, keeping his aim on target and sustaining the kinetic volleys as the bolts thundered from his hand, adapting to the new rhythm of shimmy shimmy bang bang, and the roaring Luminous Gatling pattern of:

Buh-du-du-du-du!

He'd expected the rest of the team to be up and running by now, but if Lucia needed more time, then more time she would have! Unceasing, he laid into the Bear with a constant, furious flurry of homing bolts while bolting around himself at top speed to stay out of leaping-maul range. A great majority of his current barrage exploded in a spectacular fashion! Demonstrating all parts of the Bear being damaged, rather than just the part struck. Bendsy even staggered! "That volley looked spicy! Time to check the damage!"

Ding!

———

Error Log! Hypocrisy, clashing values.
  Protection: Lesser Resistance to Sonic and Electric Damage.
  Vulnerability: Lesser Weakness to Thunder and Lightning Damage.
  Vulnerability: Weakness to Kinetic and Melee Damage.
  Resolving: Lesser Weakness has a double thematic similarity to the Lesser Resistance. Neutralizing both entries. No further conflicts are detected.
  Commencing Damage Log.

———

You have hit: Area Boss: 'The Bends' Barotrauma, with: Luminous Gatling.
  Impacts: 120.
  Kinetic Lightning Damage: 698.
  Explosion Damage: 700.
  Components affected by Explosive Damage: 10.
  Total Explosion damage: 7,000.
  Multiplier: Weakness to Kinetic: Damage times 4.
  Total Kinetic Lightning Damage: 2,792.
  Total Damage: 9,792.

———

Artorian smacked his lips as those numbers were pieces of candy to savor and enjoy. "Now that tastes sweet! Those were great results! Shame the numbers stopped popping out of Bendy's head, that would have been funny. Must be another Pylon limitation? Honestly, they can just turn it off. It's cute, but that's really reminding me I'm in a game. Wasn't there something about immersion that was important?"

A confirmation chime played in his ear, and he dropped the commentary in favor of running another lap. His subsequent multiple passes did not do nearly as much damage as that particular second of time had accomplished. He mentally smashed a mug, the sky filled with music, thundering kinetic bolts, and lightning flashes of purple rain as Less Than Three and Bendsy played a dangerous game of cat and mouse. This thrilling joyride of figuring out the enemy, and then beating them, was what the game should be. He liked it! "Another!"

Buh-du-du-du-du!

Ding!

————

You have hit: Area Boss: 'The Bends' Barotrauma, with: Luminous Gatling.

Impacts: 120.

Kinetic Lightning Damage: 411.

Explosion Damage: 241.

Components affected by Explosive Damage: 10.

Total Explosion damage: 2,410.

Multiplier: Weakness to Kinetic: Damage times 4.

Total Kinetic Lightning Damage: 1,644.

Total Damage: 4,054.

————

"*Mmmm*! Tasty!" His mana and stamina remained topped off, and he was feeling pretty good about life while well fed, well hydrated, clean, and using only his regeneration metrics as expenditures. If this was all this boss fight was going to be, he was going to be able to solo the— *K'zap*!

A stray aquamarine lightning strike from Fuyu No Arashi caught him right on the noggin, tearing apart Sanctity, Integrity, and Tenacity all in one go. He lost his footing, missed a step in his run, and tumbled from his cozy circling corner all the way down. He slammed into the snow before he had control of his consciousness again, at which point he instantly rolled left and used a platform to push himself off faster. He did not see the flash coming, but surely it was time for the shimmy part of the pattern. Dodge!

A purple lightning bolt honed in on his exact, prior position. With a *kra-kow*, purple rain grazed his Shield for a clean four-hundred damage. Not direct damage either; that would certainly have hurt a whole lot more!

Artorian got to his feet on the snow, then realized just how *big* a Gargantuan creature size actually was as Bendsy grinned ominously at the turn of events. This sixty-four feet tall, one-hundred twenty five tons heavy, massive lump of a thing angry specifically at him. One of those teeth was far larger than Less Than Three. "Nope! Haulin' butt!"

He turned and ran for the crags as the Bear roared and beelined for him, already Rubber Banding and guaranteeing a victorious pursuit as Artorian instantly saw angry red text begin to pop up in the top left of his vision, his Acuity heads-up display warning him of bad tidings. Barotrauma was no longer something he was able to contend with, and life was about to thoroughly be abyssed. "Toast, toast, toast, *toast*!"

He tried to increase his elevation, but the nausea slapped him back down for trying. He covered his mouth with his free hand, but could already feel his stomach turn and vision twist, going wonky. Like the world was lilting. He gripped the brooch hard for comfort. "Momma Bun! I hope that was enough time! I'm about out of time!"

Lucia's voice crackled back through his brooch. "Jump! Now!"

Artorian was not in a position to ask questions, and leapt in the air! Bringing him just high enough to be in perfect mauling range. A capital opportunity that Bendsy instantly cashed in on, his massive claw going for a swipe. Artorian was certain that a single smackaroo was going to do more damage than the full juice stored in the jar of his shield value. Which made it such a pleasant surprise when Lucia dove between those massive, tower-sized claws like a ray of light shining down from the heavens.

Ember, mounted on the Glitterflit's back, grabbed him by

the scruff of the jacket mid-twisted-leap! Acrobatically shoving him right into the spot in front of her. "Gotcha!"

Lucia barrel-rolled herself to safety and kept on running without landing flat-footed. Artorian had half a mind to ask where Dasein was, but when an equally Gargantuan Shadow Reaper rose up from the Bear's back wielding an equally impressive, onyx black and Tuscan yellow scythe, he felt his question was moot.

A new question occurred when he saw the scythe swing in an attempt to decapitate the area boss, only to shatter against its fur and do absolutely nothing. The impact resounded with a sharp, metallic *ping*!

The Bear rounded on the Reaper and mauled Dasein to pieces instead, immune to her hunting claws, blackfire, scythe, and Death effects. They didn't know about the protections!

He grabbed his brooch, then looked up and behind him at Ember. The first thing he noticed before speaking was the trail of dry blood that lined down both of her ears, cheeks, and neck. "Sugar, can you hear me? That thing is immune to dark damage!"

Ember winced, her grip on him tightening. She looked down, clearly having recovered enough to hear something, but beyond muffled noise, grasped no details on what he said. Artorian remembered the tidbit in the inspect field about sensory damage, and instantly pulled up a fresh screen to write the same information down with his finger.

A furious look crossed Ember's face as her eyes devoured his words, followed by her poking herself hard in the chest as her other hand moved to grasp Lucia's fur, as their Glitterflit played dodge-the-Mauling. Bendsy was already on their trail and tail as Rubber Banding had allowed the area boss to immediately catch up from putting Lady Death into the snowy dirt.

Ding!

Warning! One of your party members has died, and has been sent to respawn!

———

Dasein was not going to be happy about that, but that needed to be a problem for later. Ember was asking him why her damage had done nothing, and what she could be doing instead.

He had that answer.

Artorian furiously wrote out the Bear's protections and vulnerabilities in shorthand while talking to Lucia, relaying the same information verbally since she could not read his prompt right now. "He's vulnerable to kinetic and melee most of all, which... Momma Bun, what's his health at? I've been laying into him, but there's no signs of Bearsy slowing down."

Lucia chanced a sharp dive, turning hard and straining her shield with some damage to gain line of sight to the area boss, then laughed like mad as she zipped between all four of his legs and made him tumble head over heels. "Ha! Four!"

Artorian didn't follow. "Four... four what? Four thousand? Forty thousand?"

She shook her head, a grin on her Basher face. "No, kit! Four! Exactly four! One more solid hit and we win! You did good! He had about a hundred-fifty thousand something before Bearification, a good chunk more after."

"That's ridiculous!" The health remaining provided Artorian with a sudden epiphany. He couldn't pull the mental bandwidth together to fire off a Kinetic Bolt, but he didn't have to! Artorian pulled the screen close, and wrote down a message for Ember that said, 'Hold out your hands, you only need to hit it once and we win!'

When she did, he reached into his inventory, and directly deposited Halcyon Nights into her waiting grip, accompanied by a giant smirk.

Ember read the message as the weight fell into her hands.

She looked at the weapons once, confirmed the information with a quick glance, then kissed his forehead before launching herself straight up from Lucia's back like a vengeful rocket.

A roar from behind them made Artorian divert his attention. Bendsy had recovered from his dumble-stumble with a quickness, and was already almost back on Lucia's tail. The Gargantua Mole-Bear leapt to strike and pulverize them, but Artorian was not paying attention to the claws! Through Lucia's protective shield that was giving the angry red additions in his Acuity a fantastic breather, he was watching the Integrity and Tenacity shields on Ember flicker to life.

She was directly above the enemy, poised to strike.

She spun in the air, her rage manifesting as she exploded into a being of living flame. Twisting like a tornado, she kicked off from some unseen ceiling and shot down like a spear hurled from the heavens. With a volcanic howl, her martial arts maneuver guided a tonfa straight into the top of the Bendsy's cranium, cracking it to bits and doing significantly more than four points of damage, instantly sending the gargantuan beast to its knees as physics demanded its due. The Bear's mauling swipe went wild, and missed.

Artorian ate up the damage log like it was a buffet of desserts.

———

Astarte, Goddess of War, has hit: Area Boss: 'The Bends' Barotrauma, with: Halcyon Nights. Using: Martial Arts Maneuver - Volcanic Piledriver.

Impacts: 1.

Kinetic Damage: 6,208.

Volcanic Damage: 6,241.

Multiplier: Weakness to Kinetic: Damage times 4.

Multiplier: Weakness to Melee: Damage times 4.

Combined multiplier value: 8.

Total Kinetic Damage: 49,664.

Total Volcanic Damage: 6,241.
Total Damage: 55,905
Area Boss, 'The Bends' Barotrauma, has been killed.
End of Log.

———

Notice!
Hidden event completed!
Your party has killed an area boss in the Beyblade Crags with a Spinning Technique.
Bonus awarded!

———

Ember landed dramatically in a full three point hero pose, smack in front of the collapsing body of Bendy, the Gargantua Barotrauma Mole-Bear. She got up right as her inflamed form released its effects, showing her to be made entirely of diamond!

Shoving one of the tonfas into the air victoriously, her diamond body ability sparkled as the collapsing boss behind her hit hard snow, then exploded into colorful, shining particles, illuminating both her warrior's form, and claim to her victory and prize.

Ding!

———

Quest Complete! Bear-o-Traumatic.
Congratulations. Dramatic finish!
Reward: 100 Adaptive Pylons.

———

Artorian would not, could not, and did not stop applauding while whistling loud as Lucia pulled up to the scene. He jumped off right away, dancing like a cheerleader while being as loud as he could to celebrate her winning hit. Making a big hurrah of it like he was handing out vanilla ice to desert C'towl. "*Whooo*! Glory to Astarte! Go Goddess, go Goddess, go! Go Goddess, go Goddess, go! *Go! Go! Go! Go!*"

CHAPTER TWENTY-SEVEN

With the boss down and dead, the music ending, Lucia had plenty of time to focus on healing Astarte's ears. As a pleasant addition, any unsanitary touches that Barotrauma had caused her were swiftly cleaned up by Less Than Three's Cleaning Presence.

Now that the trial of mad dashes was over, Lucia shifted back to her human form, pulled out a lantern, and let it float as she cast her spell. "Serenity."

A pleasant Journey-style wind chime played. From the glowing, glass-steel lantern, a bubble of runic scripture expanded to include them. The bubble repelled the latent effects of the boss's annoying effects, while nullifying Fuyu No Arashi's ever less random cold, zappy strikes. That moody cloud was definitely cheating, especially when five strikes hit the shield dead on in quick succession.

The lantern hummed with light, Lucia's static defense absorbing the blows like a lightning rod. Artorian recognized that this particular medium left them stuck in place in order to enjoy this safety, and that wasn't great long term. For the moment, with only the cloud to assail them? This was excellent.

She had definitely done this before. He added Serenity to the list of unknown Shield spells, alongside Integrity and Tenacity. The moment was not right to ask.

He pulled up a screen to write so he could speak to Ember, her ears still muting the world. As he wrote, he spoke the words out loud so that Momma Bun was in on the conversation. "You did great, honey. Beautiful final blow. I loved the showmanship."

Ember smiled at the corner of her lips as she was still coming down from her adrenaline rush, replying with a wavering tone of voice. She could neither hear herself speak, nor had all her faculties back yet. "It was... releasing? Fulfilling? Weight and anger off shoulders. How much health did it have left?"

Artorian smiled like a sly fox, proudly holding up the screen with his reply as he narrated the answer. "Somewhere between three, and forty-three thousand! You killed it dead, dearest! Wonderfully done. I'm especially happy that you feel rejuvenated from getting all that upset out. Loved seeing you flex that prowess and might. You looked amazing. Star of the show!"

Ember blushed deeply, looking away as she brushed rogue strands of red hair away from her face. She tried to push him away with her other hand, but he was too far away for her to even touch him, making the act all the more adorable to Artorian. She looked like a C'towl pawing at the air, and he filed that away to tease her with later.

Lucia was giving him some serious side eye, joined with a secret smirk to the side of her lips. She knew Abyss-well that the boss only had four health, and here this romantic little monster of a boy goes and plays her up, purely to place the girl he liked on a winner's pedestal to make her feel good.

She reached over, rubbing his head. "Good boy."

He winked at her, cheeky as could be! Knowing exactly what he did while Ember looked puzzled between the two of them. She checked her own damage prompt to see how much carnage she'd actually caused, then adorably squee'd and clapped when she saw the huge number. Fifty-five thousand plus oomph to the skull was one Abyss of a cracker.

Artorian adored this, then remembered he had something for Lucia as well. He reached out, and upturned his palm. Her bow appeared as he pulled Heartstring out of his inventory. "Don't think I forgot about you, Momma Bun."

Lucia chuckled, about to go back to healing Astarte's ears as a glowing warm light enveloped her hands. She paused mid-turn, her spell fading from her fingers as her eyes went wide. The other hand slapped in front of her dropped jaw and open mouth. "How did…?"

Artorian didn't let her fall into self-pity, or let her wallow from losing the bow in the first place. That had never been her fault. He deposited the bow right into her hands, and followed up with an instant hug. "Wasn't your fault, Momma Bun. Was never your fault. The traffic cone took it from you. The art from your babies is back in your hands now. That's all that matters. You never lost their **Love**, and you never lost this either. Look at how it came home to you."

Lucia strained his shield from how tightly she hugged him back, Lenity cracking from her grip, her face hidden so he couldn't see. Artorian instead worked a hand onto her head when he felt her shoulders weakly bob against him, whispering and being supportive. "Awful day for all this rain. It's so loud, I can barely even hear it all come down. So good that your shield is keeping us dry, Lucia. Good job. We **Love** you, Momma Bun."

She nodded into his neck and shoulder, sniffling. Wiping her face with the back of her hand, Cleaning Presence had her all pristine when she let him go. Lucia grabbed his cheek, and kissed his forehead while clinging to the bow with her other arm. "Good kit."

Their healer stowed her bow, moved to Ember, and half-leaned on the team lead while pressing both hands over those long ears as the glow returned to her palms. Ember gladly held the bun up, quietly giving Lucia that extra time as Artorian innocuously turned and checked some prompts.

A quest was completed, his inventory was far lighter, a bunch of skills were rebuked, and their fourth party member had died. Dasein was no longer listed in their grouping information. None of his tools had ranked up, but the flickering was no longer anywhere to be seen in his heads up display. Out of curiosity, he sent an inspect at Lucia with an intent to see her health and mana pool, but got... nothing? That was strange.

He then looked at his own hand, flexing it. "Things are broken in the holds again. Inspect isn't working right. Also, this really should be listed somewhere? Status and inspect are both abilities that we have that aren't cataloged... anywhere? You sort of just have to know that you can do that."

Ember rubbed the side of her head, but shrugged as her ears popped alongside a sudden wince. "I heard that. That was kind of the point? There's a whole host of hidden commands that serve as developer tools, rather than player tools. I'm sure some commands might leak out, or the language will end up being the same in the future, or we end up sneaking new players the language so they try it. For the most part, the intent is for people to use the abilities to patch those gaps. Like Lucia's Acuity. Not everyone is going to figure out terms like inspect and status, so someone with an ability to show them their information suddenly has a valuable skill. We don't want to take away from the support classes, but we do want the tools just in case."

She rolled her neck. "Sure, some people will rely on it forever when they find it, but so what? Let them have it. Let people enjoy the secret, unlisted toys. It's a nice feeling to find something special. We've already subdivided inspect rankings, anyway. Let me try, I'm sure it's fine. *Inspect.*"

Ember waved her hand at him, then placed her fists on her hips as the information came up. "*Huh.* Nope. I'm wrong. That's broken. I'm not seeing half of the information I should, and your health and attributes didn't come up at all for me. I should have that, and a lot more. I'll ask what's going on when I can, but I can't say I'm surprised. I've seen a lot of Pylon banks get replaced, and things just... turn off for a while. It'll be back. If you need a workaround, we have Lucia."

The healer in question posed like a flexing bodybuilder, showing off her strength. "*Hmpf*! Glitterflit might! Always in the fight!"

She then posed all cute, and shifted into the large Basher form. "Let's get to New Haven. I got a quest alert that there's another boss fight we have to head straight into. We're all topped off, and our fatigue and need for sustenance and sleep is manageable. If we get there soon enough, we may be able to knock that out before a nap, and a trip to Vanaheim!"

Artorian nodded, then checked with Ember. "Dear? How are you?"

Ember stretched, her back popping. "*Oooh*! Much better after that set of happy noises from my spine. I'm doing well, sugar. My hearing is getting back to where it used to be, and I am looking forward to a big meal and a long sleep. Which you will not escape from. There will be a cuddle puddle in New Haven. Which I would like to get to! We should not be too far. On the way, you get to tell me if that was a Shining Ray I saw."

He turned in place, marching right to Lucia to staircase-stroll his way up and sink into his designated spot. "Tim cleared its use, and said Vanaheim was too busy to bother us. One more ability back in my pocket! Even if it wasn't useful this time around. Honestly, resistances are crazy!"

He shuffled about, then offered a hand for her to take.

Ember hoisted herself up and flopped into place. She checked her inventory for a moment, summoned the tonfas to look them over, then stowed them again. "These were great, sugar! Nice to see a goodie that is compatible with all maneuvers. There's not many of those."

Artorian pat Lucia. "We're all set to go, Momma Bun."

He then sank back into Ember's chest as her arms went around him. "Keep them. I had to give up all my melee skills and toys up to Tim so that my Pylons would stop overloading. I'm not happy about the trade, though I'm happy about having gotten to make the choice. I can't even use them right without a good… what… three hundred more points in strength? I'd need to Ad Astra… I mean, I'd need to Trans Am just to hold them both. I will find other weapons when I have the Pylon space, and some other kind of safety blanket to wrap around my singular hit point. It's cramping my style."

"Your Pylons were overloaded?" She grumbled the words, squinting as Lucia recouped her Lantern, ended her stationary protection spell, and got to jogging. "That's not… It was that roasted pyramid, wasn't it? He set your bank up so Runescript in your Pylons could be double or triple written, and make them catch fire and blow up."

Ember kneaded his chest like a C'towl, reading up on other prompts she had received from upper management. "Well done stabilizing your Pylons, sugar. I'm sorry you had to give things up, but there's a custom note here from Tim that specifically states you were keeping a promise to me. That makes me happy. I think you did well. We used to stack writing in order to save space, but I read the reports of what happened with the spawning Pylons. All we were over by was a couple thousand points, and suddenly *vwoom*! They flash fry together into that Amalgam. Messy."

Ember hugged him tight as Lucia ran across fresh snowy landscape, leaving behind another broken battlefield. Breaking her first sound barrier, she zipped out of Fuyu No Arashi's range as fast as her paws could take her, picking up extreme speed now that she didn't need to worry about others. Her big shield kept them all bundled, and that brought Lucia a unique, pleasant comfort as she hit Mach one.

Boom!

Mach two, three, and finally Mach four also seriously cramped the style of any monsters that popped up, as they neither survived a direct shield impact, nor had any hopes of catching up as Team Sleep exploded on by.

Lucia saw their destination first. "New Haven, straight ahead."

Their team leader sighed in relief, giving the order. "Run around it a few times to find and confirm the causeway. Take us in."

CHAPTER TWENTY-EIGHT

Lady Duchess stood a sentinel's watch upon the rimward march of New Haven. The tallest tower was ever less of a glacier as she kept herself well-wrapped in a sherpa bundle. In the turbulent wind, her stance remained stoic. Steadfast. Undaunted and unmoving while she held a looking glass in her hand, her attention momentarily diverted from flashes in the far distance.

She observed water pouring from what had been a taller outcrop, the frosty tip of the glacier now level with her nose as the sun chipped away at it bit by bit. They were going to need to be concerned about structural stability soon.

One day, she believed she would miss the frozen times of The Pale.

Today? She relished in watching that accursed, hardened cold die and pool at her feet. Her nose remained upturned at the water, the Iron Lady's gaze more frozen than what was left.

Her expression softened when a bright red volcanic clap on the horizon stole her attention, her eyes snapping to the event. Flipping out her looking glass, she spied the scene of combat beneath Fuyu No Arashi in time to see the Mole-Bear turn into particles. Her lips curled into a grin. "A victory, well won. Excellent. They will be here soon."

Satisfied, she handed the looking glass off to a shrine maiden before throwing part of her sherpa clean over her shoulder. This eased her walk as she turned to heel-click her way to the opposite edge of the march's top-most railing, where she had become accustomed to making declarations.

Since she'd sent off the first few New Haven-approved questing groups right before dawn, Lady Duchess had already found comfort in the new patterns now that dusk neared, used to these new people showing up. These *travelers*, as she had begun to call them. She breathed deep when enough were gathered below, repeating the same speech she had rehearsed by doing it live, several times. Lady Duchess was certain she would be delivering this welcome speech several times more.

The edge had left her voice since the first few versions of the speech. The reason hadn't been the repetition. That would have only gained in sharpness had the circumstances remained the same. The first few groups had been people and creatures of incalculable power, and then... *children*. Smiling, laughing, cheering *children* had been sent over to her New Haven. To play the game. To have fun. At *her* New Haven. For *fun*.

Lady Duchess had been so upset about the thought earlier that day, and yet the moment she'd heard that first, young, pitched fit of laughter? Her senses had been glued to the courtyard below. A girl named Ra had chased around a boy named Sett. They had tumbled and crashed into others of their ilk. Who, instead of admonishing them for the rough and tumble? The disruption to people's work? Laughed all the louder and joined the horde of activities. Sharing self-made games that showed a complexity and camaraderie found only in the kind of souls that spent all their time together.

The all-powerful? The adults? For these, she felt no affection. But for... that other side that her mother, Katarina of Duvetia, spoke of? To send their children? *Here*? The parents from that other place thought it *safe* to send their children *here*? Her heart was made of turmoil from the thought. The horrors of The Pale assailed her vision, and yet her fears found no foothold.

There was no starvation now.

No rationing by the calorie.

No clawing for one more inch of space.

No screaming winds and cutting ice.

No oppressive cold to tear the heat out of a heart.

No great sacrifices that ate blood, sweat, and tears.

No trials that demanded her Iron soul, and raw grit.

She extended her hand and caught some sunlight on her palm, relishing the warmth of it. This brightness that, even now, still stung her eyes. A detail which she wasn't sure she'd ever get used to. Looking at her palm, she could swear that a liquid made of light had gathered, even if perhaps she imagined it. Looking down at her shadow, she then couldn't help but notice the darkness it held. Some metaphor being pointed out? How absurd. There was no sheath for the sword she had become. The heart of Lady O'Dachi would always have teeth.

Her eyes lifted when her ears lingered on the origin of laughter. What music. Such a soft, happy noise. Two flickering still images of herself appeared in her thoughts. The Pale Duchess faced The Sunlight Tsarina. Words that had been thrown at her from the travelers, to her disbelief, had stuck. The identical women faced each other, judged one another, and were each appalled at what the other saw.

The Pale Duchess lifted her hand. Within it, she held a mixture of frozen slop, rusted gears, pieces of coin that had only been half-turned into pipe, an iron insignia of a sheep, and the cold, cutting, empty feeling of what it meant to know hunger.

The Sunlight Tsarina lifted her hand. Within it, she held a piece of hand-sewn cloth. The first dew flower of a spring never seen. The tingling pain of limbs waking.

Lady Duchess, daughter of Katarina, joined the duo, and lifted her hand. Within it, she held liquid light, and no more, before her mind released her.

"Travelers! Hear me!" Lady Duchess breathed in deep, about to repeat the same speech again, until her voice paused, words faltering. She would introduce herself as the Lady Duchess, the monarch of New Haven. The arbiter of the quests, and allowances of direction in a world that these travelers all believed to be a game. "My name…"

For a moment longer, she was in her head again. The circle widened, as a smaller, younger, more innocent version of Lady Duchess came forth. The girl held a sheep-shaped plushy, bound in father's wool. She looked up at the three versions of herself, and recognized them now as versions that she did not wish to be.

The three old women lowered their hands, offering the young one her pick. The child began at she who was Pale, and took the iron insignia. She then reached for the Tsarina and bypassed the flower, wanting only the cloth. Lastly, she looked up at Lady Duchess. Rather than reach, she stepped in and took the bottom of her wrinkled hand, drinking the liquid light to make it a part of her.

When a shrine maiden touched her shoulder as Lady Duchess stood on the edge, having paused in her speech, she returned to herself. She glanced at her open hand, and found it empty. Her eyes turned to her shadow, and she found a swirl of light that twisted and lived within. Churning. Fighting. Hoping.

In her mind, the three old women each placed a hand on the child, and let her walk, proud and of her own volition, right to the front. Through an opening in their castled mental chambers, and onto the physical, real edge of a balcony.

"My name…" She observed the crowd, the children enraptured regardless of her pause. Many of them had their character screens open, having already figured commands out. Some were obsessed with maximizing certain numbers. Most smiled. Excited. Happy to be here. Like it was some escape from a dreary life of repetition, while here there was challenge, excitement, and a liberty they could not find elsewhere.

That was enough.

She let go of the child, as did the others. The girl was now free to speak of her own accord. Her voice did not change, but the light in her soul did. "...is Lenore."

A strong breeze of warmth pushed through New Haven, parting clouds and bringing down fresh rays of the sun as all eyes drew to the cinematic experience. The Lady up high looked healthier now. The cold edge to her eyes had more love in it, dulling the cut when she swept them from person to person.

People who had previously heard the speech stopped what they were doing, as the de facto ruler of New Haven had never introduced herself as something other than her position before. The children, observant and primed, noticed that something was different from the norm. Particularly when others around them outright ceased conversation and stopped what they were doing, bringing their attention all the more onto Lady Lenore's words.

"I am diplomat. Arbiter. Ruler." Lenore's grip squeezed the balustrade, the rough metal no longer wrapped in cloth to protect from skin-destroying cold. "Welcome to Eternia, *travelers.*"

Her voice cut with the hunger from The Pale. "I expect great things from you."

Her voice shone with the smile of a Tsarina. "I am glad you are here."

Her voice mediated, as the Lady of the region. "I welcome you to my New Haven!"

Lenore then decided it was fine to smile. Her expression no longer needed to be that of the unmoving statue, the iron reminder that times were harsh, but she was harshest still. "May you find a home here, at the warmth of the fires. You are free to explore the mysteries within the labyrinth of pipes. You are free to leave these walls, and return at any time. You are free to descend deep into the forests of Murim. You are free to roam, and seek your destiny. New Haven is a place of new beginnings. I welcome you to yours."

A sound from behind her made Lenore turn her head.

The sight of a blip of light tearing into her region, followed by a stop and turn that caused a sonic boom, demanded her attention. The natural protections of terrain around New Haven had only increased, as the sun had time to lay on the heat. This had increased the size of the chasm protecting an entire flank of her society from a chunk of the world, but to a very fast Glitterflit who could lap all of New Haven in record time, that was moot.

Several stable in and out locations had been secured, with the causeway among them. Though they didn't look the same after so much ice melted. Lenore had to puzzle out why so many loops were being made, until she saw The Eminence slow down more and more. That made sense… one couldn't simply walk into the front gate at top spe— "Did she just jump?"

Lenore's abrupt break in her speech brought eyes to bear over the wall, not that the wall was a notable obstacle as people learned that 'bunny jump good.' From New Haven's perspective, a large golden rabbit was clearing the tallest outcrop of the rimward march by an easy three times over.

A bright blue and white flash atop the golden streak stole the show, then stopped their movements in place as the forward force was turned centrifugal. The blue and light took hold of the golden and white glow, twisted with a turn, and sent the bunny realmward before a red and white glow followed The Eminence's lead.

From Team Sleep's perspective, they couldn't manage to figure out where the causeway was. Or any of the other entrances. With too much ice melted, they were unable to recognize enough landscape features that were still similar enough to get a grip on the supposed front door. This difficulty had, on the other hand, provided Less Than Three an easy solution. "We can still see the rimward march! Plus I think that's Lady Duchess I spot up there? That's where we need to be anyway. Momma Bun, jump it! I'll turn my anti-gravity feature on and we can coast right over that wall. Afterward… ideas?"

Astarte cackled. "Trans Am it, platform stop in place, and chuck us down!"

Lucia giggled, on board with this dumb idea. "Seconded. Axes away! Maybe when all our quests are over, we can find a tavern and throw real axes for relaxes? I miss the old club activities. Oh, I see a nice ramp! Three, get ready! Launching Bun Force One in three… two… nyoom!"

Artorian toggled Wisp Flight, gripping both Ember and Lucia's wrists as they used him as an anchor to coast. Realizing why Trans Am had been mentioned, he gleefully toggled it on for extra strength and control, then used platforms to add spin and throw them down towards the top of the tower. "Trans Am!"

He burst with free-floating particles. Celestine cosmetic effects rolled out in force as he was shrouded in blue glow, accompanied with white particles as his statistics doubled and made the effort and control portions of getting his team on the ground pure child's play.

Lucia landed first, thumping into a three point hero pose before standing in her human form, her arms crossed as she beamed out the biggest grin. Astarte copied her right away, slamming down in the three point pose as well before standing and also copying the crossed arms pose and accompanying prideful smirk.

Artorian couldn't well let them down, now could he? If they wanted a flashy entrance, he was going to deliver! Rather than fall straight down, he used his platforms to add some fancy forward flips into the mixture, so that when he landed, it was nice, clean, and like a C'towl's first fall. He ended right on his feet! Rising from slightly bent knees and a hunched posture, he crossed his arms like his team, and joined their merry facial expressions.

Artorian flicked off his Trans Am, beaming at the crowd and giving them a good wave. "Good news, everyone! The spawning Pylons are *completely* busted. Travel in groups!"

He then turned to Lady Duchess and squinted. Something was different, but he didn't figure it out until he saw her shadow, at which point he couldn't help but smile. "Well, would you look at that! Who's the Child of Light now?"

He grinned wider as that comment sank into Lady Duchess's face. "I hear there's a Mechanicus Steamlord problem? As it happens, we seem to be short a party member. Come with? I figure of everyone who might have some grievances with the Generator? You're it."

He glanced at Ember, who snickered and flipped Lady Duchess a party invitation. She thought that was a grand idea, and was all for it.

Lady Duchess stared at the invitation, never having seen such a prompt. She reached over in disbelief to press accept, never having expected the chance for retribution. Her name was added to the list, and Artorian looked up from the screen with a welcoming smile. "How interesting. It is very nice to meet you, Lady Lenore."

She couldn't help but smile at the use of that name. The sound was warm. Pleasant. That Sunny, the Sovereign of the Sun, was the first to ever say it? That filled her with a love she would always keep to heart. Lenore looked at him, and nodded in approval.

This would do, but she did wish to be honest. All her prowess was specialized, and molded purely to the form and use of the O'Dachi. "I am afraid, I must admit… that I have no official class. Merely a profession."

Less Than Three then spread his arms wide, a moment of luminous constellations flickering around him before another prompt appeared next to Lady Duchess. He spoke as a divine for just a moment. "A nonexistent setback, if you do not wish it to be."

She read the entry, held back tears, squeezed the cloth in her grip, and pressed accept on the prompt. No class had ever seemed more perfect. "Thank you."

Artorian beamed, ever so proud. "Welcome to Team Sleep, *Paladin* Lenore."

CHAPTER TWENTY-NINE

The crowd cheered for Paladin Lenore as she rose from her feet, glowing bright gold while cosmetic fireworks erupted from her being and shot right up into the sky. The world itself celebrated her advancement! Once the brightness faded and her feet once more touched the ground, she raised a hand for a dainty, queenly wave as people howled excitedly.

Artorian took that opportunity to lean on the balcony, spotting Ra. Rather than cheer, she was squinting right up at him, her finger pointed in his direction with clear suspicion.

He saw her mouth the question. "Grandpa?"

Snickering in response, Artorian momentarily reached for his deity options, pulling on that lever so he could go all constellation-y for a moment. He waved back in the long-bearded old-grandfather version that she knew, enjoying that she'd spotted him in that short moment. High perception ran in the family! He liked it! Mug smash! Another!

Ra screeched, now violently pointing. "I knew it!"

Laughing, Artorian dropped the divine visual effect and returned to being plain old Less Than Three. Casually, he hopped from the railing and dropped all the way down to the courtyard, landing with a soft thud. The distance of the drop was small potatoes for his attributes. "Hello, granddaughter!"

He smirked wide on approach to the young adult, thinking of something very cheeky. "Or should I say, Ra-torian? *Hmmm?*"

Ra's words died in her throat, as her arms curled in and pulled to her chest, defending herself physically from the question. The rest of Lunella's children shrieked with laughter, many pointing at each other and cashing in on age-old bets. Ra's actual reply originated from deep-rooted panic, mixed with whatever her mind gave her as a solution. "I don't wanna go to school, I just wanna break the rules!"

That made Three pause and close an eye. He was missing context here, and imagined her saying that to Lunella while kicking and screaming. Artorian then shrugged, and smiled at her. "I don't mind, Ra. I just want you to have a good time. I never did get to spend as much time with you as I wanted. Keep up the Ra-torian thing! Find yourself some champions! But please, do not feel a need to try to copy me. You're more aggressive than I am; it's okay to let that flow."

Ra instead felt her mind snap into place, the correct question rolling from her tongue. "Can I pick you as a deity option? I want health regen!"

Artorian cackled hard, shaking his head to the negative. "Nope! I'm stepping out of that arena as much as I can and want other people to step right on in. My goodies are for the natives and NPCs only. You go the deity route! Make some of your own bonuses. If I don't need to step in to solve problems, I would be very happy about that."

A whistle from above made them turn and look up to see Astarte waving at them, followed by a thumbs up when she had her boy's attention. He nodded at her, then turned to Ra and opened his arms to offer a hug. "It was good to see you. Bump into me more when there's time? I've got a teleportation platform to go unclog."

Ra sputtered, but smiled. She hugged her grandfather-in-child-format, and both tried and failed to crush him hard, ending up hurting her own arms and chest. "I'd like that. Also, what are you made of? *Ow!*"

He laughed, that cheeky expression right back on his face before he waved at the rest of Lunella's brood. He received both grins and waves back. There was no time for a better meet and greet just yet. "Nothing much! I am but light."

He turned when ready, smoothly leaping from their courtyard level back onto the top of the tower, balancing on the railing's edge before hopping down, meandering the scant few feet to be back with the group. "Present!"

Lenore touched him on the shoulder when he was present in their circle. "I am calling the location of the boss encounter to us, rather than us descending down to the teleportation platform's level. I have always wanted to know what that button did and how it worked."

Her words were information rather than a question. She was not asking for input, but making a declaration. Just as her following words to the crowd were a declaration. "Clear the courtyard! Team Sleep will be engaging in a boss encounter. You may all observe, but not interfere."

Her words carried, and people scuttled and scurried out of the way, leaving the pentagon-shaped courtyard vacant and ready for use within the minute. Nobody, it seemed, was going to tell the only person who could assign and approve their requests *no*.

Lenore opened some windows, pushed the requisite buttons, and made an orb of light appear in the center of the courtyard. The orb scanned the available area by throwing out walls of light that spun, then retracted those panels when finished to ping green. Winking out, the entirety of the courtyard adopted a weary look, the appearance of ichor and dark metal sinking in. A deep industrial theme riveted itself into place as an overlay over the existing area, joined by sounds of heavy equipment doing work.

An unseen team of Wisps changed the look and theme of

the available space, enjoying adding their personal touches. Artorian's Truesight spotted them regardless, but he kept his mouth closed.

From the floor, a large metal panel cracked and opened, revealing an outpouring of roiling steam. To the sound of industrial trumpets, the Mechanicus Steamlord elevatored in. Artorian recognized many of the design elements from the Generator, mainly the heat and steam vents. The sharp, unfriendly pipes. The angled edges to make that blocky front into the shape of a demon's face also felt telltale and done with purpose. Other than that? The Steamlord appeared rooted to its position, having traded its mobility for… Well, he'd find out.

He scratched his head, leaning on the railing. The themes were pretty, but the mechanics seemed… odd. What was the difficulty with an opponent that didn't move? "Is Gennie going to merely sit there? There are both fish in a barrel and the broad side of a barn somewhere that make for a more difficult target."

He glanced at the party, needing some reactions. Lenore was frowning, the sight not what she expected. She also turned to the more seasoned veterans in this kind of affair. Lucia shook her head no, as she wasn't sure what was going on either. Astarte was holding her face, and thus all eyes went to her. She sighed, dropped her hands toward Less Than Three, and kept it simple. "Sugar? Jump in there and shoot a few times. You'll… you'll see. You're not going to be happy."

Confused, but intrigued, Artorian hopped into the arena to… a lackluster reception, and complete absence of fanfare. Not a notification or interesting visual element to mention made entering this boss encounter feel like it should have the gravitas it deserved. He looked back at Ember to be sure that he could just dent the boss a few times, but she nodded without any enthusiasm.

He pointed his finger at the Mechanicus Steamlord, and popped off a few kinetic lightning bolts. The first thing he noticed was that while his rounds made the normal thumpy popping sounds, there was a disturbing lack of impacts received. There was no satisfying reaction when the bolts hit the Steamlord. They struck, but ebbed away like they'd hit something else.

That the Steamlord didn't budge or attack back…? Alright, now he was fully lost. Pulling up a damage record, he groaned loud. "Damage reduction? Against melee, kinetic, lightning, and… *Forty points*? It has forty points of flat damage reduction, against everything? Before my bolts hit whatever 'shield mode' is called? I didn't even hit the shield! What am I going to do against this thing? Throw sand and insults? Shining Ray is too dangerous for the indoors, lest I put a hole in the city, and with Gattles the Gatling being moot… uhhh. I can stand here and look pretty?"

When no answer was forthcoming, he looked up at the tower where Ember was fussing with her Silverwood Bracelet, something clearly being wrong. He bent down to jump up, but shortly after his launch, he hit his head on an invisible ceiling with a **dengggg**!

Artorian fell like a sack of potatoes, groaned when crumpled on the metal floor, and held his head. "*Owww…*"

His shields also dropped like a rock, but aside from losing specific protections and Prosperity starting its countdown to patch up Lenity, the Steamlord wasn't attacking him at all.

Artorian rubbed his noggin and sat up, shooting one Abyss of a confused look at the Mechanicus boss that was very visibly and obviously keeping quiet, while also having moved mechanical parts to denote that the boss had its many eyes on him. Compared to the Mole-Bear, this was weird. "I need several explanations."

Astarte, The Eminence, and Lenore hot-dropped in and entered the arena as a group. Still, the Steamlord passively observed them, lacking both hostile intent and any interesting activity. The point where the crowd thought something more had gone wrong had already been passed, the murmuring getting loud as people started checking screens.

Still rubbing his head, Artorian made his way to Lucia for refreshed shields and related effects, even if it didn't seem necessary. Their healer laid her paw on his head, allowing him to turn and work out what was going on with Ember's bracelet. "Can I help?"

Astarte grumbled, but held the item out by stretching her arm. "I'm not sure. I stopped feeling all the contents? But in the sense that there are no contents to feel because no space is connected. I think my warehouse location disconnected from the item key? I had all my stuff in there, and now I can't get to it. I can't reach my weapon tickets, Damocles, Halcyon Nights, Surtur… nothing."

He ran his fingers through his own hair, holding up his own bracelet to ponder solutions. "Want to use mine? We can share space."

Ember snapped her attention to him, her free hand pressing to her chest. "Are you asking me to merge item pools with you, sugar?"

He smirked, coy. "Are you saying no?"

Ember blushed, grinned wide, and clicked her bracelet against his. "Yes."

Ding!

———

Notice! The warehouse keyed to your Silverwood Bracelet has been keyed to a secondary controller. Both bracelets are now able to store and take from the same warehouse. Due to both parties having hard item limitation pools, your shared 'World Boss Plus' Titles have been upgraded to 'World Boss Duo.'

———

Title: World Boss Duo.
    Requirement: World Boss character trait, shared warehouse space.
    You may no longer claim an area as your dungeon or base of operations,

and will always be considered a Roaming World Boss. Your shared maximum item limit is set to 30.

―――――

Ding!

―――――

Inventory Listing: Less Than Three.
   Autarchy's Wonder. Count: 10.
   Archimedes. Count: 1.

―――――

Inventory Listing: Astarte.
   Autarchy's Warmth. Count: 8.
   Spider Autarch's Brooch. Count: 1.

―――――

Inventory availability. Count: 10.

―――――

Lucia and Lenore both softly clapped in gentle applause, each nodding at the other that this scene had been both sweet and wholesome. Ember then successfully crushed the life out of Artorian, whose next sound was **glrk**!

"Baby bun!" Lucia fussed about needing to redo the one-hit shields *again* as they all popped like balloons. With the boss still sitting there and watching them without taking any actions, Lucia had both the time and the mana for the refresh. "Are we still doing this? Or is something else going on? Normally boss encounters trigger by themselves, and rarely when players are ready. This one is sitting on its paws, waiting on us."

"Conversation." The bellows in the Mechanicus Steamlord wheezed hot as it spoke, flame and heat flaring from its many vents as it gutturally uttered that one word, eating through coal and stolen mana to do so. Its observation slits shifted, looking directly at Artorian. "I know of your tales. Wandering Sun. I remember you. Administrator. I recognize you. Accords maker. I request parlay. Realm-Breaker."

CHAPTER THIRTY

Artorian considered this development. "I can't say I'm unhappy about a game giving me the option to talk my way through a boss fight. That's a massively effective tool for keeping me engaged."

He began by turning to Lenore. "Lady of the House? I do not wish to deter you from—"

She instantly shot a hand up, pausing him. "Less Than Three? You are a good boy, but I wish to see this difficulty laid low. It does not matter to me if that is through physical violence, or verbal violence. I am well past the age where I feel the need to do things myself, to cross the Is and dot the Ts on my documents. If I never have to draw my O'Dachi for this Generator to submit, then you shall find me thoroughly pleased. Do I desire this catharsis? Of course. Do I require it? No."

Less Than Three replied with a polite nod when her hand dropped, checking the expressions of his party. Lucia provided approval after giving his shields a twice-over and being satisfied with the results. Astarte? She was grinning like a wild tiger!

Ember was happy to observe this hunt while bouncing on her toes, her free hand fiddling with her Silverwood Bracelet while distracted and blushing. "Get 'em, honey. Go set their world on fire."

With approval, and thoroughly enjoying Ember all bubbly, he strode to the middle of the arena where the Mechanicus waited. Artorian crossed his arms once in front of the sassy Steamlord who was refusing to fight. "You understand, before we begin, that I have had it up to here with demon shenanigans of all kinds?"

He moved his hand above his head, showing he was over capacity for their brand and flavor of Abyss.

"Comprehension." The bellows in the Mechanicus Steamlord wheezed hot once more, further flame and heat flaring from its many vents. Looking directly at Artorian, its coals were quick with the terms. "I shall submit, if defeated solo."

Artorian squeezed the bridge of his nose. Demons were always funky, but this one was dancing to music that he couldn't hear yet. "Let me guess. You want to one-versus-one me? Specifically me."

"Affirmative." Heat wheezed from the Steamlord, seals flexing and bulking before fusing back into place as the hot metal cooled. "Interest arose from an earlier challenger. The man with two swords, and pot on head? Particularly persistent. Similar challenge desired. Stories of the Cathedral of the Luminous Prism, prevalent. Dual-wielding Divine of Speed, rumors disbelieved. Proof, necessary. Solo duel, *challenged*."

Ding!

———

Notice! You have been challenged to a duel!
   Challenger: New Haven's local area boss: The Mechanicus Steamlord.

———

Artorian squinted. He squinted hard. Something was *off*, and it wasn't the Steamlord's reluctance or conditions. The side of his nose tingled, and that was even more suspicious to him. He inhaled cautiously, speaking with suspicion. "Is this person... present?"

The eyes of the Steamlord, or what was artistically being formed to represent them, moved to the stands. Artorian moved his eyes to catch the boss's sightlines, spotting the poorly dressed individual in possession of two swords while wearing an upturned pot over his head.

Intrigued, Artorian turned his gaze to his party, and answered their unspoken question with a swift nod. He was going to accept this engagement. Ember would not have encouraged him had the challenge been too great, or would have stopped him when the very visible prompt came up, that screen hanging next to him. Therefore, this Steamlord must be a lesser threat than the Mole-Bear.

Lenore grabbed hold of her blade at his nodding motion, and offered her legendary weapon when she grasped his intended direction. Instantly helpful. "You have my blade."

Lucia had already turned, but her ear swiveled on her head at the mention of Lenore offering her O'Dachi, suddenly remembering that Three had no weapons. Copying the move, Lucia held her Heartstring bow out a mere moment later, not going to be outdone by their freshest addition to the team. "You have my bow."

This action was flanked by Ember holding up one of the tonfas. Two was too much, but he could certainly handle one. "You have my beatstick."

Sound from the stands erupted chaotically at the sight, followed wholeheartedly by the onlookers as people unsheathed weaponry from every direction, offering it to the warrior in the arena.

Artorian looked around when those sounds filtered in en-masse, his attention wavering away from the boss as his jaw dropped at what the people were doing. Echolocation burdened him as he could see the weapons being offered, regardless of many of them being behind him.

He had yet to form a reply when four glimmering blades shot down from the sky and added themselves to the collective. Thumping down in a clean line, the weapons embedded themselves into the arena, slicing into the floor like ships pulling into port.

Separated by exact matching distances waited **Sorrow**, the black Katana. **Compassion**, the celestine Albion Principe. **Pride**, the rainbow Claymore. And **Explosion**, the nitroglycerin Assault Nagamaki. Each concept weapon mentally saluted at him as if reporting for a duty that was long awaited.

He was touched, but a thumping beat from the sky demanded his attention while too many things happened at once, as they often tended to.

Roaring through the clouds, the blades' method of transportation broke into the scene from above with noise and fanfare, heralding the uncanny timing and arrival of the group You've Yar'd Your Last Har. Here to yee their first haw. Artorian recognized Zephyr in ship form instantly. Crewed by... Oh. *Oh no.*

Both his hands slowly held his head as the realization and horror sunk in. This was a disaster in the making. She was glowing a sequential set of colors—red, green, and blue—but that was garnishing compared to the crew.

Hans himself started the headcount, dressed up as some oblique pirate captain named Morgan, his leg dramatically pressed up on Zephyr's bow. Hans Jr, dressed identically in the silly pirate getup, sat and rested on his father's bent knee while held tight, happily waving a toy sword around while making what must be happy, screechy sounds.

If only those were audible over the thumping madness of the Gnomish musical team present on deck, each acting as a roadie to a Wisp named DJ. That giant sign was hard to miss, outlined in neon as the music thundered out from the amplifiers of Zephyr's hull. Maybe those concentric circle designs on her hull had something to do with that? Wouldn't be a surprise.

Riding this wave of music, Megheara the bard belted out a

matching song! As Meg sang to her heart's content, he spotted Oak in a makeshift crow's nest. Artorian spoke to nobody, and everyone who could hear him at the same time. "Please don't do this to me."

The sound of belted song and thumping music was carried on pinkish cotton-candy clouds that poured free from Oak, the Ancient, most innocent of Wood Elves. Could this disaster get any worse? No… No, don't ask that. Don't *think* that.

Snug in their nest, Oak was once again floating on a fat host of pink fluff while giggling to himself… Or herself. Who knew. They giggled like they had heard the funniest joke in the universe, and couldn't get a hold of themselves. The vivacious pink fumes also appeared to increase Zephyr's speed, filled with sparkles for effect. Artorian suddenly doubted the sparkles were for effect, and turned to Lenore. "Could you…?"

Stern and stoic, Lenore became ice and iron. "I'll deal with it."

He nodded, holding his hand up to kindly pass on the weaponry. "Thank you, everyone, for the offer. I do not wish this assistance, but it warms my heart to see so much **Love** and kindness surround me. Stow your armaments! I have a plan."

Artorian then dropped his attention on the four swords, having more specific requests for them. "If you wish to assist me, curtail the airship crew. I bet they are armed with something silly. Such as Leave Enemies Distraught weaponry, while the Wisp up there is likely going on about how his weapons glow… With the Gnomes snapping back that their weapons *work*."

He slid into sturdier footing. "Zephyr is trouble enough. Meg only amplifies that insanity. Adding Oak to that mixture is no different than adding Hans to it, and it appears they are *both* present. I cannot handle the amount of rogue-laden sass coming my way."

The concept weapons mentally saluted, acquiescing to Artorian's will. They pulled themselves free from the metal-coated ground without difficulty, twirling in place before shooting back to the sky.

Ember snickered, watching the scene as she stowed the tonfa. "You say that like it's a bad thing. My concern is what Zephyr is carrying. There's an entire SCP foundation—a Spotter Collection Program—waiting to disembark. I can see their bald heads all piling out of the aft portholes, and those maddening smiles speak volumes. They're going to break... all the things. Poor Tim."

She chuckled, having a thought and providing the content to her boy. "Honey, for this upcoming fight, since you're going to do it unarmed...? Remember my lecture on strength. Recall how a Mage draws Mana into their bodies to strengthen themselves, and dilate time."

She smirked wide, her expression warm as sunshine. "I think I know what you're going to do, and I can't wait to see it."

Ember then gripped Lucia by the shoulder, and helped drag the Momma Bun from the arena when she wasn't taking the initiative to leave, following Lenore's iron-powered strides.

Artorian released a thick sigh.

How tempting that had been. Particularly his curiosity with the Assault Nagamaki. There was a mind in there now? Who was it? Could he hope it to be Majev? No. His nose always knows, and his nose was leading him back to the Mechanicus encounter. Rolling his shoulders, he waited for the arena to be clear of everyone save for him and the Steamlord.

The thumping music from above worked to his advantage as Zephyr circled on high, accosted and distracted. The next part of their conversation would go unheard. Good. Less Than Three slid both his arms against his spine, holding them against his lumbar as he properly flickered on Truesight and confirmed some suspicions, his blue eyes shining a bright cyan. "So... Can you tell me what you *really* want to tell me? It's about time you drop the act. Your shadow doesn't match your appearance, *Lady* Steamlord."

Caught, the boss pushed on its armored confines from

within, the protective walls cracking, bending, bulking to pop their rivets. To the tune of Tim's dark mechanical organ music, busy humming the Caestus Metallican, the area boss broke free from its stationary bunker. Revealing a smooth, advanced, equally Tim-inspired Mechanicus Golem that strode calm and confident onto the arena field. The Steamlord attuned to the form of a battle-armored lady, complete with an instant change in voice.

Where previously the Steamlord spoke gutturally, as if from the forge and bellows, now the sound was smooth and easy. A touch of metal in the throat, sure, but definitely feminine, hostile, and just as direct. The boss repeated herself, pinging Artorian's duel prompt with a glowing border. "Mechanicus Steamlord Melania challenges Less Than Three. Do you accept?"

Adopting a martial stance from a skill he currently did not have, Artorian prepared Deny the Blow, uncaring that he currently did not possess his 'No' style, as far as the system was concerned. What he wanted to accomplish in this bout had nothing to do with damage dealt. The system did not dictate what he did and did not know, a pink and cyan glow gathering about his being. "I accept."

A chime whistled in the arena, the duel accepted. Not as a bout between a player and a boss encounter, but as an engagement between equals.

Melania shifted her pose, adopting a combat stance. "Opponent confirmed. Noting lack of dual wield weapons. Own weaponry will not be restricted. Access to duel listing granted. Confirming identity. Pass. Identity confirmed. Maximizing output. Engaging."

Artorian rolled his shoulders, bouncing on his toes as he watched the Steamlord manifest two bizarre—but thematically fitting—blades of steam in both of her hands. Their sudden appearance began with a shrill call, accompanied by an outpouring of heat and angry wet air. "You would have gotten confirmation of who and what I was regardless, Mechanicus.

That brings us to the exchange of our conversation. I will fight you, if that is what you need."

Artorian squeezed his hands into fists one digit at a time, Voltekka's cobalt lightning coating them as the electrical charge licked and danced between his fingers. "Make no mistake, Steamlord Melania. During this little bout? You will tell me everything on how a demon falls in **Love**."

CHAPTER THIRTY-ONE

The Steamlord fumed at him like a boat horn, releasing a steam-based breath attack that was more show than harm from this distance. Charging from her position hard enough to put a dent in the metal floor with an array of sparks, she sliced down with her left steamblade, denying his accusation with clear anger. The intelligence in her words, on the other hilt, rose! "I am *not* in love!"

Her immaterial sword swung, but struck only blurred imagery. Her metal wrist met and countered flesh. Melania's swing was sent wild as Less Than Three appeared in her face mid-spin, elbowing her in the head with his free arm. The blow sent the Steamlord staggering off, physics functioning as they should. Her body twisted unnaturally to stabilize, able to twist on a central core rather than a spine. This increased her recovery speed and footing prowess, returning to the fight moments after being blown out of it by physics.

"*Uhu.*" Less Than Three appeared from nowhere next to her head a second time, already in the middle of a roundhouse kick that immediately hit spicy paydirt as sparks and electric effects fizzled. The golem stumbled to the side as the same spot on her head got kicked, her frame skidding across the metal floor. Scrambling for support as her forced trip sent up a shower of sparks, Melania recovered with a repeated set of small hops after unnaturally voldo-twisting to be upright.

The damage from both strikes had been minimal, her exoshell not even dented, her health bar barely nudged. Her opponent, on the other coal pile, was rolling his arm and opposing ankle as if those impacts had hurt him. Several of his layered shields were already missing as a pulsing field played over the main one. Damage being repaired?

Damage being repaired.

Artorian checked himself so he did not wreck himself, coping with the creepy method Melania used to recover her footing. He was too used to people with normal spines. Lenity had taken a scratch, so Prosperity had gone off to start patching. He could already hear Lucia groan, their Momma Bun shouting from the stands. "Not even two minutes? Not two minutes!"

He snickered at her reasonable outburst, but focused on the fight. Melania was on the offensive, her voice shrill. "Demons do not have feelings!"

Artorian turned his head to look over his own shoulder, villainously hanging his head back so she could see his taunting expression, and knowing grin. "Liar."

Steam burst from Melania's seams, her golem body wrenching from within as her Demon-housing steam core handled that accusation poorly, the seals on her frame glowing a hot red from pure tension. Vents opened from her legs and back, propulsion applied to her steps as she charged him with a speed that would have blindsided any Midgard-leveled opponent. With a precision swing, Melania vengefully cleaved the head off her opponent.

It wasn't until the steam from her own attack cleared that she saw Less Than Three had squatted down, unimpressed. Arms on his knees, she interpreted the way he looked up at her like he was reading a book. Filtering her existence out by the numbers and reducing her to—

"What's his name?"

Stumbling and missing her combination strike as the boy slapped her with broken expectations, another sharp whistle fumed from within. Her slash altered to a lunge with several dexterous backsteps, but he was gone when she came around to dedicate the point straight into his heart.

A fizzling, electric *thumph* originated from behind her. Grabbing her leg, Less Than Three used her existing momentum against her. Flipping her over and letting her spin like a wheel a few times, he stepped in sharp and fast. One pushy palm-strike to the abdomen later, and Melania the Steamlord was sent sailing into the domed shield keeping the arena boxed in. A loud *deng* resounded on impact, with shimmers of movement coursing through the dome that ebbed out, like a droplet striking calm water.

Artorian rolled his shoulders, happy with the cloak. "Well done, Archimedes! Loving this Shunpo, flash-steppy thing."

The stun did not appear to have taken effect this time. He was certainly using it. Did he need to use the damage effect as well for it to work? That was worth a try, but first, he had a thought that needed an answer. He gripped the brooch, squeezing it. "Team? Is Lady Duchess… I mean, is Lenore in earshot? I need to know what kind of shield we're domed in with."

Lucia's voice answered him through a crackle. "Asking."

Artorian glanced at the stands. Lucia made it to Lenore at the speed of light, but what caught his eye was that the poorly dressed man with the pot on his head was gripping the railing hard enough to indent it. He stepped to the left when Melania charged, walking the few mere steps to be out of her direct-line lunge. Electrosense had filled the confines of the domed arena, and now felt comforting as he did not need to keep line of sight on the Steamlord to know where she was.

He saw Lenore open screens with Lucia present, checking

information before she leaned in to talk into Momma Bun's brooch. "The Voice of the World says 'Absolute.' Nothing in. Nothing out. We seem to have been able to leave due to not being the intended target of the duel, but you are stuck there until the duel is done."

He nodded in appreciation, tapping the brooch. "Thank you, Lenore, that's what I needed to know. How's the show from up there? Satisfactory?"

Lenore cackled, amused that he felt the urge to ask. "Curious what you're up to, bright one, but enjoying the smack-down nonetheless. We can't hear what you're talking about, and I'm not being provided spoilers. Astarte has this knowing grin plastered on her face, and I hunger. Otherwise? I was worried when you had no weapons, but you're making a showcase to all the newcomers that one needs no weapons. All we need to do is *style* all over our opponents."

In full agreement, he spun on his heel, twirling past another charge from Melania, who was seriously sick of his attitude and behavior when it came to this fight. He was clearly playing around. She fumed at him, burning through shrill speech. "Fight. Me!"

Artorian raised an eyebrow as he watched her feet screech over the ground, metal sparking against metal. To emphasize his feelings, he stuck his hands into his pockets. "I'll repeat myself. What's his name? What did he do to catch your attention? What is your real name, Demon? Will you tell me? Or will I find out the hard way? I guarantee you, I will know within moments, either way."

He ducked below another angry, wild swing of a steam weapon. The shape of a halberd was adopted this time, before the gaseous expulsion morphed back into twin blades. He backpedaled and played the dodging game, alley-ooping around the trajectories of weapon strikes.

To the crowd, their exchange of blows was a rapid, heated flurry of attacks and dodges. To Artorian, he was watching the wet blades come at a speed that gave him enough time to play a round of Go Fish before needing to pick where he was positioning himself to get out of the way.

He didn't have any true dilation abilities, but the gap between their attributes was too much, and Ember's reminder of the strength lecture was too on point. What was the math on perception versus action speed anyway? Just how much of a difference between the numbers mattered? He was sitting at seven-fifties in terms of attributes, and he felt about... six or seven? Seven times faster than Melania. With a healthy dose of 'ish' added, in terms of how much he felt he could exert in order to make the difference matter. Why had he never tried this before? If this worked with intent, why had he ever needed the ability? Or did people simply not think of filling their Mage body with all their energy to get the most out of it?

Granted... Ember had needed to specifically tell *him*. Best not to be hypocritical, as he'd failed in his own assessment and assumption. From a different viewpoint, this was instead an excellent trick to learn.

An excellent trick that suddenly made the end of his stamina bar turn red, the edge flashing in his Acuity's heads up display. A trick that cost chunks from the maximum value of his stamina bar? *Ah.* There was the rub. Exerting like this dealt burny damage, like to his mana bar.

He windmill-struck a steamblade blow away, denying the attack as he spun while upside down. Being able to run in the middle of the air on platforms, with anytime footholds on any surface, provided him a mobility that Melania simply wasn't able to match, regardless of her contortionist curiosities.

When conveniently positioned in the air above the Steamlord, Artorian snap-kicked Melania in the back of the head to send her crashing down to a knee. As much as he was in the fight, he was distracted by consideration of the prior topic. The hypocrisy may be exactly it? A mortal would never think to inhabit more of themselves merely because some numbers went up. They would be happy with the increased numbers and use them, but they wouldn't truly *be* them. That required experiences as a cultivator, with self-empowerment as a minimum, and knowing what it felt like to be a Mage as a more averaged out sensation.

Ember's description of using strength, versus *using* strength, had been critical. The thought was minor, and small, but the difference in output was breathtaking. Alternatively, dilation had been baked into the game on some level, and he was being allowed to play with it?

Hard to tell. "Ask Tim later. Smack a Steamlord now."

The ground was still trembling and vibrating from the sheer force Artorian had used to make the Mechanicus golem bend the knee, when she countered him. The boss swiveled her head around, once more reminding him that the word 'spine' was not in Melania's lexicon. He dodged the surprise steam-breath attack that she unleashed.

A clever ruse! Shame he was faster.

While the Steamlord got up and spun its body pieces to be back in a more-correct orientation, he used another Shunpo to appear directly behind her once more. The golem air-swiped with a scythe made of steam, but he was on ground level, the strike clearing a full two feet above his head. Melania clearly couldn't see behind her like he could, otherwise she'd have known that. A two-step staircase advance, and a *deng* impact of his knee to the back of the skull, sent the machine down into a prostrating position. Head slammed to the floor, hands and knees touching the ground as the metal flooring under the boss buckled, indenting at the pressure points.

This should be enough? There was a limit to poking a hornet's nest, and he should about be there. Artorian glanced at the pot-helmet man, seeing the railing under his hands thoroughly destroyed. That was, in fact, confirmation enough. He swung his sight back down to the Steamlord, and made good on his threat. "Inspect."

———

You have encountered: Area Boss: Mechanicus Steamlord. 'Melania.'
  World: Eternia.
  Realm: Midgard.
  Region: New Haven.
  Terrain: Metal Courtyard.
  Circumstance: Area Boss Encounter.
  Local Event: Official Duel.
  Unique Properties: None.
  Racial Template: None.
  Species: Demon inhabited Golem.
  Demon Name: Mallorca, the Scarlet Aeonia.
  Cultivation Rank: C.
  Attribute Bonus: 24 to All.

———

Detected Trait: Three Stage Encounter.
  Detected Ability: Armaments of Steam.
  Detected Ability: Reconfiguration.
  Detected Ability: Demon Mode.
  Detected Skill: Melee Mastery.
  Detected Skill: Adaptive Protocol.
  Detected Skill: Adaptive Steam.

———

Damage Reduction: 40 Versus All.

———

Protection: Immunity to Status Conditions.
  Protection: Immunity to Dark Damage.
  Protection: Resistance to Heat-themed Damage.
  Protection: Resistance to Water-themed Damage.
  Protection: Resistance to Pressure-themed Damage.
  Vulnerability: Weakness to Electric-themed Damage.

Vulnerability: Weakness to Frost and Cold-themed Damage.

———

Attack 1: Flurry of Blades.
   Attack 2: Steam Lunge.
   Attack 3: Steam Breath.
   Attack 4: Waterfowl Dance.

———

"Again with the horde of resistances. Is electric-themed damage different from electric damage directly? I'm losing my grip here. I already forgot what that other prompt said." Artorian sighed and stopped the information from rolling in before the system prompts could turn into another Full Inspect. He hadn't wanted a Full Inspect. Just her name and, maybe if it worked, her attributes and… oh, there those were! "Persnickety little system, aren't ya?"

———

Characteristics of Mechanicus Steamlord. 'Melania.'
   Stage 2: Lady Steamlord.
   Strength: 124.
   Dexterity: 123.
   Constitution: 250.
   Intelligence: 55.
   Wisdom: 35.
   Charisma: 33.
   Perception: 38.
   Luck: 34.
   Karmic Luck: 0.

———

Ding!

———

Warning!
   Mechanicus Steamlord: 'Melania' has activated Demon Mode.
   Updating values.

———

Characteristics of Mechanicus Steamlord. 'Melania'.
   Stage 3: Demon Mode.
   Strength: 248.
   Dexterity: 246.
   Constitution: 500.
   Intelligence: 110.
   Wisdom: 70.
   Charisma: 66.
   Perception: 76.
   Luck: 68.
   Karmic Luck: 0.

———

Artorian… didn't know what to think. Impressive for Midgard values, probably? Was this Melania's… No. There was no reason for him to use that name anymore. Was this Mallorca's big super move? Why did this feel so… human? So simple. This was one of *his* tricks, and he dismissed his information screens to see what happened to the Steamlord. "I feel like this multi-stage silliness is going to come standard with boss encounters…"

Melania's chest buckled open from within, the burning black demon-core exposed, covered in tar, the black goop spilling out from within, the dark-aligned ichor aggressively spreading and covering the Mechanical Construct with smooth, blackened material. Like a Venom that burst forth and coated her mechanical body as a shifting symbiote of muscle and slime. He'd seen this trick before, and plenty. Zeus's little minions inhabited by their Demons had this effect in spades. She likely gained regeneration of some sort, and a sudden weakness to Aura, had Mallorca not been inside of Eternia.

He shrugged, and finished his sentence as he Shunpo'd directly in front of her, this time with everything active. The stun was blocked by the golem's immunity, but the damage got through just fine. Even with twenty-one percent burnout, he had a solid 28,144 value mana pool. Five percent of that still dealt a whopping 1,407 damage, minus a meager forty.

His hand snapped forth and grabbed her tar-covered face, shifting into his own next form as he activated Trans Am with feeling. The Demon reflexively grabbed his wrist with both of its own hands, but the act was futile.

Supplanting the vague prior glow he'd been sporting, the blue and white particles of Trans Am poured free from him as his fingers squeezed, the metal beneath the tar stressing, buckling, and cracking.

"Speaking of boss encounters, you should likely have picked the target of your duel a touch less pridefully." He growled rather than spoke as his attributes overpowered the souped up Demon's, having no issues whatsoever with putting the fear of the divines deep into the symbiote, happy to break her claim that Demons didn't have feelings.

"After all, Mallorca. I *am* one."

CHAPTER THIRTY-TWO

From Mallorca's perspective, this was insanity.

She unloaded another steam-breath attack directly into his hand, but the wet heat licked against her opponent's flickering shield. She was definitely doing damage, with her breath attack dealing an easy two-hundred steam damage a second. Two hundred and a bit.

For her trouble, she was thrown to the ground with an unceremonious *p'thank*! No thankfulness was found in the sound as she once again found herself pancaked onto the floor. Twisting with mechanical contortion, the symbiote tar tore from her mechanical frame due to the wrenching movement. The harm was superficial. The ichor reassembled in a wet and goopy blanket of seamless connection after safely backflipping away, but safe was a relative term.

One moment she had eyes on him.

Then *pop*.

A fizzle of electricity, and in a flash he had stepped away to be elsewhere. Her world spun against her will when another roundhouse kick caught her from a blind angle, the hit cracking undershell in the left segment of her upper ribcage. Mallorca was not liking these odds, and she always calculated them.

As a Mechanicus Steamlord, she had usurped immunities and resistances that most could only dream of. She had the vaunted and all-praised damage resistance versus all. In her first form, bunkered up? Those values had been multiplied by a factor of ten, allowing her to measure and assess her opponents before transforming into Melania, the second stage of her Steamlord form. The original host. While she lost those bonuses in form two, she gained her entire offensive arsenal in trade. An arsenal that, up to now, had laid low every comer and every taker.

Her time as a stationary being of contracts most ill was at an end. She could claim and taste oppression over others directly now. Why bother with the difficulties of slowly siphoning mana when one could relish in the gifts of the system when defeating another? Bringing the hand-delivered morsels directly to her not only for free, but in *reward* of her wanton murder.

She desired zeal and death against the breakers of words, who had slipped from her contractual grasp, of course. Such as the Lady Duchess. Those were tantalizing treats, if only they offered themselves. Yet they remained treats, for she had never been bested in her second form... but once. By that accursed, unyielding, unforgiving, unbreaking pain in her core with that dumb pot on his head.

She charged at the luminant one, clad in particulates of white and blue. Yet the strike lacked focus. As a Mechanicus, her stamina was infinite. If she hadn't been harangued by moves that specifically toyed with physics and tossed her around like a mechanical ragdoll, she would have been able to lay waste by laying into her opponent with endless, flowing combinations. Endless barrages. Endless waltzes.

Instead, in her third and most powerful form, she was as powerless as the weakest specter of the Abyss. She should perhaps have recalculated when her measurements had shown that this divine was at its weakest. Missing tools, devoid of weapons, pathetic in level... Honestly, a level *one* divine? Could there be an easier, more delicious morsel to sup upon?

Hubris, Mallorca thought, was a trait in which she had invested too many skill points. Demon Mode allowed her to bring out the full force of her pre-game prowess. To coat the stolen body in her true self, and heal from wounds so grievous and obscure that it would confound the most serene of minds... And here this boy was looking at her the way she looked at food.

An electric fizz popped. Her vision collapsed to the ground. More movements of hurried separation and the making of space followed, returning her to the pre-existing stalemate.

Another electric fizz popped. Her vision collapsed to the ground a second time. Faster. Sooner. The opponent was losing patience, and her health bar...? Her health bar was not liking that instant bite of well over a thousand damage each time he appeared unseen, taking big, meaty chunks out of her with the gnawing force she reserved for her own meals. Was this just desserts, perhaps? To have finally bitten off more than she could chew? To have miscalculated? Or was this all, truly, and purely because she was not answering questions?

An opportunity?

A worthwhile experiment. Mallorca filled the voice box of Steamlord Melania with her ichor, and spoke using the oppressed creature's cadence and words. The Steamlord's own mind and voice within the core attempted to struggle, but that tiny thing was muffled easily enough. "Why do you care?"

That appeared to perk her opponent right up! Instead of appearing from nowhere, the child held his chin, and pondered. This provided Mallorca opportunity after all, reconfiguring her steam armament into a spear. Slashing weapons had no merit. She could not finish the arc of a swing without there being enough time for her opponent to turn it back against her. That passive fighting style of his was beyond infuriating. His physical strikes were doing nearly no damage, but all that force was translated into physics, and tossed her about or cracked her interior.

An electric fizz popped, and Mallorca dared not believe that it caused her to *flinch*. The boy, the divine, spoke to her from behind, leaning on her shoulder while laying sideways on vacant air, as if there was a convenient bench there that she simply couldn't see. His words were measured, full of inquisition. "I care. Are you... going to tell me? Or do I have to begin persuading you?"

Another flinch struck Mallorca. That was impossible. She was *immune* to conditions. Especially physical conditions. Surely this upstart had not scared her so that the Voice of the World, working its infernal systems, saw fit to allow this behavior a bypass to those metrics? The Voice of the World was impartial. The Voice of the World was **Order**. It would not allow itself to be swayed. Least of all by some child.

The Steamlord twisted to stab with the spear, but its immaterial tip stopped inches short of his chest. The boy had grabbed her wrist, and by raw, brute strength, stopped her cold. He leaned in slow, whispering to the location an ear should be, even if that didn't matter to the Demon. "Convincing, then. Do you see the man with the pot on his head? Shall I point him out to you?"

His arm crawled around her neck before he spoke, the boy pointing his single finger towards the challenger that had been coming to see her non-stop. The challenger who had persistently returned to her, again, and again, and again, of his own volition. Undaunted by death. Undeterred by loss. How something inside of her ached with pain and filth at the thought that she enjoyed that so. "Let me provide you with an incentive. If you *don't* tell me... I change targets. Like so."

Something flipped inside of Mallorca.

A lever she hadn't known, or been aware of, or realized had

an existence. The words of the child, combined with a truly ominous color that gathered in a blob of light at his finger, aimed *directly* at the man with the pot on his head. The sight turned her world upside down. If... If the divine could best her with raw strength, as if she were no challenge whatsoever, and he was suddenly a caster instead of a hand-to-hand fighter? That changed all the variables. It changed them for the worst. Physical damage was doing nothing, because this magician couldn't deal physical damage. He'd been appearing all around the field, and *that* was doing the harm. He was no fighter! He'd been tricking her! A direct attack from a caster would be utterly devastating.

Mallorca felt sick.

Truly, awfully, disgustingly sick. As it fired—this beam of light, bubbling with blackened red—made her reflexively shove all her might and body mass into the hand and wrist of her opponent. To force the beam to veer off course. To force it to miss. To force it not to hit. Anything, except for that beam to hit! "No!"

Panic gripped her. Fear took hold. She couldn't budge the wrist, not even slightly. Her head turned to look at what this terror of a child was looking at, but to her own horror, he was looking directly at her. The beam doubled, then tripled, then quadrupled in width as it fired off in full force. He spoke to her like an aged wise man, with the voice of a child. "**Love** can be cruel. Especially when you don't realize you're about to lose it."

Mallorca's insides felt like they were breaking. Twisting. Tearing. She was sickened, physically, at the sensations roaring through her. She was appalled, mentally, that he could... possibly have been right. Her mind blanked, her calculations frozen. Mallorca screamed, not knowing why, nor understanding. Her blades fizzled out, backplates and every panel along her spine breaking wide open. A torrent of steam exploded from the back of her body, all force concentrated on his wrist to move it even a little. Just a little. Just a little before the beam could hit... before it could hit...

She heard the impact of beam to dome. She heard something shatter. She imagined, horror upon horrors, that it was the dome. She imagined the beam tearing through the challenger that had come to see her, to face her, again and again. This singular being who came to her, not because of anything she could offer. Not because of anything he could take. He came purely for the challenge. Purely to face her. Purely to see her. He came just for her and that was important. It was so important.

Her voice broke, the sound of tears heard in the tone even if her body had none to shed.

"...No."

The beam attack ended, and she felt broken on the inside. She couldn't bear to look. She couldn't bear to turn. To face reality. To allow her calculation engine even the option or possibility of the thought that something she had gained, and ended up enjoying so much after all, was now gone. Likely along with the entire wing and wall of that side of the arena.

She raised her fist as the child eased down to stand on both feet, her balled-up metal and ichor hand falling and striking the shield covering his chest without any damage being dealt. She couldn't muster force. Her attributes meant nothing. She felt hollow. She felt like she wanted to break apart and ebb away. She crashed her fist on his chest again, but incurred no damage. There was no strength to the motion. There was only emotion. The sickening feeling in her core was overpowered entirely, by a category of grief so intense that Mallorca couldn't speak.

Instead, her ichor dripped down from the head of the Steamlord as her tarry form melted, suffering from a complete lack of focus. Her tears were simulated even if she otherwise had none to shed. Her fist rose, and crashed down. Fruitless. Her fist rose, and crashed down. No damage dealt as she hiccupped through utter confusion. "How could you? How could...?"

Nothing made sense. She was a Demon.

She should relish in this pain. Celebrate this suffering. Cheer for the death of an enemy. When she finished an opponent? They came back. Those were the rules of this place, challengers could come back. To be removed by a divine? There was an assumption of permanency in her head that she could not shake, and the thought of that particular challenger being gone overpowered all the feedback loops ingrained in her. There was only a feeling worse than death, and her words spilled forth freely, no longer barred by her hubris. "He was the best."

Mallorca raised her fist, thumping it harmlessly on his shoulder as she slumped against the child and began losing footing. "He came back. He kept coming back."

The fist thumped, the shield hummed. "Not for a prize. Not for a deal. He came back for me. He only ever kept coming back for *me*."

Her fist thumped, but the shield didn't even hum from the impact anymore. "A million deals. A thousand contracts. To retain anyone. To have anything I could call mine. To possess or feel like something was mine. That some rancid, worthless little corner of the world could be *my* rancid little corner of the world."

Mallorca tried to raise her fist, but lacked the strength to do even that. The ichor was leaking from her mechanical sockets, pooling at her feet as she lost the ability to keep her symbiotic form together. Her eyes unfocused, seeing through a lens of wetness. "He came back. For me. Just for me. I looked forward to it. I counted my minutes by it. He comes, we fight, he grows. He bests me slightly more each time. I clear the arena quickly when I know the timer is close. I empty the queue so it can be his turn. I relish the company more than the bout. I win, and I… I *yearn*."

Her fist trembled on his shoulder, the boy's particulates of white and blue fading away in favor of a soft, warm, pink nimbus. His hand was on the exposed core easily available from her blown out back, where she had put more force than was ever safe in an attempt to… do something stupid, she supposed. "Now he is gone, and I am empty. I am so empty."

A rough set of clinks and clanks decoupled the steamcore from the Steamlord, and Mallorca found herself removed from its center as the pink glow extracted her. Existing instead as a concentrated puddle of shapeless, inky blackness that looked like it was melting from the side of his palm.

The boy clank-clinged the core back into the Steamlord after, then held up a finger to signal a pause. When Melania, the actual Steamlord, once again had control over the Mechanicus frame, the Steamlord took one look at the situation and bowed its entire torso to nod at Three's motion. The genderless being then took clunky, ungraceful steps away.

Mallorca felt hollow as she was carried in blob form to the edge of the arena. The boy spoke, but his tone was gentle. Anything but harsh. "Do you yield this duel, Mallorca?"

The blob shrugged, out of it. The puddle bubbled to speak. "Nothing has merit. I yield the duel."

The dome fell away, the courtyard swiftly returning to its prior, non-metallic counterpart. Mallorca barely noticed, hearing only the boy's voice. "Excuse me? I am in need of a pot. Would you happen to have a spare?"

That detail sat... oddly with the Demon. The puddle of blackness looked up, needing no eyes to do so. Mallorca then saw reality, her insides a spinning framework of feelings. The challenger took off his helmet, offering the pot to hold the puddle. He was striking. Handsome. Too good for an ugly puddle. She couldn't fight when the child placed her in the pot, and then didn't want to fight when the pot was handed to the challenger. Why was he taking her?

The challenger's smile was soft when Mallorca, the blob, looked up. His eyes, brown and gentle as the most nurturing of earth, was a sight she could get lost in. He spoke, and that too was gentle and sweet. A warrior filtering his words through the heart. "Your name was Mallorca? Nice to meet you. Would you maybe... like to spend some time with me?"

Mallorca raised her arms, but only measly tendrils of ichor replied to her will. There wasn't much to her in this form.

There never had been, as a mere C-rank Demon. The gesture, however, appeared to be enough both for her challenger, and the divine still hovering in mid-air next to them. The challenger may have been standing on solid ground, with his helmet balanced on the railing, but the child was *hovering*.

Her challenger locked eyes with the divine, and offered his hand. "I… I'm sorry. I got carried away. Thank you for not… Well. She does mean a lot to me, even if our engagement is a strange one. My name is Solo. Just Solo. No affixes or suffixes."

Mallorca watched the child grip his hand, introducing himself with a name unfamiliar to her. The word he used evoked that awful feeling at her very center. Except that this time, there was a fluffy, sparkly, warm bliss accompanying the term. "Nice to meet you, Solo. I am **Love**, and it is so lovely to see you both in it. Please, do take good care of her? She's still finding herself, and doesn't have the know-how on how to be honest with herself yet. Nothing that some of your time and pleasant communication can't fix, *hmmm?*"

The challenger smiled, chuckled, and nodded. "That was… always the intent. I fell not for the Steamlord, but for… someone hiding inside. Someone I met more and more as our blades clashed, and it was our blades that spoke. Mallorca has… This is going to sound odd, and I can't really believe I'm saying it to a child. Not even a divine one. But… Mallorca has a beautiful smile. There's this laughter when she fights that sings, and I've never felt that through my blades before. I yearn for that song."

Mallorca could cry even more, verklempt and overcome with emotions that she was ill-equipped to handle both as her species, and a person. Solo reached down a digit, and she curled her tendril around it ever so barely, not having the dexterity she wished that would allow her to grip his hand whole. To crawl up and hug this man, and not let go.

"That's alright. I understand." The child placed his glowing, nimbus pink hand on her blob of a head. For a moment, the child was gone, replaced by an ancient, long-bearded grandfather. A being made of pure constellations, and the most **Loving** of light. This light burned her presence, but it burned away things she didn't hold dear in the first place.

Her perspective rose until she was tall. Until her tendrils were arms, hands, and fingers. Until she stood not as a puddle of a blob, but on dark legs made of ink and... stars. Gone was the ichor as the light pierced through her, the divine writing her into existence as he molded the ink of her being. As if her existence could be determined by words on an empty pane.

Then there she stood in front of the railing, dressed in clothes of solid ink, and shaped as a human, her featureless being a monotone dark. Mallorca lacked any personalized aspects, but that would change with time.

The ancient became a child once more, speaking fondly. "I've given her the template. The rest, you two will need to discover. I recommend carrying her? She does not yet know how to walk. It's a common problem with new bodies. Bit of an expert on that one."

Mallorca watched the child wink, then turn and walk away on panels of hard light, humming some old song to himself about not wanting to set the world on fire. "I just want to start. A flame in your heart."

Artorian eased out a few of the lyrics that he'd picked up from Dawn while en-route to her, finding it most fitting for this brand new ink-spot of a person.

She listened until her attention was fully captured by Solo, which happened purely by her turning her head, and the challenger standing right there. With that look on his face, and that warm smile in his eyes. "Hello. I'm... Solo."

Mallorca felt the pull of the Demon inside of her. She reached out for it, grabbed the feeling by its ugly little throat, and stifled any sound that it could make as she spoke as someone entirely new. Someone unfettered by the dark, now that her chest filled with pleasant, warm fuzz. A bright, fresh flame had found its way into her brand new heart. Her voice, to her own surprise, was sweet as sugar. "Hi… I'm Mallorca. Would you have a duel with me?"

Solo picked her up to carry her, his reply equally sweet as he walked away from the courtyard. "I would *love* to have a duel with you."

CHAPTER THIRTY-THREE

Ding!

———

Quest Complete! The Archmage Of Bonkmancy.
Congratulations.
Reward: 100 Adaptive Pylons.

———

Ember smacked Artorian's shoulder when he returned to their circle, a massive, beaming, proud grin on her face. Before she could open her mouth to say what she wanted to say, his Lenity shield shattered in front of all of them. He cringed and held his own arms, curling in on himself in very noticeable discomfort. "*Mmmmm…*"

Ember hissed in a breath between her teeth, pulling her hand back to her chest fast.

Less Than Three mewled. "I need my momma."

Lucia was on scene and on the ball! Their healer bunny-paw-bapped him with a quickness, shoving a brand new Lenity onto him after that nailbiter of a fight, because he clearly had not been paying attention to when Prosperity had run out. That steam-breath had done serious damage to his protections, and like the doofus he was, he had not taken proper stock that his own physical attacks were damaging his shield. Or, if he had been paying attention, her kit had cut that far too close.

She chittered at Three, but otherwise didn't verbally chastise him as she held her kit tight to her chest, furiously kneading her hands through his hair. His retribution for making her stressed was swift, a freshly shielded Three becoming Lucia's stress ball to squeeze and cope.

Mushed tight, Less Than Three's reply was muffled.

Lucia let him go from her squeeze, but reluctantly so. "You're going to give me white fur, kit."

Their boy repeated his words that had gone unheard the first time, the Momma Bun still firmly keeping her protective paws on him. "Where did Lenore go?"

Lucia aimed her gaze squarely at Astarte, who was innocently trying to twirl her finger through her hair. When the burning baby bun's hand finished adding a whole curl a moment later, Ember pointed back down at the courtyard. "Lenore is having a one on one with the Steamlord. Or had. She won."

Artorian leaned to the side so he could peer past Lucia, his eyes slowly returning to their normal blue colorations. Already? He just got here. That was far too fast for a duel, and especially an area boss encounter.

One glance at the courtyard allowed him to see the artistic brush-stroke of the single blade movement Lenore had flourished, the after-effect of the O'Dachi's lingering damage field painting a victorious curve in the air.

Like a case study, all of Lenore's technique was on full display, the story legible from that brush stroke of her blade. From her instant draw exemplified by the thin starting line, into the forward step of the long stroke. Followed by the sudden widening of the line as she unsheathed her weapon and cleaved through the Steamlord in a single slice with her O'Dachi.

One draw.

One hit.

One kill.

The upward arc of the blade's damage field then tapered off as Lenore had come back down from her jump. She had claimed the part of her vengeance that hadn't been provided by her divine, satisfied by the personal victory.

Returning to the group with clicking heels, Lady Lenore smiled with clear relief chiseled on her face, glancing over her shoulder to see what they were all studying. "I call it the swoosh. The lingering damage effect is semisolid, so if I catch someone with it then they're stuck. So long as that field is there, the swoosh deals full blade damage every second. I'm not sure what the Arcane damage type is, but that's what it does."

Artorian studied the blade, or this movement of it. "Impressive that the swoosh is still there. When will it dissipate?"

Lenore snapped her fingers as only a seasoned ruler could, bringing to heel an entire nation with the movement of her wrist. Her tone once more iron, her gaze cold as the swoosh vanished with the same motion and speed that the shimmering field had been made with. "When I deem it to be so, Less Than Three. When I deem it to be so."

Lenore then reached over, taking over the head-petting duties that Lucia had surrendered. "Why did you not kill the enemy? Based on what you showed, that would not have been difficult. Mind you, I don't mind. When I discovered that I needed to sink my sword into something after all, the Steamlord was happy to oblige. Something about death being the only way to fix the blowout injury. We've also made a soft agreement, but that's for New Haven's benefit. I am down one obstacle, and up one reclaimed Generator. This time, without a contemptible contract."

Artorian winced before remembering the new shield was up. He relaxed afterwards, letting the iron lady pet his hair. "I have a history with regrets, Lenore. When I play the game of *what could have been* in my head, I see narratives of what the world might expect. Of what onlookers think they want me to do. I stride through that field of eyes, undaunted. All that matters with the past is the decisions I made, and that I must shoulder them. Who I have become is dependent on those lessons. All that matters with the future is the decisions I want to make, and that *I* must make them reality. Rather than allow the flow of reality to dictate what my actions may have been."

Less Than Three leaned into the head rub. "Too often is it the case that my boat has to go down another's stream, but I want control of my own paddle. When I realized just how tempered an area boss that Mechanicus was, yes, I admit, I could have crushed that Steamlord with ease. That would have been the flow of reality, had I no other motivations."

He held Lucia, comforted by the touch as the discomfort of having been without a shield for a moment ebbed away. "I sometimes believe that I am cursed, Lenore, to notice more than I am able to affect. To know that even if I could be in all places at once, that it would not be enough. So when I see the ray of light, no matter how deep it is buried in the dark, and I see that I am on the path and could do something? Then the flow of reality will bend, and curve to the movement of my will."

Having had enough, he pulled away, extricating himself from the hands so he could stretch. "I saw **Love** smothered. That it was a Demon who discovered it is a philosophical problem for tomorrow. For now, I am content to have been proven wrong, that even a Demon could know **Love**, and be absolved. That the methods are strange, and the means odd? Who am I to judge? There was **Love**, and that is what I stand for. That is my hill."

He looked at Lenore, smiled weakly, and shrugged in apology. "A kill may have been more satisfactory for you, but to breathe life into **Love**, to place my hand on the backs of those who feel they are alone in that fight. That is my place."

A quick wink at Ember and an offered hand quickly followed. "Astarte figured it out fast, but she also knows me the best. That's why she didn't want to tell you anything. Spoilers."

She took his hand with an eager smirk, lacing fingers and tugging him close. Cupping her hand to his ear, she whispered time-sensitive and pertinent information. "That was lovely, sugar. Now for the bad news. The airship crew is looking for you. They made you a *song*."

Artorian's expression turned from reminiscent, to concerned, to meek, to appalled. His words became breathy, peeping like a mouse. "*Danger dooting*? We must flee."

"I have no such luxury." Lenore squeezed her forehead, an irritated tone buzzing from her throat. "Sunny? I love the class, and was delighted to be invited to the party regardless of my time in it being short. If there is the opportunity, I would enjoy a second attempt at a group bout versus a local foe. For now, I must step out of it. Responsibility is a heavy mantle, and these adventuring groups require logistical management."

Artorian felt bad that Lenore hadn't gotten her moment to shine alongside them. The Steamlord victory was spectacular in its own right, but the intent had been skewed away from a desired outcome. He wanted the group bout, but he'd wanted to tackle his devoted concept even more.

Less Than Three held his hand out to shake hers. "I am glad to be on the same team as you, Lady Lenore. That local group listing won't change that."

Lenore could read his thoughts on his face like they were an open book with big lettering. She accepted the handshake, taking that moment to leave the party. "The enjoyment is all mine, Less Than Three. I would give you warnings, before you go?"

Artorian was sad to see her name vanish from the Team Sleep list when he checked it, but when he refocused on Lenore, she had a smile on her face while looking at the same screen on her end. "I will, of course, take warnings, but currently my curiosity is focused on why you aren't feeling the sense of loss and lacking that I am feeling. I still feel torn."

Lenore considered this, and turned her screen. Hers did not show her current team like he thought, but rather the history listing of the teams she had been on. In the first slot, proudly listed, stood Team Sleep. "I do not feel a sense of loss or insufficiency, sweet boy. Because for all of time, I can say that the first team I was ever officially on was yours. How many Paladins or Champions can claim to have been in a party with their own divine? There is no blame to be placed here."

She turned, ready to leave as she collected herself, stepping more into the persona of the Iron Lady when preparing for less savory interactions to come. "I will repeat myself, my divine. When there can be a next time, let us rehash this event, and resolve that feeling if it yet persists. Now take this, and leave through the south gate. I'm fairly certain this is system information that I should not have. Put in a kind word with the Voice of the World for me?"

A sense of relief came with the repetition of Lenore's words, which Less Than Three allowed to sink in. The first mention had not been enough, but the repetition helped. He waved as she walked away with her sheathed O'Dachi in hand, then opened the prompt he'd been provided while between Ember and Lucia so they could both read the contents as well.

Ding!

———

Directory: Adventure Party Allotments.
   Secret Files: Current configurations, Import Data.
   Key: New Haven, Order of the Iron Sheep.

———

Group Designation: Team Sleep.
   Artorian.

Ember.
Lucia.

————

Group Designation: Nightshade.
  Chandra.
  Rose.
  Brianna.
  Amber.

————

Group Designation: Predator's Territory.
  Raile.
  Snowball.
  Manny.
  Halcyon.

————

Group Designation: Beef and Book.
  Tychus.
  Grimaldus.
  Sarcopenia.

————

Group Designation: IcyHot.
  Tom.
  Yuki.
  Shaka.
  Valhalla.

————

Group Designation: Magnitude.
Hawthorn - Discord.
Hawthorn - Chaos.
Hawthorn - Entropy.

———

Group Designation: The Oldest Woods.
Mahogany.
Rosewood.
Birch.
Snowdrop.

———

Group Designation: The Old Woods.
Olive.
Baobab.
Eucalyptus.
Sequoia.

———

Group Designation: The Young Woods.
Apiculteur, Peach Tree Wood Elf. Hive Mage.
Maya, Beech Tree Wood Elf. Moss Mage.
Airos, Quaking Aspen Wood Elf. E-Ranker.
Crooked, Sycamore Wood Elf. D-Ranker.

———

Group Designation 1: Definitely-Not-a-Date.
Group Designation 2: Nature's Secrets.
Chandra.
Tatum.

———

Group Designation 1: You've Yar'd Your Last Har.
Group Designation 2: The Pirate Crew.
Group Designation 3: You've Yee'd Your Last Haw.
Zephyr.
Oak.
Hans.
Meg.

———

Group Designation 1: Four White Mages.
Group Designation 2: Four White Mages in a Trench Coat.
Richard.
Adam.
Irene.
Craig.

———

Group Designation: Beasts and Beauties.
Jüvra.
Astrea.
Blanket.
Voltekka.

———

Group Designation: Blood and Stone.
Emilia Nerys.
Kellen Shadowbeard.
McShane.

———

Group Designation: InkSplash.
  Lucky Luca. Art Mage.
  Eri. Art Oni.
  Piano the Evanescent.
  *Tsuu. The Heavenly of **Art**.*

———

Group Designation: We're Just Visiting! Honest! Quickly Grab the Thing and—
  Tibbins.
  Jin.
  Tarrean.

———

Artorian had many questions. Such commentary. Why was the formatting not uniform? Why did some groups have so much more information? How did you get a second team name? All of those questions had to wait when the sudden addition of dangerlicious dooting threatened to round the corner.

Lucia, her ears on a swivel, reacted first. With a shimmer and flash, she transformed into her big Basher form, ready to bolt!

Ember acted second by a fraction, picking Artorian up and throwing him over her shoulder like luggage before his busy mind could spool down to deal with reality. When she noticed Lucia was in Glitterflit mode while both ready and set, she hurled herself onto the bunny's back instead of taking off herself. Gripping golden fur tight with her free hand as the sound of song came up from the docking bay stairs, she gave the order. "Go!"

In a blitz of light, Team Sleep was *gone*.

CHAPTER THIRTY-FOUR

Ember shifted to be in her assigned spot after Lucia turned a few sharp corners in quick succession. The bun ran on walls, curved paths, pipes, and even ceilings in order to have a clear enough pathway to vamoose. Ember dropped Artorian in front of her and gripped him like before, one arm acting as a safety belt. Once saddled and set, she let their healer know so Lucia could slap on the speeeeed. "Secured!"

Cranking the nyooms, Lucia sonic-speed pipe surfed and spark-grinded rails until she ducked from the south exit to be gone with the wind. Their bunbun's voice carried through the brooch after her shield flared to life and the wind stopped beating them wholesale. "I was really hoping for that snack and nap. Anywhere else we can go before the Arcoplex? New Haven seemed kind of it. In addition, as a reminder, I need ground to run on. I'm no good up in space."

"I don't." Ember grit her teeth, not having good answers. Her fingers followed suit to match her mulling, making worried biscuits on Less Than Three's clothing. She calmed when his hand pressed over her, softly taking her fingers into his and squeezing them in a supportive, gentle grip. He was smiling when she looked down at him, looking both snug and comforted.

Artorian's words provided relief. "I do."

Gripping his own brooch, he rolled some dice. The odds felt in his favor. "Zelia? I need your help."

A crackle pulsed through his brooch, followed by a similar crackling sound from Ember and Lucia's communication pieces. They all glowed with a soft galactic light, then turned a dark magenta. Artorian heard and felt some odd details with his senses, as if multiple channels in the brooch were being clicked through in order for the object to connect directly to the Autarch.

The pleasure in Zelia's voice was thick when the connection was finalized. "Then I am pleased to be helpful, my Dreamer. I am delighted that you thought to ask. What are your needs?"

Artorian wondered if he should ask why the background noise of Zelia's end sounded like a whole lot of feet had just come to a dead stop. He decided against, relaying his troubles. "Some Eternia hiccups that I have no reasonable way of getting around, without help, have come up. We can't get to Vanaheim. Arcoplex or otherwise. Last time we had Bifrosts, this time we have hurling ourselves into space. Before we consider that option, we're in need of food and sleep. New Haven stopped being an option when Zephyr showed up with…"

Zelia performed that soft laugh where it was clear she was hiding her face with her sleeve. "Hans, his youngest, Meg, and Oak? A quintet of joyous, innocent songs, to be sure. Have you considered Demeter's Dream? That was to be your resting station and berth, after all."

Artorian looked behind him at Ember, confused. He still held the brooch to keep Zelia looped in on the conversation. "Didn't that get eaten by Brother Moon?"

Ember made an uncertain face, but Zelia had a clear answer. "Only the outer shell and some of the outcroppings. A few latent cheese Penguins may linger? Otherwise I recommend that location. It retains air and gravity, plus the pre-planned supplies. Would you like a Slipstream?"

Artorian beamed when that offer arrived on the table. "Yes and please, Zelia. Whenever you're——"

Vwup.

"——Ready."

Lucia power slid to attempt a hard stop, her large hexagonal shield eating up disgusting numbers of damage so she could come to more of a halt before dangerously crashing into the main stairway of Demeter's Dream. Her ears shot right up, panic and surprise heavy in her outburst before her head *thunked* into the lower level anyway. The hexagon lattice shield flexed, bent, and shattered into glass shards before becoming energized particulates. "Wow!" *Thunk*! "Ow!"

While Lucia saw spots, Ember and Artorian were launched from her back, rolling up the stairs from all the crazy momentum and velocity they still carried. They slammed into the base of the central statue all the way at the top before coming to a stop. The head of which was still damaged from when Ember had used the face as a launching platform to punt the first cheese Penguin.

They copied Lucia's words in tandem, agreeing with her statement of pain while horribly disoriented. "*Ow.*"

Artorian reached for his brooch, his ribs bruised from hitting the statue sideways. That four-thousand damage blip in his shield also didn't feel too good. "Thank you, Zelia. Li'l rough of a trip, but now we know that Slipstreaming retains momentum. Why do I feel like you did that to me on purpose?"

Zelia's pride was easy to pluck from her tone. "I did do so on purpose, my Dreamer. I have been going over the records of your attempts at 'Dale'ing it? I discovered surprisingly effective results. You will be learning Slipstreaming to make the trip to Tisha, unless you discover alternatives. Consider that a *memorable* primer, with love. Enjoy your nap, my Dreamer."

His brooch returned to its simplistic metallic white configuration, the connection to Zelia ending as he could hear her giggle. That was plenty for him to push himself up and stand, still holding the brooch. "Everyone unharmed after that chaotic little hiccup?"

Ember had already been up, grumbling as she brushed herself off. "Fine, sugar. Would have been happier with more of a heads up, but we're here and that's what counts. Was wondering when Zelia was going to start playing around. Momma Bun? You alright down there? I can see the metaphorical canaries flying circles around your head."

"M'fine!" Lucia slurred her speech as she got up in her full Basher form, then flopped onto her side while still making the movements as if she was getting up. "Never mind. Bun needs a bowl of greens."

Artorian was well enough to make his way down to the lowest level, rubbing over her large head. "Is a bowl of greens going to help with our sudden exit?"

Lucia made a grumbly, groaning noise from the back of her throat. "I'm in denial about how much my head is spinning. Let me be in denial. No casty casty yet. Spinny spinny go wheeeee. Casty only makes rainbow vomit if cast now."

Trying not to chuckle, he rubbed her head considerably softer, laying her large, floppy ears over her eyes so it was less awkwardly bright. Inside the Grecian rest stop, the nautical twilight effect was in use, the world a soft hue of blue. A bubble around the place prevented the addition of natural sunlight, making Demeter's Dream a little blue world.

Whispers passed his ears, and he copied the melody. "Da dum die da dum da."

Lucia groaned louder. She bopped him on the head without looking, and mumbled out her discontent. "Shut up, Urtu! I know that was you with the dumb blue song!"

"Ow!" Holding the top of his head as the bun had bopped him a little hard, but within the realm of well-meaning intentions, he wrenched his thoughts to the whispers. Right, those were Heavenly-typed tricks. They were being watched, weren't they?

Leaving Lucia to lie still until she decided she had the physical comfort she was happy with, he pressed his hands on his hips. Looking straight up, he flicked on both True and Profound Sight, providing him enough sensory information to suss out an odd spot in the air above them. He peered right at it, then began to frown, and frown deep. He spoke a single word to inform the onlookers how he felt about Urtu's little... intrusion, the voiced displeasure thick. "*No.*"

The hole visible with Profound Sight soundlessly closed itself, prompting him to dismiss the effects and rub over his eyes. "Now we can have some peace."

Ember curled her arm around his neck, her temple pressed down to his as she melted into his side. "You alright, sugar?"

Artorian scowled, pointing at the sky. "I forgot entirely we had oglers. We now no longer have oglers, but it still bothers me to have forgotten. I'm not sure how I feel about having an audience. Feels invasive on one hand, but I like the transparency on the other? Had I been bed bound, I too would take great delight in watching Ra roll through her adventures. I'd want to spoil her, though. The task of a grandfather, upheld."

Ember continued to lean her head against him while Lucia took her sweet time getting upright, her paws on her head and toe-beans rubbing circles over her skull. "Do you mean that you'd be more accepting of being a show if the audience was able to participate?"

That direction wasn't where Artorian's mind was heading.

The cart in his head came to a halt, turned around, and went down Ember's pathway instead. T'was far more interesting! "Honey? I think that was an incredible suggestion. That may just be it. Being watched like this is... icky? I didn't mind in Avalon. Here it's different in a way that I can't put my finger on. Being involved with the watchers and doing this activity together? Now there's a loophole I can get behind."

His stomach loudly interrupted his current quandary. Looking down, he pressed a hand to his chest. "I hunger? Even with my race merits?"

A swift check to his character sheet also showed that the tired debuff was back again. "Already?!"

Ember poked her nose in to learn what he learned, then tugged him up the stairs. "C'mon. There's sous vide to make. I've got a hankering for Bear flank."

He reached for Lucia before following along, the Basher easing into her human form as brightly colored spells finally flowed from her fingertips, followed by deep sighs of blessed relief when the effects found purchase. When she saw him reach out, she waved her hand dismissively, wanting them to go ahead as her ears flicked about. "I'll be joining shortly. Just because I'm up doesn't mean I'm awake. It's noisy up there."

Artorian felt that statement in his bones. "Celestial feces. Preaching to the choir, Lucia? You take your time, Momma Bun. We'll be in the same place as last time. Or next door? I remember the house came down on you when that music showed up."

"If I hear Lacrimosa play again before some sleep, I am breaking things." Ember tugged him up, an eager smile on her face that betrayed she'd noticed something he hadn't yet, or he wouldn't have set the broken house as the meeting point. Stumbling up a few steps before trailing along, he squinted at her expression before looking back up at the statue they'd crashed into.

Recognition dawned on him when he recognized the faces of the sneaky people already standing here! The clashing duo had walked over when the kids had run down the stairs, instead of toward them as expected. They had a full bonfire up and everything! How had he not seen them? "Yuki! Shaka!"

Shaka fixed his dashiki, then slapped his hands onto a drum he carried under the arm to begin a jaunty tune, laughing in welcome while thumping out inviting music! He was the hot, opposing contrast to Yuki's cold and impassive stare as she stood silently next to him. A glacier looking down her nose at a dancing desert. "*Ha-haaaa*! I knew it! Tom. Tom! Throw mo' Penguin on da fiyah! We be feastin' on da cheeeese!"

Yuki closed her eyes, her folded hands and stern pose clearly at its limit with Shaka's brand of enthusiasm. She gripped him by the ear, and walked off at a glacial pace while refusing to let up on any of her frozen grip to his twisted tragus. That piece of his ear was in dire danger as Shaka was forced to stumble and hop along while failing to keep his drumbeat steady. "*Ay, Ay. Yu— Ay!*"

"She will not listen to you, brother!" Boisterous laughter overpowered Shaka's futile whining, followed by the clashing slam of a burning warhammer impacting the thundering crash of another warhammer. *Kra-kow*!

The overly polite voice of Tom, the Norseman, resounded. "The Lady of Ice quenches even your flame, friend. See to the evening meal thyself! I face the Mistress of all Valkyries in honorable combat once more. My hands are tied!"

Tom, now a B-ranking Mage of **Fire**, squared off against Valhalla, Odin's liberated Chosen who had found her own path in life. That path involved very big hammers, applied to any nail that remotely resembled Odin's quirks. They traded hammer blows once more after the sudden interruption of newcomers crashing in. When those newcomers had proven to be disoriented old friends, they'd gone right back to their sparring bout. Hammerfalls flew with the dexterity of sparring rapiers, and all the force of Dwarven mountain breakers. The mutual impacts thundered with outbursts of hot flame.

Kra-kow!

Valhalla howled in glorious combat, her face and deep tone one of mighty delights as her wings beat, carrying her back into the fray to meet force with force, fire with thunder. Thud to Mjolnir. "Focus, firestarter! Your blows soften when you distract thyself. Swings like that won't shake a bed frame, much less an opponent."

Kra-kow!

Tom sputtered at Valhalla's provocations, too good and pure of a man to meet her on that verbal battlefield just yet. "Valkyrie! Language!"

She laughed loud and proud, knowing full well how it unsettled him. "Language you can clearly understand, Tommulus! I shall continue speaking then, so your ears may continue to redden, and your win count continues to dwindle against me. Use all available tools at your disposal, future divine! Do not expect your enemy to give you grace and comfort."

Ember and Artorian both watched them for a few swings. Lucia ended up catching up to them as they took in the show, holding her large ears down to her head with a bothered expression. She nudged them with a clear headache, motioning to the fire, the smell of meat and cheese thickening in the air as they moved closer. "Momma wants her greens. Where's Momma's greens?!"

Ember placed her hand on top of Artorian's head, who was now also holding his ears as his Echolocation was not happy, thinking there was something to be done about that. "Sugar? The level inside of the building below us is a hydroponics segment. *Uhh…* indoor farming? How about you get Momma her greens, and I make the banging noises stop?"

Her eyes cut a burning line toward the sparring Valkyrie and fresh Mage, both enjoying the Eternia game with their characters. "Those children believe themselves to be combat experts? I feel a passionate need to go *humble* them. For fun."

Artorian giggled, finding that far too funny. He pecked her forehead, then veered off in search of Momma Bun's greens. There was snacking and napping to do, and he was happy to do his part. Away from the noise. "Best of luck! To them, I mean. Best of luck to them."

Ember grinned wide, her heart aflame from getting a forehead kiss before she turned to rush the sparring, hammer-y duo. Her body glimmered, becoming one of diamond and deep flame when she interposed herself and interrupted their blows, negating both strikes and forcing their hammers to a standstill with a wicked grin. To the horrified surprise of Tom and Valhalla, whose weapons continued to roil with power as both hammerheads were trapped in Astarte's palms.

"My turn!" Her smile blazed with infernos, eyes torrenting out heat as her face was replaced with an effigy of war. Only her smile and all-consuming eyes remained visible above the coronal-crimson combustion blotting out the rest of her features. Astarte's voice burned with anticipation, both her arms coming alive with solar heat trails as a halo crown of northern heat formed above her head. "*Corona Borealis.*"

CHAPTER THIRTY-FIVE

Tom and Valhalla made good seats.

Ember came to this conclusion after much trial and error, having determined that the seating arrangement was best with Tom on bottom, as he was hard and sturdy. Then Valhalla sandwiched in the middle. Those big wings made great padding for her butt! She leaned to the side, arms crossed as her effects faded. "Are you both certain that you don't want it to be your turn again? We can keep doing this for as looooong as you want."

Weak mewling was returned, prompting Ember to nod and hop off the hammer-loving puddle. "Another time, then. Momma Bun? These two may need some medical attention."

Lucia was busy, face-deep in a large metal cauldron of mixed greens and cauliflower, and her absolute favorite food: Timothy hay! Her large Glitterflit body was splooted next to the bonfire as she thought on how that wasn't quite true. Bananas were her ultimate favorite treat food, and grass hays more of a staple food that she wanted as much and as often as possible.

Happy *nyom-nyom-nyom* noises resounded from within the cauldron. Her ears twisted in place when she heard Astarte speak, the rest of her face thoroughly engrossed and buried in seasoned deliciousness. Everyone heard a *mllmmrmbml* leave the pot, but most of them had no hope of deciphering the sound.

Shaka leaned back from his spot at the fire, translating while attempting to mimic her voice with his. His hands were full of Bear-flank that was being prepared for sous-viding. "She said: Just a minute!"

Shaka then paused from his work with the seasonings, eyes landing on Less Than Three as the boy laid against the Basher's fluffy side, taking a breather while snacking on fried cheese Penguin on a stick. The outside of the meat-coated cheese stick was hot, crunchy, and breaded. The inside was all... well, cheese! Pretty tasty.

Artorian turned his head lightly while flopped in place, feet wiggling left and right. Chewing on his food, he met Shaka's gaze. The Heavenly was inspecting him curiously. He raised a brow, prompting the other drum-lover to speak.

Shaka gleefully accepted the opportunity. "Ma apologies, sunshine. It is a wonder to me that, even in da game, da mana love-loves you. Not because of your **Law**, either. More than anyone else, you care about Essence. You see the possibility for minds and assume it, then treat them like ya do people. The air around you is shaped as Winter Wolves, tails waggin'. Tongues trying hard to lick your face. I gave Dawn—or was it Corona at the time? It's Ember, currently?—a whole lecture on the substances of layers, knowing some of it was going to only be useful for your ears. I wonder now if it was even needed."

The Heavenly reached for creatures that Artorian could not see, his fingers making the motions that he was petting through a thick coat of heavy fur. "Don't chu worry your big toothy mouth none, Fenri-ri. He be back with you soon 'nough."

Shaka clicked at the air, fussing back. "Don't chu whine at me none in that whimpery tone! Ev'things gonna be ey'rie. Ya whiny baby."

Artorian had difficulty understanding Shaka when the dark

DENNIS VANDERKERKEN & DAKOTA KROUT

man dipped deep into his accented speech, but picked up enough context to be happy with the conversation. He leaned forward when he felt his backing shift, Lucia done with her bowl of greens.

Stretching out before getting up, she took her sweet, sweet time to mosey her way down to the crumpled heap of Tom and Valhalla. The Eminence shifted into her human form while plodding along, pressing her hands into her thick hips before looking down at the duo. "Tha's what you get givin' a lady a headache with that hammer-y racket of yours!"

She specifically eyed the winged Gatekeeper of Asgard like a scorned nurse. "Valhalla? Don't think I've forgotten the whoopings you used to hand us in the before-times neither. Consider this a lovin' blessing for how to treat healers."

Artorian pulled his attention away when a Greater Lenity went off. Regardless of Lucia delivering her healing with a whiplashed clap to Tom's ass. The big man yelped! Pleading for what he did in a high-pitched tone, when it was Valhalla she was upset at.

Artorian nodded sagely, knowing everything was going to be alright as he heard their Basher Nurse fuss. "Now git on up!"

Ember had joined the bonfire group in the meanwhile, taking over sous vide duties from Shaka to finish the part he was working on. He could have it back after. "Gimme. Mine."

Artorian was going to strike up more conversation, but paused when Shaka and Ember both suddenly sat up ramrod straight. That didn't tend to bode well.

"Settle down." Yuki glid as if across ice from one of the open doors, a basket filled with salt in her hands. "It's just Tim. He's joining me for dinner like I asked. I'm still busy. Joining later. Eat when food is ready. Don't wait on me."

Eternium complained by making an inhuman noise from inside of the Grecian home, his schemes spoiled and surprise appearance ruined. The rotund, plump man pushed the door open with a large hand to stroll into the light. His clothing was exquisite and flawlessly tailored, betraying their simple appearance that he held the profession of seasoned bar patron. Sighing with the power of a Dwarf, he snapped a hand up at the wrist, causing the appearance of chairs, benches, and tables. Including a considerable upgrade in quality from haphazard bonfire to stone-built fire pit.

The new pit even matched the decor!

Artorian clapped his hands along with the others at the display of dungeon modification prowess, then worked himself upright as Ember pointed to a seat. She'd returned the cooking task to Shaka, her hands full of the same bread-fried cheese stick he'd enjoyed earlier. They both chose to occupy the same chair, Ember busy inhaling her dinner at the same time. The reason for the seat choice was simple. That particular lounger was laden with the most pillows!

Tim thought that was a capital idea, and dropped himself in a sturdy lounger as well. A hefty sigh of relief escaped him as he melted into the cushions. Nothing like some handmade comfort. His accent was thick as usual as he spoke, the relaxation seeping in. "*Ahhhh...* That's the stuff. Artorian? Your love for pillows? I *get it* now."

The person in question shot his small arm up, flashing a thumbs up while still clad in his wintery attire. The old man in his young-child format was busy trying to get cozy against Ember's matching outfit while she finished up dinner, making her settle and sit higher in the big lounger so she could do both. "Glad you found the light! Or in this case? The flooooof!"

Artorian then swiftly added an apology, feeling that Tired debuff knock him on the head. "I ate too much, too quickly, Tim. Cheese Penguin on a stick is very tasty and extremely filling. I'm starting to fade. Are you doing well? Anything pertinent?"

Tim accepted a plate of salted herring from Yuki. A delicacy that Artorian was convinced did not fit his own palette, but to each their own. He then immediately backtracked his assumption, and wanted to try it. The part he liked most was when Yuki didn't leave, instead turning her cheek and tapping it twice in clear expectation. He beamed when Tim pushed up to hold her opposing cheek, and kissed the tapped side.

Yuki found that most acceptable, sliding back indoors without a word after being provided her due payment.

Tim also looked behind him. The dungeon almost leaned too far over the chair to see Yuki, draped in her icy hanfu, vanish into the structure and glide down the stairs back to the hydroponics. He sat back down proper after, a big smile on his face as he made another salted herring vanish with thoughtful bites. "Hmm... *still* needs more salt."

Artorian didn't want to think about that statement, kicking the segue in his head over to an entirely different topic. "Yuki looks happy. As much as Yuki can look happy, that is."

Tim nodded enthusiastically, his mouth full of the treat tailored to him. "*Mhm!*"

He swallowed, rubbing his thick fingers over his large stomach before his attention turned to Artorian. "Definitely needs more salt... She is! I never imagined how well the concept of **Kenopsia** and I would get along. She's a marvel when it comes to inhabiting her **Law.** Must say that I loved time with her when it was just us two in my Soul Space. She would have broken into the S-ranks several times over were it currently possible. She's enamored with how I see plans through, and how I don't boast about things I can't actually do. I'd boast about her all day, but she'd come right back up to smack me if I started. Yuki being my happiness aside? Work, work, and more work."

He folded his digits over his chest a moment, thinking back. "The Pylon holds look like an expressive painting of cognitive dissonance. Works, but it doesn't look pretty. There's more spaghetti code present than I want to admit, but we're finally making headway on clean, structured, organized banks. Now that we know how far to keep them distanced from one another to prevent that daft heating issue."

Tim pointed at Artorian specifically. "Yours are doing much better after we cut your coding down to under the allotment, but I'm sad to say I still don't have a good fix for your Bone-scripting. Nor do we seem to be as able to connect you to the mundane network as we wanted to. It's a shame we can't make you start over from scratch again. That would save us so much headache."

Artorian considered that thought, pushing himself back up a moment. "Then make me start over from scratch, Tim. I'd be happy for a third do-over. I even have ideas for new mechanics to run by you, especially if I'm going to stick to the roaming world boss role. That's really not as big of a setback as you're making it sound."

He yawned hard, having trouble hanging on. "Maybe with attempt three, I can actually earn my own goodies based on what I want to do, instead of being gifted everything per what I have to do? The imported goodie I wanted to play with is gone, and most of my toolkit is... present? Sort of? If it wasn't for the single health point, I think I would have been happier sticking to the duelist themes. I had a great time in my solo bout versus the Mechanicus, even if I flavored it as playing the role of a villain so my opponent wouldn't be the wiser of what I was up to. "

Tim dropped his finger, half curling his digit in as he'd not expected that response. "One moment. You're fine with another restart of New Game Plus?"

Artorian motioned at himself, then at the broken hole in the asteroid shell of Demeter's Dream above him, feeling it made for an apt metaphor and comparison without needing to elaborate further.

The dungeon picked his salted treats back up, chewing on herring while thinking. "That does add some conveniences... Do you—?"

The large man cut his words short. Artorian had drowsily laid himself back down, and when he'd nested into Ember's winter plush, had fallen right asleep. Tim chuckled to himself, attention turning to Shaka and Ember. "Look at him. So peaceful and innocent when dozing. Are you both doing well, **Fire** and **Sun**?"

Ember still had her mouth full, holding up her vacant cheese stick to signal a positive response. It was enough.

Shaka held up his successful attempt at sous vide as well, the culinary creation smelling divine. He would be devouring that shortly. "Da Shaka is fantastic! I am having a great time bein' alive. Playing da game. Having something silly to do. I like da party mechanic too! Tom and Valhalla are a hoot, and Yuki keeps me on my toes. Shaka likes! No complaint from me about the troubled state of this world either. I could go on for hours to tell you how *good* it feels to be part of something big where I can see the improvements happen before my eyes. Feels good. Feels *very* good."

That detail improved Tim's day, a satisfied smile growing on his otherwise always-serious face. "That does warm my core, Shaka. Do you think the other Heavenlies share your perspective?"

The Heavenly of **Fire** plated his meal, added vegetables with a side of cheese Pengy fritters, and tore in with enjoyment. Tim waited patiently for Shaka to savor the chewing, amused by his unique noises of hyena-laughing happiness when the food went down. "*Ja, ja!* Shaka happy. The rest of the Tower that's here is very enthused as well. We're all used to being involved on the same project, and this time we get to play instead of run!"

Shaka went into some details, to the enraptured attention of Tim. "What makes us all happy is seeing the fixes, the improvements, the repairs. The overhauling of the holds. The remaking of storage warehouses. The intricacies of your synthetic Pylon networks! There are so many ideas that seem so simple now that we can look at the physical examples of them working. We have usually opted for the more complex, energy-only variants of solutions, because that is what we have had to work with. There's no such thing as solid Quintessence, but that may only be because nobody ever had the thought to try. Now?

Now *we* are in arguments over what the Tower could be doing better."

Tim just about wiggled in his fluffy lounger. "Glad to hear! Dawn, what about—"

His words once again faltered, seeing her breathing just as quietly as Artorian. Her cheek was pressed to the top of his head with her arm curled over his side and shoulder, while he was nested into her chest. Ember was even still holding the skewer in her other hand like it was the mightiest of weapons. "Well, that's just *too* adorable. That's getting a statue."

Shaka nodded in full agreement.

Lucia walked around the corner from having patched up the hammer twins to poke her head into the scene. Momma Bun instantly hand-motioned signs of approval while rapidly nodding her head. She then bunny-bapped on her own knees excitedly when an idea struck, her ears shooting up before she pointed at the current central statue. "A replacement for the one with the head-dent?"

Checking the statue to survey the damage, Tim slapped the armrest of his seat. "Capital idea!"

One clap of the hands later, and that statue was replaced with a carbon copy ice sculpture of Ember and Artorian's current positions in the pillow-laden chair. Skewer and all. Once again, the peanut gallery clapped politely at the display.

Tim gladly made miniature bowing motions from his seat without getting up, his hand pressed to his upper sternum. "Thank you, thank you. I'll be here all night."

He then sat back to find comfort, taking a deep breath. "That does change my plans somewhat. I was hoping to talk to Dawn—I mean Ember—about transitive and intransitive game mechanics. The rock-paper-scissors cycle only goes so far, and we've got some clear balancing issues. Or was that the second topic? I remember having notes on the emptying out of stamina and mana bars making a person sick, weak, or pass out. As that's the closest, actual representation of their bodily health that we have."

Shaka got up from next to the Grecian fire pit, washing his hands by sticking them directly into the hot coals. Using the licking flames as if they were water, he even splashed some on his face, and thought nothing of the act before sitting down in a free lounger next to Tim. "Perhaps Shaka can be of some assistance? Da children need their sleep, and Shaka has thoughts that drum in the mind."

The Heavenly of **Fire** paused himself by pointing at the healer, who was forcibly keeping herself upright and awake. "You too, young lady. Get some shuteye. You need it."

Lucia felt her inner brat rise with a powerful vengeance at being told to do something she didn't want to do. The Glitterflit then saw the fire in Shaka's eyes, thought better of it, and turned on her heels to curl up in the pillow-laden seat next to her young charges. She mumbled out her reply, both huffy and filled with pouty behavior as she pulled pillows over, bunkering herself into a makeshift warren. "Yes, *sir*."

Shaka stifled laughter at the cheekiness in the Basher. "Ha! Shaka likes this oversized rabbit. She has da fiyah!"

Tim quirked an amused brow at Shaka. "Who, exactly, is going to tell a Heavenly the word 'no'?"

Shaka grinned wide, content to let everyone else sleep while he chattered with the local dungeon about this game world they were all in. With so much room for improvement, and the burning down of inefficient systems. He especially liked that latter part. "According to the local news? Exactly that one! That bunny been smackin' around both Urtu and Hella from what I hear! With a *ladle*! So, like I says? Shaka likes!"

He clapped his hands together, getting down to the heat of the matter. "Now, 'bout this game balance that's bothering you so? Shaka has also already had conversations about the topic concerning the energy bars. Shaka wishes to share."

Tim spread his arms wide, the invitation as open as his reach. "Share with me your wonderful thoughts, Shaka of **Fire**. Eternium of **Order** delights in your stoking of the flames."

CHAPTER THIRTY-SIX

Artorian woke with his face buried in fluff, still feeling drowsy. His ears picked up the voices of Tim and Shaka, deep in debate. Something about 'wives' tale wisdom' proving true?

There were many more in the Grecian Dream now, and the hammering had picked back up as well. Tim's voice was prominent when Artorian was able to filter the sounds from other people talking.

His excitement was easy to pick up while he was going off on a tangent; Artorian tended to do that himself. "I'm telling you, Shaka, the Hyperkinetics, with their abnormal involuntary movement? Put both them and the attention deficit disorder sweethearts on horses. Calms them right down. Their focus changes. Hippotherapy works! It's slated for immediate inclusion. Sleipnir is on board, and already taking some of the people who haven't taken the Soul Space journey so well on six-legged walks. I didn't expect that the utilization of the natural movements of a horse to provide both motor and sensory input would work so well, but look at how happy they are."

A hum sounded, some observation windows being closed.

Shaka provided feedback on what must have been the prior

topic, speaking with calm and measured notes. His heavy accent was incredibly subdued for clarity of speech. "Have your hippotherapy, Tim. I am still focused on the false decisions game mechanic. You will encounter the same issues I brought up before. Once known, experienced players will always ignore the choice, knowing that there is an objectively correct route. While new players face a dangerous learning pitfall."

With Tim pensive and focused back on the topic, Shaka delved deeper. "People seek optimality in decision making. If two skills can be obtained, and one is far superior over the other, then why would anyone choose the inferior one? Think of a graph. Benefit to cost. Slash in a linear curve. Adjust as needed with spikes for where the difficulty hurdles make a leap. Anything above the linear cost curve will be considered over-powered, and therefore desirable. Anything under that curve will be considered underpowered, and therefore undesirable."

The Heavenly drew an example in the air using raw heat. "However, you show that curve to players indirectly, based on what abilities and tools are available. What they can talk about amongst themselves. What they can see others do. This leaves you some wiggle room if you are separating difficulty zones by realms."

Shaka adjusted some coals in the fire with his bare hand, refreshing the heat stored in his fingers. "If every ability deals a thousand damage, then that is not overpowered, that *is* the linear curve. That is the basis. The rest of the game then becomes difficult, or easy, depending on how it treats that thousand damage. If your weakest monsters have less health, and your most lesser tools remove it as a threat instantly? Then that is the bar you have set, and how your players will feel about continuity. If the early enemies are difficult? Then you set that as an expectation for the rest of the game, and you knew that. Which is why we were having the earlier conversation on high difficulty being beneficial. It sets *expectations*."

Tim grumbled, but must have made 'go on' motions, because Shaka breathed in and trekked right on up the mountain. "Intransitive gaming is like… your rock-paper-scissors? Where every option is better than some other option and there is no single 'best' move. To contrast, in transitive games, some options are flat out better than others in terms of their in-game effects. We balance that by giving them different costs, so that the better things cost more, and the weaker things cost less. As discussed, the problem stems from a lack of good grounding. How do we know how much things are meant to cost? That is why letting people play, regardless of how crazy their abilities are, is not a detriment. If the output is above the curve, you can alter the cost, alter the output, or attach some secondary cost, or another effect as a balancing mechanic."

Tim grumbled again, but had a reply this time. "Not the first time this has come up, but always nice to hear it with fresh ears. I understand that standpoint, Shaka. My current debacle stems more from wider balancing issues than the basic cost to effect ones. When increasing in level and attributes, or whatever an ability may be keyed to? That has the potential to fundamentally change how a tool is used, because the costs became negligible. Take Artorian's Energy Gatling as an easy example?"

Tim pulled up the schematic of Luminous Gatling, with an easy twenty different variations to the norm being presented like a folder. "That ability only does what it does because he has the regeneration metrics to fire it off without emptying his stamina or mana bars. Which would make him very sick, or exhausted, or the like, when we re-implement those systems. I'm fairly convinced that I'm going to. To anyone else using that Energy Gatling? It's not so great of a tool. The ability does little damage when it can't be properly spooled up, and the initial math on it was ten energy for a ten-sided-die worth of damage."

Tim's chair creaked, the dungeon sitting back and letting his weight sink in when Yuki came by and made a motion for him to relax. "That means I also have to account not for the upper end of the formula, but the lower end as well. If a person only had a hundred stamina, and they use this ten times in succession, only to get terribly unlucky and only deal ten damage with ten bolts, they'll feel horribly cheated, and collapse in place from having expended their entire stamina bar. Now there's a case of the rainbow-vomits, and they did essentially no damage to a foe that now gets to murder with cheap shots. That's a lose-lose for me, because now I've damaged their encouragement and placed the burden on personal willpower, rather than faulty tools that need attention."

The dungeon made a half motion at the asleep-looking winter duo. "So while my cost curve didn't change? Due to who is using the tool, the cost to benefit analysis is entirely different. One ten sided die worth of damage suddenly becomes a lot when you can reel them off without consequence. Does that mean I should be adapting tools so they always have consequence? Or do I let the person play? To see what they come up with, knowing that they're not using that ability on par to their realm, and that we're only seeing results to a lower realm, which skews the data. The background teams have already had to throw in higher realm opponents against Team Sleep to get the old data uncrunched so they could re-crunch it. That Storm Mole was originally slated for Vanaheim."

Shaka picked up a hot coal from the fire, scribbling directly onto the white Grecian stone to make notes and chew on napkin math. "For that reason, Shaka believes, you are using intransient properties when it comes to certain tools being more or less effective against certain targets. Such as with your resistances and vulnerabilities. While you focus on transitive tools for the players, specifically because you did want their tools to grow, change, and adapt. With some tools, when acquired in a more difficult zone, having better base attributes to build up from? They offer the promise of greater heights. My only recommendation is to try it."

The conversation came to a grinding halt when a sandy *poof* occurred.

Conversation dulled to the point where Artorian pushed himself up enough to see through bleary eyes, spotting a confused Red Goblin in the panic stance. The mob awkwardly posed next to Shaka's chair, as if the Goblin too did not understand why he was there.

Tim leaned on his lounger, speaking flawless Goblinoid. While gibbering whooping came out of his mouth as far as anyone listening in was concerned, the dungeon made a swirling motion, activating translation services.

Tim addressed the Red Goblin again, his words understandable on repetition when the first words only got as far as getting the Goblin's attention. "What happened?"

In a squeaky tone, perfect for the walking embodiment of trouble, the Red Goblin answered with normal words. That the way his mouth moved didn't match those words was unimportant. "Yolo jump on leafs!"

While that seemed innocuous and unworthy of attention, the Red Goblin's tone immediately turned teary, like the after-effect had been devastating. "Leaf *no crunch!*"

Falling to his knees as the tears streamed down his red face, the hiccupping mob wept. The poor Goblin was entirely distraught. "Burn the world. All is lost. Death to the soggy!"

The bigshots had no idea what to say.

How does one handle a sudden, distraught Red Goblin?

Artorian, dramatic and full of terrible ideas, raised his hand as he spoke like a crone, croaking out his words to enact his narrative. "Yolo? Crunchy leaf pile. *Hidden.*"

From that raised hand, a single digit emerged to point up at nothing. His voice alternated between conspiratorial and breathy. "Secret place of true crunch. *Close by.*"

Gasping loud, as if being provided revelation, the Red Goblin peeled his hands from his stained face. Looking up through wet eyes at this speaker who knew of the crunchy leaf pile, and how it must always be crunchy.

Artorian pushed himself up far enough to see the hope build in the Red Goblin's little eyes. His face mouthing 'make a pile of dry crunchy leaves' to Tim. As his hand began to descend, with the Goblin's gaze locked on his digit as if observing an act from the heavens.

When Artorian pointed to a place behind the Goblin, Yolo turned to see a pile of dry leaves three times as tall as him! A blessing of the true crunch. The fall leaves present in a multitude of colors, with some rogue fluttering still adding to the heap from above.

For a moment, the Red Goblin, clad in naught but his leathery loincloth, looked back at the enigma in blue for confirmation. The voice of the crone child commanded him to fulfill his heart's deepest desire. "Go."

Releasing a Goblin's famous *reeeee*, Yolo hurled himself into the pile. The most satisfying of crunch noises followed, and all was right with the world when Tim disappeared both the Goblin and the pile of crunchy leaves back to the innards of Muspelheim.

The dungeon then paused, narrowed his eyes, and felt the gears turn. "Why would the leaves inside of Muspelheim be *soggy*?"

A look of horrible realization then came over his face, blanketing him in a dire and sudden need to leave. "I must go!"

He shot up from his chair, turning right to run. The plump man stopped hard, then turned left to run. Realizing something else too late as thoughts cascaded, Tim ground to a halt a third time to rush back to Shaka and grab his shoulder. "I need Team IcyHot! Come with me!"

Before soundlessly vanishing with the rest of his team, Shaka managed to get out a confused, uncertain response. "Yes?"

This left that space around the fire pit vacant, as some hammering noises in the background abruptly went missing, Tom and Valhalla whisked away along with Shaka.

Artorian dropped his hand, no longer pointing at a leafy pile. Thinking this was all some very amusing dream, he pressed his face back into Ember's winter attire and fell right back asleep.

Tim popped back in moments after, frantically searching for the bundled winter duo. When he spotted them, he immediately clapped his hands, making Team Sleep disappear. Loungers and all. "Can't forget that! I am *not* dealing with Slipstreaming Pylons if I can help it."

He then turned in place to shake his fist at the open hole of Demeter's Dream that let out to empty space. "You hear me, Zelia? I know what you were going to do, you oblong ball of **Chaos.** No, I say, no! There will be **Order**!"

Tim then vanished as quick as he came, leaving a very startled and confused Halcyon behind as she'd just barely stepped from the open doorway of the kitchen home. The Orca in human form held a massive pot of fish stew meant for ten. She looked down at the steaming pot of bouillabaisse, looked around, then shrugged as she created her own solutions.

"More for me!"

CHAPTER THIRTY-SEVEN

"Sugar?" Artorian woke again, this time to the sussy smell of cheese and Ember's gentle prompting.

A dissatisfied, throaty *mnnnnn* left him as he indignantly rose from his most cozy of pillow-laden spots. His eyes were bleary until he allowed his Cleaning Aura to patch that up. Blinking the spots out of his vision, he indulged in the significantly fresher air, smacking his lips together to taste a lack of flavor. Artorian considered that a vast improvement before turning to Ember. "Mmm?"

Ember rustled her digits through his hair. "We're in Vanaheim."

That detail needed a moment to click in, his response nearly identical. "Mmm."

Should he be surprised? Should there be some sort of outcry? Should he question how he ended up in the intended location, or should he approach this like a gift horse and mouth kind of situation? The decision was made to instead lean his head into the head rubs that had evolved to become scratches, his response once more of the laconic and noisy sort. This time the sound was filled with indulgent enjoyment. "*Mmmm…*"

Ember smiled, stifling a chuckle while whisking her claws back and forth over his scalp, the rhythm nice and slow. "Honey bunny, you know I'm fluent in grunty noises, right? I used to speak in them exclusively."

The well-organized pillow pile in the lounger next to them exploded from within. The pillows flung all over the place when Lucia shot upright, her ears bent at awkward, crooked angles. Her state of being was not any more awake than Artorian's. "D'someone say bunny?"

Lucia was up and on her feet before she was lucid. Mid-wobble, she shot her finger to the air, as if recalling the proper order of things. "Flasks before tasks!"

Patting herself over, she sobered up and woke up more the longer she went without being able to locate said flasks. She squeezed her eyes shut, exhaling deep in momentary lamentation. "Right, that was… long ago."

Ember's groan pulled Lucia's attention to the other chair. Their team lead was currently copying Tim, and shaking her fist in the air. "I had some, too!"

Lucia's ears twisted in confusion. "Flasks?"

"Flasks. Sadly, we're not short on tasks." Ember sighed, working herself out of the lounger when her boy made grabby motions at the ground. Once the team stood together in a huddle, they performed group stretches, and shared buffs.

Less Than Three scrubbed them all clean, Lucia made them all glow colors with a bevy of shields, and Astarte added some kind of red halo over them all that doubled as a damage booster and light source. Then they pulled up their character sheets, and shared information round table style.

Artorian began by poking at his Nuts and Bolts bar. "The red smidge has diminished. I've recovered one percent of bar damage in both metrics. Sleep fixes burnout damage? Or what are we calling it? Too many things are called burnout as is. I'm sensing a theme here either way."

Ember found nothing off with hers. "No official name. Not yet. Bar damage is not really a feature we want to keep; that visual was implemented as a sign for something actually going wrong. Remember how prompts used to have discolored text? Same difference."

Artorian hummed, rubbing his chin. "Shame. I rather like the idea of wailing into an opponent without doing direct harm. If I can fill up their entire bar with a different kind of damage, turning it... blue? Or something. I'm not fussy on specifics. That would be nice? I am more interested in treating my time as a world boss as some kind of lesson, rather than just another checkmark on a chart. I'm fond of providing health regeneration as a bonus, and I think I'd want to teach people how to deal with the opposite if they wanted to encounter me. No health regeneration. No healing. No stamina or mana recovery."

Lucia tilted her head, her ears laying down flat. "Seems harsh. What's the lesson? To be aware of how best to use your limited resources? Or... or is it because of how you're feeling right now? Throwing out abilities like you are, and how—"

The Basher frowned, gaining concern. "Kit, I can only guess that you feel something is lacking?"

He nodded demurely, Momma Bun in possession of secret momma-powers with how on the sniffer she got her guess. "That, and a few other feelings. I was never a fan of needing to hurt people or creatures that I truly didn't *need* to hurt. So if I can mitigate that using system mechanics, that will improve my time here. The burnout portion of the bar made me think about slapping someone on the back of the head as they fought me. Lecture them into doing it better. Appear next to them and copy what they did, but with the improvement they are lacking. Then whap them again and repeat the process until their entire health bar was blue, and thus unusable or something. Preferably, I'd want them to fall asleep."

Ember leaned on his shoulder, a half smirk on her lips. "You with your single hit point?"

He shrugged at the mention. "Even with my single hit point, honey. Honestly? That could be a fun, rogue twist. Players meet an old man, roaming about. On his way to wherever with more enthusiasm than is good for him. Most will avoid me. The smart ones will get confused on why an NPC with a suspicious single hit point is doing that. They'll think it's a secret escort mission or something, and I'll lead them to whatever my boss grounds end up being…"

Recalling the limitation from his trait, he had to change that answer. "Or I'll likely pick someone else's based on what kind of stuff or skills they need? Then surprise that party at the end when they get through the ordeal. The old man was the boss fight they've been looking for the whole time, and had no clue! Something fun like that. I'm sure I can convince whoever the actual boss of the area was supposed to be to take a breather."

A pleasant thought occurred, Artorian leaning to his dearest. "In addition, hon? Maybe we can do something with that Duo Boss title? If we can work in some wiggle room that they have to beat us at the same time, or we won't stay down, or something? That may get around our annoying limitations if they persist. Bonus if we don't even have to be in the same arena. We can sneak the victor their rewards and fancy title while the other sits in the stands. Then, when a party happens to get me? You can come pick me up in whatever gazebo I come back to. Perhaps after some kind of cooldown period? I don't know how the boys upstairs have it slated, but I'd like to *not* get my Pylons wiped, unless I choose to have them wiped? Now that they're improved, it's not like Dale can touch one by happenstance and make them all blow up."

Ember loved this, her expression bright and alive. "Yes, yes, and triple yes."

A confirmation chime played so loud that Lucia's left ear snapped right up, prompting Ember and Lucia to both look around. Ember squinted at empty air, trying to find the source. "The Abyss was that?"

"The confirmation chime?" Artorian pointed at himself for ease of everyone's mind. "That's been following me around. Whoever is controlling and adjusting my prompts seems to be making it. If not, then I don't know. They haven't introduced themselves, but I've guessed it's not Tim. The chime keeps happening as I say ideas out loud, or things I believe I'd want, or improvements. I'm growing to like it. Unlike with the other onlookers, the chime makes me feel like something is getting done."

Lucia and Ember both rubbed his head in response, satisfied by the answer. The character sheets went down, and now was the time to check the environment.

Their team lead stuck her finger into her mouth, popping the digit free and shoving it to the air as if that was going to give her detailed information. "We're in Eternia, the realm of Vanaheim, oddly twisted into ball shape, and puzzled together in a horribly mismatched kind of way."

That pleased her, her fingers weaving in the air as she brought up a menu with fourteen whole map types, each offering different information. Though purely to be coy, she kept them visible only to herself for now.

Ding!

———

Map selector: Please choose your map.
Basic Maps:
Topographic Maps.
Political Maps.
Weather Maps.
Economic Maps.
Resource Maps.
Population Maps.
World Maps.

———

Advanced Maps:
Road Maps - Major and minor pathways.

Thematic Maps - Special purpose data points.
Cadastral Maps - Division by country, state, or municipality.
Navigational Chart Maps - Depth contours, tidal streamlines.
Time Zone Maps - Disabled.
Geologic Map - Distribution of rocks, soil, and sediment.
Bathymetric Maps - Ocean floor topography.
Heat Maps - Death locations, unit activity.

––––––––

Selecting the cadastral map first, Ember got everything she needed as she filtered through them. "Excellent! Horrible mismatch is how we wanted to put realms back together. We're in quadrant C-seven. I already know that we need to be in quadrant H-four to be in the same square as Tisha. So that's our goal."

Pressing her hands into her hips while the other two gawked at her from getting all of that from some airflow, Lucia and Artorian both gave her the look that they believed she was cheating in some way at the same time. Ember smirked, and made her maps visible so she could share, and point at what she was talking about.

Her party members both hugged each other in relief that Ember had just been teasing them.

She stifled a giggle, and continued planning. "According to the heat maps, nobody knows we're here. Geologic maps say that the buildings are made out of granite, marble, and a mixture of other sedimentary rocks. Predominantly gneiss and basalt. Unless we use brute force, we're not breaking any of this rock with our toys."

A concerning thought struck, her fingers tapping on her chin as she consulted population maps. "We're likely to encounter sentient buildings if we travel on the top layer. They're all moody and swing like bricks. The big downside with aboveground travel here is... while we're quick, we can't really damage them back. If we travel underground, then we immedi-

DENNIS VANDERKERKEN & DAKOTA KROUT

ately need to worry about vampiric templates, and flamberge mosquito swarms. If we plunge into The Depths? That's going to be Cheese Penguins, and Arachnoids."

When her third digit went up, her party happily ate up her tactical intel. "In terms of difficulty, we're dealing with Vanaheim modifiers. Six-hundred is the player attribute cap for first timers, but mobs don't have to adhere to that rule, and the spawner is still broken... Momma Bun, what were the difficulty jumps again? I've got my realms out of order."

Lucia groomed her ears while rattling the answer off. "The difficulty jumps are as follows: Midgard, one. We count both Alfheim and Svartalfheim as the same step, two. Jotunheim, three. Then Vanaheim, four. For Vanaheim difficulty, we multiply Midgard health by four, after their other bonuses kick in. If you don't know an opponent's health, merely expect enemies to take at least four times longer to kill."

"Thank you, Momma." When her fourth finger went up, Artorian and Lucia both pulled up a lounger, sharing the pillow-nest to sit and learn. "We jumped some realms, and the difficulty spike is going to bite us. Exploiting vulnerabilities is paramount to go fast. Unlike per the expected game progression plan, we do not have a good variety of tools to exploit differing element or damage types. My carmine halo gives some local light, but more importantly it allows you to turn your damage type into fire."

She pointedly looked at her boy for a detail before he could ask. "Yes, sugar. Thermal-type damage gets turned into fire-type damage, and no, I don't really understand which category is supposed to supersede the other at this point. If your prompt controller is still listening, can we get that cleared up? A hierarchy chart of some kind would really help."

A confirmation chime played, and everyone liked that.

Astarte crossed her arms, mulling over their options. "I don't feel good about The Depths. Penguins are weak, but as numerous as the Arachnoids. Their cheesy comedic counter move puts us at significant risk, since it can whack-a-back anything we happened to throw at the Penguin. Arachnoids are a mystery opponent, but my hips don't lie and neither do numbers. There's a lot of them crawling around down there."

Thinking of delving even deeper to avoid all three routes, she realized that wouldn't be an option. "Going after Brother Moon feels equally as questionable... We'd have to get in The Depths, then through, and then get back out from The Depths? Bad deal. That's like detouring to BlightTown to get fresh air. Let's not do that. That leaves the aboveground route, and the underground route."

Opening a fresh window, Ember slid her fingers into her red hair to pace and crunch some numbers as Lucia snuck Three a snack out of her pouch. "Living buildings have a bunch of physical damage reduction, and ridiculous energy resistances. We could still punch through and play the head-jump game?"

She paused mid-stride, Artorian munching as Ember planned out the battle. "No, there was something dangerous about the high road that I can't recall. I just recall it was so bad I didn't even want to consider it. I'm not seeing anything on the maps though..."

The weather map, of all maps, had her answer. "Ah. No... There's no air. No atmo above the buildings at all. One wrong jump and we free-float in space."

She chewed on her options. "The real problem above-ground is going to be... Actually, with what the road map is giving me, I better show you."

Walking away from her screens, she opened the basic wooden front door of the Vanaheim home. Rather than exiting to open air, a solid brick wall barred their way. She then pointed at stairs that went up to nothing, and a hallway that cut through several open rooms from a separate, oddly connected home.

When she opened the window next to the door, that exit opened to a street. That street led to a cul-de-sac, and equally went nowhere. "We can't trust anything that looks like your normal door or window. Streets are going to dead-end without warning and we'd need to cut through buildings without knowing which structures have a route that lets us progress. Fast is not an option. Elevation is an optical illusion. Getting lost is a serious concern. The map, even as flawless as I have it, is of limited help if I need to always have it both open and be nose-deep."

Lucia and Three shared a look, thinking this had a fairly straightforward answer. Artorian chimed in first. "Is there anything about the underground that makes it a pain in the rear? Or are you worried we'll run into El Mosco?"

Ember froze in place, confused. "How did you even know that…? No. Never mind. El Mosco is the worst enemy type to run into, yes. The problem with the underground is that…"

She shuddered, feeling unwell. "*Ugh*, it's a *sewer* level."

Artorian dramatically twirled his arms before pointing at himself. "*Ta-dah*! Living aura of scrubba-lubba-dub-dub, at your service?"

Lucia snickered as she watched Ember come to that realization, their team lead having forgotten entirely that they weren't being accosted by the bad cheese smell right now. "That… Yes. Point for the underground route. Bonus is that the sewers are set to reconfigure themselves to fit properly, unlike the city above which is subject to the sewers taking priority as city pieces shift. We can have a jigsaw puzzle city, but not a jigsaw puzzle sewer. Sanitation has to actually work."

Dismissing her screens and maps since she ended up not needing it, Ember took their expressions as answers. "Nidavellir has similar underground service tunnels that double as their illegal racing venue. I take it we're opting for that choice? The sewer route is going to be filled with swarms and other unpleasantries."

Artorian stuck his finger up, motioning extra dramatically with the rest of his body before his other hand settled on presenting his pointer finger. "May I present to you the fondue maker of the great undo. Laser extraordinaire and what have you? The Shining Ray boogaloo! What am I gonna do by using it at this point? *Annoy* the moon?"

The ground rumbled below them.
Ding!

———

Warning!
   Brother Moon remembers you.
   Your presence has been noticed.
   You have annoyed Brother Moon.
   Brother Moon is considered the controller of Vanaheim.
   Vanaheim has been to 'Hostile'.
   Character: Less Than Three, has been set as a specified hunting target.

———

Artorian inhaled hard, his hands sliding into his hair. "Crackers and toast."

Lucia cocked her head, her ears tilting to show confusion at not knowing the history of that phrase. "To eat all the cheese?"

Ember bent over laughing at her boy's awestruck face, unable to stop even as the first of their enemies began to break a hole into their hideaway's floor from below.

CHAPTER THIRTY-EIGHT

Lurching free from a broken floor that erupted like an over-excited fondue volcano, a cheese-filled Arachnoid burst forth with a maddened screech. The quadrupedal warrior bug—approximately three meters long and five tall—was camouflaged in yellow and brown stripes to match their specific terrain. Its powerful, vertical, pincer-like mandibles—clearly capable of crushing rock and metal—were grabbed by Astarte as the bug got too loud.

With a broad smile still on her face, the shrieking noise promptly ended via a squishy squeak and crackly crunch as she messily ripped the warrior bug's exoskeleton in half by the Arachnoid's oversized mandibles.

The fondue goop splattered about and gushed free from within the bug, all hot and bubbly as the cheese poured down the ripped halves. Pleased, she tossed the broken remains over her shoulder before the remnants turned to particles. "*Ahhh,* I needed that. Thank you, bunny-bun."

She leaned over the edge as the splattered fondue vanished from their surroundings along with the torn exoskeleton, her attire becoming immaculate while her hand pressed to her hip. "Honey? That's our way down."

Less Than Three, in the middle of looking at an inspect screen on the Arachnoid, had the prompt follow him as he platform walked directly above and over the open hole currently shrieking with unwanted activity. He looked down along with Ember, whistled at the storm that was approaching, and had an idea.

Without moving from his spot above the well where multiple cheese-infused Arachnoids were wrestling to break free first, Less Than Three discharged a clean Shining Ray from the bottom of his right foot. He was surprised to see his idea functioned, both from change of firing location, and that he was standing on a platform while doing so. A double success? He felt plenty happy about that! "Does that work because it always works, or does that work because of my socks? A curiosity for later."

The Arachnoid's massive mandibles snapped out of the open space to eviscerate him, but were instead met by ominous omens bearing down as the beam of burning energy passed to and through the packed-in warrior bugs.

The shrieking and gnawing noises threatening to bulge from the opening were replaced with a muted, humming fizzle. The impending swarm of bugs disintegrated from sustained exposure to a smooth one-thousand fire damage per second.

The descending lull of screeches that vanished into the deep as Shining Ray ate up more and more targets was a far more welcoming music to their ears. Everyone loved a blissful silence.

The sound of forgiveness.

The energy investment ate into his reserves a bit, but Three didn't need to sustain his beam for more than five or six seconds before the ramshackle tunnel had been turned into a two-meter wide, seared-clean borehole. The walls of which were piping hot, glowing orange, and going down far deeper than the original pathway had allowed. He'd need to be careful with aiming down. Too long of an exposure and he'd damage Brother Moon directly, and that would likely be met with a far more intense response than merely sending some cheese-controlled extras.

That the cheese could take Arachnoids over at all was a bad sign.

What was it with evil being so synonymous with the taking away of another's agency and autonomy? Sure, the bugs likely hadn't much of it, but still!

Artorian leaned over to look at his glowing footsie-work while the heat from below made his clothing flutter, then shot his dearest a thumbs up. "Done! Even made it warm."

He turned his inspect screen to his party to share some quickly gained information. "These aren't so bad by themselves. In groups, I see why they'd be annoying. We got lucky with the weakness. If my mental napkin math is right, these crawlers have about twenty thousand health each. That's a lot! I'm very happy that rebalancing is an ongoing process."

———

You have encountered: Warrior Bug Arachnoid.
   World: Eternia.
   Realm: Vanaheim.
   Region: Quadrant C-Seven.
   Terrain: Urban.
   Circumstance: Living World.
   Local Event: Call to Mandibles.
   Unique Properties: None.
   Racial Template: Pasteurized.
   Species: Arachnoid.

———

Detected Trait: Nerve Stem.
   Detected Skill: Mandible Mastery.
   Detected Skill: Clamber.

Detected Skill: Hostility.

———

Protection: Resistance to Melee Damage.
Vulnerability: Weakness to Fire Damage.

———

Attack 1: Eviscerating Mandible.
Attack 2: Severing Strike.
Attack 3: Shriek.

———

He had to dismiss the screen before having a chance to enjoy the details. Lucia had adopted her golden Glitterflit transportation mode, and Ember had taken *his* spot on the back of her neck! "'Ey!'"

A few deft steps saddled him into Ember's spot on Lucia, his arm adopting the hold across Ember's outfit that she usually kept on him. Their team leader focused on having the right maps up, in places that didn't block her line of sight. She didn't have to add commentary for her boy to grasp that they had switched more than physical places, and he was going to do the path-clearing this time around.

That suited Artorian just fine, peeking at a screen she had up about Brother Moon. "Cheese is weak to fire, but not thermal? The carmine halo gives us fire, so that's sorted. My cleaning effect should keep the worst of the smell away from us, and I don't want to imagine what the air is like outside of my field. That was a lot of cheese I just burned."

She made a noise to ask if he was set, and her response was a kiss to the top of her head that made her smile wide before he followed with verbal confirmation. "All set! I sees 'em? I beams 'em!"

Astarte nodded, but had her hands full and eyes occupied as they snapped from map to map. She was already strained trying to grasp the labyrinthine trail ahead of them. "Momma Bun? Shield up, dive in! Second opening on the way down is the one you need. It's right below another opening, but that one is full of angry red dots that waddle. I bet they're Penguins, and I want to avoid the Penguins. Zoom it!"

The hexagonal shield buzzed to life around Lucia, interlocking shapes clicking into place. With a hop, skip, and a drop, she nosedived the glowing borehole. "Second star to the right, and straight on 'til morning."

The first revelation Team Sleep discovered on the way down was that the Arachnoids did not care about taking damage, or being on fire, or that the walls were destroying their exoskeleton as they burgeoned from below in ridiculous quantities. They clambered uncaringly past the corpses of their disintegrating brethren, bled goopy yellow fondue, and shrieked as soon as their targets were close enough for their liking.

Ember pressed her digit to a map while Lucia made an unhappy keening noise. They were diving straight into wide open mandibles. "We'll make it before they intersect. Go!"

Lucia's shield sheared against the wall, bruising with sparks. Compressing the field closer against the Basher and her riders to go faster by reducing drag, their healer bought them those extra two seconds. Having to hunch down for their protective eggshell to neatly fit and carry them through the borehole was a cost nobody on the team said a word about. Lucia saw her turn come up based on some parts of the descending tunnel that didn't glow, ominously close to snapping mandibles approaching from the other direction.

Without time to second guess her team leader, Lucia kicked off against the wall and re-vectored them into the second available opening, relying on her shield to eat some of the momentum damage while crushing the head of an ill-positioned Arachnoid, flattening the bug on the way into their new sewer path. Her next obstacle after that was much harder to deal with. "Rubble!"

Lucia saw the blockages a smidge after Less Than Three had, his beam unleashing when her outcry ended. Having had it primed, Shining Ray seared open the path that a significantly lesser amount of Arachnoids of the worker variant were trying to break their way through. The workers were turned to particulates along with the rubble, adding another borehole that Lucia considered favorable pathing, regardless of the steady shield damage. "Thank! I'm going to need to use my next tier of shields if this keeps up, kits. The heat damage is too much for my class feature shield to eat up."

Small crevices didn't work well for large creatures, but something about the cheese spilling out of them was giving them all the creeps. When that cheese, associated Arachnoid, and rubble clogging the sewer line all disintegrated into particles along with any refuse that may have been there? That did a lot for their mental wealth and hel-being.

"I'll find you a spot, Momma." Astarte snapped her head up from her maps. "This… Honey! After Lucia has her new shields up, I'm going to give you a marker. Drill a path in that direction and ignore the existing pathing after. You're making a far better route than the Labyrinthian Abyss I was trying to navigate had available."

"Ready!" Less Than Three dropped his beam emission down to match his stamina regeneration value when he felt some strain. The laser would still undoubtedly bore through the gneiss, and hopefully would still be fast enough to make pathing faster than Lucia caught up to the open space. Bonus that they'd have to deal with even less bugs.

From the front, at least. He wasn't sure what to do about the back until he thought of Astarte's weapon kit. "Dearest, do you still have those cluster grenades that multiply? We're going to need improvised caltrops on the swarm chasing us if I'm focusing on drilling."

"Can do!" Dropping a few hundred explosive presents

behind her right away, the team lead pressed her free hand on top of their Basher's head. "Bunbun! Slow down. A sharp turn is coming up, and we're cutting through a big empty cavern after, that I have serious doubts is actually empty. I bet it's stuffed and there's just no movement right now. Looking for a detour, but I have an Artorian-quality crazy plan. If this works, we're about to make a very ugly tunnel that bores through The Depths after all, based on planet curvature."

When Lucia slowed down, Astarte continued with directions. "We're about to hit a diverging path. Take the next right hook and filter your shields; don't enter the open cavern. We've got maybe a minute before they're on us, and I need to calculate pathing to place the marker."

Lucia laid her ears flat. "Got it! Talk through what you're thinking, kit. It's no good being stuck in your own head. Pretend I'm a tiny yellow duck if you have to, I don't know where I overhead that works, but I heard it works."

Ember knew full well of the magic trick that was talking about Pylon code to the tiny yellow duck. "Map wise, we need to be five sectors right, and three sectors down to get to Quadrant H-four. Sugar, cease fire. We need them to not know we're taking that turn."

She grumbled as she tried routing line after line, only to run into the same problem as Artorian paused Shining Ray and let his stamina recuperate. The glorious sound of explosions graced his ears immediately after, the explosive presents finding eager wrapper-tearers. "All that empty space in quadrant G-four is turning my coals. The line will connect... No, we can drop a quadrant to draw a clean line and then go back up. C-seven, to D-six where we dip into The Depths at the end, to E-five where we're in... far too close to the core. We'll need to be very fast. Then F-four where we break back into the underground, to G-three where we coast through until we're at the middle of that quadrant's square. Then we need enough speed to wall-run a cavern, to redirect the tunnel up and left and we'll break from quadrant G-three into H-four when the drilling kicks back on."

Her hand tensed on Lucia's head. "Momma? As soon as that shield is done and I mark, be quick, dirty, and don't stop or slow down for anything until we need to make that wall-run turn in G-three. Sugar? Blow up the cavern. I do not care how, just make it empty. We're not going to have the speed to tear through whatever's there, and there's too many death marks on the heat map for my liking. Expect an area boss."

Without being able to look at the map, the references to quadrants made for difficult directions. Lucia, ever the Momma, moved one of her big ears so it pressed down over Astarte's hand. "Just tell me the turns, kit. We'll make it. Bashers are great in tunnels! If it wasn't for the debris blocking the way, this is just one big warren. Taking the right hook, stopping in five seconds, we'll be out of shields in four, three, two…"

The hexagonal, interlocking, egg-shaped shield was dropped as Lucia padded down from her run into a jog, and then enough of a walk to bring her higher tier shielding abilities to bear. All before they turned the corner and entered that vast, perhaps not-so-vacant cavern. It was merely quiet. Too quiet, considering the shrieking behind them that should also be in front of them and wasn't.

Artorian considered his options, slapping himself for giving up his spells. Of course it was going to come up that all of a sudden wide-area explosions would be useful. Of course! He came up with an idea, considered it a bad idea, and set it in motion because they didn't have time right now. Getting caught in a swarm slog would not be fun. "Back in twenty seconds!"

He leapt from Lucia's back to land in front of her, wasting zero time. "Trans Am!"

CHAPTER THIRTY-NINE

Blooming with blue and white particles as Trans Am hit full output right away, Artorian blitzed into the cavern, illuminating the place, and instantly triggering the area boss and all associated minions. Compound eyes flared a bloodied, hungry red all across the chamber as the remaining darkness filled with ominous, hungry lenses. The largest pair of which originated right from the center—several times larger than their mini-ito counterparts—as the Greater Mosquito Swarm woke, and woke hungry.

In their midst, El Mosco spread his many flamberge appendages and multiple, sharp buzz-kill wings. The many giant blades were merged to each limb, all gleaming before becoming drowned in the dull, darkened red of old blood.

He didn't need to drop an inspect to know what was going on there. "Of course the area boss gained a vampiric template. Sure. Why not? Why should it be easy?"

Being a speedy boy while lighting the cavern up, he created clear lines of sight to all his opponents purely to know his enemy. At his current speed of nyoom, it took two out of his twenty seconds to get deep enough into the cavern to get to the correct vantage point. The ground shattered under him from the sheer force applied when he forgot to use platforms, but that mattered little compared to discovering what he was dealing with.

Vampiric Flamberge Mosquitos. Lots of 'em.

A clean score of one-thousand five-hundred in all attributes was nice and all, and probably gave him double whatever El Mosco had. Attributes, unfortunately, were not what cracked the cookie in Eternia. They helped, but skills and abilities were the meat of the pie, and he was short one very meaty pie. He did not have a big bada boom. Without a method to funnel the Mosquitos that didn't create a bad circumstance elsewhere, Shining Ray was not going to catch them all, and Luminous Gatling was not going to pin all these enemies to the wall. Not before they pin-cushioned him first.

That made it time for his terrible idea.

His loved ones wanted to help, to the point Zelia had to come drive the stake in and grind the point home. So, alright. He was in a pinch, and if there was ever a time to ask for help, that time was certainly now. He filled his lungs with air, and shoved mana into his yell as he opened and closed his fingers in rapid succession, sparking the cobalt electricity.

"Vol-tek-ka!"

That got the attention of his Pylons. Specifically the dinosaur speedy-boy with a love for the zappy zappy. The lightning in his hands, that luminous energy coursing between his fingers, pulsed out a devastating wave of thunder. He had been heard, the Teslasaur answering its favorite person with a reverberating roar released from mountainous lungs, translated through the rampaging wave leaving Less Than Three's fingers.

Artorian collapsed his hands together in reply, releasing a follow up thunderclap as a mist of pink fuzz swirled in between his blue and white Trans Am lighting effect. A pink symbol of a roaring sun coated his back as his words were released, Artorian being painfully honest with his feelings, and speaking them into being. "I need you!"

The Greater Mosquito swarm cared little for his antics. They only cared for the delicious blood-filled morsel that they were all about to turn into a snack. The sound waves passed over them with little harm, the thunder damage a nuisance at best. They were a vampiric swarm! Only vampiric weaknesses affected them now, and a sole intruder into their hive was not considered a threat. Regardless of how their boss, El Mosco, displayed himself by posing as a fabled vampiric lord from the stories. Wings all draped over himself, and weaponized limbs coiled in to guffaw over the fate of the interloper.

Bards were always treasured, and so good at giving away their location! How pleasant their stories were, before the dinner feast served them up whole.

The third thunderclap changed the mood, and caused a few members of the swarm to falter in their charge. Both the illumination inside of their cavern, along with the shape of the interloper, altered. Packed tight in a form of energy and overlapping the shape of the tiny, running creature that had already lapped their cavern—who was almost back at the entry point he must have slipped in from—ran the outline of an electricity-crackling Teslasaur.

The Carnosaur basis Voltekka had begun with all those years ago had grown even more! The Beast now looked much larger, and much more threatening as the speed-obsessed dino took pages right out of Artorian's playbook. The silent lessons of Artorian's pattern were engraved into Voltekka's being. Just as the other Chosen had retained parts and memories of him, so had the dinosaur taken home memories and experiences to make his own. Happily roaring after getting to go on a swift run with Artorian, Voltekka snuck his favorite person a delicate treat that had been wanted for a very long time.

Voltekka hadn't accomplished this feat alone, but that was not important. The copper **Law** of **Aeris** that Artorian had connected him to was far too talkative for Voltekka's liking, regardless of the guidance usually being good.

Tekka didn't have the burden of planning his actions out

farther than needed. When Voltekka became hungry? He ate. Simple. When Voltekka wanted to play? He played. Simple. That he was as a Pylon, or an energetic shape, or a fleshy dino-beast? That was all completely irrelevant. He was will, energy, hunger, and drive. When Voltekka needed something? He got it. Simple. When Voltekka's favorites needed something? They got it. Simple. So when Voltekka's absolute favorite person in the world needed him? The memories of having his head pet while safe in Artorian's lap as fresh in the mind today as if they'd happened yesterday?

Voltekka was there.

All of Heaven and all of Earth would scoot and be put to the boot if it did not get out of the dinosaur's way. When the energetic outline of Voltekka ground his head into Artorian's temple before accumulating himself into the shape of a ball, and flowed into Artorian's chest?

Voltekka found a wholesome, warm welcome waiting for him.

Buzzing to life, the dormant Beast Core within Artorian gained a new use as a storage center, the Teslasaur protectively curling around his favorite person from within. There was a reassurance in being called, that he was wanted, and could now protect what he needed to protect. The notification that Arto-rian got with that feeling, filled him with a serene, **Loving** joy.

Ding!

————

Living Item gained!
Armored Core: Voltekka.

————

New mechanic gained!
Flash Rune: Voltekker.

———

Artorian grinned from ear to ear, and didn't bother reading any of the descriptions, warnings, costs, or effects. Nothing. He placed both his hands over the spot in his chest Voltekka currently occupied, and whispered, fiercely proud. Not only had Tekka instantly come to his aid, but Tekka had been ready with help.

"I'm proud of you, my good boy. Welcome to that Beast Core I wasn't using anyway. It's you and me, Tekka!" He fed mana into the feeling, mentally rubbing his hands over the Teslasaur's head. Of all the choices he could have expected Voltekka to make, this had never even been in the calculations. Never in the expectations. He felt the pulse of the dormant Core reverberate between his two hearts, Voltekka replying with one shocker of a tail waggle.

Thankfully, a harmless one! The knowledge that Tekka was aware of the damage he could do there, and had restrained himself? That was a worry gladly shed. Artorian beamed, relishing in the opportunity to let Voltekka show off as he felt that dinosaur tail whip about with increased excitement. "Show me what you made."

A roar of delight peeled from Less Than Three's skin in the form of copper thunder.

Deep, primal energy built under his hands as the snapping pulses between his fingers altered their coloration. First from cobalt to copper then, as if aged over time, the lightning turned dark, hunter-green and balled up in his palms.

From the center of that energy, pulsing to his heartbeats, a bright, neon-green core blipped to life. Filling in the very center of the dark, but healthy hunter-green ball that grew in size, crackling with copper electricity across its exterior. The sight was gorgeous, and only the beginning. The sight, unfortunately, drew the ire of the swarm in the room. Particularly the area boss, who wasn't in the mood for a shiny bardic performance today.

The greater swarm charged him as El Mosco screeched impatiently and swung out a fancy wing, commanding the troops. Their spear-proboscises were aimed directly at his hearts. They would be on him in seconds, and his shields would do Abyss-all against that many successive stings as an easy hundred-plus horror-shows flew right for him, charging as a swarm with that inane buzzing sound. Possibly thousands? Attempting to count was fruitless, and not the focus of his thoughts anyway.

Artorian felt Voltekka grin a hungry, sharp-toothed smile inside the Core. While the dinosaur spoke no language, Artorian grasped the inherent message. Voltekka was saying, 'Watch me.' As if the buzzing threat coming his way didn't meet the mettle of what the Teslasaur had put together.

Energetic armor surrounded Less Than Three as the dark, hunter-green energy pooled free from both his hands, shooting up his arms and rapidly coating him as the threat approached. First as the shape of a Teslasaur, nearly identical to his Auric Liger form previously used in Cal, the living energy then morphed to fit his stature as a suit of the tightest, most seamless full-plate armor. Modeled in the air-tight style after Marie's Battle Tyrant set, but with a far different thematic presence.

The green, white, and silver suit that solidified into a physical mixture of Mithril, Iridium, and Silverwood was indicative of a warrior that did not lead from the back, but stood at the front. The slim and dexterous, wide-shouldered design of the armored core was secondary to what the piece represented. A living beacon. A flag. A symbol, as the sigil of a roaring sun burned to life on his armor's back like an oversized halo. Shining bright for all to see.

He felt a mental prompt prod him for the amount of mana he wished to use, but Artorian was adamant to make his Chosen boy's creation as powerful as he could make it for its first use. When his voice came out of the armor, it was distorted. The voice of the loving grandfather that Voltekka knew was all that played when Artorian spoke words. Regardless of his age under the suit, he would sound like the person Voltekka adored, because Voltekka adored hearing that voice so very much. "All of it. All of the well over one-hundred thousand mana from the Trans Am buffs. Take all of it, Tekka! Show me what you made!"

Artorian matched his dinosaur's grin under the seamless helmet, enthralled at experiencing what Voltekka had done, his expectations so utterly shattered. His curiosity burned as bright as the sigil on his back.

Voltekka, of all the ideas that the boy could have, had chosen to become his armor.

Voltekka had *made* him a Flash Rune.

Voltekka, of all sources that Flash Runes could come from, had been *first*.

Voltekka, who suddenly roared that he was ready.

The suit burst at the seams to grow and expand, filling the volume of Artorian's stature to that of a full-fleshed adult. The large shoulders opened like Voltekka's mouth, revealing the kind of cannons that seemed ripped directly from the ancient tomes of Karlussen and Peterovia. That madlad pair of scholars that had provided his Auric Liger form equally insane weaponry. The feeling that built in his shoulders was similar to Karlussen's Projectile Particle Cannons.

As a bonus, he could already feel that just as Saint Karlussen had discovered a love for the kabooms, Voltekka had adopted these most excellent traits too.

Slamming his fists together for thematic effect as he followed the flow of the movements that Voltekka required, Artorian felt the shoulder-maws burgeon with light. The gathered hunter-green lightning condensed into the hungry cannon-maws. Merging together with the mana provided by Artorian, the annihilation spheres almost instantly reached critical mass.

Artorian felt the moment when it occurred.

The eye slits on the armor flashed with copper force, as bright, white light majesty particles poured from the armor's frame to join Trans Am's thematics. The armor's duration was sapped by the instant use of Voltekka's super move, rather than the armor being used as armor, but Voltekka clearly thought the attack to be more worthwhile as he taught his most favorite person the primal feelings involved.

Voltekka taught by feeling, instinct, and raw intuition. The thoughts associated with the process. The movements of energy. The hunger and wants. What the attack represented. An unopposable, annihilating roar of force and power that would make the land tremble. The ground quake. The inhabitants fear. Their enemies would know primal terror, or they would know death, and break.

Knowledge flowed into Artorian like a Wood Elven gift, and unlike when he borrowed from Heavenlies, this knowledge was his to keep.

Pulling his fists apart to spread his arms wide in welcome of the incoming threats that had begun to impact his shields and cause them to shimmer, Artorian understood all the steps of Voltekka's Flash Rune.

The energy flow. The intent. That the pattern of the roar to come was not a pattern of an attack, but the pattern of Voltekka himself, expressed as an attack. His Teslasaur had made him more than armor. His Teslasaur had crafted him a labor of love.

Both sword, and shield.

Artorian's solar sigil flared pink as the links of sympathy clicked in, the real Mana around him howling in a mixture of affection and approval.

The pattern of Voltekka was made real to the world around him for a fraction of a moment. Running through all the steps of the process in an instant, the effect expressed itself on to reality as Artorian invoked the words and pattern. Flashing in the shape, design, and complexity of an intricate three-dimensional Rune that formed around him.

Artorian's first Flash Rune, true and whole, went off with a kaiju's roar. "Vol-tek-ker!"

CHAPTER FORTY

Existence erased itself where the wild roar of annihilation ripped through, the twisting copper and hunter-green colored Voltekker tearing through matter like it barely mattered, reducing whole quadrants of Vanaheim to dust in addition to the comparatively meager threats occupying what used to be the deadly cavern before Artorian.

El Mosco, self-proclaimed vampire lord, managed to strike a pose before being turned into particles. Accepting death with dignity as the Voltekker saw his vampiric resistances, found them amusing, and then rolled over and through them with sheer, raw damage.

Fueled by the power of well over a hundred-thousand mana, the brutal efficiency of a Flash Rune put spells to shame. Flash Runes amplified the output of their effect to levels that real and true cultivators all paid attention to. The sight caused gawking. Artorian's release of power and primal might wasn't merely the example that his idea could be done, but was the proof of concept that it could be done well, and with spectacular results.

Runes had been the great staple. Spells a gorgeous refinement by Cal. Script a mighty amplifier. Now Flash Runes, the Aura format that contrasted the mechanical means by which Runes and spells were formed, lived, and shone bright for all to see.

While onlookers fiercely applauded in many other places from the pure spectacle, Eternium's jaw dropped at the numbers. Not those of the damage done and devastation incurred, but those of efficiency and cost. Enacting that effect, with that Rune, had been *negligible* for him. The output hadn't been free, but this type of method where a Rune or pattern was expressed with Aura. Even in game format, it would guarantee that a C-ranker could damage and severely hurt a Mage. An actual, honest to the Abyss *Mage* now had reasons to fear C-rankers.

Plain mortals!

The revelation that this particular bag of tricks, that he had just confirmed mortal minds could both learn and handle, worked? Tim had to get up from his chair and pace, his hands pressing to his head before running them down his skull, muttering to himself at the implications.

The status quo had shifted, because guinea pig Artorian had once again put his mouth where his pie was, and bitten in to chew. Tim had been hopeful for good results, of course. Being hopeful for good results and good results staring him in the face were two different things entirely. He didn't even care that Vanaheim was in dire danger of breaking up into realm pieces again. Let them! This news eclipsed that event entirely, and he rushed from his workspace in the Enclave of Information to call Cal immediately.

He had the most *excellent* news.

If they could slot this method into one of their most critical projects, then their efficiency problems with the Exodus Cores to exit Cal's Soul Space, to exist in a world devoid of Essence was solved! Instead of hours spent outside, they could have *years*.

Such was the power of Flash Runes. The proof that a full pattern could be established and expressed externally, in full, separate from the self. Crafting patterns to create effects inside oneself was a common enough Mage trick, but one *had* to be a Mage to do it. Their bodies were made entirely from the energy they were using.

This development changed everything. Runes and spells were great, but needed to be placed in internal arrays or physical scripting to make the project viable. That combination of intricate work pulled the cost back up. Even if the output of the current results could be duplicated, they couldn't be duplicated while also accounting for the space problem.

Space was limited inside of the physical Cores that had been prepared for exodus. If they had the option of external Rune applications, then the space inside of the Core could be repurposed to be a pure battery, holding more Mana instead of being stuffed with sensitive, miniaturized script.

This could not wait. Cal had to know. Luckily for Eternium, Cal did know, and was rushing toward Tim at exactly the same time. This required instant prioritization. No longer could Flash Runes be a background project.

Tim exploded his words out first before their bodies collided. "Cal! That daft old fox did it! I've already found who helped that dino-brain put it together. It was **Aeris**, of copper!"

Slamming together as the impact of two frying pans, Cal's choice of scholarly frame and Tim's meaty body both staggered back. Wisps turned to wonder what two hunks of metal had thunked into one another, before seeing the two dungeons embrace, laugh, and spin.

Cal found his footing first. "I know! I told you he's useful to have around! Never know what to expect with the odd ones out."

Cal's expression on the scholar's face then faltered. "Oh no, now I owe him *even more*. I don't even have anything of equivalent value that I can give him at this point! He's never cashed in any of his rewards or dues that he's owed properly, and the tab just keeps getting fatter with the tally he's racking up!"

Tim laughed boisterously when he recovered his own footing, curling an arm around the scholar who'd buried his face into his hands. "*Bwahahaha*! Don't fuss, bud. I've got an idea for you concerning that expensive nugget. There's a Golden— I mean, a Heroic Age that I'd like to pitch you."

The older dungeon grinned, full of mischief and well-ordered planning. "Come with me! We have much to review and many delicious goodies to discuss. Including what you did to *poor* Klendathu. How did you make an entire planet cower in fear using *only* Dale? Look at it, it's got anxiety! I had half a look at mobilized infantry as a class, and I need to have words with you about beam weaponry. You have single-handedly done all of the testing we were going to prepare a division of people for. I need stories."

Cal looked over his shoulder before being dragged off, seeing several large screens all focused on Child-torian. The Armored Core had been depleted, Voltekka falling into a deep slumber as all the Teslasaur's effects and associated bonuses faded.

Before being joinked into the Enclave of Information, he saw Less Than Three stagger and fall to a knee, Trans Am deactivating as his mana plummeted to rock bottom. His Administrator was accursed lucky that the lever on passing out hadn't been flipped yet. Though, with some of the subsystems running, he was going to be horribly sick.

From Artorian's point of view, it would have been better if that lever had been flipped, because he felt utterly awful. Heaving and coughing, he held both his hearts by clinging his arms to his chest. He barely felt or experienced the world around him as more than an artistic wobble, seeing spots, swimming terrain, and exactly what a sudden deficit of mana did to a person, Particularly when you spent more in one go than your current bar could even hold, as his big mana bar from Trans Am shrunk back down to his existing one, devoid of juice.

His regeneration metric was churning along, but he had a disgusting deficit to catch up on now that the maximum amount from Trans Am was no longer remotely as sizable, and his Nuts metric was stuck at zero. "*Bleh*. This feels far too much like being afflicted by that stuff from last time that burned up my mana supply all the time. I don't even remember what it's ca—"

Struck by a pang of mental vertigo, he held his head and groaned.

Glitterflit Lucia—trailed by many lanterns and a mystical, tassels and hanging flag adorned curved floating roof over her head—padded over to press her big paw to the top of his head. "Veracity."

The mana deprivation sickness and associated debt didn't go away, but the terrible feelings tacked on with them did start chipping away. Lucia promptly nipped him in the back of the parka, hoisting him onto her back after. When emplaced in his spot in front of Ember, he was clearly not in a state to be useful for a while.

Ember curled her arm around its normal spot, holding him with concern as he babbled while holding his head, utterly incoherent. He seemed to think he was having a full and proper conversation, but drooling toddlers could string words together better. "Looks like he's not feeling that awfulness anymore, but he's not back with us yet."

She rubbed his head regardless, Young-torian suddenly collapsing against her chest as his consciousness flicked out. "Took more than twenty seconds, but you scared off the Arachnoids, and that cavern sure is empty! Also *gone*, but certainly empty."

A swirl in the dust-laden air above them stole their attention, as El Mosco popped back into existence. Exactly in the spot he'd been defeated, holding the same dignified pose and all. Confused by his own reappearance, the area boss looked around, looked down, saw them, and buzzed his wings as a question in the unlikely event they knew what just happened.

Ember looked up, raised an eyebrow, and chuckled. "Well,

that looks to be an accident, but you're about to have a bad day, sunshine. Good morning!"

El Mosco did not 'do' mornings. As a devout creature of the night, living in realms far away from the accursed sun! He—

—Was very confused as to why it was so bright and dusty. Until a wayward breeze blew the dust away, exposing him instantly to a direct hug from the sun. The utter lack of ceiling added an unexpected variable of considerable difficulty to his vampire lord plotting. Particularly the part where El Mosco vanished in a sudden wave of dust himself, instantly devastated by the full force of direct solar exposure. There was even a sad *phuh* to accompany his second death.

Lucia copied Ember's chuckle verbatim. Rather than taking off, she sat on her butt, her attention on Less Than Three's abysmal state. "His status isn't getting better. I know he did what you told him to, and we really want to break this Tisha person out of whatever predicament she's in, but we can't really continue without him. Thoughts?"

Ember ran her claws through her flaming red hair. "The plan's wrecked. I wasn't expecting this sudden reprieve, nor the frankly unimaginable damage to Vanaheim. Brother Moon is currently too busy uncurling like a roly-poly pill bug to have the attention to send more things after us."

She tapped a few screens, trying to keep up with the turmoil in the mapping system. "Based on the maps and how many quadrants were annihilated from the stunt my boy just pulled? Vanaheim is going to be a floating flat realm again. A literal Arcoplex this time, rather than an Ecumenopolis. There's such a big rent on the planet that the map representation looks like my boy ripped its spine out."

Lucia rubbed her horn with a paw. "I don't remember what those words mean."

Still trying to think of solutions and new plans, Ember rattled off the explainer of how it had been explained to her. "An Arcology is a self-contained city in one massive building. An

DENNIS VANDERKERKEN & DAKOTA KROUT

Arcoplex is a whole city of buildings. An Ecumenopolis is a city planet."

She toyed with her Silverwood Bracelet as the ground shifted under their feet, the entire realm rumbling, warping, and bending to straighten out as the buildings above were crushed and mushed together.

Their environment was busy falling apart around them, and they couldn't easily outrun the realm they were standing on. "We may have to completely back out. Tactical retreat to the Faith Foundry. The original plan is a bust. Both with the terrain overhauling itself, and our boy out of commission. He also needs more serious medical care than we can give him with Vanaheim's sudden interest in yoga. A mana deficit that big did bad things to him, and then he passed out. Those systems weren't supposed to be active, so I can't help but feel this is another latent Task Manager present."

She squeezed her hand into a fist, gathering mana into her bracelet. "Tisha's a big girl. She's held on this long. She'll be able to hold out a bit longer. As a bonus, I know exactly who to ask for help now that we've got a much clearer shot to her. I vote that we bail."

Lucia groaned, not wanting to go back to being the Eminence and dealing with Heavenly babies for any length of time. Especially not Hella and Urtu. "*Fiiiiine.* I vote that we bail. Take us out. I don't want to go, but we need to not be here more than I don't want to go. It was such a good crazy plan, too."

Ember laughed, flicking her Silverwood Bracelet to have it ring out that pleasant chime. "That it was, but we're rolling with Artorian. Plans change. I like that about him. The punches come, and he rolls with them."

Her bracelet hummed with light, primed and ready. "Alright, Momma Bun, I see buildings starting to collapse and fall. Exiting Eternia on my mark, since I wanted to mark something. Three… two… one. *Mark.*"

With a pop, blip, and a *vwump*, Team Sleep left Eternia,

leaving Brother Moon with the biggest crick in his back, and a dire, sudden need for a chiropractor as all of Vanaheim bent and did what it could to stretch out, reshaping to fill the missing gap of space with other pieces of the realm. Where was the moon-turned-living-city with a core of cheese going to find a chiropractor?

One thing was definitely for certain. If Brother Moon ever again met anyone with dinosaur heads, anywhere on their body, the fight would be *On. Sight.* There would be riots. There would be picketing. There would be a lot worse happening than meteors going on strike. He'd had enough of this getting his cheesy behind kicked! Brother Moon threw his building-covered tendrils up high in the air like he just didn't care, and turned over a new leaf in life.

There were *children* running around able to set all of him on fire, and blow entire chunks of his back out, erasing perfectly good armor right out of existence. Just *barely* missing critically important parts of him that the child had no idea it had almost gotten?

The planetary mass of sentient cheese was giving up his aspirations of eating all there was and becoming a farmer or something. He'd grow flowers, maybe. The word tulips came to mind. If right when new food showed up, and the lights were turned on, this is what he had to contend with? Then the Brother was peace and the Moon was out.

Actually, an even better thought occurred.

Taking control of one of the many Cheese Penguins that had long ago infiltrated places it should not have been, Brother Moon waddled the little guy right into the Enclave of Information as if he was supposed to be there. For some odd reason, nobody stopped him. Not one Wisp or Gnome even asked why he was there, allowing him to waddle right along to look for someone important. This was one of the places they tended to be, and the duo in the middle of all the screens likely with the fondue bill.

Taking the time to form his voice box and method of speech

since Noot Noot wasn't going to cover it, the Penguin inhaled with freshly made lungs as it addressed an unaware Cal and Eternium when he waddled to them. Because it was obviously a great idea to sneak up on both of them at the same time. They had the most potent energy signatures about them as well, so they must be in charge. "I would like to surrender."

By the time Cal and Tim stood around the crater of what was left after their very impromptu explosive rebuttal, they were both confused on how the Penguin had left Eternia and snuck into the Enclave. The delivered message was small hat by comparison.

Cal scratched his scholarly head, fully distracted by the smoking crater. "I'll fix this, you fix… that?"

The **Acme** dungeon then smirked, suppressing a giggle, clearly having thought of some terrible pun. "Hey Tim, why can't you trust cheddar cheese?"

"Because it's no gouda." Tim squeezed his brow, starting to feel Artorian on the topic of pain in puns. Wanting to escape the punnery before it began, the older dungeon stepped out through a door of **Order** to have words with a planet. "I'll fix that, you fix this. Rogue cheese is not a problem that can stay on my plate right now. Moony! You better brie-live in magic, because—"

Tim stood still in empty space on arrival, facing the underside of Vanaheim which exposed Brother Moon's imposing octopi mouth. He stomped on a platform of his own making, realizing what he'd done. "Celestial feces, Cal, now I'm doing it too!"

Brother Moon wasn't sure what to think when all of space around him broke down in high-pitched laughter that couldn't control itself. The sound of wheezing and a table being slapped followed, before Moony's attention turned onto the portly man holding a hand over his eyes. Uncertain of how to act on its newly turned leaf, Brother Moon's only recourse was to match the vibe, releasing a single Cheese Penguin that was brought close with a tendril. He used the creature to speak, attempting to be... supportive? "I Swiss you the best."

Given that whoever was laughing in the background of space sounded like they'd fallen out of their chair, and were afflicted with a second fit of laughter, Moony figured he did... good? The person in front of his Cheese Penguin speaker was now using both his hands to cover his face. Progress?

CHAPTER FORTY-ONE

Artorian woke up from having trouble breathing. Finding Lisette, the Goblin, sitting on his chest with her arms crossed answered his question of why.

She showed her sharp teeth as he blinked and moved his arm to cover his eyes, welcoming him back to the Faith Foundry's pavilion with a mocking grin. "Morning, kitten!"

Artorian heard the statement, his mortal mind grinding to a halt as his face twisted into an expression of scrutiny. "Did you just call me a kitten?"

"Sure did, pussycat!" The Goblin prodded her stubby green fingers into his forehead, unmoved from her cross-legged spot on his chest. "Given you're out of the bag and all! It's not like I'm sour about it. Giving me the slip? That makes you a very good Goblin. If you weren't all set to head back into game-land, I would be dragging you to the next zone. You're also *actually* injured, so I won't give you the verbal smackdown I chased Lucia around with. That girl can run! She thinks she's clever hiding out in the old Flasks Before Tasks hideaway, but *oooooh*, Lisette's gonna do some bunny-hunting. My bow is ready."

One of her green ears twitched, her earrings shifting.

Glaring over her shoulder in the dimly lit room, she growled at the darkness, then slid off his chest and walked to the wall of the room. When her back pressed against a hanging blanket, the archer huffed indignantly. "You have a visitor."

Artorian pressed his hands to the bed to work himself up. His vision was only beginning to adjust, so he was working on feeling for now. His covers felt familiar. Present in the same bed that he normally occupied in the Faith Foundry's care room. The lack of strength as he tried to move was noticeable. The leeway from Eternia missing. Only good ol' muscle was available for him to push himself up right now, and he did, in fact, feel sore all over. The pain sensation was firing like his meridians had cramps.

He grasped that he'd been evacuated from Eternia easily enough. The memory of Voltekka doing him proud followed. The use of the Voltekker caused him further aches, discomfort, and a not insignificant pain spike in the skull. He rubbed the base of his head, breathing in to taste Cal's air. "Good morning to you too, Lisette. Is it anyone I know?"

She scowled at the darkness, her body language distressed. "In a way, yes. They said they knew you very well. An old friend of yours, they said. A healer."

Artorian checked himself, finding no bodily injuries, which didn't account for the fairly consistent feeling of misery that kept building like a drum in his head. Nor the pain flaring through his nerves that felt strangely metaphysical. Moving was a bad idea. "Well, don't leave me in suspense. Who is it?"

Lisette pressed her hand to her chest, politely bowing to the darkness before letting herself out of the care room. As the door creaked closed, she paused before clicking it shut, answering the boy. "**Death**."

A larger Goblin slid from the dark at the invitation. His robes were pure as the whitest snow, with a matching skull painted on his dark visage. Artorian frowned, the only recognition of that face and the associated shape shooting to the forefront of his memories. "Bob?"

The deeper voice that answered him, old and patient, was filled with optimism. "No, old friend. Though he did have words for me concerning a long-beard that hates going to war. I am not Bob. I am **Death**."

Interest turned to monotone concern, Artorian's stomach performing the pretzel twist. "Do I have long enough to grow that beard out again, or is it lights out for me?"

The Goblin moseyed over to the large bed, moving a small field of flowers, get-well notes, a variety of trinkets, and hand-crafted toys that Artorian hadn't noticed before the Goblin had to interact with them. When **Death** noticed that Artorian's attention had shifted, looking around to see the walls covered in drawings of him, he motioned at the far wall coated in mementos.

Artorian rubbed his eyes, seeing countless patches of sown cloth, embroidered with suns. Works of his deeds littered what had clearly become *his* care room. The other beds were used solely as storage for more flowers. So many flowers.

"From the look of it, spry lad? I can have you when I *earn* you." **Death** sat on a stool, grunting as he pulled his clean, soft, snug multi-layered robes about him. "The amount of souls trying to keep you alive is frankly… intimidating. Then again, I'm not here to take. Bob was a favorite of mine, and you have kept totems draped in storied honors of him sprawled across Calcium's Soul Space. Or was it Calcite? Calcutta?"

Artorian leaned heavily into the pillows supporting his back, wishing he had access to his Soul Item. These just weren't fluffy enough. "We call him Cal. He likes that. The term used to be overlord, and he wasn't so fond. Tried Cale for a while? Didn't go over well. If you're not here to spirit me away, how can I help you, **Death**? I'm Artorian, or currently Young-torian. Though I will apologize, I'm completely taken by the fact that you're so kind, and were introduced as a healer."

That apology amused the Goblin, who did not take it as a slight, and even pondered the perspective. "Death is kind, and those who know death have no qualms healing the living, to stave it off further."

The Goblin shrugged gently, reaching out for Artorian's head, which the old man trapped in a youthful body did not fight. "The embrace will happen eventually. Why not let them go when they have more stories to tell, and let them stay in the meanwhile? A healer of death is the kindest soul. Unjudging. Ever neutral. Ever kind. They do not see life as any kind of race, and neither are they smug for already having won. **Death** comes. It is the living who need us most. To weep. To mourn. To grieve in our robes. To be told their loved one is in a good place."

The Goblin traced his dark fingers across Artorian's skull, the pain inside being sapped away. "Because, **Love**. A healer of death is ever kind, and I neither needed an introduction, nor needed to be told. I see the snappenings in your past. Such a distaste you had for raider necks."

Death smiled. "While I can't see your future, I see the lives entangled within yours. The red strings wound around you as the central ball. All you have saved. No, Artorian, I'm not here to do you harm. I'm here hoping to make a friend. It's rather lonely over on my side of the bench."

The Goblin extended a hand after taking it off Artorian's hair. "My name is Mortis, friend of Bob. The best of all Goblins. I wear the mantle of **Death**. I was hopeful that you would let me attend to your health? The curators are adorable, with this little game of theirs. It does, however, affect you directly. What you need, grandfather, is *not* more life injected into your being, but to have that which is dead removed from you. Your existing, assigned healer cannot help you with this. Your damage requires excision, not repair."

Artorian reached out a hand without really thinking about it. There was no need to think about it. "I would love another friend, Mortis. Thank you for your healing attention, and insight. I would be glad to be under your care. You did, after all, scare away my gatekeeper. Even if I love that she sneaks me giant flanks of meat. Sneaking out will be all the easier this time!"

Mortis took his small hand, slowly and carefully, before giving a geriatric shake. "Then I am glad to call you a friend, **Love**. Should you ever meet **Life**? Please tell her that I very much love her for all the presents she sends me. I cherish each and every one. I consider you the best messenger for such a request."

That got Artorian to laugh, his grip squeezing the Goblin's hand as a smile formed. "Yes, yes I do believe that I am the one for that task. I will let her know when I see her. I'm guessing she's a higher **Law**? I half-remember something about the lower tiers getting into Cal first, though I know a few notable cheaters."

Mortis shrugged good naturedly, releasing his hand to press and prod his fingers into Artorian's shoulder, then his upper arm, then his forearm. "**Existence** does as she pleases. She's currently busy being quite upset at having been mauled by a Mole-Bear. Ah, there's the first break. Your Bonescripting is good and well, but bones aren't meant to change or be chipped into. No amount of careful scripting, when re-scripting, is going to be healthy. Bonescripting is a once and don't touch it again affair. There's so much here meant purely to keep you together…"

Mortis sat back on his stool, his hands pressing to his knees as the script damage meant other factors about Artorian were going to start following suit. "For that issue, you are out of time. You have to decide what you are keeping, and what is dying. Your stele can't handle all of this rapidity, even if your bruised Soul is lying on the floor giving me a thumbs up, thinking that having a single hit point means it is surviving."

The Goblin winked at Artorian, making clear he was making a joke. The message passed with the jest had been clear enough. "So. Cultivator? Non-cultivator? Beast-ivator? Or whatever the youngsters want to call it. Are you a future dungeon, a Beast, or something else, my most pleasant Nascent Being?"

Artorian felt the candle snuff in his head. Time was up. The jest had been sweet, but he laid down in the bed, lacing his fingers over his chest. "I was... I was so expecting to have people throw ideas at me, and here I was given space. How pleasant, in a way."

He drummed his fingers on his chest, Mortis appearing to have all the time in the world for his answers. Artorian liked that. Seeing another Agent of Agency, preferring to let people make their own choices. That helped him settle.

The decision was surprisingly peaceful, with only the feeling of a bonfire flickering in his mind's eye. "When I play the game of 'what could have been,' I want no further regrets that could have been avoided. I am a cultivator. I am the shape of man. But I know.... deep down, once a Mage, that I am but *light*."

He stared at the ceiling, deeply introspective. "When I Incarnate? I will be **Love**. I want to hear laughter. I want people to experience joy. I want whole groups to find fulfillment. I want all that is man, and Dwarf, and Elf, and plant, and tree to discover their purpose. To hold it close. To know what it means, what it is to cherish. I want to see children play, and learn. To see their children play, and learn. To see their children play, and learn. I want to see them brimming with stories. So that in a thousand years, when I walk and roam, and I see the same faces again, belonging to other people? I see their ancestors smile through them."

Artorian squeezed his hands tight, getting lost in his thoughts, not realizing that he summoned a being with his words. "I want to see **Compassion** flourish and thrive. I want people to see neighbors as brothers. Communities as extended family. Countries united by care and kindness. A world that stands on the understanding of suffering, of the difficulties of what it means to live. To bear one arm tight across the neck of another, then to reach out with the arm they have left, and make room to let their hearts carry more. I want my people aggressively friendly, with found families galore. None of us were ever meant to do this alone."

The celestine blue Albion Principe hovered on the opposing side of the bed where Mortis sat, the Goblin wearing the mantle of **Death** unperturbed at the concept weapon's arrival. There was rarely a greater purpose than to be called by **Love**.

Coming to check on their friend, the katana of **Sorrow**, the claymore of **Pride**, and **Explosion** the Nagamaki all filed in behind **Compassion**, who was emitting a silenced staff of pink musical notes that drifted up into the air, cut by five lines.

Artorian closed his eyes, visualizing his ideal circumstance, but losing himself to a tangent as the presence of concepts influenced his thoughts. "I want to have the means, and the tools, to help everyone that I want to help. I want the power to stand up and against people like Odin, blinded by their pride. To prevent people like Hakan from existing, addicted to sorrow. To, on a day filled with rain, prevent lonely orphans from losing their only cat. For the society that forces orphans to live in such a destitute state deserves to blow up."

Death extended a hand at the weapons, the four of which respectfully backed up. This allowed Artorian to resume his thoughts with clarity. "I want to let a roaring **Sun** live in my center, as my cultivation technique. Not one of **Fire**, but one of **Radiance** and **Resplendence**. For I love her, beyond words, and there is no better place than to keep the memory of that which I cherish most alive and well than nested between my hearts. So she will always know that they beat."

Artorian drew in a breath, unlacing his fingers as he slid his small hands over his eyes, regardless of them being closed. "I want Voltekka to feel at home in the Core at the center. My good dinosaur who only ever wanted to make me proud, and chase freely, wild as the wind. My Armored Core. My good living lightning, dancing around my fingers, and running along my hands. Roaring at my enemies from atop my shoulders."

Death placed his hand on Artorian's forehead while the boy blinded himself, making it convenient for the healer to extract that which was dead as blackened energy from his still form. Mortis would make certain this did not hurt, at least. He was kind like that. He preferred it.

Urtu and Hella momentarily peeked their heads into the door as they snuck it open, checking if they could commence mischief. Discovering **Death**, unfortunately, made them close that door exceptionally gently as they fussed at one another, stressed and doing their utmost to not make the door-hinges squawk or make the lock click. Their strained expressions remained tense and combative until they successfully got the door shut, before they fled for their lives.

Mortis quietly smiled. **Holy Fire** and **Hel Fire** were both such hellions. He spoke to Artorian in soothing tones, glad the boy was letting his soul spill from the confines of his cup. Mortis noticed that Artorian's echolocation had picked up the troubling duo, and had stopped sharing due to it. "Continue, my friend? I would hear more of your **Resplendent Sun**, your ideal form, and the direction of life you wish to tread. Worry not. When you're all done, you'll have another nice nap. Then, when you wake? Drink your milk. Eat a cookie. I prefer them over your crackers and toast."

CHAPTER FORTY-TWO

Artorian woke the next morning from continued breathing troubles. Not bothering with Echolocation, he grumbled and chanced a look. Discovering—as expected—that Lisette the Goblin was once again sitting on his chest with her arms crossed. She flashed her sharp teeth as he moved his arm to cover his eyes, which didn't shield him from her commentary. "Morning, kitten!"

"Lisette, while I—" Artorian's rebuttal was abruptly cut off when a large blur tackled Lisette off his chest. A heavy thud slammed the floor, the Goblin sputtering and trying to prevent multiple wet licking noises. He moved his arm enough to take stock of his unexpected savior, seeing a large, rough-furred, shadowy beast covered in wisps of red fire pin down Lisette, while making ominous eating noises as the Goblin arms trapped below it flailed.

Given that Lisette's response to the massive thing stepping on her to keep her stuck to the floor was exceedingly giggly? His inclination for concern didn't have ground to stand on as she sputtered out laughter. "Cerbunny! Staaaahp!"

He didn't feel worry or discomfort until the three-headed,

fire-coated, black-furred Hel-Basher turned as if to see him for the first time, turning all three of its burning bunny-heads. The six bright red eyes scorched like coals as the Beast looked at him, their ears swiveling and rotating to locate his heart beats.

Artorian really should have been intimidated, but he didn't feel it. Instead, he leaned his arms out and fell sideways on the side of his bed, reaching for the Cerbunny. "Beautiful bun! Do you want some nose rubs?"

The middle and right heads retained their composure at the offer, stoic and impassive. The Cerbunny's left head shot its ears straight up when it recognized the words, before taking control of the body and dragging the other two into a straight charge!

The derpy left head barreled straight into Artorian's outstretched arms for an instant serving of praising head and nose rubs, while the other two heads had their eyes roll around in their skulls from the sudden whiplash.

Lisette sat up to jealously watch her prized Cerbunny melt, the Beast enamored with her charge. Artorian successfully caused the three-headed Beast to sploot while somehow using two hands to rub three noses. All the while baby-talking the big Beastie. Classic Artorian moves, as he studied the Beastie at the same time. The Cerbunny was sentient, but not sapient, showing no signs of being able to speak, or possessing the type of intelligence that showed more was going on in the noggin.

To Artorian, this mattered little. The Cerbunny was a pure, sweet baby, and he was going to baby the flaming Beastie as it made happy chittering sounds at him. On the topic of the Beast's fire, the big fluff was coated in flames that he didn't feel, nor appeared to burn his hands? How interesting. They certainly didn't look cosmetic, and carried plenty of heat, but he wasn't being burned. How he wished he had some paper to make notes on. This was how bestiaries began!

He chuckled at the thought. "Where's my Bolts to Ink skill when I need it?"

The door to his care room creaked open, Cal casually walking in using the scholarly body Artorian recognized and knew. The dungeon snapped his fingers and shot at him with crossbow-hands, side-stepping the four floating concept blades keeping guard. "Buddy! Heyyyy!"

The inflection and elongated way in which Cal stretched his words and then rubbed his hands together was too reminiscent of the moment where Tatum had earned the nickname Ricky. Something had gone wrong and Cal was trying to patch it over.

Artorian attacked the Cerbunny with some particularly intense head-scratches, then shot Lisette a pleading look to take over. She sighed, plodding over and picking the Beast that was four times her size right up, flinging the splooted three-headed Hel-Rabbit over her shoulder like a potato sack. "Alright Spot, that's enough. Come on now."

Artorian felt his ears twitch. "Their name is Spot? That's *adorable!*"

Lisette gave Cal a light bow, then motioned a green digit at the left head on the Cerbunny. "Didn't see the fur pattern? The other two heads have stripes and streaks. Spot has a spot, and the most control over the body. Stripes is the serious one that can't chill, and Streak is the reason they get their zoomies, but likes Stripe and copies him. They both get grumpy anytime that Spot takes body control."

Cal moseyed up to Lisette, motioning at the Cerbunny. "May I pet them?"

Artorian's ears burned rather than twitch. Did Cal just show overt respect and kindness for boundaries? Did Cal just *ask* someone who wasn't Dani for permission to do something? Was he dreaming? Had Mortis killed him after all, and this was an afterlife?

Lisette nodded. "As much as they'll let you. He's a picky brat."

Artorian watched Cal the scholar copy his nose-rubbing tricks, the Cerbunny having a great day after so much attention! That little cotton ball flame of tail became an excited wiggle. The dungeon then helped the Cerbunny sleep, letting the big Beastie snooze on Lisette's shoulder. "There we go. That's all they really needed. A good nap. You have a pleasant day, Lisette."

The Goblin archer didn't really know how to feel about the great ruler of their universe knowing her name, and knowing it personally. She politely bowed again, and left the room. The four guardian blades unblocked the door for her as Cal sat down on the available stool next to Artorian. He then figured out that Artorian had already figured out he wasn't here for a house call, purely based on the flat look the child was giving him. The words 'what did you do' were plastered on Artorian's face.

Cal raised his arms and dropped them. "Well, I tried. I got here before anyone else could, so you didn't have time to get upset with me before I had a chance to tell you myself."

Artorian laced his fingers, holding his own hands as he got snug against his pillows. He still found them to be insufficiently fluffy, writhing in discomfort. "What happened, buddy?"

Seeing that Artorian disapproved of his pillows, Cal made the executive decision that he disapproved of the stool as well. With some swirly finger motions, Artorian's pillows fluff-a-fied themselves, with the seat Cal occupied turning into a full recliner that reminded Artorian of Deverash's ultra-ergonomic Iridium seat. Except with even more plush! Now he wanted to be in that chair. Maybe after Cal left? Definitely after Cal left.

"*Ahhh*, much better." Cal stretched out in the lounger, sagely nodding at the improvement in comfort. "Yes, try it after I flee from this place. If you think that it's preferable over chasing me. I absolutely didn't do this on purpose or anything."

Artorian inhaled deep and sharp, biting his lip. Of course. Of course it was a ruse! "What happened, Cal?"

The dungeon waffled on how to begin. "Dale was very enthusiastic about spending time with me. We had fun testing beam weaponry. Dale was mostly happy that he was getting my attention and we could finally talk, and get his questions answered. He had some worries I was able to put to rest. When you left, Tim and I were—after handling a sticky situation—

able to make a trip to your personal Pylon hold. I had to use Dale as an intermediary, with the whole *not imploding* thing and all. You get it? You get it."

Artorian made motions of understanding, rolling his wrist so Cal would continue. Cal checked his exit points, then did so. "Dale is now no longer as enthusiastic about spending time with me. While we were down there, I asked him to touch one of your Pylons. A detail looked squirrely. Your, um… your Pylons did not like that. Dale has a new body? Minya's fairly miffed at me, but I tided her over with a path in the game towards a specialization advancement called Arcane Loot Lord. She can start as an Archer, hop into Seeker, belly-slide through Treasure Lord, and bam, end goal! For now? I've staved off her wrath. And Dani's."

The scholar shuddered. "I fear ladies night. I love Dani, of course, but I once made a comment that people should critique those in power, as a comment to something else, and she very much took it to heart and has no problems throwing me right off the mountain and under the cart at the same time. I have to admit, with some pain, that it's effective. She's my Wisp, and being my Wisp well. Oftentimes to much applause from the group, which I can't say I'm unhappy about. I like how it makes her smile."

Artorian scratched his head. "How do you know about the applause? Sticking your nose in to sneak a peek at her expression?"

Cal snapped his fingers. "I forget! Every time! That you are a perceptive little snoot. You are Ex-Spelled! Yes, they've thrown the window closed on my nose a few times. Dani taught all of them how to discern all the methods that dungeons use to peek. Either to be or look from somewhere without trying to make it obvious."

Artorian pressed his fingers to his chest, acting terribly coy. "I'm expelled? From what? Did you decide on a different Administrator? Have my farming days arrived? Are you the reason that Hans came after me, on Zephyr, with *Meg*, and *Oak*?

One of those bardic heathens is enough to derail an entire narrative, and I am being chased in Eternia by four of them. Hans by himself would surely have sufficed for the joke. Four of Hans? *Four?*"

"No, no, and also, surprisingly, no?" Cal held up both his hands, crossing and uncrossing them to motion he wasn't the culprit. "Ex-Spelled. Banned from casting. In my game, Flash Runes mean no spells. I was told you gave them up due to discomforts, but it turns out that if you have one, you *cannot* use the other. Synthetic Pylons are like bad farts. The Runescript is either in or out. We either keep the energy charge on the surface of the Pylon, or inside of the Pylon, and it's wherever the Rune isn't."

Cal then shook his first in the direction of the Silverwood Tree. "And *one day*, I'm going to find where that Abyss-blasted smell is coming from!"

He flopped into his seat, melting into the recliner like he was descending into his favorite puddle. "Oh, to be a small rock in a tiny pond once more. How simple a life. Supping 'pon the mosses."

His hand fell towards his Administrator, Cal sighing heavily. "When we can get your Janitor class reinstalled, can you come down to the Pylons hold and help find what's going on? Or help clean the smell? Or, honestly, help with the growing rat problem? We found there's more than one Amalgam, and also found where Pag went missing. If you were at all curious why he hasn't been around causing trouble, it's because he *has* been causing trouble, just like the rat that he is!"

CHAPTER FORTY-THREE

Cal fussed, venting his frustrations. "I am going to *hurl* that boy into a volcano one day. After I turn him into a big snake, or something. I'm going to lock him in as a world boss to a lower realm and make him deal with players coming to give him grief the way he gave me grief."

Artorian rubbed his thumbs over one another. "I can't say I understand the flatulence reference, bud. But if you say that it's one or the other, I'll work with it. I take it that the bad news you came to deliver is that my Pylon bank went boom, after all the work I put in to make it *not* go boom? Therefore I do not have the means to rescue Tisha like I wanted, because unlike Tim's idea to build a copy and transfer me to it, there's now nothing left to make a copy from?"

Cal waffled his hand in a so-so motion rather than take his chances with speech. "*Ehhh…*"

Artorian slid from bed, sitting on the edge in his Faith Foundry designed pajamas. "Tell me, Cal. You're making a facial squirm that says it gets more complicated. You're hiding it better, still not quite there."

The dungeon deflated in his seat. "We have to redo your

stats. The growth and flat bonuses thing? Fantastic, but too much. Choosing a single one for a class, maybe two? That ought to be it. Three, if I'm feeling generous. I'll let you pick, bud. You can customize the Janitor class that way. My personal curiosity comes from a different test I need help with."

Artorian made positive hand motions, so Cal nodded and spoke, glad there was no anger. Then again, there was rarely anything but help and care from the old man, child-form or otherwise. "The point of keeping statistics even, attributes wise, is important to ease people into a sense of artificial Magehood. If I want to give them Mana bodies, real ones, through the game, then I need that measuring stick to be equal and even, and the players need to get used to the feeling of what that means. For purely playing the game, on the other hand, with people that have already passed that stage? Maybe not so necessary, it turns out. I have a whole batch of Gaston Pylons in play meant to penalize players who deviate too much from evened out attributes. But I need tests from people who are willing to let them vary wildly."

He frowned, trying to recall terms as he began humming the tune, needing to get that out of his head. "I need to see some… what did the kids call it? Min-maxing? Yes. That. Also! I very much liked what you did with your world boss moves. I know you didn't choose that route, but I am very entertained, and would love to see more. I'd even like to send whole parties after you."

Artorian thought about this as Godhand-clan gauzy white curtains billowed into the room from a passing cool breeze.

Some light entered the room along with fresh air, the window opened from outside as Somnus, the Cheshire cat Heavenly of **Sleep** got cozy on the windowsill. A loud *mrowl* from Somnus changed Cal's tune, who remembered a sudden detail by daydream. "There *was* a concern mentioned by your loved ones. A good quote, actually? You either die a hero, or you live long enough to see yourself become the villain. I intend to safeguard your heroic nature in reality, and work out this alternative end in my game. I happen to be in need of some villains! They don't have to be evil, merely competent. I've asked Odin, and been given positive responses, but... y'know. It's *Odin*. A name he's sticking to until the Grecian realms are done to play in, then I'm told he's going to go plod around as Zeus again. Something about practicing being a major deity before decanting? I don't know, I slipped out early from his speech. I think it's still going?"

Cal momentarily looked over his shoulder at a sight Artorian could not see. "Yup, still going."

Artorian sighed, hanging his head. So much for all his progress and all of Zelia's hard work. "My secretary's not going to be happy about my player character, and Yuki's going to sharpen ice when she finds out about Odin."

Cal could not puddle into the chair further then he already had. "I got an earful already. Zelia said she's going to be there for the next version of your game-self, and the next, and the next, and the next. We did salvage some Pylons from your hold, but your entire specialization tree is gone. Luckily, Halcyon has a full copy of the critical hit specific specialization in her greedy little Orca fins. I badly need that not to happen when we roll out of beta. Pylon banks going boom is fun in theory, but even I am getting tired of that specific brand of fireworks."

The young scholar then lifted his head from his Iridium lounger after a moment of silence, peeking over the edge when there wasn't a snappy comeback. "Not upset? Was expecting an upset."

Artorian shrugged, conflicted. "I finally understand what Tom meant so long ago, when he said something was missing? I shoot things, and I feel pressured and frustrated, but rarely do I feel satisfied. The satisfaction came either from revenge, which is not a feeling I want to cultivate, or feeling glad to have been done with the challenge."

He shook his head, disappointed. "That's not what you're looking for, is it? I entered expecting to have some fun, then quickly had to take the game seriously like it was a second life. I am now noticing that I am feeling stress ebb away because I'm no longer there, rushing towards the next objective. Since you mentioned it? The best time for me was in fact momentarily pretending to play a villain. That bit in the metal courtyard to pursue and enable **Love** between two souls that, in their own weird little way, worked together? That was meaningful to me."

Cal sat up more as the entire chair shifted to accommodate him, the dungeon holding his own hands and moving one of his legs over the other as some gorgeous and clean game prompt screens opened next to him for notation.

Artorian held up a hand, starting a count. "Voltekka's Flash Rune? That was meaningful to me as well. That's progress on a problem I've actually wanted, and circumvented my worry of me having no idea where I was going to find the ten...? Twenty plus years to sit down and study? Practicing like the old days. My sense of progression is on fire, and yet those woods are drowning. I'm getting confused, Cal. I remember sitting on a mountain for years, recovering to go out on the adventure to get my grandchildren back. I remember how difficult it all used to be. I simply can't get used to how easy it all is now, and am stumbling over my own feet."

Abandoning his counter, he motioned out the window. "In that same vein? I love that we have this, especially for the kids. I never expected my Aura-practice Aquarium to get the kind of attention it did. Cultivation was a persistent death threat to anyone on the path, the success chances abysmal, and the casualties counted in raindrops. Now look at what you've done here. A place where everyone who wants to is almost guaranteed to become a Mage. If someone dares say you didn't succeed in your own version of making a utopia? They are blind."

He reset his hand for a fresh count. "I'm still burning up to get Tisha and get her back into Gomez's arms, but without the means... What am I gonna do? I am letting that sink in, and there's an odd peace that comes with the lack of responsibility. If I could do the thing? Then my noblesse oblige makes Goblin *reeee* noises."

Artorian loosely motioned all around him. "Now I'm a powerless... what? Twelve? Fifteen? Am I fifteen? I have no idea. A powerless fifteen year old in a medical ward, who everyone is sending flowers and trinkets like a celebrity. That thing I never wanted to be. I want my quiet office back, with my paperwork and my grumbles and yelling at my quills about some silly nonsense a planner is trying to propose. I want to take walks around the societies and see how everyone is doing. I want to poke my nose in and cause chaotic good mischief. I want to stroll into Chasuble like the enemy stronghold it is, no more than a handful of coins to my name, and utterly devastate any corruption I might find while robbing them blind as I walk out."

Artorian paused to open and close his hands at that memory, his feelings worn on his sleeve. "I want to sit at the bonfire every night and make pensive noises while I rub my beard, scheming and shipping people together in the right harbors to foster more **Love**. Scarfing down honey pie. Laughing and drinking with my Dwarves. Chattering up a storm about cultivation with my Elves."

Artorian apologetically turned his head to look at Cal. "I don't want to be divine. I don't want to rule the world. I want to enjoy life and everything in it, savoring the details and seeing that each next generation has it better than their forebears."

He eased his arm over Cal's recliner, offering a hand. "I do a lot of complicated things, bud, but I'm simple. I've got problems with authority, chips on my shoulders with people who don't grasp that everyone has to win for individuals to win, and overall just want to see people happy. That's it. That's all."

Cal took him by the wrist, holding him to support his young Administrator as Artorian released brain-worries.

Artorian's other hand slapped the bed, emotions flaring. "Because, by my big, fluffy longbeard, I want to have tea with Heavenlies and meet every last one. I want to know them, each and all, so I know what kind of place to make next to the fire. I want to pet every variation of Essence and love it like a child to welcome home. I want to carry Mana in my arms and rub its tummy. I want to hug my loved ones and squeeze them tight, and to not let go until they deemed it enough. I want to get everyone I care for that's in a bind, out of that bind."

Some anger found room on Young-torian's face. "All this clever hoop-jumping is from situations I find myself in where my values clash with the circumstance, and so far I have for the most part managed to step on the circumstance. But, Cal? I confess, Marie was a blow to me."

Cal did not interrupt, nodding and notating while remaining supportive. "I still don't know if she said some of the things she said out of anger, or because she was serious. Or purely because those words would make me feel a certain way? She still said them."

Artorian very much liked the steady handhold, squeezing lightly. "That I got lucky in puzzling out how her **Glory Law** worked, mostly from seeing her sit on a pile of Mages and Henry blabbing, when she had infinite Mana and **Glory** reasonably shouldn't have triggered? Yet she was *clearly* getting **Law**-use practice? That plays second fiddle."

Cal waffled his spare hand. "Some of the challengers had higher **Law** tiers than her, and qualified for her **Glory** triggers. They ran out of juice, and she did not, changing the math. So she won. I did like how you got her stuck using infamy. Because she wasn't trying to advance using infamy, but that's what she ended up getting. Infamy-gain did nooooot match her intent and expectations. Much less the results! **Glory** definitely didn't like the hypocrisy, and got fed up, I think. Haven't had the chance to talk to **Glory** about it. I'm curious about the details of the interaction. I'm guessing there's only so much leniency that a Heavenly is willing to give you before they get upset that you deviated too much from *their* meaning and interpretation of a **Law**. Regardless of the infinite flexibility that the **Law** itself might have."

Cal squeezed his Administrator's wrist twice, changing the topic. "What plays the first fiddle?"

Artorian squeezed Cal's wrist back, the tiny detail one of great comfort. "That I lost a friend, and not because they died. Immortality is normally the curse of watching everyone else die. What is it now, brother? What is immortality to us now? With our pile of growing mistakes that we cannot avoid, or hide, or get away from."

With serious concern, and a not insignificant surge of emotion to the sudden change in relational qualifier, Cal sat up, still holding Artorian wrist to wrist. "You're not okay. This is more than the game. What's wrong?"

Artorian smiled weakly. "It's all the setbacks, bud. It made me think of what Henry and Marie said about needing to start over, and over, and over. I had so many game tools that I gained, only to need to give them up again, that I feel frustrated with the system. I was given so much, and yet my tools felt hollow. They were gifts, but they weren't mine. The more I put my own tools together, the less I wanted to. I miss achieving something and getting that adorable list of selection options. Where I did not know what anything was, and had to pick based on what looked most enticing. Then I got to discover what it did, and feel a sense of progress? I like the tools increasing in effect as they rise in rank, but special new little effects that can be chosen. That the overall quality of the tool changed depending on where you got it sounded fun."

The Administrator's mind wandered. "I overheard Shaka and Tim gabble about curves and averages, and I like the thought of being able to find the same ability in a more difficult realm that has a better basis for me to build up from. That's like finding a more efficient attack technique in cultivation. It's *exciting*. I want the kind of gains that make me gasp, my eyes glitter with stars, and run to show off what I just got. I might have the body of a child, but when it comes to the game? I want to *feel* like a child. To be allowed the indulgence of that sheer, raw, dumb happiness."

His thoughts drifted back to Henry and Marie. "I don't want to repeat that cycle of loss if it is not required by the normal rigors of life, and I now have insight on what would make them not want to repeat it either. In my eyes, I failed them, Cal. That's why I'm currently not okay. I lost all my power, and now that it's quiet, dark, and I feel alone? The regrets are piling in."

Cal was up from his lounger in a blink, his arms curled around Artorian's head. His hands pressed against the small back as he held the mortal child close, Cal's voice suddenly became fatherly, and soft. "Hey, *hey*, no. None of that. You're okay. That was not your fault. That was my fault. That's my burden to bear. Not yours. Mine."

He sat with Artorian on the bed after letting go when the child tapped him. "Let's talk about something else for a bit. Something that would cheer you up. Give your head something to hold onto that isn't the endless tasks. Got anything?"

Artorian adored the surprise hug, having squeezed Cal's scholarly form back. "Thanks, bud. *Umm…* Yes, that sounds like a good idea."

A good idea promptly jumped to the forefront, presenting itself with a salute. "Would you mind talking about your original dungeon? I never did get to see it. Not really."

Cal beamed and clapped his hands together at Artorian's request. "Oh boy, do I ever!"

CHAPTER FORTY-FOUR

Outright delighted at the request, Cal showed off one of his proudest creations.

His original dungeon!

Represented by a fully interactive, three-dimensional map. Complete with tags, color outlines, notes, pins, and version iterations. All excited, Cal swapped right to the last version. Artorian saw something about 'Shroomish' before those dropped down on the list as Cal excitedly rambled. "Normal Bashers on the first floor, with a squad of advanced Bashers as a boss. Dire Shrooms and Vampiric Moss are also on this floor."

Hyped up from the topic change, and the sudden chance to gush, Cal leaned heavily into the model. He zoomed in on several parts to point while showing how to control the object, before pushing the model into Artorian's hands so he could fiddle with it and ask questions about his layout. That failed to keep Artorian's attention away from what his eyes were drawn to. The threaded cables of crystal, ore, and gemstones coated in warning labels.

Were some of those Essence transfer pipes tagged as *radioactive*? What was radioactive supposed to mean?

Artorian mouthed the names under his breath, though Cal heard him regardless as he read some of the associated notes on his Administrator's distracted voyage through the dungeon model. Some of the notations were very recent additions, while the original notes were from Bob. Cal then realized that seeing Bob's tags was catching Artorian's eyes, likely due to Mortis having visited. He, too, missed his most-bestest Goblin-buddy.

Once he'd repeated the names, Artorian read the descriptions about these dangerous corruption-transference materials all bound in Osmium tubing. "Air Affinity. Arsenopyrite is arsenic ore, or iron arsenic sulfide with a brilliant steel-metallic color. Often found in hydrothermal vents, gold deposits, and pegmatites. Despite its usefulness in insulation, fire resistance, and sound absorption, the mineral dust is deadly if inhaled. Air Essence and corruption-absorbing."

His vision dipped as a frown furrowed into being. "Water Affinity. Chalcanthite, or water-copper ore, is toxic due to sulfur compounds. Chalcanthite kills everything in blood. Blood cells, bacteria, nutrients, and leaves behind pure water when suffused with the mineral."

Concerned, the frown even deeper, he read on to the entry utterly plastered with excessive fire corruption warning purity seals. "Fire Affinity. Cinnabar, a deep-red mercury-sulphide mineral, amalgamated with sulfur. Deadliest mineral in the Old World."

He stopped himself from reading the rest of the label, glancing at all the unpleasant effects cinnabar caused before moving on with clear discomfort.

"Earth Affinity. Torbernite, a mineral composed of hydrated green copper, phosphate, and uranyl. Also called uranium ore, it decomposes skin on contact." Artorian shot Cal a face full of fear before reading any further. "On *contact*?"

Grinning wide, Cal should maybe have dampened his enthusiasm and excited head nodding. The scholar was just about clapping.

"Cal, your dungeon is showing. Mr. *Altruist*." Artorian

snapped back to the notes to continue, horrified, but unable to look away. "Celestial Affinity. Heliodor is an ore for beryllium, otherwise a yellow or green beryl gemstone. However, exposure to beryllium or beryl dust disrupts biological processes. The body has no methods to remove beryllium and death from toxicity results after five years of exposure."

Artorian was so glad he was on the last entry. "Infernal Affinity. Opal. The transfer rate of infernal Essence and corruption along opal is more powerful than any other type by a factor of three. Additional notes... redacted? Additional testing compiled by Soni, The Moth-er Mageous."

"Altruist? Oh hush, you walking lexicon." Cal leaned over to look at the notes his Administrator was reading off. "Ah, yes. The Bat Demon! You remember Soni from your alpha-run days in Eternia, don't you? Soni took on a Moth form when they changed their lot in life."

Artorian gave Cal a look that said he wasn't about to forget Soni, his tone sassy. "You're the lexicon, Cal. An altruistic lexicon. If you find another word that starts with a C, you can even spell your name out with it all clever-like. I remember Soni. I'm stuck on why we're using Demons for projects."

Cal now needed a word that began with a C, to make the setup for another glorious pun. In the meanwhile, he rambled off his reasoning. "With Demons being ancient and mostly immune to death, lost knowledge of natural Essence conductors became a delight to rediscover and continue research on. Corvid has a jumble of a gemstone collection that Soni rifles through and organizes from time to time. I'm told it's so that he can 'borrow' from it for portal experiments. They've even got this amusing category system from the Old World."

The scholarly dungeon looked entertained as a memory surfaced, recounting the event. "Soni once saw one and dropped everything they were holding, then tried to play it off as if their find was no big deal. Soni said, 'Oh, that one is hard to find.' When I asked why it was marked as 'common rarity,' Soni made me laugh. The Moth said, 'Not shiny enough in nature for Corvid to add a ton of it to their collection.' I sputtered, but had to see this collection."

Cal swirled his thin finger, conjuring an image of a pile of minerals, gems, and rocks so tall that it almost made the singular smug bird sitting atop the pile invisible among the mess. From the top of the image, the pile had the appearance of a six pointed star.

As a time-lapse played, Corvid flew into the image, dropping even more shinies onto the pile, then flew away. Soon after, Soni snuck onto the pile, the Moth seeming to almost burrow in as he threw items towards the different points. The image slowed and zoomed in, showing that the items thrown to the points were the more useful conductors, like heliodore, while less ideal conductors, like emeralds, were thrown less far. Non-useful shinies were left in the center, creating a mound while some of the useful shinies disappeared into Soni's pockets. The thieving Moth looked around for Ludere and hurriedly flew out of the image before the time-lapse stopped.

Cal didn't stifle his giggling at all. "Oh, if the Wisps and Gnomes ever got wind of this organization system, there will be another war. Until then? This is my personal little bundle of controlled chaos to savor."

He then clapped his hands together, overly excited once again. "Let's get back to my dungeon now!"

Reclaiming the model, he swirled it around to focus on his floors. "The squads of advanced Bashers on the second floor have secret tunnels and hidey holes to maneuver through. Third floor? Those were my Goblins. Large fortifications were emplaced, along with various types of Boblins."

Cal waggled his eyebrows at Artorian, but the Administrator did not take the bait when it came to his word flub. You couldn't force flubs, and it was too obvious. Cal moped when Artorian replied with a flat look, shoving his small nose back at the model for Cal to carry on. "You fussy baby! More dungeons, it is. The boss of the third floor was particularly clever! Dani posing as the Goblin Amazon, a body without a mind that she could inhabit. Bob did most of the heavy lifting on floor three, really."

He moved to the next floor, not wanting to linger on Bob again. "Fourth floor. A cat labyrinth littered with traps, with Snowball the steamboat as the boss. Each branch in the labyrinth corresponds to a different elemental affinity. The fights here were particularly noteworthy, so I added a large panel of glass in the ceiling of the boss room, purely so those on the surface could watch. I loved showing off so much in those days."

Artorian finally cracked, laughing. The steamboat comment hadn't hit the barn wall, but Cal pretending he no longer liked showing off? Please. "As if you don't love showing off now?"

Cal grinned, succeeding in his objective. He highlighted passive dangers. "Floors one through four are outfitted with the standard trap allotments like pitfalls and spikes. The fifth floor? All Manny the Manticore. With holes in the boss room for Manny to maneuver his tail through. Complete with a clever mirror, and an alcove above the door for him to hide himself. This is purely a boss room to weed out problems."

That got some understanding nods, so Cal kept going. "The sixth and seventh floor are experimental ideas that I tried to implement, but hit snags. Tower Tier representations, with Golems on each platform that used their associated effects. I tried designing floating platforms to match the Ascension process, but it took so much room and energy that it ended up being not particularly cost effective. Plus, after Chandra ranked up the Tier of her **Law**, I began having doubts about having those floors at all. Her going from **Plant** to **Nature**? That was a *yeowch*!"

Artorian understood, curious about the next floor. "That makes sense, very costly. Sudden Essence costs punch you in the stomach. I'm familiar, having done that to you myself a few times now. Say, this next floor looks familiar. Don't I know this one?"

"You do!" Cal beamed, focusing the model on the design of

the Mage's Recluse. "Eighth floor! Mage Recluse. Pillows, beds, and a bunch of other goodies specifically crafted to cater to B-rankers and up. I didn't get much use out of the place, but it had so much potential! My real, main problem was getting Mages to want to stay put, or having the time to get them to stay put. There was always too much to do that ended up needing a Mage. Speaking of!"

A sudden genius idea struck Cal. He knew how to cheer his Administrator up! "Do you remember all those pillows you entered with? I still have the patterns and designs for all of those."

Artorian perked up instantly, pointing at a relatively empty corner of his stuffed care room. Cal laughed, clapped his hands, and let the Skyspear Pillows from his students of old, each lovingly crafted, rain from the ceiling. The downpour of fluff lasted until each and every one had been accounted for. His Administrator clearly loved it, his spirits visibly improving as Artorian began to get nostalgic and stuck in his own head.

Cal shot his finger up, recalling something. "I do have one more, but I understand if you don't want it."

Reaching behind his back so Artorian couldn't see what he was reconstructing, Cal offered Artorian a tiny throw pillow. Plucked from an empty crib in the Old World, the item had made it into Zelia's claws before once more entering Cal's possession. Sown through with ancient, painful memories, the throw pillow even had the same smell that Artorian remembered.

A smell that hit him like the sky falling on his head.

The sight and sensation split Artorian's hearts in half, both of his hands reaching for the pillow as he stole the small, hand-sewn thing from Cal's grip, cradling it between his hearts before protectively curling in around the pillow.

Cal attempted to reach for the boy, but Artorian felt unfathomably distant, regardless of physical proximity. "I... Maybe not the best... I can undo it."

Artorian shook his head, his voice empty. "No. Let me have this. Talk about your floors."

Conflicted, Cal pulled his hand back, having little recourse but to continue as he worried he'd just done the opposite of help. Some altruist he was. That thought stung, and he didn't like it. "Aright, bud, but if you need something else?"

Artorian nodded, but was no longer present, lost in daydreams of ancient times.

Somnus, the Cheshire Cat of **Sleep**, tutted Cal with a half-awake stretch as she rose from the window, her back arched powerfully. "Tsk-tsk-tsk. You were doing so well."

Coming apart line by line, she was suddenly gone from the windowsill, and sprawled behind Artorian. Somnus served as a chonky backrest as the lines filtered back in one color at a time. A backrest not used until she put her paw right onto Artorian's small head, and tugged him down to be nested in the cat's fluff.

Somnus let her paw lay on him before yawning wide, showing off a mouth full of sharp teeth before tugging the lost boy in against her belly like a baby kitten, protectively moving a leg over him. "You can do that with Mages, dungeon. If you do that with mortals, their minds will run right into a brick wall, and they'll get all sad for a while. Unable to stop the feeling, or do much about it, until they have allowed it to happen and pass."

Somnus pressed her nose to Artorian's head, sniffing. Confirming he was beset by the sads because the memories associated with the small throw pillow had pushed him down into a spiral, her large tongue came to bear to groom him. The little sad kitten lacked responses, his eyes open, but his gaze far away.

Cal sighed, not knowing where he went wrong. "Did I do bad?"

"No." Somnus was surprisingly curt with the answers, but didn't withhold them. "You thought of something that might help, recognized it could be a problem, then provided your gift without a preamble. The step you missed was explaining to the boy what the questionable gift was, allowing him the agency to decline you. Instead you made the object exist, and shoved it into his sphere, forcing him to deal with the memories regardless of him being ready, or prepared. Much like that game of yours? The process of pleasantry is missing steps."

The Cheshire Cat paused her grooming, her fat, fluffy tail flicking before she looked up at him as her face changed entirely. "Not bad. Merely inexperienced. The best of intentions do not always yield the most favorable results. One must balance good intention with measured forethought, and considered action. Then you will find the outcomes you seek will come much more easily. You have now learned more about being a person. What an odd path for a dungeon to choose, but who is Somnus to deny you your **Dreams**? I know what hopes you harbor, Cal. What visions of the future plague you so."

Somnus reached, placing a cat's paw on the dungeon's knee. "The plague of technology. The moment when you become more. Where Essence and Mana return to the world. That life-giving energy flowing free once more. The golden age of knowledge, thought, and peace that can follow. You are plagued by the nightmares that only you can save them all. The only way anything from the Old World survives. You dream of the best possible outcome, yet you dread the hardest of choices that you must make. The reality that you may not be the best choice of grand savior. Just as my little kitten here has realized and laments that he cannot do it all, as you lament it."

Cal slumped, deflating like a balloon with his exhale. "I was really hoping never to have to hear those words spoken out loud."

Somnus patted his knee to console him. "You must hear the words, Cal, so you can face the door. So you can come to terms with the awful nature of what it means to end your ley lines. Artorian knows that he will be a poor ruler, no matter how much everyone would love to see him take the seat. You know that you make a poor overlord."

Somnus provided the dungeon with her telltale Cheshire

smile. "Much like our favorite Dreamer, you treasure agency. The choices of people. Their unpredictability, guided by their patterns and inclinations, is what you treasure. You do not seek to oppress or rule, so you wonder just how this age of peace is to last, when you know that you will not enforce it. Or the grudges from the Old World would not be playing out once more, between Nidavellir, Atlantis, and El Dorado."

Cal ran his fingers through the hair of his borrowed body. Back-talking a Heavenly was fruitless, and she wasn't doing anything that your average housecat wouldn't. Walking all over people was the cat thing to do. "Abyss, you know far more than I'm comfortable with, Somnus. Do you have anything you can aid me with, or is that paw of yours just going to press down on my soul?"

The Cheshire Cat ran her large tongue over Artorian's forehead, then yawned violently wide. "You have been helping yourself this entire time, Cal. I, of course, suggest a pleasant **Sleep**. Perhaps calling the Astrea girl, as she specializes in **Nightmares**?"

She lounged on her side, seeing the dungeon didn't find that very helpful. "You wish for immediate gratification? Very well, Curator. Continue telling this Dreamer of your creations. You will find that in sharing, you heal wounds you did not know you had. Time may heal what reason cannot, but nothing will heal if healing is not what you seek. There is my aid, Cal. **Sleep** on it."

When Cal moved to ask a question, he was met with a cat-paw to the face. "*Shhh*. No wake-y wake-y. Kitty Momma naps now. Talk to my kitten."

CHAPTER FORTY-FIVE

There was really no coming back from a paw in the face, and Cal couldn't help but find amusement in the visual. He had a great sense of humor! He searched for Astrea's whereabouts since the Lady had been mentioned, and found her easily enough. She was set to stay one floor down, in treatment for... Nightmares? That was too on the nose, even for Cal. Wasn't that her thing? Her current location was... *Ah*. Well, that made things easy, now didn't it?

The Cheshire paw left his face when Somnus fell asleep, which took very little effort. That paw instead curled in around the kitten she was protecting. Cal saw himself doing the exact same thing to Grace as a memory hit, far more understanding than he was letting on. "Astrea? You can stop listening in with the rest of that big huddle of people all pretending to be very quiet in the hallway."

A scuttling of individuals could be heard all flittering out of the hallway adjacent to Artorian's door, which peeped open just enough for Astrea to poke her nose through. She tried to smile and play off being innocent, but it was clear from her sniffly voice that she had a cold. Which was a second odd thing… Why did a freshly minted Mage of **Nightmare** have a cold? "Hiiiii. Fancy meeting you here, Bossman."

Cal chuckled, motioning at the recently added pillow pile in the corner of the room. "Slink past the guardian blades and plunk yourself down. I won't fault you for listening in, though I admit to enjoying being surprised. Not having myself spread out to pay attention to everything at once has upsides."

Astrea hissed in a breath, pointing at Artorian all bundled in under the big cat's paws instead. "Oh, that's alright. Can I—"

Cal was already making the 'come on over' motions, more interested in what was going on with her Mage form. "Do you mind if I check you over while you check your grandfather? You're also taking his current appearance surprisingly well."

Astrea slunk into the care room wearing her own Faith Foundry pajamas, making Cal think they doubled as the outfit for patients. "Go for it, Bossman."

She reached for Somnus first, scratching under her chin while pressing her own forehead to the cat's head, copying a purring sound as best she could. Somnus clearly liked it, the half-asleep cat grinding her large head into Astrea's, before a long singular lick was dragged up Astrea's cheek. Followed by a *mrooowl* that anybody could translate as 'want to sleep.' "Goodnight to you too, Somni-ni."

Cal found the issue fairly swiftly, though his find left him with a new problem. "*Huh*… Are you having trouble cultivating after leaving the C-ranks? You're so low on Mana that your Mage body is creating sickness symptoms. You've got your C-ranker reserves, but that's it? Also, congratulations on the transition! Did I congratulate you already? One moment, congratulation time."

Making a silent shower of confetti that evaporated as it hit the floor, he politely clapped with a big smile while solidifying balloon-words that read 'congratulations' and 'praise'! Owner of the Soul Space or not, upsetting a Mother Superior came with downsides. He then motioned his finger between Astrea and the cat as they ground their foreheads together. "You know each other already?"

Astrea pulled her head away, sitting on the edge of the bed next to the large Cheshire and the ancient in youthful form. "That's a lot of questions at once for a sick person, Bossman."

Cal reached over to gently place his palm on her head, filtering in Mana to bring her up from rock-bottom B-rank zero to the threshold of B-rank one. He watched as Astrea blinked in confusion, her symptoms and terrible feelings clearing up at a speed that was visibly noticeable on her body. The luster returned to her skin. The shine to her eyes. "Better? I did note that your chart said you were in treatment for what should be your own bonded **Law**. Please put a pin in that and tack it onto the answers list."

Astrea flexed her hands in the same manner that Artorian did. Cal couldn't help but smile at the odd little family traits being passed down. He adored seeing silly little mannerisms transfer. So cute! "The… **Law** problem… is that my power controls me, rather than me controlling my power."

Astrea's voice gained more clarity to it as the difference in Mana caused her great relief. "Yeah, better!"

Adjusting her pose, sharing came more easily. "Somni and I bonded over our shared thematic. Somnus to people who she isn't close to, if the name was confusing. I don't consider it strange that the Heavenly of **Sleep** would be close to those of **Dreams** and **Nightmares**. And no, Bossman, the family and I have long come to terms with who Grandpa is and the way Grandpa looks being mixed up. I've seen him as a Dragon, a Liger, a cloud, a literal ray of sunshine, and then several stages of a person. You get used to it? We actually had to go to Corona to ask how old he really was. We started having doubts that he wasn't five-hundred years old or something, when we knew him as children in the Fringe."

Cal pressed his hand over his mouth to stifle a hard laugh. "Oh, this codger. You're all so alike. Reminds me of something he said to me once. Let me try to copy the mood."

Sitting up slightly more, the dungeon made a dramatic face to be funny, speaking to the room as if lecturing to copy the sly old fox. "My boy, never misconstrue a person's age with their ability to be a complete child. The correlation has no bearing. Was I not proof of concept enough? It doesn't matter what age someone is when having fun is on the table. We never truly stop being children."

Astrea sputtered with a smile, needing to cover her own face before pressing her fingers into her own chest, taking a moment to breathe and exhale. When she breathed in again, Cal steadied himself, because she was about to have a lot to say. "I really do feel much better. Thank you. Maybe that will make all my headaches and uncontrolled nightmares clear up as well. Thankfully, they haven't been as bad as they could be because of Grandpa. Cultivating has in fact been a problem, but it's my own fault. I got so used to the constant influx of free Essence in the C-ranks and down that I'm now having trouble drawing Essence in. I mean Mana."

She sat up straighter, composing herself. "Pa's Aquarium zone worked utter magic on our problems with Aura, letting us see and feel our fields as if they were tangible all the time. I think what may have bottlenecked me currently is that instead of dividing Aura the way I was used to, I now have Presence, with all of the layers merged. People warned me that existing as a Mage would be so incredibly different, but going about it as a mortal doesn't cut the sandwich. Not even a corner of it. I need Mage classes."

When the Mage remembered that breathing was a polite thing to do in social company, Astrea stopped talking even though she realized that she could easily continue without a pause in stride for much longer. The ears of others were not so lenient. "All those stories about new Mages learning how to walk? We laughed, but now I'm in that boat, and my rear is bitten. I have been thoroughly humbled, especially after my troubles with the basics. Pa made such a fuss about it during his lectures too. So, like I said, it's my own fault."

Cal slid on oversized glasses, jotting down notes on a pad that hadn't been in his hands previously. Just for fun, he put on a silly little accent. "I see, I see, and how does zis make you feel?"

Astrea sputtered again, a smile breaking out on her face as she reached down to run her fingers through Artorian's hair, who had latched on to the sound of their conversation rather than the conversation itself. The company was clearly helping, even if he couldn't be helped directly yet. "I'll be fine, Cal. It's my Pa that I'm worried about. I know what happened because I listened in, and I only understand what's going on because Corona had an evening at the bonfire to hold me tight while she told us the story. His first life? He's been through a lot, and keeps trying to shoulder it by himself."

Astrea sighed, enjoying the feeling of the breathing life under her fingers. "It's like he knows we're here for him, but something is preventing him from using those bridges. Like he's not doing enough, if he's not doing it all. Hearing Zelia gush, all proud he asked for her? That was a pleasant surprise. Having seen the moment where he called Voltekka? That brings me joy. It gives me hope he'll ask for me one day. Shouting my name to the skies. I know I would drop everything to come running. Everything."

The dungeon grinned wide. "No more Bossman? I'll take it. Cal is better."

Cal took off his glasses, folding them to fit the silly thing into the front pocket of his attire. When he realized this robe did not have a front pocket, he considered it an affront to clothing, and promptly added pockets. "This is the bit of the savior complex where I feel out of my depth. I want to help. I do. But I put him there, and that bites. I know every molecule that makes a person, but I've never been one to explore the mind. I understand why the pillow sunk him into the mire, but I cannot grasp how to get him out without directly reaching into the brainpan and changing the chemicals."

"You're doing it right now." Astrea's words gained strength

and confidence, her fingers opening and closing on Artorian's head as she affirmed that he was on the right path. "You can tell by the glaze that's going away from his eyes, the way his ear points at us, the lack of nail-deep grip in the pillow. He's not hearing our conversation, as much as he is hearing comforting voices, while physically aware that we're around, with Somni providing back support. He's got all the psychological needs ready and physiological needs provided for. So he's going to recover fast. He's also predisposed to be able to get himself out of these kinds of situations. You just happened to hit him hard when he was vulnerable. As the **Nightmare** person, it's what I would have done. **Dreams** and **Nightmares** are two sides of the same coin. I think it's why they're back to back on floor twenty-two of the Tower. They're meant to help you cope or process something your subconscious is trying to tackle. If you're truly unlucky, something your consciousness is struggling with. If it's even worse than that, then you're in a battle with your conscience, and I'd feel bad doing anything to that person at all."

She stopped when Cal put his glasses back on to peer over the rim.

Her words petered out, confused. "What?"

"Breathe, Astrea." Cal soothed the newly minted Mage, a small smile manifesting. "Breathe."

"Right!" She slapped her own knee, admonishing herself for forgetting. "I should cede ground. I overheard Somni say to keep talking about your layout?"

"In a moment." Cal had another question that needed an answer before he could focus. "What was that about Artorian helping your nightmares? I know that aside from the bit of time where he was in bed in Avalon, he hasn't been back."

Astrea frowned, then realized that Cal truly did not know. Before she could answer, she looked down when Artorian's small hand reached out to grip her robe. She slid her fingers back into his hair, petting his head. "You're okay, Grandpa. We're here for you. You take your time, okay?"

His small nod was returned with a happy smile, even if he didn't see it. "This is going to be odd to explain, Cal. In my dreams, they're not always *my* dreams, but I experience the viewpoint as if I am the person who they are affecting. In Jiivra's nightmares, it is often the case that I find myself stuck under the old Skyspear Academy, buried in a dark hole. I hear the sloshing from the walls that steals my fellow students away. The hungry scratching on the ceiling as it rushes to close the distance to me."

She swallowed, needing a moment as the difficult part was over. "Then right before it gets me, there's a brightness. I open my eyes, and there, at the beginning of the tunnel sits a pink, glowing outline of my grandfather. In his fancy lapis lazuli blue robes. Then I shift, and I am Jiivra, and he is still there, but in Skyspear robes. The scratches recede. The sloshing can't get past him. I can breathe. I can stand. He looks over his shoulder, smiles at me, and runs his hand down his beard going *fu-fu-fu.*"

Astrea couldn't help but smile at the memory. "Like he knows that Jiivra didn't want to be given a hand getting up. She wanted to stand up all by herself to face this threat. She wanted to overcome this with her own strength. So Grandpa sat there, proud of her. He didn't reach out a hand, instead he gave her what she really needed to do as she wished. He bought her time. I feel strength fill my chest, and…"

Astrea lifted her hand, blowing air over her palm. "And like that… he is gone."

Cal leaned in to ask about the energy, but Astrea answered his question before it left his mouth. "It was him. Not the him we know, laying under Somni's paw, but him all the same. All of who he is, packed into his Mana. Like it learned who he was, and then chose, for itself, that that's who it wanted to be. Like all his Mana picked up what he could no longer bear to carry, and carried it for him."

Her hand rose, walking it over Somni's fur like a tracker through tall grass. "I have followed this weave of love. Through the dreams of others, I have seen his Mana coil an arm around

Grim's neck, keeping company to the lonely. I have seen his Mana wrestle with Tychus, giving pointers. I have chased it into the dreams of Ferrets and Red Pandas, where he becomes golden and glowing, matching their form. I have seen his Mana sitting with children, weaving baskets, listening to them weep and speak. I have seen it hug Brianna's head, when she needed to hide her face so none could see her stress. I have seen it stop, and turn, and look at me, knowing I was there."

She sailed her hand through the air like a ship bobbing over gentle waves. "Sometimes pink, sometimes celestine blue, Grandpa's spirit walks the horizon, and smiles when he sits with you."

CHAPTER FORTY-SIX

Cal looked down at Artorian, reminiscing on his history. "You wholesome little monster."

Astrea grinned wide, stealing his attention while he sought the opportunity for a pun. "Yeah, but he's our wholesome little monster, and we love him."

They both looked down when Artorian poked Cal in the thigh, having gotten the terrible nose-tingle that punnery was about to be afoot. That couldn't stand. "Map."

Cal chuckled, smiled, and pulled the map closer. He glanced at Astrea, but received nods in turn as she leaned over to pet Somnus instead, the Cheshire Cat's tail altering in fur patterns while flicking. "The ninth floor of my original dungeon is a double corkscrew gravity cone filled with Elementals. Or artificial Elementals? Semi-sentient ones. There ended up being a big difference between natives from another plane, natives from this plane that had been consumed by an affinity type, natives from this plane that happened to have an elemental-quality affinity connection, true Elementals, and my artificial Elementals."

Distracted by those old experiments, he then half-chuckled,

stuck on a dichotomy. "It's funny. At the bottom of the drill-shaped cone that descends, I made an artificial **Love** Elemental that became a boss mob in the strangest way. The other Elementals all wanted it the moment that Elemental Core was added, more than anything else. I'm seeing a lot of similarities with Artorian, save one pertinent thematic detail."

Astrea frowned, curious but not following. "What do you mean?"

Cal wasn't certain how to explain. Moving the three-dimensional model to the side, he pulled up his archives. Represented by a bookcase that he pulled into reality, opened, and removed a file from, before dismissing the entire thing. "Well, I held a battle royale on the ninth floor. That got me some very interesting results. My tenth floor was a Mana control testing room with several levels where, if you didn't get your Mana control perfect, you died."

He paused, waggling his hand to backtrack that statement. "Die is a strong word. Mostly I stole Mana to allow Mages to pass to the best Mana-dense spot I had for them to cultivate. I loved free snacks! I should bring those back. Mages would pay an arm and a leg to use those for practice!"

Astrea raised an eyebrow. "Don't you own everyone's arms and legs?"

Cal turned sullen. "You would not believe how often that comes up to dampen my day."

Distracting himself, he played a file from his archive. "There was a time where I started working with an Elemental Core in my testing lab, frustrated with recent setbacks. As an Ascended of **Acme**, with access to all the flavors of all the **Laws**? I could shift around the composition of the Core, altering the Mana type and quantity."

Cal grumbled at his own file, narrating as he unpacked it and put up screens of moving pictures. "I wasn't trying to make a specific Elemental, I wanted something that could improve all of them."

The dungeon turned, pointing at Artorian. "Then I

encountered an interesting result when I made a particular top-tier Elemental. The first oddity was that, unlike the other Elementals who had a decently consistent size, this one was half as big as even the next smallest Elemental on the docket, and whoooo-boy, was it built differently! Not a bad difference? Definitely different. Then again, I had no idea what to expect from a **Love** Elemental."

He swirled his hand, bringing close the image of a gold-tinged, pink blob, the Mana-matter surrounding an Elemental Core. "I put it in the box with the others to see how they would play. When this gold-tinged, pink blob came into the sensory range of the other Elementals? It instantly put any and all taunt Runes to shame, which was not what I expected. Normally they either acted cautious, or aggressive."

Cal centered the image on his fighting pit, and let the results play. "Everything near the **Love** Elemental charged at it for no reason I could discern, brutally attacking all the other Elementals trying to get to it. Our pink blob rolled toward the edge of the pit, and I watched with utter fascination as the Elementals destroyed themselves trying to reach that edge first. My pit was pandemonium. The little love-bubble saw this scuffle, disregarded the melee, then decided it was going to do its own thing and went *wheeeee*! Much like someone we know. The Elemental hopped into the open air above the pit, ignoring gravity, then as if holding onto an umbrella, descended at a leisurely pace."

Cal paused the recording when a watery-yellow Elemental snagged the **Love** blob right out of the air. "Imbrem Aureum. Nasty bugger, mixture of Celestial and Water. Once it… not consumed. Not ate. Merged is a better word? That still misses some nuance. Imbrem expanded, taking on a pink tinge while trying to integrate the **Love** blob. To my surprise, Imbrem then compressed back down. Currently I think that has something to do with the Mana density increasing. I originally thought Imbrem had absorbed the **Love** bubble, but now I have doubts. Certainly got a lot stronger though!"

Cal increased the clarity of the image to show off that, as

the improved Imbrem moved, the spinning droplets that coagulated and formed Imbrem's body sliced through the corrupted
stone floors with ease. "I love this next part! Not the bit where
my dungeon took a beating, Dani had words about that.
Imbrem is going to fight another boss down there called
Aranea. Diametrically opposed Mana types butting heads
makes for a cataclysmic show, as Aranea is mostly Infernal, Fire,
and a smattering of Earth. To clarify, Imbrem Aureum
combined Celestial, Water, Wind, and conceptual **Love**
energy."

Astrea watched the recorded display, the spider-style
Elemental taking the offensive with a sharp lunge as Aranea
won initiative. The water glob knocked those bladed legs off
course by lashing out with a compressed water whip and slicing
them right off. The residual water turned sticky, glued to
Aranea, and creeped up the other Elemental's leg nubs for a
sneak attack. Aranea showed surprising intellect, slicing its own
limbs off at the root before rolling away and unleashing a cone
of black fire at Imbrem.

For the most part, Imbrem got out of Dodge, some of its
floating orbital droplets not being so lucky as those evaporated
when the conical black beam struck them. That display ended
up being far from the impressive one, as Astrea spotted the
background losing whole chunks of matter on contact with the
infernal cone. The attack moved uninhibited through corrupted
reinforcement like the most potent acid eating away at tasty
treats, but as fire!

The watery Elemental glob learned a new trick on the fly,
shooting itself forward as a directed stream as Aranea worked
on positioning to catch Imbrem in its cone. Adapting to swim
through the air in a perfect laminar stream, Imbrem circumvented the attack entirely. The newfound speed was too much
for the leg-lacking spider-Elemental, who had its Core plucked
right out as Imbrem pierced straight through the darker
Elemental's center mass. The Elemental spider dissipated in

motes of black energy without its central power source, falling apart from within as the conical attack sputtered and died.

Astrea watched intently as the remaining black motes were being reabsorbed by Cal's dungeon influence. She remembered that phenomenon, but it had been ages since she'd seen it. Her head snapped to Cal when he spoke and caught her attention. "Now the best part!"

Twitching and shaking erratically, Imbrem changed upon acquisition of the third Core. Astrea didn't know much of anything about Elementals, but if it was anything like Beasts, this was where one would eat the other. Expecting the black-and-red Core to be dissolved and consumed, she squinted and saw a pink light wrapping around both Cores rather than any of them vanishing.

Instead of one of the two major mixed-affinity Cores over-powering the other, the two larger Cores began orbiting the smaller pink one as a central keystone. The fiery body of Aranea regrew around the three Cores, golden water swarming around it like a regal Aura.

Cal wrung his hands together. "Aranea Imbrem. The new version and this boss mob, and best of both worlds. Dani translated the words to 'Spider Shower,' which gave me the most incredible idea for a trap that I want to make another version of."

Astrea liked the story, but was hoping there was more to it than merely a story. That must have been written in crayon on her face when Cal glanced at her, as he quickly created those three Cores on his palm. "Now the cool part."

Funneling Mana into the inert Cores, he re-applied the same mixtures as displayed in the recording. The Infernal, Fire, and Earth Core sprang to life first, hovering higher. Followed by the Celestial, Air, and Water Core that hovered up next to it, the two Cores exchanged upsetting sparks between them and vibrated as if to start a fight. The third, smaller Core then pulsed bright pink, hovering between the existing two Cores that stopped harassing the other. As in the recording, the two larger Cores began to orbit the **Love** Core, their feud ended.

Cal made a dramatic hand motion at the artificial Elemental, but the effect he'd been planning for did not happen. He squinted at the Cores in his hand, then at the recording that he pulled back to replay, clearly seeing the fiery spider body reform and gain the regal Aura. Looking back at the Cores floating on his hand, they had done nothing of the sort. "Odd. They recombined normally every other time I recreated this. It's even *fighting* me. What gives?"

A grumble from below them distracted all eyes away from the Elemental Core, Artorian wriggling himself free from under Somnus. He got halfway out before running out of energy and flopping. Reaching out an arm, his fingers opened and closed. "Gib."

Cal initially thought that giving a **Love** Elemental Core to a currently-not **Love** Mage was a bad idea. He then reconsidered that stance, and thought it was a great idea! He had no idea what this was going to do! Now, of course, he had to know. "Sure thing, buddy! Here you go."

Failing to keep the overly friendly tune out of his voice, Cal cheerfully handed the Cores right over like a Spotter expecting a glorious disaster moments before the kaboom.

Astrea helped Artorian get the rest of the way out from under Somni's paws, getting him to sit up on the side of the bed while she stood, so he could use both hands to accept Cal's current experiment. The moment his fingers brushed over the Infernal, Fire, and Earth Core, the pink glow coating all three Cores pulsed brightly. "Hello to you too, my sweet."

Cal felt enraptured at the energetic signatures pouring from the Elemental Cores, seeing with more eyes and types of sight than merely the mundane. The moment Artorian touched them, they came alive with energy, pulsing out wavelengths of sound that carried all the hallmarks of synesthesia. Artorian was hearing the Core through the tunes it radiated, but was seeing those sounds as images. Images that cleared up to shape a far different form than the fiery spider he'd been expecting.

Cycling vision types, Cal had to stop cold in his tracks when landing on Mana densities, and the local forms they had taken on. The care room was utterly filled with Wolves, Fenrir, Liger, and C'towl. All formed from the latent A-rank Mana Artorian did not have access to while in this mortal shape. A tight-knit pack of found family and energetically-bonded Beasts. They saw him when he saw them, their eyes filled with the spark of intelligence. Both sapience, and sentience. This Mana was *alive*, in the full sense of the word. Guardians of the being that would one day become the vessel for them to return to. Artorian's multiple ranks of Mana.

Cal was so caught up in the scene of being observed by living energy that was so calm, so collected, that the Cores being taken from his hand had not registered. When he looked down, Artorian wasn't visible due to having no Mana. He had to cycle back to normal view, then saw a pink orb had formed around the three Cores, with Artorian holding them against his tiny throw pillow and chest, while he petted the pink ball and whispered to it.

Before Cal could ask his million questions, several things happened in rapid succession. The Elementals consumed Artorian's throw pillow at his prompting. Immediately after, the Cores swirled into his Silverwood band, causing his bracelet to hum and glow as Artorian held up his arm and squeezed his hand into a tight fist. Pink light pouring from between his fingers. "Astrea."

She wrapped her arm around his shoulders, sitting on his side to keep him close. "Grandfather?"

"This is for you and Jiivra, if you two so wish." He breathed life into his closed fist, and opened his fingers to reveal a marble of Silverwood, clean and polished. Unseen to him, one of his living Mana ranks stood, darted forward, and leapt into the core, adding a healthy, luminous, loving resplendence to the Silverwood marble.

Cal gawked at the marble. "That is the cleanest Silverwood Seed that I have ever seen. Where'd my Cores go? Is that them? What happened to them?"

Artorian reached over, placing the marble in Astrea's open hand before he closed her fingers around the object. The act appeared to give him great strength, the color returning to his skin. He breathed in deep, and saw the world with clear eyes once more. He then tapped her closed hand, and smiled up at her. "I had lovely dreams, after I got out of my mire. Who is that lovely little girl sitting between you two, I wonder? Holding both your hands, while you soar through the skyland seas on Blanket."

His grip squeezed her hand, pink light escaping from between Astrea's digits. "I can't help but feel like that wasn't *my* dream that I was having, oh wandering **Nightmare**."

Flicking his blue eyes to the window, he winked at her when she grasped what he meant, and what dreams he had seen. "Go."

Cal hadn't caught on yet, but Astrea was up from the bed and flying out of the open window in less than four strides. It was no mystery to Artorian where she was off to. Silverwood pollen was potent enough. A mixture of Elemental Cores not wanting to be what they were assigned to be, who had explicitly requested they wanted to be part of a family? Say no more, fam. That gave him great hopes for Astrea's happiness.

A happiness he was most certainly going to support! He rolled his shoulders, getting on his feet. "I feel much better. Cal? I'm going to want words later. For now? I need Decorum. I'm going to get Tisha."

CHAPTER FORTY-SEVEN

Cal was trying not to add seven sudden new projects to his frankly already impossible to-do list. Unable to get a word out as he was busy reeling in said to-do lists to do more than look dumbfounded as Decorum's giant Liger face suddenly occupied the opened window.

Darkening Artorian's assigned care room by popping up like a storybook wafer when a page was turned. The Liger's booming voice was accompanied by a fang-filled smile as Gomez greeted Artorian with all the aplomb of challenging him to rapier duel. "Brother!"

An upset, bellowing cry from the Mother Superior instantly followed, her upset Basher voice shuddering through the entirety of the Pavilion. "Decorum! Boy, I swear, if you rolled in my flower garden again, I will have your hide and wear it as a coat!"

Sparing no moment at understanding there was very little time before the Mother Superior found he had in fact been rolling around in that pile of catnip, Decorum flowed from his Liger form into that of the well-dressed, stately human that tended to suit his needs as Gomez more.

Decorum had come to mean more to him as a Liger, while Gomez fit his comforts on the humanized social platform much more smoothly. A platform he'd always wanted to be mingled with. "I was already looking for you when I heard you call for me, brother. I encountered a minor distraction."

He brushed some catnip from his shoulder. "I was informed we can rescue my dearest love, Tisha? Are we leaving post-haste? Does anyone require a good mauling should they yet stand in our way?"

Artorian pressed his hands to his hips, rearing back for broad laughter. "*Aha-ha*! Brother! Good to see you. Hugs now! Plan on the way. I think there's a small crowd of fans about to break my care room door down again. We can Bracelet-plop out, but brother, I have no more capacity in Eternia. My character Pylons went boom."

Gomez strode right over, got down on a knee, and swallowed Artorian up in a heavy hug. "I know, brother. I finished getting the last of the Squirrels out only recently. They're all speaking with Curator Caladrius, that Celestial Hawk, to get back in and get back to work on your new bank. There was a great uproar over quest rewards received that you never got to use. Many are upset on your behalf."

Cal blinked the other topics away, hearing some concerning names. "Wait, wait. That Squirrel Cabal was hiding in *your* Pylon hold? Why am I even surprised? Why is Caladrius helping? He was assigned to complete other projects. I thought with his Tier one-hundred thirteen **Art Law** Heavenly showing up, he'd be too preoccupied trying to sneak out to meet them. Or sneaking over to one-hundred seventeen again to ask for more **Luck** with people visiting his pure-celestial affinity **Art** dungeon."

Cal crossed his own arms, shaking the new set of rogue thoughts back out of his buffer. He pulled a communication brooch from Zelia out of his pocket, and thumb-flicked it to Artorian with the flair of flipping a coin. "Too much to do. I'm glad you're well, Administrator. Take this, and poofles the fookles on out of here. Mother Superior is already up the stairs and on this floor. You must flee. We'll talk later."

Artorian caught the brooch out of the air and affixed it to the neckline of his white care-pavilion pajamas in one smooth motion. Grabbing hold of his brooch, he dropped an open hand toward the four guardian blades, the weapons hovering in place while representing the legend of his links to the past. "Do you four want to come with me?"

The four blades all felt like the heavens parted before them, the light streaming in from the open balcony behind Artorian appearing outright angelic as he offered them a place. **Sorrow**, the black Katana. **Compassion**, the celestine Albion Principe. **Pride**, the rainbow Claymore, and **Explosion**, the nitroglycerin Assault Nagamaki all twirled in place before speeding over to dance and spin around him. Each concept weapon then lined up in front of Artorian, mentally saluting as they could finally, properly, report for duty.

He extended his Silverwood Bracelet, letting them each bump against his arm to be stored, before he took hold of Gomez's fancy suit sleeve. He matched his countdown to the stomping coming up through the hallway. "Three, two, one, *wheee!*"

The door to Artorian's care room slammed open after Cal had strategically chosen to leave along with Artorian and company. Only Somnus remained on the bed, now all sprawled out as if to attempt to claim every corner with sheer mass.

The Mother Superior turned beet red, shaking her fist at the open balcony, the remains of her garden strewn about the floor. "Decorummmmm!"

Decorum could swear that he heard the Mother Superior all the way from Cal's Soul Space, feeling the shiver roll across his skin to the point where he needed to rub his arms. Eternia was safe enough. Right? Right.

"*He-heyyyy!* Look what the C'towl dragged in!" With a clap of his hands, Hans initiated his harlequin scheme the moment that Decorum and Artorian appeared in Eternia. The damage from Less Than Three's Voltekker had been greatly amended, leaving Decorum and Artorian standing in a town square on Vanaheim's surface. Rectangle. The town square was shaped as a long, thin rectangle, on its way to becoming a proper plaza.

Hans's questionable welcome was filled with a lurid, oozing personality that sent concerning shivers down the spine of all except Decorum, who already had it going. The still-pirate-dressed bard lounged over the edge of Zephyr's fancy airship hull as she hovered low in the vacant Vanaheim skies. "I guess we can recall Meg and Oak! We got this far and then lost track of you. Like you vanished from the world entirely. Guess you did! Now that you're back, though… I, the Great Hans, master of the brown pants and flame, destroyer of reputations and seamstress of lute and song, must regale you with—"

"Zephyr!" Artorian's clear, sudden, unyielding call silenced Hans outright when the airship stopped lilting and hovering at an odd tilt so Hans could be dramatic. The ship lowered herself to the ground more and more in anticipation of Captain Sparrow stepping off her prow and onto whatever could serve as an improvised dock as if she was sinking beneath the waves. Hans swaggering his way across to their intended target!

Zephyr had been very successfully bribed into this plan with a black pearl coloration scheme for her vessel form. Instead, Zephyr outright landed and deployed a boarding ramp when Artorian followed up on calling her, causing Hans to stumble. "I need you."

"*Zephyyyyy, noooo*! We must stick to the plan!" Hans's whining could be heard from the deck as he got himself back on his feet, tackled down by Hans Jr. in a matching outfit who thought it had become play time when Daddy lost his footing and did a little dance. The child threw himself right onto Hans's stomach with an innocent, naive giggle, knocking the air out of the bard as he had to catch his son before being able to catch himself. Wrecking himself rather than checking himself.

Zephyr paid Hans no heed, as there was a time for fun and a time for serious. She manifested herself a High Elven body, dressed it with just barely enough clothing to be considered modestly garbed, and pushed open the door of her own main cabin to stride out and walk over her own deck. It was odd to be both the ship and the person at the same time, but the freshly minted **Neon** Mage was much more comfortable with the entire affair after Ascension. Being in Eternia did little to hamper that comfort. It was how she had gained the status, after all.

Once at the ramp, she folded her hands as the black pearl color scheme of the pirate-themed vessel overhauled itself to that of the Administrator's faction. Her bright turquoise and green mermaid dress was easy to spot on a ship adorned in healthy, welcoming hues of whites, browns, and golden filigree. Making her quite the standout as she herself definitely carried the High Elven hunger for vanity and good looks.

Zephyr's tone, on the other hand, was still the young Elf Artorian had always known. The nerves, shyness, uncertainty, and eagerness to prove herself were still on clear display, regardless of her otherwise robust confidence. "Administrator. How can I help?"

Artorian boarded with Gomez in the lead, who politely greeted Zephyr with a bow. With Gomez having a permanent office in her hull, that was likely not necessary. It was, however, very polite. Zephyr gave Gomez a nod, but really needed to know what she had been called for. Artorian rarely-to-never asked for help, much less stated that he needed her. A statement that had sent her into a moment of paralysis before an overwhelming sensation of pride mixed with duty had flooded her.

She had instantly righted herself, not a second thought spared to abandoning the longstanding, well-planned out plot that had been in motion against him for some playful grief. When he raised his arms to her at the top of the boarding ramp, Zephyr eased to a knee to hug him gently. She repeated herself, much more softly, her voice concerned. "How can I help?"

The grip on her back made her aware of clear discomfort.

Something was wrong. He didn't feel at home in his body, and the small hands on her back shook with twitches. When he spoke, his voice was strained. "Hard transfer. Don't have a character sheet. Feel like I'm surrounded by sharp prickles all over. Need to sit. Need to get to Tisha. Call Lucia and Dawn. They know the location. I'm not sure if I can help. Need to be there anyway."

That was more than enough for Zephyr.

She scooped him up like a paperweight and carried him right to one of the abundantly luxurious loungers on the portside of her vessel. "Gomez, I'm turning the empty office into a tactical room. Tell me everything you need when the others get here, and expect party favors to linger around downstairs. I'm cleaning those up last. We had a whole setup ready to surprise Artorian, which is being scrapped. As soon as I have coordinates on Tisha, I'm applying thrust. I'm taking off right now."

Gomez certainly appreciated her sudden snap to action, leaving his brother in High Elven hands as Zephyr was already tucking him with a luxurious blanket of exotic quality. She rubbed his head as he struggled with being in Eternia without being connected to the requisite Pylons. That had to be uncomfortable in a world of **Order** that lacked the flexibility it used to.

As if on cue, Tim stepped onto her hull through an unannounced alabaster portal of said pure **Order**, his heavyset, well-dressed, portly form not making a dent on her hull as he carefully controlled his density. "This should be the… Yes! Artorian! There you are! Glad you're back, I need to assign these to you, or rather, your bracelet, pronto."

He strolled right towards the Administrator, grabbing Hans by the face when the bard slid like snake oil in front of him to speak in an instant attempt to schmooze and kiss butt. Tim didn't have time, depositing Hans on his feet to his left on the way by, muffling the brown flame's mouth until he was past. "Hlmm inn mft!"

Tim reached for Artorian's bracelet. "Could I please?"

Nodding while still feeling covered in pins and needles, he got the bracelet off, but that was the limit. The limit was enough for Tim, who took it in a hurry. He updated a small hoard of information to change what the bracelet was keyed to as a small library of screens flickered into being and scrolled down around him. Tim used the object as a gateway, helping it back onto Artorian's wrist when the screens all winked out. "Connecting… and… success! No more risk of you dying in here. If you are defeated, the bracelet will snap instead of you, and you will be tossed back out into Cal. You'll lose all your stuff, but *you* will be fine. I will make backup bracelets so Amaterasu does not do to me what she did to Marie."

He shuddered hard. "What is it with all these lady powerhouses? They would have torn my old dungeon a new back door. Here, let me get this back on you."

The moment the Silverwood Bracelet was back in place, Artorian felt right as rain, the prickling sensations of all his limbs falling asleep at the same time subsiding. "*Whoo… oooh*, that was uncomfortable. Much better now, thank you, Tim. I need to call for my team, but this feels like big changes? I like the safety blanket."

"They are big changes, but this solves the problem. I'll find them for you. I've kept track of Team Sleep." A wave of the hand opened another Grecian-themed, alabaster portal of **Order**. The checker patterned black-lit gate with its stark white portal stood there a moment before Ember ran through at a full sprint, the gate closing behind her before anyone or anything could follow.

She ground to a halt on Zephyr's hull and left skid marks that made Zephyr's High Elf form cringe in place as she could feel her deck being stained. When at a stop, Ember pulled a bag from her bracelet, upending it to reveal the pocket-sized Basher form of Lucia as Momma Bun fell out of the bag. "Bag-out!"

Their Glitterflit healer hit the floor, bounced, and stood up in her human form with her hands held high. "*Whoo*! Safe! That is never going to get old!"

Something felt out of place as Lucia wrinkled her nose. She traced her fingers over her face, then felt the Basher-spike that was present on her forehead, the bladed white horn crisscrossed with kintsugi-like striations of gold. Pressing her finger to it, she managed to repress the horn at the cost of her Basher ears flopping right back out of her head. "*Aww*, Abyss. Well, rather my flopples than the horn, I suppose. Too many bad jokes come with the horn, and there's been some unpleasant talk concerning the kintsugi thing going about. I'd rather not be affiliated with this Marie person."

Lucia looked around to check where they were, detecting and recognizing the cheesy odor of Vanaheim right away. Without Artorian's cleaning effect, its presence was painfully pungent and obvious. She found her kit easily enough when Ember was bunding herself into the big cozy chair with him. Already half-entangled and pulling the blanket over herself as she worked his arm around her shoulders so she could nest her face into his neck, a happy noise purring from her spot the moment she got settled.

Ember was clearly happy about this notable improvement. "I get to be on a boat, *and* be with my boy? Two of my favorites."

She then, for just a moment that she clearly didn't have spare based on her expression, addressed the ship while pointing. "Zephy? Tisha is in that direction. I'm sharing my map information with you about the quadrant. She has moved and is now in K-9. Castle of the Great Howl, which apparently has nothing to do with wolves. She's in the sub-basement under the sewer lair, or sewer layer? I can't tell if that's a typo. While I hear we no longer have beef with any of the cheese denizens, we still have plenty of insects in need of a good swat. Map says Decorum is on board. Share my maps with him while you're at it? I've set the permissions already, and now I wish to bury my face into my Artorian's neck and not be bothered."

She then slammed her head back down where it was, and

refused to be engaged with, as she put all her effort into maximum cuddles.

Artorian held Ember snug and tight, pleased to find he could successfully throw up his character sheet version three. Four? It had a V and three at the top, so, sure… three. He'd have to pick a name other than Less Than Three this next time.

Happy to hold his dearest close as he whispered to her, he received a hand on his mouth for his trouble as her cheeks burned red. He smirked under her palm. All according to the plan.

Zephyr undid her High Elven manifestation and returned to being purely the ship, changing her sails to the colors of her mermaid dress. She was more fond of that these days; a luxury cruiser had far more options to accessorize with!

From a porthole, Zephyr, as the ship, announced their departure. "This is your ship speaking. The spare room has been converted into a tactical meeting chamber. The presents have been removed from my hull and hold. Everyone strap in or strap on. That means you two! Oak and Meg! I see you speeding towards my aft! I'm throwing you some rope but you better catch it, you dingy cotton-cloud surfers!"

She did unspool them some rope as promised, performing a cursory check while altering her prow to face the correct heading. There wasn't a lot of atmosphere in Vanaheim before one hit vacuum, but needing to ride the fine line between danger and death would only make Zephyr lick her lips in anticipation.

Tim appeared to have grasped Hans by his lapels and was threatening the man with divinity and responsibility if he kept these stunts up, while Hans Jr. was kept steadfast and firm in Tim's other arm, fast asleep from sheer safety and comfort. When Meg and Oak grabbed hold of the rope from Zephyr's aft while screeching about her waiting before launch, she chose to launch right away regardless.

Meg and Oak both had a hold of the rope, after all. The rest could be a heroic rescue by… someone. Someone would probably do it. She had places to be, and engines to engage.

Her perspective moved to Artorian for just a moment, who perked up and appeared to notice when she did so.

Artorian turned his head to look right at where she was looking from. The boy didn't have more than attributes on that fresh character sheet. How was he doing that?

He then shot her a grin, tapped the side of his nose to say that attributes had nothing to do with knowing, and dropped two fingers forward. "Engage."

Zephyr replied with an all-ahead full, her neon thrusters lighting up the night sky.

CHAPTER FORTY-EIGHT

Vanaheim had changed.

Out was the extreme curvature of the landscape. In was a flatter, more traversable variation. Though littered with interlocked buildings of all kinds, all the same. From his spot on Zephyr's deck, Artorian could see structures clearly meant to be stores mangled together with tall houses. Including the exact opposite combination, and mixtures of buildings thereof with main roads and thoroughfares cutting right through all those structures without any concern for privacy or the ideals of proper architecture.

The most interesting mélange was a castle and a cathedral that had fallen into one another, remaining connected at the roof and upper floors while the entirety of the ground floor was major roads and intersections. "I suppose that's what happens when you mush multiple maps of buildings together, and add in the roads last. Based on the sewer map, they made that layer connect and work flawlessly, while everything on top was made to suffer and work it out."

He tugged Ember's other local maps closer, having been given access before she went on a trip to nap-land. While trying to make sense of the cluster-cluck that was Vanaheim, he praised whichever Gnomish genius had put the quadrant map together. That was the only screen linking the rest of them together, giving him a semblance of peace and order.

People could certainly live in Vanaheim, but the detail that the local currency listed had become several varieties of cheese hadn't escaped his notice. Neither had the glaring sights of Cheese Penguins hard at work putting broken structures together as they built, according to the map, the Spine of Vanaheim. He wondered for a moment how the cheeses were ranked in value, but the thought fled as his eyes were hungry and hard at work.

Seeing the Penguins merge into the building foundation to prop them up while acting as the mortar between bricks made Artorian feel a bit squick inside, but he had to commend the effectiveness. Funky, city-planner-nightmare architecture or not, all these structures would stay standing with living cheese inside of them keeping them upright. Some even had a surprising amount of flex to them, which was the only time he even saw the cheese once a structure had been repaired. "Tim? Of all the things I expected with Brother Moon, from throwing Muspelheim at it like a giant bomb to giving it indigestion, this was not one I expected. End-game boss fight thing? Absolutely. Eldritch cheese horror from beyond the stars surrendering, and joining the team? Color me surprised. Happy, but surprised."

Tim leaned over from his own seat, easing in with his arms crossed to mirror where Artorian's eyes were looking. He was more interested in the integrity and quality of the maps than their contents, and there was nothing like seeing them used and interacted with live. "Brother Moon became surprisingly amicable after being informed that he could still eat and grow as initially intended, given some changes to the menu. I do need Vanaheim to get bigger and be population-worthy, and a silent overseer where players may plumb the depths only to encounter more and more horror is something that appeals, as I didn't properly have that category before."

His chair creaked, the big man leaning back while enjoying the view of the realm righting itself. "The closer they get to Moony's center, the more absurd and stomach-twisting the adventure, filled with subtle changes to the environment the deeper they go. I've already poked my nose in, and even the starting phases are a chef's kiss. Cosmic horror is hard to pull, regardless of how cheese-flavored it is, and the Penguins did have some curious abilities that would throw a serious wrench into the plans of any player getting too big for their britches. Particularly since Cheesy Comedic Counter works against *everything*."

The dungeon chuckled pleasantly. "I can't wait to see some rogue fireball be stopped, a Wisp pointing and poking at the rules with an upset light, and that fireball promptly turning around and returning back to sender with a new flavor. Or larger. I hear Tatum is fiddling with something called Rituals. If one of those went awry because it accidentally hit a Penguin? That would be hilarious."

A flashing window demanded Tim's attention while Artorian chuckled, the dungeon pulling it forward. "Of note, Curator Caladrius has been unassigned from you. They need to focus on their pure Celestial dungeon, regardless of their **Art Law** having more than merely Celestial as an affinity. The Nuttelator has been cracked, and you need a new calculation engine. I have a list of high-end options for you if you'd like. Or is there any dungeon you know that you'd like to assign your number-crunching to?"

Artorian paused his studies to think. "Zelia is proud of Incursus. The one who helped with Grecian themes, ordinance tests, and my second character sheet."

Tim scrolled down the list of high quality dungeons, and did not find Incursus on the list. Doing a vague search, that answer changed. "Ah, well, if you like him. I must inform you that Incursus is on the high end of the lower tiers. Close to the middle tiers, but not there yet. Are you certain? He will struggle."

Artorian thought his initial response had been clear enough, but he repeated himself for posterity. "Zelia is proud of him."

The portly man threw his big hands up in an 'if you insist' motion, and assigned the Curator to Artorian. Incursus would certainly not complain, but the information was going to trickle in slowly when he received prompts. "One moment, the Momma Bun is coming by again."

Lucia dragged Meg and Oak by the ear around the deck, berating the both of them for hidden surprises that had been left below decks, and Zephyr hadn't thought to clean up. Neither he nor Artorian paid attention to the words after about fifteen minutes, but neither he nor Artorian would have been particularly pleased to have an entire vat of particularly sticky rice milk dumped on them from above, either. Which had come mere minutes after Lucia had been the one to rescue them from their ropy predicament.

Sympathy for the You've Yee'd Your Last Haw group was at an all-time high of zero.

Lucia was tearing Meg and Oak new ones at all the time it was going to take to get that rice out of her hair and fur. While the spankings were coupled with healing effects, the sonorous *clap* that accompanied them caused Artorian to suffer from the kind of breath-sucking hisses that wrote home about how they ought to be avoided. Meg and Oak's begging and screaming was secondary. Nobody was coming to help them.

Decorum cared for none of this, glued to the prow of the ship and squinting into the distance as Zephyr sailed, bobbed, and weaved between roofing like sharp coral shoals, flying low enough for atmosphere, but high enough to avoid picking fights with living structures. He smoothly altered his weight and balance as if surfing the large ship, his tailored suit immaculate and spotless as his main hand hard-thumbed the hilt of his rapier. His breathing was the only thing unsteady about him, his heart beating faster and with more purpose the closer the map showed they were to the icon representing his Tisha.

Woe to whomever, or whatever, was still in their way.

Tim saw the drive in Decorum, the Liger in the shape of man. He too was curious what the Amalgam currently creating all the random encounters was going to spit out. Though, given how busy it was on Midgard, and how it hadn't needed to pay any attention to Vanaheim with the still-ongoing invasion of Arachnoids that were not remotely done hatching from frozen hunks of ice-clumped comets... He could probably do it himself? He didn't do much personal game-mastering after chasing Artorian with an Apocalypse in the alpha run.

He plucked some dice from his pocket, working them around in his hand. His ear picked up some lamentation from Hans before he rolled them. A good rescue should come with a good fight. If the dice were with him today. The dice had not been with him lately, and he couldn't help but feel it was due to drinking Lady Luck's strongest potion in front of her, and claiming it needed more kick. His own fault, really. Tasty, though, but needed more **Order**, and better balancing.

Admitting to curiosity of whatever was going on belowdecks, he checked Hans's activity log, then pulled up the prompt giving Hans such grief.

———

Dear Sir,

It is with great confusion that we must inform you of your expulsion from New Haven's Magic Academy. The confusion arises as this has been exceptionally difficult to do as you are not even a student at our school yet, but we feel that you would take some pride in knowing that you are the first in all of the recorded wizarding history, which extends far further than this iteration's recorded history, to have been expelled before admittance.

Congratulations?

May we never see you in our hallowed halls,

Chronomancer Axon - Headmaster.

P.S. All golems and guards have been provided with a description of your appearance, and will remove you on sight with extreme prejudice.

———

That name sounded familiar.

Tim did some rooting, finding that Axon had abandoned his Gnomish Tchaikovsky character when given the option for a redo due to extravagant Pylon failures regarding horological issues. Chronomancy was time magic, while horology was time science. Synthetic Pylons didn't appear to like science. Whelp, the Gnomes would fix it. Seemed like their kind of bag. He couldn't be unhappy to see that more and more players were keeping their own names for their game characters as well. It certainly made the entire mess easier to keep track of. Multiple names for the same person just got so tedious after a while.

He glanced at Dawn, strategically kept his trap shut, and made the wise decision not to upset any more ladies on this fine day. Instead, why not roll some dice? He already had them in hand and everything. See what kind of boss battle was triggered for this final part of their trek. Yes, that sounded excellent!

Artorian was still busy sorting out his new character sheet, and likely wouldn't be participating, but oh well. Decorum was raring to go! Tim rolled the dice with a big grin on his face. "Alley-oop!"

CHAPTER FORTY-NINE

Burgeoning free from a sudden, solar-light blocking cloud of dark, buzzing mosquitoes, the great, the one, the only El Mosco spread his many flamberge appendages, flourishing multiple, sharp buzz-kill wings. The many giant blades that made up his limbs all gleamed before becoming drowned in the dull, darkened red of old blood. As fog set in around the area boss, he spread his appendages wide in dramatic performance before draping his wings all over himself to uphold an air of mystery.

Opening his act with a guffaw, El Mosco splattered against Zephyr's prow as she barreled into him at full-speed ahead, running him over without a thought being spared to El Mosco's presence. While the self-proclaimed vampire lord didn't instantly become a stain, the impact and subsequent keelhaul was a total buzzkill.

El Mosco was getting rather sick of this treatment, stabbing a flamberge in Zephyr's keel to come to a hard stop. He was majestic! Full of prowess and poise! Unfurling his multiple bladed limbs, he quickly scurried like a bug up the way he came. Returning to the front of the prow to pose imposingly on Zephyr's nose with a dynamic entry! The vampire lord's wings and blades out so he could pull the fog close, screech to commerce the area boss challenge, and—

Stab.

—look down in confusion to see a rapier had effortlessly pierced his chest and heart, destroying the full armor value that protectively coated his health bar. That metal shell had prevented him from taking damage as his specific vulnerabilities hadn't been penetrated, and being run over hadn't done enough damage to break it. Damage to his pride notwithstanding.

When El Mosco looked back up, he was met with the stern face of serious countenance, and pure decorum. His buzzy, nasal voice communicated his mood flawlessly. "Well, that's not fair at all."

Decorum sliced his rapier free with a tiny *splurt* from El Mosco's chest, sheathed it, and replied by releasing some steam from his mouth. "Oh, I'm sorry. I don't give an Abyss."

A statement preceded by Gomez adopting his full Liger Prime Beast mode, consuming the majority of deck space, before politely following up with an invitation to the local ball. The dance was located in a most pristine location of High Elven repute and glamor, accompanied by a free serving of *instant mauling* at the door.

Decorum's fang-filled mouth snapped around El Mosco's oversized mosquito skull, busy rip-tearing it from the rest of the insect while providing the mosquito's two red and glowing compound eyes a front and center view of the inside of Decorum's mouth. El Mosco had to give surprising credit to the health of the Liger's teeth, they were all sparkly white and pristine and—*Oh Abyss*, priorities, Mosco! Being eaten!

Decorum's massive, air-infused claws shred and mauled through Mosco's rapidly diminishing health bar, the mosquito utterly pinned and at the mercy of the Beast with far more mass and strength in the good ol' relevant attribute score.

This mangled the area boss, who flailed in panic and slashed into Decorum's hide with oversized blades. Finding a moment of clarity, El Mosco countered! Attempting to pierce deep in a massive, multi-pronged synchronized stab. "Sanguine Censure!"

In ordinary circumstances, those blood-drenched blades would have leached and siphoned the health right back into El Mosco when they plunged several feet of flamberge into their feisty foes. Rather than meet flesh and bone, his appendages encountered only an unsatisfying *ping* when the bladed impacts plinked off against one of Lucia's shields.

The Glitterflit in Basher form fumed with a nightcap on her head, Lucia busy picking the remaining pieces of rice out of her fur after a High Elven luxury bath that she could definitely get used to. "Momma Bun was *just* about to lay down for a nap. Wrap this up, children!"

This distraction and moment of invulnerability as his wounds healed with a swiftness provided Decorum plenty of time. Whirling around to hurl El Mosco out in front of the ship again, Zephyr delightedly ran him over.

Gomez spared an over the shoulder glance at something his brother was holding up, which appeared to be a party screen belonging to Team Sleep. A prompt came up for him to approve, and he tapped it without much thought.

One **ding** later, and his name was on it! Marvelous!

Back to murder, now.

While El Mosco got run over a second time, he did not appreciate Zephyr's sudden addition of black-pearl bad-girl keel-spikes. Keelhauled for actual damage as he was cut to ribbons, the area boss turned irate! The ireful litany of cursing that followed gave the giant Liger time to bound to the back of the ship while keeping easy track of his opponent, where Zephyr was clearing out a flat platform for him to plant his feet.

Mid-journey across the keel, El Mosco the now very bruised mosquito vampire lord failed to stab Zephyr in the keel again, an act that she was still going to take vengeance for. When the massive mosquito with blades for hands tried to clamber up her portside hull, she slammed open a gunnery port, revealing a fully charged Staravar-Class Macro-battery Beam Cannon.

A neon beam which Zephyr, accompanied by a menacing grin that formed on the front of her hull, fired off without warning as a *bwaaaaamp* cut through the air. The Macrobattery swiveled to slice the area boss's way as the mosquito attempted to escape his fate of being dragged deeper into the lands of damage and disrespect.

The neon beam nearly took off all of El Mosco's legs, but the dastardly blood-sucking rogue activated his Nimbly Dodges trait, and wiggled his way free like the evasive mosquito he was. The trait allowed him complete evasion from any attack! Once per ten minutes. Recently purchased from the boss monster's 'Tricks and Gimmicks' store. Now having a sale, everything is thirty percent off storewide, or forty percent with a coupon. Specifically to counter his equally recent Abyss with... just his luck? Beam weaponry!

He hated these energetic fly swatters!

Unfortunately, that brought El Mosco up right behind the aft of the speeding luxury cruiser. That positioning by itself wasn't such a bad thing, but being in Decorum's effective range was another.

The Liger was ready to prove that point. Rearing up with his head to the sky once on the back aft where a rogue rope was still trailing and snapping in the wind, Decorum gathered the winds in his maw.

El Mosco had enough of this! He would recover from this blatant disrespect, his pride burned and streaked with neon scintillation right on the booty. His attire was ruined! He would not falter, and rebuke both this rude kitten, and its dastardly Boaty McBoatface of a companion! He was already bearing a grudge. "Swarmageddon, Fallen Dark!"

Mosquitoes gathered around the flamberge mosquito vampire lord, his minions consumed by the thousands to restore his own health at the cost of his wealth. Which would have been a fantastic solution had Decorum been in the mood to play. Instead, Gomez's only thoughts were on Tisha, and this *gnat* was in the way.

The Liger roared forth the true, the pure, the original. "Shining Ray!"

A roiling star of hyper-concentrated air formed in Decorum's open, fang-filled mouth. Released at the drop of his head, the rupturing beam launched forward came accompanied by a calamitous outpour of bright white starflame. Courtesy of his brother's luminous influences, Gomez had trained in the ways of all that was bright.

The power condensed into a tight line before breaking from those confines, unleashing a Primal Shining Ray onto the realm of Vanaheim as a roaring beam measuring fifty meters tall, and fifty meters wide. The roiling star fired in line-format encapsulated and vaporized El Mosco, destroying him for the third time in a row. Minions and all.

El Mosco once again thought that this wasn't very fair, and once again received a death notification that he had been killed by Team Sleep. Team Sleep?

Team Sleep?! For a third time in a row?

Et tu, Eternium? That they got credit for the sunlight kill was bad enough, but the oversized kitten with claws for days, that used his head as a chew toy, and vomited energy beams from the mouth as if they were hairballs? That one was a sleeper as well? Forever accursed would be all that was related to pillows.

Grudge? Forget a little grudge.

When he was back again, he was going to carve murals to their downfall in every backwater shrine he could get his flamberges on. He was going to erect crooked cathedrals and dark castles with the deepest of dungeons, raising armies of bloodsuckers purely for the purpose of satisfying his newly minted vendetta against Team Sleep.

If only the reputation Pylons worked! He would have known their location at all times. Curses! Did they think that bosses and boss encounters were all singular instances? No! Bosses remembered, and would most certainly ignore other targets in favor of the ones that had drawn their ire.

Team Sleep had most certainly drawn his ire.

They would rue the day that they had crossed… vampire lord, El Mosco!

So went the last thought of El Mosco, the unfairly murdered mosquito. Which would have been a great grievance, if there was such a thing as a mosquito that didn't deserve to be murdered, and given the clap on sight. All mosquitos deserved to be chancla'd.

No exceptions.

Tim was busy holding his forehead and covering his eyes when he got a pop-up message from Brother Moon. The top of Vanaheim's new housing district had become a bubbly, boiling variant of the local fondue, with several Penguins reduced to molten heaps on the street from residual backlash alone.

One did not unleash Asgard-quality Aeroblast-equivalents without expecting severe collateral damage. Worse still, because it was environmental damage rather than direct damage, the Penguins had their Cheese Comedic Counter go off on the environment rather than Decorum.

So the big cat wasn't even being punished for the big bang attack, and several copied Aeroblasts had shot off in a variety of directions as that was what the Pylons responsible for collating thought the Penguins had been hit by, except their target was 'the air.' Resulting in a windy show, and a sudden new town square. Or maybe a parking lot. Either way, there wasn't anything left in that spot.

The message's origin that Tim tried and failed to ignore was easy to discern, the window colored a smooth, cheesy yellow. The message within was equally clear, spelled out in all capital letters as Vanaheim felt a need to hide all the new yellow snow, comment on the sudden need for a second spine, and request brown pants.

———

"COULD YOU PLEASE NOT?"

———

Tim exhaled deep, his face buried both his hands. "That did not work out as planned. I'll bar beam abilities on Vanaheim or something. This is how everyone keeps getting anxiety. That was not at all the boss battle I was hoping for. That mosquito got murdered."

He looked to Artorian to be consoled, but the boy's first response was to shoot him an odd look. "Between a boss encounter, and a person going all-out for **Love**, who exactly do you think I'm going to support here? I would have supported the odds to be even more skewed in Gomez's favor. I'm a biased judge here, bud."

Artorian leaned over to pat Tim on the back as Gomez, in well-dressed human guise, passed them to return to the prow. The lounger-bound Administrator poured forth his support. "Good show, brother! We'll be with Tisha soon."

Gomez's stern expression remained unbroken, but he nodded and knew that to be true. He couldn't be back at Tisha's side soon enough. He would be, for certain, back at her side. The world would break before he succeeded in this quest, just as in the story of the Guardians of Cadia.

Where the planet broke before the guard did.

Gomez stepped his foot back on the prow, his fencing hand pressing gloved digits down on the hilt of his rapier as his words growled out of him. "I am coming, my love. Your Gomez is on his way. Fight, and live, oh light of my life. So I may dance and duel with you under the affection of the sun. Oh, most beautiful of daywalkers, the flame in my heart. My dearest, adored, cherished Tisha."

His gaze steeled. "I am coming."

CHAPTER FIFTY

Artorian turned his attention to Tim, who was all sorts of sullen as he turned to the last chapter in the notes he was currently perusing. The big notation titled 'Balance Sheet' at the top, filled with more red text than anyone wanted to see, caused some discomfort.

Artorian had to address this. There was help to be provided, even if he was purely the yellow rubber duck of the conversation. "What is going on with the balance in this beta run? It's all over the place, bud."

Tim sunk into his seat, puddling almost exactly as Cal had when in the care room. The resemblance was striking to Artorian; they must be spending time together.

Good! Friends time is a great time. "We lost reference Pylons I would rather still have had, Artorian. All that old data is gone, we have to start from… mostly scratch. Bulky hard copies of information are the only way to store information that is to be used on a mass scale. Try this with a memory Core and you've got an instant bomb. The more miniaturized or packed in the encoding, the worse the boom, and the more sensitive the trigger. That's part of why Pylons are so big, crystalline, and see-through. Easier to study the Runes and inlay for problems when something goes wrong."

He stretched his hands above his head, placed them down while laced on his scalp. "We have conditional backups in the Pylons that used to be creatures, people, and whatnot. Those were masterpieces compared to what we have to work with now, but I'm not the kind of evil sycophant that enjoys taking that much agency away from that many. We could have everyone in the Soul Space be a processing Pylon, and for Cal's game, that would still be insufficient."

Artorian did his best to rub Tim's shoulder with the limited reach he had. "Any good solutions?"

The portly dungeon folded his thick fingers together, resting them on the divinely soft fabric coating his food-loving stomach. "Plenty! Few of them are good. Volunteers would be optimal. Though that has more to do with a decanting problem we're going to run into when it's time to exit Cal, and the Chains are sorted."

Tim shimmed in his seat. "Currently we have, at most, wiggle room. The Chains can't be removed, that's a random event. Zelia and her ploy to make the Chains of Chaos that are binding Cal be uncertain if they should be working or not, and flubbing about with the probability thereof, is tricksy business. Once they're off though, well. Everyone is going to want to leave, right?"

Artorian nodded, seemed sensible enough. "As a C-ranker, I hear? To reconnect with the Tower so we're no longer using Cal's **Acme Law** as an intermediary for Mana and cultivation gain. Allowing us to grow properly in what we are affectionately calling the real world? It's all been feeling plenty real here to me. You went off on a tangent, Tim. What do you mean 'volunteers'? Why can't everyone decant? You wouldn't mention the topic if it wasn't a problem."

Tim scratched his head with a wince, trying to think of a nice way to explain this. "You know we can make bodies of a variety of races, with decent ease. *If* they're made out of energy.

You know that the energy problem is not one we need to contend with. Equally, making synthetic Pylons has become an automated process, so the problem of quantity will be solved. It is simply one that will be solved in time, and not right now."

He drummed his fingers on his belly. "What we don't have is infinite manpower that is immune to mental fatigue and burnout. Cal and I unpleasantly discovered that dungeons aren't immune. Even Earth Cores—and I assure you, I love throwing myself into the finest, most minute details of a problem—have a limit, and have discovered the benefits of a nice nap."

Tim pulled up a chart, showing a timeline. "Rough estimation, from Moonfall's daring rescue to final exodus? We're looking at half a billion years of time having passed. Billion, bud, with a capital B. Five, hundred, million years. There's going to be nothing left of the world we knew. Anything made with Essence or Mana is long devoured, and anything physical is dust and dirt, or buried so deep it will never see the light of day again. We'll be lucky to recognize a single mountain."

Tired, the dungeon closed his eyes to frown and cope. "I know what it *feels* like to have the mind smell like burnt toast. Cal and I have been up and running that entire time, and aside from a few notable breaks? Cal actually getting broken for a bit, and the speed of time flow being experienced as a wibble-wobble not counted? We haven't been taking breaks, and we haven't gotten nearly as far as either of us wanted to. Then there's the setbacks…"

He sighed, deep, feeling like he'd been happier with even more time rather than having moved at such high relative temporal velocities. "The problem with decanting during exodus isn't that we can't do it, it's that we can't do it all at once along with everything else going on."

Artorian leaned in for the details. "Cal and I are taxed well above capacity with tasks, and we always will be. Every dungeon, Gnome, and Wisp has been pulled in for background duties and services that we have been forced to offload, and we are now gathering intelligent Beasts to pick up the slack that even they can't handle. We are straight up accepting any Heavenly that states they want to help, and yes, I know they're all still being children. We need the help that badly."

Tim motioned at another chart as he pulled it up. "A main issue: if everyone goes mortal at the same time, our problem is twofold. One, we won't have non-player characters to station in the game world, to help make sense of life and existence for the people we expect to be trading places with. Two, while we have the resources to grow everyone a new body, that's the hiccup. We have to *grow* it, the *slow way*, and these bodies need to be tailored to the person whose mind is being transferred over."

The dungeon's thick digit stabbed a screen to make it stop whining at him. "As soon as we move them from a memory or seed Core to that body, that's also the last and only chance we get to do that. Unless they die in Cal, and we re-Core them, but that is now expensive and time consuming."

He motioned at a third chart. "We don't care about expensive things right now, but time consuming issues are a dangerous cost."

Tim snapped his fingers, pretending to be excited in a very mocking manner. "With the fun follow up problem that bodies from either Cal or I simply won't…"

The dungeon squirmed with a groan when realizing a detail, stopping himself. "Dang it, Cal… you and your puns."

Artorian hadn't caught the pun, so it was explained to him. "Cal or I shortens to calorie, and that was a conversation recently. Cal said, 'I'm proud to say I burned a lot of calories today. Forgot to turn off the stove while making dinner.'"

Artorian made an undesirable face, grasping the majority of the content, which Tim painfully agreed with as he got off that topic. "I'm going to specifically muck up the word order and get the language wrong so I can say this with a straight face."

Fixing his train tracks, he righted his locomotive and chugged on. "The bodies that me and Cal made won't be able to exist long term in the outside world. Not without that external power source we've been so gung-ho about. Your mad Flash Runes idea helped. A lot. Tekka had help from a Heavenly—who almost exclusively did all the work on it—but I don't think I care about unfair division of labor here."

Gleeful, Tim pulled up a rolodex of patterns that were in progress of being turned into Auric expressions of the Rune-quality measure. "This Rune format is incredible, and I despise not having had it sooner, because the one I made was nothing like that. Mine was crumbs on the napkin compared to Voltekka's scrumptious chocolate chip cookie. I had the foundation ready, but **Aeris**, the Heavenly of **Copper**? She did so well with what she baked that she's still smirking after seeing our reactions. That woman humbled us. *Us*, Artorian! Put Cal and I straight on th—oh, Abyss with the pun!—put me and Cal straight on the humble bench."

The gear-grinding got to Tim, his cheeks reddening. "There's nothing we can't do, and then, this, just, *ooooooh*."

The dungeon scowled as he blew out air. "Now we owe her a favor. That's going to be costly. Back to topic? We need volunteers for the kind of system that lets us keep some people in Eternia, so the game doesn't fall apart and people can pretend to play their roles as best they are able. Earning tokens for time levered or tasks completed, before handing their shops, or tasks, or jobs, over to the incoming crowd, so they can all leave."

He waved a dismissive hand at his second chart. "Leaving with a Mana body that they got here is useless. It will fall apart outside. They're not going to be able to cultivate, having the reverse problem as we did on initial entry. Those forms are bound to Cal, and only work in Cal. We have plans for more permanent Mana- and Spirit-based forms, but you have to start that process as a person who doesn't have a center to make the conversion work, and we have none of those. We're just expecting to get them. It's a workaround for all the people who we can't connect a center to, because most of the influx we're expecting will consist of individuals who aren't going to have souls. You need a center as glue to keep all those components together, and anyone who wasn't born, or didn't grow up in an Essence-laden environment simply isn't going to adapt to naturally have one."

Eternium pulled up his nose, not looking forward to that bag of bones. "Which is going to be an *oh, so, fun* problem to handle."

Sifting through a few diagrams, Eternium then pulled out a massive chart filled with rewards and services to be rendered, with 'Real Exodus Body' listed right at the tippy top for best reward to cash tokens in for. "My game balance is kaput, and I don't have the spare bandwidth that I did last time to finetune it all myself again. I need cultivators, people, inhabitants, anyone willing and able to come pitch in and give the background teams more raw data. Because otherwise we're going to keep having repeats of the current issues."

Artorian nodded, indicating he understood and was following, but wanted Tim to keep venting. He'd clearly kept this in for far too long, and playing the role of yellow duck appeared to be helping as Tim carried on. "Testing things with your level of attributes was a great notifier for problems you simply should not have had, and that we have a ridiculous reliance on skills and abilities going on."

Tim waffled a hand, not having the time to expound. "We're going to be able to fix that going forward, and have plans for the future, but unless we make things granular like with Cal's complicated formulas in that one prompt you saw? I don't know how we're going to be able to keep a steady progression going. Thus, we need… everyone? Abyss, we need everyone in Cal to come play this game, and many aren't going to want to. Most do, but some are very against it, and we need them as well."

Deflating like a balloon, Tim released steam from his ears and sank into his seat. "Which is project number… pick a hat to pull out of another hat so we can commence the process of pulling a number out of a hat."

He laid his arm over his face. "Excuse me as I feign being energetic."

Artorian hummed, still rubbing Tim's shoulder. "*Mmm*. So no boss fight?"

Eternium shot the entire way up from his seat, his arms thrown forward to the prow of the ship where Gomez stood as the vanguard of all. His voice was exasperated, fueled with heat, and yet utterly disappointed. "That *was* the boss fight!"

CHAPTER FIFTY-ONE

Artorian couldn't help but laugh.

The schadenfreude got him.

Tim was unamused, but had little he could do about it. Luckily for him, Artorian's giggling woke Ember. She instantly growled, pounced, and bit him in the upper arm like a wild animal. Punishment for him moving around too much.

The sight broke the straw on the camel's back, which was probably the right idiom, as Tim thought that was too perfect and too much, devolving into his own giggle fit of schaden-freude at seeing Artorian's panicked face and screeching reaction.

Artorian was pure panic, no room in the brain for common sense as he was being bit. He might still only have one hit point! "Emby! *Emby*! Health pool! *Health pool!*"

The sight remained funny to Tim for the exact amount of time until Ember coiled herself up like a cat and lunged for his stomach, claws and fangs first. Tim's very unmanly sound then murdered Artorian's funny bone, who had freshly recovered from being bitten, only to succumb to a second round of giggle-fits. Who then, of course, was accosted by a very *bity* fire soul.

"Not the nose!" Artorian flailed, failing to escape as he made it as far as out of the chair before being caught. Ember saw fit to bite him in the nose. "*Aaaah*! My nose!"

When she released her chompers, Lucia was at his side in Basher mode, half asleep with the nightcap on her head. She sounded exactly as a mother did when woken in the middle of the night to yet more rambunctious children breaking something. "Argh… *Kits*… It never changes does it?"

A quick bop to Artorian's head with a glowing toe bean and he was right as rain. Lucia's healing shield provided him the clemency from Ember's morning wrath, as she curled right back into his spot. Stealing the entire blanket, and tugging it over herself.

He was not getting that back.

Artorian got up from the ground, having spilled from the seat in his attempts to flee, in time to see Gomez discover that they had arrived at the entrance to the Darkest Dungeon. Which was no different than a big volcanic-looking hole in the ground, and about as friendly and inviting. Tisha's icon blinked directly below them on all the maps.

There was no hesitation from Gomez, who leaped face-first from Zephyr's prow, his blade drawn and ready to fight the very air if he had to. "I am coming, my love!"

Artorian threw his hands up, unable to follow. "Celestial feces! Decorum."

The Administrator hurriedly snapped out a command. "Zephyr! After him!"

Their ship shared Gomez's lack of hesitation. Though in Zephyr's case, that l'appel du vide of plunging straight down into the dark, burning hole below them had more to do with a call and craving for danger and adventure.

Artorian had to instantly hold onto something as Zephyr's horizontal orientation became her vertical orientation, and her thrusters hadn't bothered reducing output or oomph in the slightest. Those solar sails of hers were getting plenty of Mana from sunlight to keep chugging through the stars for hours longer yet, as she plunged into the depths of the Darkest Dungeon. Sailing bravely past the horrific, and the unknown, towards the very heart of Brother Moon.

Tim caught Artorian, not keen on letting a little hiccup cause undue deaths. Nor would he allow all his freshly finished work to be undone. He had just finished that Pyrite-blasted bracelet upgrade! "Gotcha, bud!"

Artorian groaned in mock exhaustion. "When I was told that my entire trip in Eternia was going to be nothing but fighting, I didn't believe them. Nobody told me that it wasn't the monsters I was going to fight the most!"

Zephyr pulled the kind of aerial maneuvers in these wide, underground string-cheese tunnels that would crack the keel of ordinary ships with the kind of Gs she was pulling. Only Lucia's expertly cast mass shields and a floating lantern from her abilities hovering at everyone's side was keeping them all relatively safe and unharmed from a ship-sized case of Goblin *reeeee*.

Lisette would have been proud.

Eternium cackled, holding Artorian. "Pretend this is halfway! You're going right back into the fray as soon as your character sheet is sorted, and we'd better get on that if you want to have any hope of helping Decorum!"

Artorian hung his head, releasing a feral noise to the air before focusing on the task. "Let's get to it then! Also, why haven't we caught him? Aren't we faster than Gomez?"

Tim grinned wide, realizing that either Artorian didn't know, or Decorum had never let him see. "You don't know? One of a Morovian Liger's main affinities is air. Kitty can *fly*."

Artorian blinked, and looked over the edge to spot Decorum in his large Liger form having zero issues navigating a vertical space, the Beast utterly coated in raw, directed wind that vectored him where he needed to be as if he was running on a stream of playful leaves.

Artorian saw this all while clinging to Tim for dear life, even though Lucia had him bountifully covered with all her shields. She herself stood on the deck with a half-awake look plastered on her face, that floating mystical roof with tassels present over her head again. The screaming belowdecks was promising as well, but Artorian was convinced that Hans, Meg, and Oak would be fine.

He did spare Lucia a look concerning Hans Jr, but she nodded knowingly. "I shielded the baby. The rest of them get to fend."

That caused a round of chuckles between Eternium and Artorian, before Tim put the Administrator back down when Zephyr's orientation and mad dashes through impossible terrain evened out, with the crow's nest yelling. "*Whooooo*! Made it!"

Artorian leaned over the ship's edge, watching Decorum crash into and break a bright red gate of preposterous size, covered almost entirely in black soot. Some streaks gave the underlying color away until the entire left gate was torn off the hinges and tossed like an unwanted crayon. Followed by a call for Tisha from Decorum that reverberated through these dark, underground, creepy canyons that he could swear were undulating in the shadows. "Whelp, I think I found what you meant by creepy. Wasn't Tisha in the Castle of Howl, or something?"

Ember growled from under the blankets, the cloth distended from having pulled up a map screen. "*Was*, yes. She's in the dungeon now. I don't see Howl's Castle on the map anymore either. It must have walked off or something."

Artorian had questions about a whole Abyss-crackled castle 'walking off,' but he had other priorities. "Tim, what do you need from me?"

The portly dungeon smiled and shrugged. "Exactly the same as last time, just with less freebies. There's also a bunch of notes."

He summoned that window, sharing details. "Cal mentioned that you only get to pick two attributes for continued flat and growth testing. Having all of them was too much. Your stats no longer have to be even, and you will be able to redistribute them once after the A-rank cultivation bonuses kick in. We need to know how that works for people who were once

Mages, and are currently not. So, the more imbalanced you can make version three, the better. Min-max me something. You'll get a version four character sheet when it's time to get serious, at which point you will have import access from all three of your prior character layouts. You get three choices again this time for character version three."

Artorian's eyes sparkled, his smile brightening and going wide as he thought of the options for version four. "Accelerator?"

Tim laughed, slapping his knee. "Ha! I won the bet! Yes, Artorian. Accelerator. Luminous Gatling. Any and all skills or abilities you once had. The works. We'll have it working by your fourth iteration. So for this one, have fun. Do what you actually wanted to do in the first place. Muck with the attributes. Sprinkle in some **Chaos**. I certainly won't begrudge you your time with Zelia, but let's also not pretend that I do not know what she is about."

Artorian had ideas. Such beautiful, gorgeous, maddening ideas. His smile widened by an entire inch. Genius struck him. "And just like that, I am having fun."

"Good!" Tim enjoyed that tremendously, watching Artorian pace and mutter to himself.

"Stats don't have to be even? I want to do the opposite of what I'm known for. Everyone expects me to go the mana-heavy route, but no! I want to spar with my beloved, and learn the ways of the smack. I want to focus on weapons, martial arts, skills, and Flash Runes! I want high physical prowess, low mana, and to brush up on all the skills I never had the time to furnish. I will always be a Mana-Loved, wily old fox!"

Stars twinkled in his eyes. "As a Mage, I will once again have that. There's no reason to overlap when I could learn new things. How to actually fight! Abyss, Tim. Throw in some experiments! Combine mana and stamina into chi or something. Give me no abilities, only Flash Runes. Maybe some Auras. I like Auras. Can I take on the one hit-point curse for a special bonus of some kind?"

Artorian was nearly vibrating through the deck as if he'd downed a gallon of coffee in one big gulp. "I am positively brimming with ideas this time. I wish to play the Janitor once more! Praise Shai-Hulud, First of the Allsand. Bless the cleaner and his broom. Bless the coming and going of him. May his passing cleanse the world. May he keep the world for his people."

Tim had a fantastic idea, manifesting two items and tossing them to Artorian, one of them a big pillow. "Here, your starter kit!"

Artorian caught the ordinary-looking pillow, and the broom of Shaka. The Boom Shaka Laka. "*Ah-ha*! A mop! The true implement of the Janitor Supreme! Now we're cleaning with mana! Right! Cleaning Presence! Some sprinkling of an oomph-increaser boss trick. Trans Am or Ad Astra! Or a third, if you have one! I want to go fast! That's my bread, jam, and butter all in one!"

Ember leaned over the edge of the lounging seat, her cheek leaning on her palm with a big smile. "Now that's what I have wanted to see! Finally, my boy is here in full force. His enthusiasm and *joie de vivre* is back. My Artorian. My *bon vivant*. Now we can truly go fight everything, drink in every mead hall, party in every city, set fire to things where fire should not be! Rescue all of our people!"

Artorian fell in instant agreement. "Yes! First Tisha. Then Rip and Tear, Yorn and Yiba. Then whoever else needs us! Here comes A and A! We ask ze questions! With anyone who can fill the fourth spot of Team Sleep, we'll be a scream of a good time!"

Ember momentarily forgot all her worries, in love with a good scheme as the smile on her face grew. "You are a wonderful pillar, Artorian. You lift me up."

He pushed his chest out, proud as he affirmed that truth. "I always will."

Tim clapped his hands together. "Then I am all set to begin on this third version of the character, so you can chase after

Decorum and save Tisha. Though I will be ducking out after this. There is much to do and I cannot stay. Henry and Marie were just given permission to start another kingdom attempt on Midgard, and this time, they apparently asked for it. I am needed elsewhere."

Artorian stopped cold in his tracks, frozen and rooted to the spot as Ember caught on literal fire. That poor deck chair. That poor blanket! She'd found the exact places where that fire she was talking about needed to be. She was still miffed at Marie.

Artorian stammered. "Wh… what? I… Here? I… Okay? What are they calling the place?"

Tim stretched his shoulders, his entire spine popping with satisfying sounds that made the entirety of Vanaheim horrifically jealous. Brother Moon wanted that exact result too! "*Oooh,* that was a good one. They're calling the place either Albion or Ardania. Have a looksie when you're done storming the castle and rescuing all your princesses! Until then? I hope you've got a lot of Dwarven friends, and know a guy named Carl."

Tim checked the delve details. "Your realm is Vanaheim, and your zone is the terrible, indescribable thing known as the Darkest Dungeon in quadrant K-nine, designed by Wisp Howard Phillips, L. So you better prepare everything you have before you go spelunking, Artorian. I'd suggest a torch, or a Gnome named Bosco."

Eternium grinned wide, excited by what was going to come next. "Good luck, bud. You're in for an elite deep dive, into the darkest depths of the Arcoplex!"

ABOUT DENNIS VANDERKERKEN

Hello all! I'm Dennis, but feel free to call me Floof. Credit of the name now being accumulated by the vast and powerfully cultivated viking beard, that grows ever more in potency. I'm now counting my writing experience in years, so let me say it is my great pleasure that you are reading this, and welcome back to the goodness!

I have been the designer, plotter, and writer of Artorian's Archives since its inception, and look forward to gracing your eyes with ever more volumes of the story. Indulging my dear readers in secrets otherwise forever obscure.

If you have any questions, or would like to chat, I live on the Eternium discord server. Feel free to come say hi anytime! I will keep you entertained for years to come!

Connect with Dennis:
Discord.gg/mdp
Patreon.com/FloofWorks

ABOUT DAKOTA KROUT

Associated Press best-selling author, Dakota has been a top 5 bestseller on Amazon, a top 6 bestseller on Audible, and his first book, Dungeon Born, was chosen as one of Audible's top 5 fantasy picks in 2017.

He draws on his experience in the military to create vast terrains and intricate systems, and his history in programming and information technology helps him bring a logical aspect to both his writing and his company while giving him a unique perspective for future challenges.

"Publishing my stories has been an incredible blessing thus far, and I hope to keep you entertained for years to come!" -Dakota

Connect with Dakota:
MountaindalePress.com
Patreon.com/DakotaKrout
Facebook.com/DakotaKrout
Twitter.com/DakotaKrout
Discord.gg/mdp

ABOUT MOUNTAINDALE PRESS

Dakota and Danielle Krout, a husband and wife team, strive to create as well as publish excellent fantasy and science fiction novels. Self-publishing *The Divine Dungeon: Dungeon Born* in 2016 transformed their careers from Dakota's military and programming background and Danielle's Ph.D. in pharmacology to President and CEO, respectively, of a small press. Their goal is to share their success with other authors and provide captivating fiction to readers with the purpose of solidifying Mountaindale Press as the place 'Where Fantasy Transforms Reality.'

Connect with Mountaindale Press:
MountaindalePress.com
Facebook.com/MountaindalePress
Twitter.com/_Mountaindale
Instagram.com/MountaindalePress

MOUNTAINDALE PRESS TITLES

GameLit and LitRPG

The Completionist Chronicles,
The Divine Dungeon,
Full Murderhobo, and
Year of the Sword by Dakota Krout

Metier Apocalypse by Frank G. Albelo

Arcana Unlocked by Gregory Blackburn

A Touch of Power by Jay Boyce

Red Mage and
Farming Livia by Xander Boyce

Space Seasons by Dawn Chapman

Ether Collapse and
Ether Flows by Ryan DeBruyn

Dr. Druid by Maxwell Farmer

Bloodgames by Christian J. Gilliland

Unbound by Nicoli Gonnella

Threads of Fate by Michael Head

Lion's Lineage by Rohan Hublikar and Dakota Krout

Wolfman Warlock by James Hunter and Dakota Krout

Axe Druid,
Mephisto's Magic Online, and
High Table Hijinks by Christopher Johns

Skeleton in Space by Andries Louws

Dragon Core Chronicles by Lars Machmüller

Chronicles of Ethan by John L. Monk

Pixel Dust and
Necrotic Apocalypse by David Petrie

Viceroy's Pride by Cale Plamann

Henchman by Carl Stubblefield

Artorian's Archives by Dennis Vanderkerken and Dakota Krout

Vaudevillain by Alex Wolf

Made in the USA
Coppell, TX
28 October 2023

23532814R00260